The Death and Life of Strother Purcell

Also by Ian Weir

Will Starling
Daniel O'Thunder

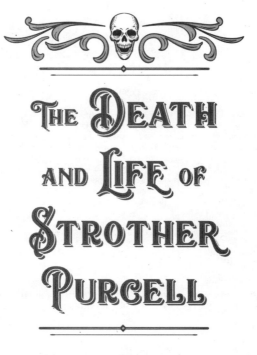

The Death and Life of Strother Purcell

Ian Weir

GOOSE LANE

Edited by Bethany Gibson.
Cover and page design by Jaye Haworth.
Printed in Canada.
10 9 8 7 6 5 4 3 2 1

Library and Archives Canada Cataloguing in Publication

Weir, Ian, author
The death and life of Strother Purcell / Ian Weir.

Issued in print and electronic formats.
ISBN 978-1-77310-029-6 (softcover).--ISBN 978-1-77310-030-2 (EPUB).--
ISBN 978-1-77310-031-9 (Kindle)

I. Title.

PS8595.E47D43 2018   C813'.54   C2018-901163-7
                                              C2018-901164-5

We acknowledge the generous support of the Government of Canada,
the Canada Council for the Arts, and the Government of New Brunswick.

Goose Lane Editions
500 Beaverbrook Court, Suite 330
Fredericton, New Brunswick
CANADA E3B 5X4
www.gooselane.com

To my mother,
blazer of trails

–EDITOR'S PREFACE–

THE TEXT YOU HOLD in your hands first came to my attention in January of 2004, under circumstances so singular as to necessitate exegesis. It was a bleak midwinter evening on the campus of the University of the Southwestern Cariboo; a slate-grey sky had darkened into night, and snow, lashed sideways by a bitter wind, drove the ghostly shapes of stragglers slip-sliding. I was at my car, fumbling with balky fingers to unlock the door and uttering faint heartfelt execrations, when at my back a voice said out of the storm: "You Professor Brookmire?"

A tiny figure stood in a bright red parka: an old woman. A hat with earflaps framed a wizened face, out of which two keen eyes peered. She had just been to my office, but had missed me, she was saying. Someone had pointed me out, across the parking lot—a student, or some such. I'm afraid I wasn't listening closely, having dropped my keys into a snowbank. Yes, I muttered, I was Brookmire. Could I help her?

"I expect we'll see. You're the Purcell fella, eh?"

"The what?"

She looked to be well over ninety. Such was my impression, in the discombobulation of the moment. An icicle depended from her nose. "The Purcell fella. Strother Purcell. You're supposed to be the expert?"

I supposed this was more or less true. I'd published two or three papers on Strother Purcell, although I wouldn't have called myself a Purcell Scholar. There weren't really any of those, given the paucity of information about him.

Strother Purcell had attained notoriety in his own time, but his fame—or infamy—had largely died with him. He had neither been exalted, nor reviled, by Hollywood. He never inspired a television series, not even in the wide-eyed 1950s, when practically anyone who'd fired a sixgun could ride into your living room; he never galloped through the pages of a comic book, or graced the outside of a small boy's lunch-box. Yet this was a gunman whose prowess cowed Wyatt Earp, and whose elemental rivalry with his own half-brother had its roots in antebellum North Carolina and a blood-feud nearly Biblical in dimension, setting in motion a lifelong saga of obsession, betrayal, lost love, and retribution.

"...And left 'em outside your office," the old woman was saying. "You left...?"

"The *papers*. Outside the door." She sounded impatient. "I made copies, eh? Just a coupla bits and pieces—there's lots more. But have a look, and see what you think. Maybe you'd have some idea what I could do with it. If you want, you could give me a call."

Having found the keys, thank God, I struggled back to my feet. But when I looked around, the old woman had disappeared. "Hello?" I called, uncertainly. It seemed to me that I glimpsed her, just for an instant: a stunted figure, jackknifed forward, trudging into the teeth of the storm. Then she was swallowed in darkness and driving snow.

I might have gone after her, under other circumstances—if the wind had not been rising by the moment, slicing through my insufficient coat. I might at least have gone back to my office to retrieve whatever it was the old woman claimed to have left. As it was, I bundled myself into my car and started it up, shuddering until the blessed heat came blasting.

This had taken place on a Friday evening. Monday morning, returning to campus, I looked for a parcel propped against my office door. There was nothing there. I felt obscurely disappointed, but somehow not surprised; the entire encounter had already taken on such an air of unreality that I could almost believe I'd imagined it.

Weeks passed. Then, in April, a colleague manifested in my doorway, looking sheepish. Something had been left for me ages ago, he said, back in January—on a Friday evening, after I'd already left. He'd picked it up and put it aside and forgotten about it, until just now, when he'd stumbled across it while cleaning out his office. He held out a battered manila envelope. Inside were two documents.

I read them, riveted. The first was a third-person accounting of an encounter at an isolated roadhouse near Hell's Gate in the Fraser Canyon in the winter of 1876—long believed to have been the year of Purcell's own death, in circumstances both fraught and abstruse. The account was attributed to Thomas Skiffings, a name I did not recognize. But I certainly recognized the name affixed to the second document. It was—or purported to be—the personal journal of Barrington Weaver, a failed journalist of the Gilded Age who had written, under the pseudonym "B.W. Colton," a series of risible dime novels in the mid-1880s, featuring the fictional Western hero "Deadeye Ned" Hartland. In these journal pages, Weaver claimed to have encountered Strother Purcell in San Francisco in 1892, fully sixteen years after the lawman's supposed death, in circumstances that were nothing short of astounding.

Stuck to the top-sheet was a yellow sticky-note on which was scribbled, in a crabbed cursive minuscule, a partial name—"Tilda S."—and a telephone number. The old woman, obviously. But when I called, the number was out of service. There was no last name, and no address. I had no way to ascertain whom "Tilda S." might be, or even if she was still alive. She made no further attempt to contact me. There the matter rested for eight years.

In October of 2012, I was contacted by J.M. Cates, a solicitor. Mr. Cates identified himself as the executor for the late Matilda Sturluson, who had died some months previously in Penticton, BC, aged 103. Among Ms. Sturluson's effects was a manuscript, along with a note indicating that, "Brookmire, the Purcell fella, might still be worth contacting. Or else possibly not." Mr. Cates asked: Was I interested?

Ten days later, a package arrived, containing 134 sheets of 8 × 11 paper, covered recto and verso with typescript, single-spaced. It had been typed, to judge by the typeface, on an old Smith Corona portable, at some point within the relatively recent past, since the pages had only just begun to yellow. But at least five separate and distinct authorial voices could be discerned. One of these was, unmistakably, Barrington Weaver's. A second was that of the mysterious Thomas Skiffings, whose "Roadhouse Chronicles" continued. Other sections of the manuscript seemed to be based upon obscure but verifiable primary texts from the sparse Purcellian canon. These included *The Sorrows of Miz Amanda and her Two Brave Boys,* a family saga from the Appalachian region, authorship unknown, written sometime in the 1870s; and the curious narrative known to scholars as *High Crimes of the Outlaw Dillashay,* dating from the same era. Other segments of the Tilda Sturluson manuscript appeared to be wholly original. At first, I presumed the sole author of these to have been Tilda Sturluson herself, although six years of editorial endeavour have led me to believe that the truth was—as truth will be—more nuanced and confounding.

But this much may be asserted with conviction: what follows is the life's work of a scholar, untutored but profoundly diligent, who spent decades researching the history of Strother Purcell, reworking and redacting multiple existing narratives, and emending these through recourse to hitherto unknown eyewitness accounts. I have chosen to present this with minimal editorial intrusion, adding footnotes only where absolutely necessary, in hopes that the reader may encounter the text as if it were a novel: as a mystery, even—for such it is. The exhumation of the tragic history of the last, lost gunslinger of the

Western Frontier, and a delving into the deepest mystery of all: the yearnings and desolations of that treacherous sonofabitch, the human heart.

To the original manuscript, a hand-written note had been appended, in the crabbed cursive minuscule that I had first seen in January of 2004. It said: "To whosoever might be reading this — it's true. All of it. Every damned word, more or less, except for the bits that maybe aren't. But the rest you can take to the godalmighty bank." It was signed, "T. Sturluson."

D. Garrett Brookmire, Ph.D.
Emeritus Professor
University of the Southwestern Cariboo
May 2018

PART ONE

–ONE–

Near Hell's Gate
Winter, 1876

THEY WERE PASSING INTO MYTH before the snow had commenced to fall in earnest on that bleak midwinter afternoon, blurring the hard distinctions of this world. So it is not possible with confidence to say where certainties begin and end.

There were three of them; this much at least is beyond dispute. Three men on horseback, ghosting their way north through the trees along the river. They had been glimpsed on two occasions earlier that day by separate witnesses, but did not seek out human interaction. A Cornishman, however, named T.E. Spurlock would in later years recall with increasing clarity that the men had stopped at his shack near Hill's Bar some time before noon, and asked him did he have whiskey. No, replied T.E. Spurlock, he did not, this being a Christian abode. T.E. Spurlock was a drunkard and known confabulist who kept chickens and a desultory pig, but he swore till the day he died that the remainder of this account was Bible truth.

They were U.S. Americans, he said, but not from Washington Territory; he knew this by the manner of their speaking. They came from somewhere deeper in the South. The one who mostly spoke was a man in the early prime of life, not tall but powerfully built, with black hair and a sullen satyr's face and way of staring that prompted T.E. Spurlock to recollect that he did possess a jug of whiskey after all. He fetched it out and told the man no payment was required.

"That is where you are mistaken," the man replied. He reached one hand inside his coat and T.E. Spurlock saw the glint of metal. "Payment is always required."

There was an instant of deadly hush, in which the great globe itself stood frozen. The moment grew more protracted with each successive telling, until by 1898 T.E. Spurlock — now a resident of Kamloops, where he maintained a position as town drunk — would recollect the world's standing still for an entire four minutes and a half, while God gazed grimly down. At last the stranger drew out his hand. The glint between his fingers was a silver coin, which he tossed into the snow at T.E. Spurlock's feet with an infinitesimal twisting of his lip.

"And I never knew," T.E. Spurlock would say, marvelling anew at each retelling of the tale. "Not once did I begin to dream who it was, standing there before me ..."

–TWO–

From *The Roadhouse Chronicles of Thomas Skiffings*[1]

Near Hell's Gate
Winter, 1876

THE THREE MEN ARRIVED with darkness at John McCutcheon's roadhouse. The night had grown vengeful. Wind bansheed from the north, flinging the snow before it in slanting volleys. The man with black hair signed the Register, giving his name as Lightburn. Mr. Lightburn, he wrote, from Decatur. He scratched it with effort, his fingers clumsy as blocks of wood from the cold.

"Decatur, Georgia?" John McCutcheon said this in a friendly manner, to indicate an interest.

"No," the stranger said. "The other one."

John McCutcheon blinked, as if having it briefly in mind to ask further clarification. On mature reflection, he did not. "Well," he said. "Well, indeed. The far-flung places people come from." John McCutcheon was himself from far-flung Nova Scotia. He had come West three years previous, buoyed by a modest inheritance and brimming with resolve, and had purchased the roadhouse from a man who saw him coming.

The house was some miles east of Yale, alongside the fabled and perilous Cariboo Wagon Road, which crept past Hell's Gate in the Fraser River Canyon and thence for 350 miles to Barkerville and the gold fields in the north. A sprawling ramshackle structure, as gaunt as

---

1   This chapter, and the chapter following, constitute the material originally left for me by "Tilda S." in 2004. — *Brookmire*.

a haunted grange in a penny-dreadful tale, with outbuildings in the trees behind and a foothold on a low bluff looking down upon the river, on which it baked all summer and was buffeted by the winds come November. It stood guestless as often as not, being scarcely the thriving hostelry of its proprietor's fond imaginings, for John McCutcheon was a man out of step with Time. The Cariboo gold rush was a decade in the past, and the traffic along the road had dwindled to a trickle. But John McCutcheon remained an optimist on principle and planted the tattered banner of his hopes upon the certainty that the railway must come. On clear nights when the moon shone down on John McCutcheon drunk on his own bad whiskey, he could see in his mind's starry eye a refurbished hotel with a dining room and a mahogany bar and a chef named Jean-Pierre imported from Montreal. At present he made do with Gimp Tom and the girl.

Gimp Tom was McCutcheon's nephew. He was the one who glimpsed the riders first, bulking into corporeality in the darkness, and knew at once what this portended.

"They'll be outlaws," he said to his sister. "They'll be killers, on the run."

The two of them were in the loft, peering out of the small, cracked window. They huddled shoulder to shoulder for warmth, a blanket wrapped around them.

"We'll be dead by morning."

He said it with a kind of relish, being of an age to be much captivated by outlawry, which he had encountered in books in all its sundry guises. He was in fact the exact sort of boy you would expect to meet in such a place as this roadhouse: as likely a lad as ever aspired to bravery and noble deeds, apart from his puniness and deformity. His sister was a different kettle of fish.

"Dead from boredom," she said. "There's no one out there."

"No, look." Gimp Tom had large uncanny eyes that glowed like lamps—so his sister had informed him—in moments of excitement. Now he pointed. "Down through the trees—three men on horseback." She began to see them too.

"Three riders coming hard, this way," said Tom. "With fell intent." He had encountered this phrase in a nickel magazine, and tried it out now for the first time. It pleased him. "They'll ask for lodging till the storm blows past. They'll want stabling for their horses, and a hot meal for themselves, and they'll be cordial enough for a time. But then they'll ask for whiskey, and when they drunk it they'll ask for more—and that's where it starts. You just see if it don't. They'll kill the menfolk first, which means Uncle John and myself. That leaves you, Billie. It grieves me to say it, and I wish it weren't the truth. But that's how these things go."

His sister watched the shadows take shape. "Well, fuck," she said.

At sixteen, Billie Skiffings was five and a half years older than Gimp Tom. The boy was her half-brother, strictly speaking; she was not blood-kin to John McCutcheon, being Edward Skiffings's daughter by his first wife, before he ever met McCutcheon's sister, the late lamented Mina. Billie had accompanied her young half-brother after Mina's funeral—the third parent she had seen buried already, in her young life—the two of them travelling from Victoria, where they had lived, by steam launch to New Westminster first and then by riverboat sixteen hours due east along the Fraser to Yale, where McCutcheon arrived half a day late to meet them. He found them on the wooden steps leading up from the docks below Front Street: the two of them sitting close together, the sister on the step above and the brother hunched below, looking out across the mud flats and the river shallows where Natives and Chinese still squatted to pan for the last specks of gold, though the glory days were in the past and white men had long since given up.

They had looked at John McCutcheon, the both of them at once. Two pinched faces, close together: the boy's great luminous eyes lost and hopeful; the sister's eyes — nearly as large — drawing narrow in appraisal. This had put John McCutcheon in mind of a drawing he had once seen: two elven children, winsome and yet somehow malignant, although Billie was more than a child. McCutcheon perceived this straightaway. She had a bold way of staring that might have come from her mother, who had reputedly been an actress at one time, or a whore, or something partway in between. Her arm crooked protectively about her brother's thin shoulders, and in that stare John McCutcheon had felt himself measured and found wanting; felt himself shrivelling and less adequate than he had been just the moment before, and Christ knows he had felt inadequate to begin with.

Now with the coming of that winter's night they watched the outlaws instead.

One of the outlaws, the youngest, had been wounded. This had been plain in the way he sat his horse: hunched down and tilted to one side, as if the next gust of wind could topple him. He came into the roadhouse gaunt and shuddering, and huddled thereafter by the pot-bellied stove.

"He's been shot," Gimp Tom whispered to his sister, in a private moment in the shadows in the farthest corner of the room, where they supposed themselves momentarily unobserved.

"You don't know that," Billie said.

"Oh, yes I do." He had read enough books to know it for a certainty. "That's a boy who's been shot, and there's a posse on the trail. Could be just bounty hunters they're running from, or maybe the Law and Deputies. Or it could even be worse than that, such as Texas Rangers."

"Rangers?" Billie said. "From *Texas?*"

An older sister would in her time hear much imbecility, but this evidently took the cake. This claimed first prize in the cake-baking tent at the harvest fair for idiots.

"But that's just it," Tom said. "That's all of it, right there in a walnut shell. A Texas Ranger don't give up—not ever. A Texas Ranger, Billie, keeps on coming. I pray for your own sake that you never find out what it means, to have a Texas Ranger on your tail."

Implacable pursuit seemed to be much on the minds of the outlaws already. The boy had set himself to watching them as closely as he could.

The oldest was a man called Cousin Fletch. So at least he said they should call him. A lean, leering man in middle age, with a cornpone voice and a grin like a tumbledown churchyard. "They's nobody coming," he said to the Man from Decatur. "Not on a night like this."

"He's coming," the Man from Decatur said. He paced to each window in turn, brooding into the darkness and the storm. The old house shook with the wind.

"Well, then let him," said Cousin Fletch. "Let the cocksucker get himself froze. They's no one stays alive in cold like this."

The wounded outlaw moaned. He had just turned nineteen years old—so Gimp Tom would presently establish—though his suffering made him seem older. Dirty yellow hair and a straggle of unsuccessful beard. In happier times, it seemed, he had been capable of a sweet slow smile, so full of light and life that you could scarcely credit the deeds alleged against him; deeds so vile as to defy earthly explication, unless you allowed that some devil had whispered him onward.

Billie Skiffings herself would not have believed it—not on that first evening, sitting halfway down the stairs with her half-brother, watching. The outlaws had clustered for warmth around the stove, on the rough wooden chairs that would serve for parlour furniture until such time as the hotel of John McCutcheon's imaginings took form.

The Man from Decatur called for whiskey. Then he called for more.

"Here's where it starts," Tom said, very low.

He had already begun to guess the true identities of these three men. The knowledge chilled him worse than any storm.

Gimp Tom knew much more than you might suppose. The boy was sadly crippled, which legacy his uncle ascribed to the Skiffings side; he moved herk-a-jerk with a queer industrious hitching of his elbows, as if the active exhortation of his upper half were required to stir his nethers into spidery locomotion. But his brain was both nimble and capacious: the McCutcheon side, very clearly, showing through. He knew the name of the first man ever shot dead by Wild Bill Hickok, which was McCanles, and the motto of the Texas Rangers.

Such facts and many more besides were contained in the nickel magazines and dime novels that he kept in a tin box in a cubbyhole beneath the floorboards, and which he studied at night with rapt assiduity. These included such works as *Buffalo Bill, the King of the Border Men,* and a memoir written by Colonel George Armstrong Custer, entitled *My Life on the Plains, or, Personal Experiences with Indians.* This famous memoir had been published two years previous, in '74. It had been left behind at the roadhouse by a man passing through with a railroad survey team. Gimp Tom would proceed to read it twelve separate times, beginning to end, committing entire passages to heart, prior to the sad events that lay scant months in the future, when in June at Little Bighorn Colonel Custer would add to his list one culminating experience with Indians.

The tin box contained other treasures as well. Some were from his earlier childhood in Victoria, in the time before his Ma grew wan and dwindled. Others were of recent provenance, left behind by passers-through on different occasions under varying circumstances, wittingly and otherwise: a jackknife and an inkwell and a fishing lure, and an old pistol wrapped in rag and tied with string. The pistol was his most prized possession, being highly illicit under British law, which restricted the private ownership of sidearms. It was an English model, a .45-calibre Deane-Adams five-shot: a notoriously shoddy piece of workmanship, as liable to explode in your own face as to spit lead death at your adversary, but similar to the pistol carried in early life by the great Wild Bill himself. He had as well a box of cartridges, with which he would in secret moments load the pistol and take dead aim at villains out the window, imagining himself a Wild Gimp Tom and performing mighty deeds in defense of his sister.

He had loaded the pistol that evening, with the coming of the riders.

Snow fell heavily throughout the night, and on through the day that followed, driven by a bitter wind out of the east. A snowfall without precedent in the memory of any white man living; prodigious even by the reckoning of the Nlaka'pamux, who had lived here since the mountains were small hills. With the onset of a second night the snowfall ceased, but as it did the temperature plunged and the wind shifted into the north. It howled relentlessly down upon them, whipping the new-fallen snow into drifts that choked the trails and wagon roads. The roadhouse was islanded now.

No one could stay sane in such conditions. Not even someone who was halfway sane to begin with.

The Man from Decatur brooded. He had been drinking steadily since their arrival; now he drank some more.

"Chrissakes," Cousin Fletch said. "He's not the Lord Almighty, stuck on a stick and rose again. Besides, we crossed the Medicine Line. He got no jurisdiction."

"D'you suppose he cares about that?" the Man from Decatur demanded. "He don't. And I've known him all my life."

He would go away, then, at such moments — a thousand miles, without ever leaving the room. He might sit immobile for an hour or more, shadows from the firelight writhing on the wall behind him and hovering above his head like the black wings of deeds he was contemplating. Then abruptly he would stand up and be jolly, calling for whiskey and someone to sing him a song.

"You." He swivelled to Billie Skiffings. "What can you sing for me?"

She'd been on her way to the back door, lugging a bucket of slops. "What would you give me?" she said.

"What do you want?"

"A dollar," she proclaimed.

"You'd sing me a song for a dollar?"

"I would."

"What would you do for ten?"

It stopped her dead for half a moment, the size of it. The implication. "Ten dollars?"

She gave a nervous laugh. She found herself considering: What *would* she do for ten dollars? More, possibly, than she might have supposed.

The Man from Decatur had that effect. He was dark as a mineshaft, but he was also Dionysus when he chose. And he took you with him. He was anarchy set loose in the world. He licensed you to be your own worst self — the self we all of us want most to be, deep down in the privacy of our heart's desire. And if you can't admit that, then you don't know your true nature at all. Or else — which is more likely — you're just a liar. As that understanding began to dawn upon Billie Skiffings, he crooked up a smile.

PART ONE

"Should I ask what you'd do for fifty dollars?"
"No," she said. "You should not ask me that."
"'Cause why?"
"You'd be wasting your time."
The Man from Decatur smiled some more.
"Then what would you do for five hundred?"
And you want to find that out. Oh, yes you do. You want to go there with him—just like Billie Skiffings, and the others who were islanded in that roadhouse for eight days in the winter of 1876. You want to follow him all the way down, and find out.

Such at least is one way to explain what happened thereafter.

Eight days and nights. Then the weather broke. And the Reckoning came.

A solitary rider, looming in the west. A long man in a buffalo-shaggy greatcoat, astride a grey hammerhead. They came through the trees and up the rise and into the clearing in front of the roadhouse.

John McCutcheon had come out with the rider's approach. He stood now stooped and squinting in the lemon sun: sallow, unshaven, working up the rictus of a smile.

Three men, the rider said. He was looking for three men. Three killers.

He might have been forty years old. His voice was thick with the South. A slow, dark baritone, rumbling ten feet up—so it seemed to John McCutcheon—from the hang of the scrotum.

Yes, the innkeeper said. Oh yes, they'd been here. But they'd gone.

"How long?"

The man only had one eye. It was ice-blue and piercing. A patch was across the other, and scarring beneath. His hair was brambled and tangled.

"A day or two, I'd guess," John McCutcheon said.

"Don't guess."

"Two days—when it cleared. That's when they rode out. Two of them did."

"The third one?"

"Yonder." John McCutcheon gestured with his chin.

The sawed-off eight-gauge in the rider's right hand had appeared out of nothing at all. He had shifted his shoulders and there it was, newly conjured into the universe: such an engine as could cut down a cavalry charge. This at least was the evidence of John McCutcheon's eyes, though the flat winter glare was a dazzlement and his vision had been dizzied to begin with by sleeplessness and busthead whiskey. It occurred to him that the shotgun had been nestled all along in the folds of the coat, just waiting to be shrugged into the sunlight.

The third outlaw—the youngest—leaned up against a shed. He was not moving, being roped to a plank around the chest and thighs and angled at forty-five degrees, as dead outlaws will be when placed on display. He might have frozen solid in the very act of rising—stiff and staring—from the grave. Round his neck hung a board on which someone in charcoal had scrawled: *One theef was damned.*

"The devil is this?" said the man in the buffalo coat. He'd dismounted and stalked closer.

"A Passage," John McCutcheon said. "The Bible, or some such."

"I can read. I'm asking: The devil happened?"

"Yes, sir," McCutcheon said, discovering his voice unsteady. "Yes, he did. That's as near as I can say myself. The devil happened, and here we stand today."

The one-eyed man's breath billowed white. The temperature had plunged again, after two days that had hinted at a thaw. Sun slanted from an empty sky and all the world stood mercilessly revealed.

"Did you kill him?"

"I didn't. He'd been shot already."

"Shooting never broke his neck."

The man with his one eye had seen that straightaway. The crick in the neck and the rope-wrenched skin.

"It was never me," McCutcheon said. "I swear."

He himself stood nearly six-foot-two, but the one-eyed man towered over him. The shoulders inside the buffalo coat were as wide as a canyon. So at any rate it seemed to John McCutcheon: as if the stranger commanded by some unquestioned right a larger share of Creation than the innkeeper had ever dreamed of laying claim to.

"Would you lie to me, friend?"

It came to John McCutcheon: Yes, he would. He would lie with great industry and application, if only he could. But this was not a man you could lie to. There was about him something grim and elemental; he was Saul or Goliath, except much colder. He was Judgement itself, come to Hell's Gate.

"God's own truth," McCutcheon said.

"Who else is here?"

"There's nobody."

"Call them out."

"No, look—you can't blame neither of them. They're just children."

But of course they weren't children at all. Not any longer—not after what had happened. John McCutcheon knew that already; he saw the recognition of it cross the stranger's face. The boy and his sister had come out of the roadhouse: Gimp Tom and that uncanny gal, ruined and shivering.

"It's true," Billie Skiffings said. She squinted against the glare. "What my Uncle John just told you."

"All of it?"

"Near enough." She stood in unlaced boots and a thin white smock, a blanket clutched about herself for warmth. "They rode out, the two of them. This dead one they left behind."

"Dead already?"

"Like my uncle said."

The low winter sun was behind the stranger now. His shadow stretched toward them.

"What road did they take?"

"The road you're on," said Billie Skiffings. "There's but the one."

The stranger looked at each of them in turn. "Here's what you'll do. You'll give that boy a Christian burial."

"The ground," John McCutcheon began to say. Meaning that the ground was frozen solid, three feet deep.

"You'll find a way. Whatever he done in life, he's paid his debt. Paid in full, which is more than you've ever done."

"Yes, sir," John McCutcheon said.

"Your boy here can see to my horse. Whatever grain you have. The girl can fetch dried meat for myself—salt pork is good. Some flour, and bacon. I'll pay you fair value, cash money, and be on my way."

Billie Skiffings said: "They'll kill you first, if you find them. Those men."

"They'll try."

"There's two of them. They'll shoot you down like a yellow dog. And mister? You'll deserve it."

"I've told you what I need from you. I need you now to do it."

Gimp Tom had not moved. He said: "I know who you are."

It was the certainty of the man. Tom would recollect this most clearly of all, about that afternoon. A vast and terrible certainty, such as he had never before encountered, and never would again.

He said: "You're his brother. You're Strother Purcell."

His uncle cleared his throat. "The boy reads books." McCutcheon said it shamefaced, as if some mitigation were needful. As you might say, *The boy has foaming conniptions,* or, *When he was six weeks old his Mama dropped him.* "Dime books, and magazines."

Gimp Tom paid no attention. He felt suddenly a desperate need to confess. To fall down upon his knees and blurt out what he had done, two nights previous and on the night before that; to confess to each ill deed that he had ever committed, on all the nights and days of his ten and one half wretched years upon this earth, and all the other crimes—too horrid even to imagine—that he must surely commit in the nights and days and years that lay ahead, if by some oversight he were to be left un-Judged and un-Smited and un-Ground into dust beneath the boot-heel of Righteousness.

Instead, the boy heard his own voice, crying out: "I want you to kill them both. D'you hear? I want you to kill both those fuckers dead, and stick their heads on stakes!"

*

His last glimpse of Strother Purcell that day was of a vast implacability, riding along the Wagon Road into the gathering shadows of the Black Canyon. He would not lay eyes on Purcell again for more than sixteen years, nor learn for a certainty what the one-eyed man had wrought.

In due course, Word would begin to filter down from the mountains of the Cariboo, two hundred miles north and east: whispers of a dreadful debt come due and a gunfight that was to have consequences beyond imagining. By the time these reached McCutcheon's Roadhouse, Gimp Tom himself had moved on, leaving behind a mystery of another kind: the question of what had transpired during those eight lost days in a storm-locked roadhouse in the winter of 1876, to have left the outlaw Dooley Sprewell dead and two children ruined beyond all hope of redemption.

Word continued to filter nonetheless. In the fullness of Time, it filtered all the way to San Francisco, where in April of 1892 it came to preoccupy the aspirations of an erstwhile scribbler of dime novels named Barrington Weaver.

-THREE-

The Accounting of Barry Weaver

San Francisco, 1892

1.

WYATT EARP was the gunman I had in my sights.

Oh, I'd heard of Strother Purcell. Strother Purcell had been from Tennessee, or Carolina—one of those backwoods places where God only knows what deviltry transpires up yonder Smoky Mountain. There'd been a blood-feud, after which Purcell achieved notoriety as a lawman in the Southwest. There'd been a confrontation in New Mexico that led to his hunting down his own outlawed half-brother— a vengeance quest that led him two thousand miles north into the frozen wastes of another country entirely, and made his name a byword for bloody-minded perseverance, against all sense and reason. At the end of it there'd been a final showdown, but—as far as I knew—it had left Purcell dead. As far as *anyone* knew. Purcell and the outlaw half-brother, too. But this had all been some years in the past, and there's only so much a man can make of the frozen corpses of shot-up hillbillies. So to speak.

What I didn't know—and had no reason to imagine—was that Strother Purcell might have survived. This possibility would not occur until the night of April 26 (I was a journalist, in those days, and kept note of precise dates and details) when two encounters took place: one with a crippled devil in a saloon, and one with an old man in a reeking antechamber of Perdition. Each of these was so unexpected and uncanny that—looking back—I can only suppose that fate had brought them upon me.

I don't suppose I used to believe in fate. At least, not Fate as those old Greeks understood it: Fate with a capital F, and blood in its eye. Fate fixed and immutable and fuck-all you can do, with great cosmic wheels turning and those Christalmighty horrors shrieking you to your destruction, those hags—what were they called?—with teeth and talons and hair streaming back, hell-bent on vengeance and ... *Furies.* That's what they were—those old Greeks called them the Furies. Well, I had no truck with that sort of thing. I still cherished—fool that I was—a young man's conviction that he could shape his own destiny. And I'd never laid eyes on a hag of retribution, not unless I counted my sainted Ma—which I oughtn't to do, not really. It wouldn't be fair.

But I *would* encounter my first Fury in that San Francisco spring of 1892, in the form of a runaway child-bride. I'd do so sooner than I could imagine, although I wouldn't recognize her for what she was. This understanding would come only later, when the disaster was already far advanced, the catastrophe that would consume us all in ways I could never have anticipated, and in the meantime—

Jesus. Listen to me—rambling and maundering, like an old drunk in a saloon.

We were speaking of Wyatt Earp.

He was the gunman I had my eye on, not Strother Purcell. And Wyatt was a different proposition. For starters he was still alive, which can be useful in a hero, up to a point. Even better, he was not yet Wyatt Earp. Not the Wyatt Earp *you* know, anyway—Earp the Lion of Tombstone. The one who rears up into your mind's eye, steely of resolve and epic of mustache, emerging through the shroud of gun smoke with reedy tubercular Doc Holliday and all that multitude of doughty Earp brothers, Virgil and Morgan and whoever the other ones were—the ones whose names their own mother could hardly keep straight, whatever her name was.² *That* Wyatt Earp would not exist for another fifteen years, when W.B. (Bat) Masterson—his old compeer from Dodge City days, now reinvented as a newspaperman in New York City—sold a series of articles to *Human Life* magazine about famous gunfighters of the Western frontier, and wrote about Wyatt Earp in the second one.

Wyatt would take his own crack at inventing Wyatt Earp in 1896, putting his name to a series of ghost-written reminiscences in the *San Francisco Examiner*. But the hack who did the writing—one of Hearst the Boy Wonder's hand-picked crew—made a botch of the opportunity. Take my word. I read the drivel, four years after having made my own approach to Earp.

Which brings us back to April of 1892.

"Your story needs to be told," I said to him. "And I am the man to tell it."

He eyed me down the side-slope of that mustache. "The hell are you?"

"Weaver," I said. "Barry Weaver. The writer."

We were side by side at the trough in the Gentlemen's off the lobby of the Occidental Hotel, where Earp had come cantering to lunch with a consortium of property developers. The Occidental sprawled across one whole block of Montgomery Street, an establishment much too grand for the likes of Missus Weaver's boy—or for the likes of Missus Earp's, if he'd just admit it. This was one of Wyatt's endless efforts to ingratiate himself into the capitalist elite; I'd been tipped to it by a Reliable Source, and arrived just in time to catch him with his business in hand.

"Don't have time for writers," he said. This, from a man who was reputed to have sat with the newspapers spread out at breakfast each morning in his Tombstone days, reading aloud any mention of his name. He hefted John Peter in his palm. "What kind of writer?"

---

2   It was Virginia (née Cooksey, *m.* Nicholas Earp). Wyatt's brothers were James, Virgil, Morgan and Warren, along with a half-brother, Newton.—*Brookmire.*

"A newspaper writer. I write for the newspaper."

"Yeah? Which one?"

"Books as well."

"Books."

"Novels."

Another slantways look, eyes narrowing. Those pale blue eyes, destined to become so famous. He'd have been in his mid-forties, at this point. Fair hair shading to silver, but still a man in the prime of life, square-jawed and handsome and six-foot-one. And that mustache. Christ. Falcons could have perched on the handlebars, one on either side.

"Novels," he repeated. It was the tone of voice that holds a word between thumb and finger-tip, as you'd hold the tail of a small dead rodent. "My wife reads novels, time to time."

"Maybe she's read one of mine."

"Possible. Don't know as I'd call it probable."

"I've written several."

"Wouldn't put it past you for a second."

Rising on tiptoes, he reeled himself back in. He wore a dove-grey suit and tan shoes and a derby hat, which he adjusted in the mirror. After Tombstone, Earp had spent several years in San Diego, speculating in the property market, until a sudden downturn wiped him out. Another man might have recalibrated his ambitions, having taken the hint that he was woefully out of his depth amongst financiers: a bully-boy with an air of plausibility and a certain steadiness of nerve, who had reached the pinnacle of his abilities as a head-cracker and faro-dealer in the boomtowns of the Southwestern frontier. Not Wyatt Earp. He picked himself up, and now here he was in the Bay Area, managing a racetrack in Inglewood, and placing shrewd bets — he knew horseflesh and gambling, give him that much — bent once again on reinventing himself a Man of Business and winning the esteem of all those sleek-bellied Republicans. This was ever the defining feature of his character. That, plus being as thick as two stout planks, and an asshole.

One last try.

"Wyatt—if I may call you—Mr. Earp. The thing of it is...you've got a story, and a story needs to be told. Tell it first, or else someone else will do it. And then *that* one becomes the truth of who you are."

The gaze was narrow and impressively fixed. For a moment, I thought I'd gotten through.

"I'm Wyatt Earp," he said. "That's who *I* am. And you?" He hawked contemplatively. Turned and gobbed: dead centre in the sink. "You look like shit brung home on a stick."

*

It was a miracle I didn't look worse.

The previous evening had begun at Sverdrup's on East Street and degenerated from there, ending in sodden ignominy on the paving stones outside a blind pig in Maiden Lane. In between I had visited Bottle Koenig's and a selection of other Barbary Coast armpits, having decided that nothing would suit the gaiety of the occasion short of getting my throat slit, ear to ear. We were celebrating my forty-fifth birthday.

I came close to achieving my goal at a concert saloon in Dupont Street, where I reared up to champion the honour of a Mormon whore named Prairie Rose against insults tendered by a stork-legged poltroon. Or so I'm told. My recollection of events being patchy, I'm going on eyewitness reports from my companions. These were fellow scribblers, for the most part, some of them employed by Hearst the Boy Wonder down at Geary Street, which is to say a clutch of dipsomaniac lying bastards who would never twist a fact when they could invent one outright, bless their hearts. Bill Lundrigan might have been one of them—I believe he dropped by, though I couldn't swear to that. If Bill came, he'd have brought Ernie Thayer with him—Mighty Ernie, author of "Casey at the Bat," the greatest one-poem wonder in America. Yes, I knew all those fellows. I knew Ambrose Bierce. There was even a rumour that Bierce might condescend to join us, but rumours are rumours and Ambrose was Ambrose, and he didn't.

The trouble began with a misreading of Prairie Rose's business card. Rose was a waitress, strictly speaking—one of the so-called Pretty Waiter Girls who plied the clientele with enlivening beverage as they savoured the artistry of the performers, who ranged from bad singers who kept their laundry on, to worse singers who didn't. But the serving of drinks was supposed to be a kind of undercard to the main event of a Pretty Waiter Girl's occupation, for which cards were at present much in vogue. Prairie Rose's was a fine one. It featured her name in red letters within a border of interlacing thorns—a whimsical and engaging visual pun, and well above the run-of-the-mill standard in such cards, which were mainly designed on a freelance basis by local hacks. Included was the address of the establishment and particulars concerning Rose's terms of service: *$2 EACH, OR THREE FOR $5.*

"And there's three of us," a voice was insisting, behind us. "Me, him, an' him. Five dollars!"

"It's two dollars for each go," said Rose. It was late and she was mortal tired already. "Not two dollars for each customer."

"Where does it say that?"

"Right there, sweetheart. On the card."

"The hell it does. The *card* says—"

"Oh, good grief. Try askin' the man who wrote it."

That's when I got involved, apparently.

I recall turning around on my stool, and squinting up at the man who harangued poor Rose. He was two- or three-and-twenty, a gangling ginger with thinning hair and a way of standing spavined and bow-legged, as if he'd just been buggered by a dray-horse. His mother, I thought, should have named him Ichabod.

"*You* tell 'im, Barry—wouldja?" Rose said wearily.

"The lady's right, friend," I might have said, urbanely. "The subject is apposite and implied, but the reference is to the act, not the actor. But look—I take responsibility for any confusion, so why don't I buy you a drink?"

Yes, that is what I might have said, if I hadn't been stinking drunk and forty-five, with a table of newsmen to impress. Instead, I snarled: "It says so clear as goddamned day, in English. Can't you read?"

Ichabod grew ominously squinty. "You wrote this? Then you're a Fucki' Nidiot. Two dollars a customer—two dollars each."

"Two dollars each poke."

"And who takes the poke? The customer!"

His lumpen companions whooped. By golly, this was logic, eh? Ichabod was further emboldened. "Two dollars for me, and five for the three of us. Black and white, clear as day, next case. And if you keep sticking your nose in other people's business, old man, there's someone gonna pull it for you."

Despite my condition, the notion nagged: this Ichabod seemed oddly familiar. I'd seen him somewhere. And there was still a way out of this dispute, if I'd had the sense to take it.

The concert saloon had gentlemen standing by to deal with disturbances—men larger and lumpier than either of Ichabod's chums, and a barkeep named Olaf who kept an axe-handle near to hand for special occasions. Prairie Rose was catching Olaf's eye already; all I had to do was keep my head down. Instead, Young Weaver reared onto his hind legs: "Oh, yeah?"

The ancient battle-cry of the Fucki' Nidiot.

Here the evening became blurry and excruciating. Ichabod had taken my nose between thumb and forefinger with more vivacity than

I would have credited. He then twisted it clockwise, looking around to his lumpen companions with a bray of triumph.

A mistake. As Ichabod brayed, Young Weaver brought his right fist up with — as the boxing writers say — a sockdolager to the coconut. And whether said fist was clutching a beer mug at that moment — as was afterwards maintained by certain witnesses — I do not presume to say. Ichabod dropped like a steer, to be lugged insensate from the field. And huzzahs were offered up to the victor, who gazed about in triumphant stupefaction.

We proceeded to several more establishments. Libations flowed and the tale of my conquest was told and retold, the adversary growing in stature each time until he was a stork-legged Goliath and Young Weaver a latter-day David. At some point I staggered back to the concert saloon. Seeking out Prairie Rose, I proclaimed that I would demonstrate the true meaning of THREE FOR $5, which feat I would perform straightway on the nearest tabletop, in contempt of five-and-forty winters on my head.

Or so I'm told. And to tell the truth I do have a hazy recollection: the whoops of the men and the bone-weary disappointment on Rose's face as I lunged to clutch her hand — *et tu, Barry?* — and I remain to this day ashamed of myself. Prairie Rose was in fact a Mormon's wife from Utah named Lucinda something — Dalkins was her maiden name, I think, or at any rate the one she went by. She had fled a marriage that had curdled; a big-boned gal no longer young who had a sad, sardonic wit and dreamed she might open a dress-maker's shop. The two of us had evolved onto terms that could almost be called a friendship; and God knows we have few enough friends in this world, without proposing to mount them in concert saloons.

I'd misjudged my lunge, however. I went clear past Rose, and ricocheting off the table staggered wildly into the arms of Olaf the barkeep, who with Nordic utterance took matters and Young Weaver in hand, and escorted him headfirst out the door.

I don't remember getting home that night. There are vague recollections of wobbling down an alleyway in the slanting San Francisco rain. Stopping to piss, and finding my fingers too numb with cold to manage buttons. Laughing out loud, and afterwards growing sorrowful and weeping. I remember staggering and stumbling and falling, and failing most pathetically to get back up again. I have a notion that someone came to my aid, more sensitive than I was myself to the inadvisability of passing out gob-down in a mud-hole. One eye in a ruined face peered at me through the fog, and two hands were hauling me upright. I recollect—or think I do—a mighty waft of unwashed humanity, and an arm like an oak limb under my armpit, and a pair of vast hobnailed boots tramping alongside my own.

When I foundered back into consciousness, it was morning. I was inside my room on California Street, sprawled in skull-splitting daylight half-on and half-off the bed. Someone, it seems, had helped me up the stairs. They'd helped me through the door and off with my clothes—coat and boots, at least, though not the trousers. These were in a sodden tangle about my shins. Evidently my Good Angel had given up at this point, though not before setting a basin on the floor beside me, into which I now vomited.

2.

My wife, Wyatt Earp had said to me at the trough. *My wife reads novels, time to time.* Meaning the lovely Josephine Sarah "Sadie" Marcus Earp, which was debatable.

Not that she read novels—I didn't doubt that for a second. And no man with eyes in his head would dispute that she was lovely. But don't try to tell me that Josephine Sarah "Sadie" Marcus was ever Josephine

Sarah "Sadie" Marcus Earp. No one else believed it either, not that you'd find anyone who'd say so — not to Sadie's face, and most surely not to Wyatt's. He may not yet have become Wyatt Earp, but he had still killed five men — six, if you included Johnny Ringo — and he had that look about him that said: Why, hell, he'd be game to make it seven, counting you. Not that anyone in San Francisco cared much, either way, whether she was actually married to Wyatt or not. Oh, there were those up Nob Hill who might *affect* to care. The Gold Rush heyday was a generation gone and the city was home to more and more with upwardly aspirations, the better to look down from a height on the likes of thee and me. That's not the same as caring, though. That's just judging.

But Sadie cared. She cared a great deal about being seen as Missus Earp, and about much else besides: exactly as you'd expect from a baker's daughter who had been born in New York City but grew up right here in San Francisco, and was staying with Wyatt these days in a leased house at 720 McAllister Street, less than a mile from the street where her parents still lived, and where Hyman Marcus had gone door to door with his baskets of newly baked buns.

This gave Young Weaver his angle of approach. "Your husband may think his deeds speak for themselves," I said to her. "The thing of it is — the problem we're facing — they don't."

"You talked to my husband already?" she said, weighing Young Weaver with her stare.

"Two days ago."

"And?"

"Today I'm speaking to you."

We were outside the house on McAllister Street. A small house, bordering on shabby, but a step up from the dump on Ellis Street where she and Wyatt had stayed on first arriving back in San Francisco. I'd done my research, though catching Missus Earp like this—first try, rounding the corner just as she'd stepped out the door—involved a stroke of luck as well. But Fortune, as we all know, favours the brave. And the well-prepared. And—above all else—the plausible.

There stood Young Weaver on this April morning: scrubbed and shaved and oiled and earnest and plausible as hell. "Deeds don't speak, Missus Earp," I said. "Deeds don't say a blessed word. It's people who do the talking. And we both know what sorts of things they'll say, if left too much to their own devices."

It was a fine clear day, but cool, with a wind gusting in from the harbour. There was frost in the air, of a sudden, and a bite of it in Sadie's voice. "I don't believe I'm following your meaning."

But she did. She followed me precisely. I drew up another brimming bucket from the Well of Earnest. "They'll tell Lies, Missus Earp—all manner of untruths. Unless you've caught their fancy first, with a truth that suits them better."

"What exactly *have* you heard, Mr.—whaddid you say your name was?"

"Weaver, ma'am. Barrington Weaver. Barry."

"And you're—what—some sorta writer?"

"I am. And what counts is what I haven't heard."

"Which is?"

"The truth as *you* would hear it."

The traffic along McAllister Street was rattling along its way. Horse-drawn carts and trudging tradesmen, to-ing and fro-ing from Market Street nearby. But we'd begun to attract slantways glances. A flat-foot at the corner was stink-eyeing Young Weaver, who began to fear that he'd overplayed his hand.

The bun-peddler's daughter said at last: "So what's in this for you?"

—

You may have seen Missus Earp yourself—or believed so, anyway. There is a famous photograph. It depicts a young woman of formidable endowments in nothing but a diaphanous shawl, which she wears draped over the head and shoulders like a novitiate's habit. Her expression is remote, the camera lens angling upward such that she seems to be gazing down from an enigmatic height. It shows you what truths the camera can exalt, Sadie Marcus being a woman who topped out at five-foot flat on the tallest day of her life. Or leastways it *would* show this, if the gal in the photo were actually Sadie Marcus. But probably it isn't, despite claims you would later hear to the contrary. I say this as someone who saw the original in the flesh—saw her *face,* I should say, having no wish to create the wrong impression. Not while Wyatt Earp is still alive.

The photograph dates from the early 1880s, a few years after young Sadie Marcus had run away from home to join a troupe of thespians that was travelling to the Arizona Territory with a production of *H.M.S. Pinafore.* A remarkable adventure, but no less than the truth, as she told it ever after. The production starred Pauline Markham, the noted contralto and celebrated beauty whose arms were once hailed by a New York critic as the lost appendages of the Venus de Milo. It must have been a memorable production, though curiously the name of Josephine Sarah "Sadie" Marcus does not appear on the company rolls. Presumably she had adopted a stage name, but the omission was sufficient to set Rumour to work. There was one persistent whisper that Sadie Marcus *was* in fact listed among several young female passengers who travelled to the Arizona on a different stagecoach in the company of Hattie Wells, who was known at the time as the proprietress of a brothel on Clay Street. In 1878, this would have been, when young Sadie was seventeen.

None of this was verifiable, of course. Or fair. But it goes to show you what a newspaperman can dig up, if you give him a couple of days and some incentive.

"Friday," Missus Earp had said by way of conclusion, that morning outside the leased house on McAllister. She said it tersely, as a woman might who did not yet trust Young Weaver one inch. "I'll think about it—what you said. If I wake up Friday in a tolerable mood, you might find me taking lunch at *La Tree-yest.*"

Her mood come Friday was downright vivacious.

"I'm seeing three articles," I told her over breadsticks. "Three at least—maybe four. Appearing on sequential Sundays."

"In the *Examiner?*"

"Where else? The best newspaper west of New York—'The Monarch of the Dailies.' Ask Mr. Hearst. It says so right on the masthead."

I cocked the grin at a rakish angle. She dimpled pertly back.

"But of course," she said, "you don't write for the *Examiner.* Do you?"

We were sitting at a table in the window. "My usual table," she had said to the *maître d'* on arrival, sweeping in on a sparkle of vivacity and beckoning Young Weaver from the gloomy corner in which they'd stuck him. Quite frankly I couldn't tell you whether she had a "usual table" at *La Trieste* or not. The *maître d'*—an oleaginous little Frenchman, all garlic and pretension—did look surprised to hear it. But there was immediately much beaming and *mais oui*-ing, and the ushering of Madame Earp and her guest to a prime piece of real estate at the front, which just happened to be unoccupied. Several other tables were unoccupied as well, owing possibly to *La Trieste's* celebrated combination of bad food and extortionate prices. There she proceeded to hold court, elbows on the red-check tablecloth, regarding

Young Weaver with a smile that would send every accordion in Paris into arpeggios.

"You've never wrote for the *Examiner,* Mr. Weaver. Not since you got here—what was it?—almost a year ago. From Kansas, or some such."

"Kansas City."

"That's the one."

The smile grew sweeter still. Evidently two days of research worked both ways.

"Missus Earp? I will be honest."

"Sure," said the bun-peddler's daughter, encouragingly. "Give it a go—see how it feels."

"I do not at this moment write for Mr. William Hearst's *Examiner.*"

This may come as a surprise to you, Dear Reader. I confess that I may have given you a contrary impression. In fact, I did not write for anyone, just at the moment. Not since I'd chucked over the only job I'd held since my arrival, with a bi-weekly rag called the *Bulletin.* Since then I'd been limping along, picking up freelance work where I could and wondering if I had the heart for another novel.

"I have never been employed by Mr. Hearst," I admitted. "But I will be, once he reads these articles. Your husband's career as a lawman in Dodge and Tombstone—the fearless exploits. The single-handed heroism and the Gunfight at O.K. Corral."

"The what?"

"The shooting scrape, Missus Earp. With the Clantons and McLaurys."

"That mainly happened outside Fly's Photography."

"No," I said. "It didn't."

She blinked. And saw. "The Gunfight at O.K. Corral," she repeated. Trying it out in her mouth. "Yeah, that's good."

"I write books, you see. About mighty deeds, and heroes."

The bun-peddler's daughter eyed me appraisingly. Then she leaned forward, a little — a trick she had, and a good one; it drew you in closer. Her breath smelled of cloves.

"How much?" she said.

"How much will Hearst pay me?"

"How much will *you* pay *us?*"

"No," I said. "No, see, you're not ... it doesn't work that way."

"Yes, it does. Or else it don't work at all."

She tilted her head in the prettiest way you could imagine. The waiter chose this moment to undulate up with the wine. Some manner of claret, ruinously priced, which Madame tasted and pronounced *très bon.*

"Fine," I said. "Ten per cent."

"Of?"

"Whatever Hearst pays me. And your husband reads the articles first."

"My husband is a busy man."

"Well, that's fine too. We'll proceed on trust, and —"

"*I* read them first. You make the changes. I read 'em again. But not for ten per cent."

"I could possibly see my way to twenty-five."

"A sharp-eyed fella like yourself? I bet you could see clear across to fifty."

"*Fifty?*"

"If you set your mind. And a hunnerd dollars in advance."

I may have sputtered. "Where would I get money like that?"

"Your relation might help. The one who sends you a bank-draft every quarter. A remittance, I'd be guessing. From a fond old auntie. Or is it your Ma?"

This was outrageous, and I said so. It was robbery. Not that I used the actual word — not out loud, and not to the consort of Wyatt

45

Earp, who thick as he was had shot the hell right out of the Clantons outside Fly's Fucking Photography, and afterwards hunted down with terrifying ice-cold calculation the cowboys involved in the killing of his brother Morgan. Including—if Rumour told true—the gunslinger John Ringo, who was thought to be unbeatable until Wyatt caught him dead-drunk on an Arizona trail and put a bullet between his eyes. That was the tale I wanted to tell, though I'd leave out the part about Ringo being too drunk to see who was standing in front of him. I'd make it the duel of titans that it should have been in the first place, and would be ever after.

And here sat Josephine Sarah "Sadie" Marcus Earp. As innocent as Cleopatra, having read Young Weaver so neat and quick you'd think his inmost secrets were as words scrawled out in crayon on a page.

"Look," I said. "You need to see—this is not about the money."

"'Course it's about the money. It's always about the money. People who deny that are either saints or fools—don't you find? And I wouldn't of pegged you for neither one, Mr. Weaver. Or have I somehow read your nature wrong?"

"Missus Earp . . . Sadie—"

"Missus Earp is fine."

"I don't *have* a hundred dollars. That is the truth. I have no way of *getting* a hundred dollars—not from my mother, and not from the Boy Wonder Hearst, leastways not until he hires me. If you have a better idea, I'd love to hear it."

Sadie cocked her head, considering. "In the old days, you could of sold some teeth. A dentist friend of my husband once told me about that. Doc John Henry Holliday. In the old days, he said, they made dentures of 'em—real human teeth. It's all done with whatchamit now—porcelain, an' so forth—so the market's dried up. And of course George Washington's was carved from wood. John Holliday tried to tell me it was cherry wood, presuming I was stupid—carved by young George himself from that tree he cut down with his axe—but I seen through that man from the get-go. He was a slinking little back-shooter with dead-fish eyes, Doc Holliday. Smelled of cabbage-farts—punk-rotten on the inside—but he knew his teeth. And you have yourself such a fine white set of 'em, too. You been smiling those teeth at me ever since we met, right up till just two minutes ago. I'd say you could part with ten or a dozen, and still have plenty of smile left over. So why not buck up, Mr. Weaver, and make me an offer?"

Sadie Marcus's teeth just now were tinted claret-red. She smiled them at me anyway.

"Ten dollars," I said. "In advance. And a sixty-forty split."

"Which way?"

"My way."

"Make it my way, and we're getting close."

"Fine."

"Call it eighty-twenty, and we got a deal."

"Eighty per cent?"

"Plus twenty dollars up front."

"That leaves me with almost nothing!"

"Depends how you reckon the rewards, Mr. Weaver. You said yourself, it's not about the money. It's being the man who told my husband's tale. It's fame and litterchure, and all the rest—not to mention getting hired by Mr. Hearst. Nice step up from *The Further Adventures of Deadeye Ned.*"

I must have made some sort of face at that. Sadie laughed merrily. "Sure, I read your books, Mr. Weaver—or Mr. 'B.W. Colton,' should I say. I liked *The Last Trail* pretty much, else we wouldn't be talking here in the first place. You can gallop a tale along well enough, though that hero of yours don't have much to say for himself. Bit boring, if you don't mind my personal opinion. You'll want to do better with Wyatt. But I just know we'll enjoy our dealings, Mr. Weaver. Do we have ourselves a deal?"

I offered up a mouthful of fine, white, gritted teeth. "We do."

The bun-peddler's daughter beamed her most radiant smile yet, and began to extend her hand. Then she broke off, seeing someone outside. "Why, look," she exclaimed, raising the hand in a wave. "It's Mr. Rourke's nephew, from the bank."

I looked.

There stood — God help us — Ichabod. My stork-legged adversary from the other night. He had stopped outside on the sidewalk, grinning bravely through the window at Sadie Marcus. He wore a banker's woolen suit, but his face above it was deathly pale; and there was a clean white bandage wrapped clear round his head, exactly as if someone had clocked him with a beer mug.

"Good golly," Sadie Marcus said. "He looks to of had some sorta mishap."

Ichabod's grin quirked wry and sheepish, as if he thought to offer some explanation, which Missus Earp might lip-read through the glass. Then he saw Young Weaver.

"The manager's nephew — do you know him?" the bun-peddler's daughter was saying to me. "Mr. Rourke, at First Union. A great friend of my husband, and a finanshul associate."

That's where I'd seen him. That's why he'd seemed familiar, at the concert saloon.

Ichabod stared back at me, like a harbinger of Apocalypse.

3.

There is a word to describe my prospects, from that moment onward. It is a fine old Anglo-Saxon word, and that word is "fucked."

It was the bank where I myself held an account. The First Union, a

redoubtable brick structure on the edge of "down town," where by day
the men of business would stride with purpose, and of an evening the
ladies would promenade past the blaze of light from store windows.
This would have been bad enough, all on its own—the discovery
that Ichabod, when not slumming with low companions in concert
saloons, was a bank clerk that I might have to deal with. But reveal
him to be a scion of wealth and privilege—the nephew of J. Pierpont
Rourke, no less—and it went to hell completely. William Rourke
could stalk stork-legged where he chose, entirely unconstrained. He
could look down on Young Weaver from the wooden railing on the
second level, where executive offices were located, with such seething
combustion that a drier man than Weaver might burst into flame.
Might shrivel right there in the line-up, and crumble to a cone of ash.
Or if he chose—and this was even worse—William Rourke might
greet Young Weaver with a cool and insidious pleasantry. "Ah," he
might say, "the fifteenth of the month. Remittance day. How is she,
your Sainted Ma?"

Young Weaver might try to eye him coolly back. "She's well,
I believe."

"Well, that's good news. Your Sainted Ma, all the way back home
in—where is it that she lives, exactly?"

"New Brunswick."

"New *Brunswick*. Well, my golly. It's a marvel to me, the places
where people's mothers live. And a regular remittance to her grown-
up boy—the fifteenth day of every quarter, without fail. She must
be awful proud of you."

Then he would stork-leg it toward another wicket, with a thin cold
smile that promised murder. This was America, after all. William
Rourke would rise. In six months, he would have an office of his
own on the second floor. In a year or two it would be a corner office,
with a prospect onto the ocean and a filing cabinet stuffed with other

people's mortgages. By the time he was thirty, he would have a house on Nob Hill and a dim unhappy wife who had once gone riding with one of the Vanderbilt girls.

Worse yet, he knew the Earps, who so desired the favour of his uncle. I'd seen it from that first moment in the restaurant. The Spectre of Ichabod staring in through the glass. The bun-peddler's sharp-eyed daughter edging back from me, the beads of her inner abacus audibly clicking. "Do I take it you fellers are known to each other? 'Cause he sure seems to recognize you."

And there went my deal with Sadie Marcus. Within moments she'd discovered how time had flown, and was promptly out the door.

And then it got worse.

That same evening, I returned to my lodging to find the lock changed, and my miserable few possessions stacked up outside the door.

"Evicted," the landlord mumbled.

He was a German, and not swinish by nature. I'd almost liked him, in his way, which was pink-faced and perspiring. A builder by trade, who had come to America to make something of himself. I'd caught him on his way out the back door.

"Rent in arrears," he said. This seemed to have something to do with it. "Un-zuitable tenant" was something else. "Drinkinks and carryinks-on."

"And you couldn't just *talk* to me?"

Apparently not. Because apparently it wasn't his decision.

"What do you mean, not your decision? You own the damned building!"

It seemed he didn't. Not exactly.

He said something about "ze mortgage." Something to do with "ze bank." Something to do with "ach" and *Gott im Himmel.*

By then he'd said enough.

This was Ichabod's doing. Ichabod's revenge.

4.

You'll have certain questions by now, I expect. Queries concerning your friend Weaver, and where he came from, and how he had managed to end up here: in San Francisco, in this sorry pass, on the night of 26 April, 1892.

I had those questions myself.

"Jesus," I said heavily, to Fat Charley behind the bar. "Jesus Christ, eh?"

Fat Charley glanced briefly in my direction, then shifted along to serve another customer.

I had gone to a saloon or two after my eviction, and now I was at Mulvaney's, leaning disconsolately against the bar. Mulvaney's was a comfortably seedy watering-hole, around the corner and down an alley from Will Hearst's resplendent new Examiner Building on Geary Street. The Boy Wonder had erected this edifice as his personal riposte to the sky-scraping Chronicle Building at the corner of Market and Kearney, and Mulvaney's was as such a noted redoubt for newspapermen. It was eight o'clock or so when I arrived.

I'd had it in mind to seek out my friends from the *Examiner*. Because I *knew* those men—I honestly did. I knew some of them, at least. I'd been badgering Bill Lundrigan, the City Editor, for months, asking the man to hire me.

"I swear, you would not regret it," I had vowed to him on various occasions.

"Well, perhaps we'll talk about it," Bill Lundrigan had replied. "Some other time, if an opening comes up."

"Did I tell you—? Wait—look here—I have a letter of reference, from an old pal of yours. Wally Palmer, at the *Philadelphia Beacon*. Did I ever show it to you?"

I'd shown it to him on three separate occasions. Each time I'd tug the crinkled envelope out of my pocket and smooth the letter carefully.

Wally Palmer was the City Editor at the *Beacon*. I'd worked there a few years previously—Philadelphia had been two or three papers before Kansas City, which was my last stop before coming out to San Francisco. I'd toiled for a good few newspapers, over the years; some of the situations had proven to be more congenial than others, and I'd never been a man for staying put when greener pastures beckoned. But Wally Palmer's recommendation had been kindly, mentioning my can-do attitude and my potential. I had one whale of a potential, in Wally's estimation. Yes, I had been seen by some as a Rising Young Man, in bygone days.

"Good old Wally Palmer," Bill Lundrigan would reply. "My gosh —is old Wally still alive? Well, you be sure to give him my best, if you happen to see him."

I'd even applied directly—in person—to Will Hearst himself, the Boy Wonder. This is a true story. Swear to God, not a word of a lie. I was outside the Examiner Building one fine September day, just after noon—this had been a few months earlier. Just lingering a bit—as one does—in hopes of bumping into Bill Lundrigan, or one of the others, on their way out to lunch. Well, the front door opened, and who should emerge but William Hearst. A dapper young dynamo, preposterously young, with unearthly blue eyes and a wisp of blond mustache—such was my first impression. He was flanked by two other men, and bound for a carriage that awaited on the street. But before he could step into it, I introduced myself and made my pitch for employment.

He heard me out, too. I had fifteen seconds of his undivided attention, at the end of which he gave me a look of piercing appraisal and asked me a question that cut to the quick of my aspirations.

Anyway. Hearst wasn't at Mulvaney's when I arrived, on that evening of April 26. Neither was Lundrigan, or any of the others.

I'd had it in mind that someone might stand me a drink, and possibly even offer up a couch where I might sleep for a night or two. Also, I may have had a notion that the men of the *Examiner* might rise to my defense, and denounce William Rourke from the Editorial Pages. No such luck. A newspaperman's tavern — and not a single damned newspaperman on the premises. None had arrived by nine o'clock, either. Or by ten. Or eleven-thirty.

Midnight found me sitting alone at a table in the corner.

I expect I was drunk, by this point. Drunk, and muttering. I'd run out of money, but had managed to cadge a last pitcher of steam beer from Fat Charley the barkeep. Stale beer pooled on the tabletop; the blue fug of smoke and sour malt sagged down from the rafters. And where was I supposed to go from here? I was homeless.

"Two kinds of men come to San Francisco, I find." That's what Hearst had said to me, that September afternoon. "There are active and energetic men — intelligent men, who come west in the buoyancy of youth, to make their fortune. And then there are those who have washed up here, on the eddy of repeated failure. So the question I ask, is — which are you?"

"God damn him straight to hell," I said.

I muttered this to the tabletop, not to Hearst. And I was actually brooding upon William "Ichabod" Rourke. As time had ticked past, my thoughts had grown progressively dark. I began thinking to myself: *Perhaps it's time to settle this — once and for all. Just the two of us, man to man.* I began to think: *I should kill him.*

"I s'pose you could give it a try," said a strange high voice.

I jerked round, startled.

Behind me, a little man sat alone, in shadow. He'd been there for awhile, I'd guess, at a low table on the other side of a pony-wall, nursing a glass of steam beer and jotting with a pencil in a notebook.

"I've had the same thoughts myself, from time to time," he said. "About killing someone."

"*Killing* someone?" I exclaimed, sputtering a little. "Who the hell said anything about killing someone?"

"You did."

"I never!"

"Just now."

Oh, Christ. Had I really been talking out loud?

There are moments in life when we see ourselves, shockingly revealed. This was one of those moments—and, oh, the prospect was dismal. Evidently, I was becoming That Person: the solitary drunk, ageing before your eyes, who twitches and scowls and mutters to himself. And we know what comes next, don't we? The swallowings of dregs from other people's mugs; the fishing out of dead cigarette-ends, and the painstaking straightening of them out; the lurches and the staggers and the outright pissings in pants.

"You're Weaver, aren't you?" the little man said. "Yes, you are. I've seen you around, here and there."

And I recognized him. Ty-something. Tyree—that was his name. So people called him, anyway. He had a corner newsstand, farther east on Market Street. You'd see him out in all weather, selling newspapers and tobacco.

"Barry Weaver," he continued, nodding sagely. "Otherwise known as B.W. Colton, creator of Deadeye Ned Hartland."

"Who told you that?"

"Oh, someone did. Heard it somewhere. Stuck in my brainpan. *The Gallows Tree, The Last Trail,* and the third one—there were three of 'em, the Deadeye Ned books, I know that. What was the third title? Never mind; it'll come to me. They always do."

He had a certain standing with the local hacks. This would explain his presence in Mulvaney's, though I didn't recall having seen him here before.

"Heard about your troubles with young Rourke. Too bad."

I shrugged.

"Missus Earp, now — there's a woman, eh? Knows her own mind. A remarkable woman in many ways, though whether she's actually Missus Earp — well, that don't signify. Not to the likes of myself, and — *The Call of the Plains*. There it is. The title." Tyree glugged a swallow of steam beer; his Adam's apple bobbed. "I just have one of those heads. Odds and pieces get lodged in there, like gristle between the teeth. No disrespect to your writings."

He offered the rough sketch of a smile. Oversized head cocked sparrow-wise on a flimsy neck, huge eyes peering through spectacles. The lenses were thick as the bottoms of Mason jars. When the light caught them at an angle they would be suddenly opaque, his eyes as void and vacant as a blind man's. Thus the name. He'd been dubbed Tiresias by newspapermen who found him to be a source of remarkable information — never for attribution, but seldom mistaken. Tiresias, the sightless seer from the old Greek play. The one who knew what King Oedipus had been up to, long before the doomed king knew it himself. Tyree, for short.

"You're better than you ever got credit for," he said. "As a writer, I mean. As a man?" That sketch of a smile. "Couldn't say. Those books of yours, though — they're all right. Considering they're not really your books."

"What are you talking about?"

"They're just books you wrote 'cause you guessed someone would like 'em. And I guess someone did, more or less. But they're not the book you were put on earth to write."

"And how would you know that?"

He shrugged at that. Eyes still void. Spindle shoulders rising about his ears. "Go ahead. Tell me I'm wrong."

I opened my mouth to do just that. Then didn't.

"The hell else do you think you know about me?" I said.

I was finding this uncanny, tell the truth. Damned near shivery up my spine. He closed his notebook, and as he did I glimpsed one of the pages. It was covered in densely compact lines, executed in a tiny, spiky, chicken-track cursive. Oh, he was the strangest creature. Those huge eyes, and limbs like sticks. You'd see him hirpling along the street, head bobbing on that stamen of a neck. Elbows pistoning, as if he must with each step hike balky legs into locomotion.

He had set himself to rolling a cigarette with a grimy leather pouch of makings. I saw now that he was younger than I'd guessed him to be, at first. Maybe twenty-seven or twenty-eight — no more than thirty. He had come from somewhere farther north — I seemed to recall having heard something to that effect. Up in Canada, I think. He'd worked at a newspaper in Seattle, setting type; had been a printer's devil somewhere else. He no doubt had a Christian name, too — something other than "Tyree" — though I couldn't have told you what it was.

"What else do I know about you, Barry Weaver?" he mused. "Well, I know what you've been asking yourself."

"Read minds, do you?"

"You're wondering: *Could I actually do it? Could I kill William Rourke?*"

That sketch of a smile. A flash of the lenses, and the eyes went void again.

I said: "Good Christ."

"Do you have previous experience in that line, Mr. Weaver? Have you ever killed someone?"

"Good Christ," I said again. "What sort of man do you think I am?

"Yes," Tyree said. "That's the question. The one we come right down to, in the end." He licked along the edge of his cigarette paper: a dainty dabbing with his tongue. Twisting both ends, he looked up at me again. "There's killers, Mr. Weaver—and then there's all the others. That's been my assessment. All the men who might kill if it came down to soldiering or just blind panic, but only if there wasn't a way around it. But there's also the first kind—men who can kill as easy as order breakfast. Men who have a gift, if you'd call it that— it just comes natural and pure, the same way other men might run like deer or sing like angels. I'd suspect Wyatt Earp to be that kind—he's a killer. There's others like that too, but not so many."

"You've known your share of pure-born killers, I suppose?" I let the sneer sound in my voice. "Broken bread with them, and such?"

He'd lit his roll-'em as we spoke; smoke curled about his head. "I met three such men in my life," he said. "One of them hardly counts—an outlaw named Quarles, out of Missouri. A killer, but only in the way that a pack of wolves is a killer, or an outbreak of smallpox. The second was an outlaw, name of Dillashay. And the third was Dillashay's own half-brother. Strother Purcell."

It was on my tongue to demand where this had been, and when, and under what specific circumstances. But before I could organize the words, he said something more outlandish still. He said: "The thing of it is—the goddamnedest thing—it turns out to be much easier than you'd ever suppose."

"What is?"

"Killing a man."

"You're not going to tell me *you've* killed someone?"

I almost laughed out loud. But somehow, the impulse died. For just a moment, Tyree was faraway. He looked more lost than I have ever been.

"It should be the hardest thing in the world," he said. "Except it isn't."

And another thought came to me, then—the most unsettling one yet, on this strange and disconcerting night. I thought: We forget how long and how deeply they've been damned. Even the very least of the lesser devils.

– FOUR –

From *The Roadhouse Chronicles of Thomas Skiffings*

Near Hell's Gate
Winter, 1876

FOR FIVE HUNDRED DOLLARS, Gimp Tom would have died for his sister and gone to hell. He could only trust that Billie knew it too. If dying alone would do the job, he'd have done it for much less. He would indeed have died for nothing at all, such being the ardency of his true heart.

But five hundred dollars would fetch you the whole hog. For five hundred dollars, he would face down the six most deadly gunmen on earth, armed only with his old Deane-Adams five-shot. Subsequently he would descend into Perdition, with joyful Hallelujahs in his heart and one tear like a diamond glistening on his cheek, dropped there from his sister's eye as she knelt weeping to kiss his cold, dead lips. He would have proclaimed this to any man—the Man from Decatur, or any other—who might ask him what he'd do for a dollar, in any of its wicked multiples.

But nobody asked him. They asked Billie instead—even though the coin came from Tom's own ear.

"They" being Cousin Fletch. He was sitting at the time in a wooden chair by the fire. "Hang on," he said, catching Tom's arm as the boy passed by too close. He peered into Tom's left ear, breathing gusts of Missouri rot. "Hey, presto!" he exclaimed, plucking with his fingers and displaying the coin. A United States silver dollar. He proffered it to Billie, who was clearing noon-dinner dishes. This was on the second day, the storm still howling outside.

"Come over," said Cousin Fletch.

"Why?"

"Sit here with me, and it's your'n." His grin was wide and inviting, by which she understood that *sit here* meant his lap.

"Not likely," Billie said.

"Why not?"

"She's got work to do." Gimp Tom spoke on his sister's behalf. He'd retreated a step or two, rubbing his arm. He and Billie were alone with the outlaws, John McCutcheon having gone outside. His shape could be seen in the driving snow through the window, labouring with a shovel to keep a path to the outbuildings open. The trails and the Wagon Road would be impassable for days, choked with snowdrifts.

"Did someone ask yer opinion?" Cousin Fletch demanded.

"No," said Tom, "but I—"

"Then shut yer mouth."

Young Sprewell, on the other side of the fire, raised his head. That was his name—Dooley Sprewell. Gimp Tom knew this, by now. The Man from Decatur was across the room, lost somewhere in the shadows of his brooding.

"A silver dollar," Cousin Fletch said to Billie. In case she was in some doubt.

"I can see that," Billie said.

"Yer too good for the likes of a dollar?"

Billie hesitated, trying to decide what she might gainfully say.

"Or just too good for the likes of myself?" Cousin Fletch's churchyard grin was undimmed. "Too high 'n mighty for a country boy. That the size of what we're lookin' at?"

Gimp Tom said: "What she means—"

"If'n that boy opens up his mouth again," said Cousin Fletch, still grinning, "I swear I may be required to put my whole arm down his throat, and rip his asshole out."

Billie found her voice. "I'll not sit down for a dollar," she said.

"That's what I'm saying. But I guess I could do something else."

"Such as?"

"I could sing."

So she did.

It was "Rose of Killarney," a song that her Ma had sung at song-and-supper taverns in London, England. Gimp Tom had heard Billie sing this often and again, in their old life, but it came as a revelation to the outlaws. In the shadows, the Man from Decatur looked up, which Billie noted straightaway. Billie Skiffings was not truly a gifted singer—a sweet voice was all, and uncertain in the higher register. But she left you somehow enchanted. That was the knack she possessed, even then: the trick of living inside a song. You'd swear that each sentiment was her own, wrung from her years in this woeful world and shared in heartfelt commiseration with you alone.

This song she mostly sang to Dooley Sprewell. He was in much pain, but as she sang he began to light right up with happiness. And it turned out that's what Billie was prepared to do for one silver dollar: to warm the heart of a wounded boy, two thousand miles from home.

*

Dooley Sprewell seemed stronger that afternoon. His spirits were revived a little, and sitting by the stove he managed to banter. He must surely be warm as toast, he said, if only he could understand the situation rightly, on the grounds that such cold as this could not exist in the first place.

"There y'are," Cousin Fletch said, with a gruesome jolly wink in Billie's direction. "This young feller's a natural scholard."

She could see that, Billie said.

"Gal who catches this young feller, she'll be popping out lawyers and judges." Cousin Fletch winked again and waggled his eyebrows. These were tangled as thickets. Coarse hairs poked out at impossible angles, as did the hairs in both his nostrils.

Billie said: "Ho, ho." She had about her an air of brittle brightness that could pass for vivacity, amongst those who did not know her.

Dooley Sprewell had recommenced to shiver. He had always reckoned himself, he said, a man fit to take on any challenge. But his Daddy never told him there'd be wintertime like this. The worst you'd get back home was a January frost. Snow was a vicious rumour up on someone else's mountain.

"Where's home?" Billie asked him.

"Alabama," Dooley said.

Toward evening, Dooley suffered them to open up his shirt, to see if his wound was healing. A gunshot wound indeed — Gimp Tom saw this clearly, looking sidelong from across the room. A bullet wound in his side, though Dooley tried to maintain the fiction that it had been caused by a sharp stick when he'd slipped on wet rocks by the river. A sickly sweetness bloomed as Cousin Fletch unwrapped the dressing.

"There's a doctor in Yale," said John McCutcheon. They could send to fetch him in a day or two; sooner, even, if the weather broke. He could undertake to be the messenger himself, he added, looking hopeful.

"This boy don't need no doctor," said Cousin Fletch.

Uncle John was not so sure. The wound had an angry redness.

Cousin Fletch just snorted. "We never had no doctor beyond my old grandmamaw — and look at me. Never been infected in my life."

"I'm fine," said Dooley Sprewell. "There's no one needs concern theirselves about me."

"Hear that?" said Cousin Fletch. "He'll be up and dancing the two-step, next."

"I will," said Dooley. "If there was a one-step, I could prolly dance it this minnit."

Cousin Fletch eyed him asquint the whole while, as if weighing the odds that Dooley Sprewell would be fit to ride a horse when the weather broke—or on any other occasion short of Judgement Day itself, when the souls of the Blessed might gallop joyful across the Fields of Heaven, should Dooley by some miracle find himself amongst them. Subsequently Cousin Fletch exchanged private words with the Man from Decatur. Both of them took dark long glances toward poor Dooley.

Dooley pretended not to notice, and was almost merry for a time. As if dark glances might go away just like the cold, if you refused to believe that they existed. "Alabama," he repeated to Gimp Tom, who had fetched some wood for the stove and lingered to talk. "A farm by the Tallapoosa River. I don't expect you ever been there."

"No," Tom agreed. "I don't expect I ever was."

It was the most beautiful place in all the world, Dooley said. But now he could never go back there again.

"You never know," said Gimp Tom.

But Dooley said with sorrow: Yes, he did.

There had been some kind of a scrape. Dooley confided this to Tom while Cousin Fletch and the Man from Decatur were preoccupied with their own susurrations. A misunderstanding, he said, except with guns, down in the Washington Territory. There'd been a worse scrape in New Mexico. Some people had been shot quite bad each time. This had not been anyone's intention, and certainly not Dooley Sprewell's.

But now he could never go home again, nor back across the Line at all. So Dooley was riding north instead, with his two companions.

They were going to be cattlemen, he said. There was land up north just for the asking, whole parcels of it, in the Cariboo. Gimp Tom had maybe heard of that place?

Tom said he had.

"Is it like they say?" said Dooley.

"I expect it probably is," Tom replied. "What is it they said?"

Dooley Sprewell had heard it was ten thousand miles of rolling grassland. Plains as wide as the gaze of the Almighty, and as green as Eden at the daybreak of the world.

Yes, said Gimp Tom. That was pretty much his understanding too.

A notion came to Dooley then. He said: "You could come with us."

"Me?"

"And your sister—you could fetch her along. D'you reckon?"

The young outlaw's eyes shone diamond-bright with hopefulness, and with the commencement of fever. Gimp Tom had seen fevers before, and knew what followed next. Dooley shivered, despite two extra blankets clutched around his shoulders.

"They got everything we'd ever need, up there," said Dooley. "Grass up there as high as your horse's belly. Kin you imagine?"

"They got winter up there too," Billie said. She had come up while Dooley was conjuring his ranch. "Got winter ten months out of the year."

Dooley's smile wobbled, just a tick. "Well, but winters come in diff'rent kinds. And maybe we'd all get used to the cold. I b'lieve I'm getting used to it already."

Billie looked surprised. "This, you mean? Why, this ain't hardly cold at all."

—

PART ONE

With nightfall it grew colder. The wind rose up again, seeping through every chink in the walls and shaking the timbers of the lodge when it gusted. They stayed in the one main parlour now as much as they could, the five of them and Dooley Sprewell shivering by the woodstove.

The parlour of John McCutcheon's aspirations would call to mind a hunting lodge in Bavaria. A roaring fire in a great stone hearth, and the mounted heads of moose and elk. A hardwood floor stained to a mahogany gleam, covered over by bearskin rugs and one of them in particular: the vast brown silver-tipped pelt of a grizzly bear that John McCutcheon had shot personally, at much peril to himself. For the present, though, the roadhouse made do with a rough plank floor and threadbare bits of carpeting. But at least the woodstove was halfway warm — excepting when someone went outside or came back in again, opening the door to a frigid blast. This was primarily Uncle John, who shouldered the Cross of fetching in firewood and seeing to the horses in the barn. Swaddling himself at two-hour intervals, to return after fifteen minutes numb and blue, his breath billowing white as he clomp-footed through the door.

Cousin Fletch looked from Dooley Sprewell to Billie. "This boy needs someone t'warm his bones." He waggled his eyebrows as he said it, in case she somehow missed the insinuation.

Billie was turning to secure the door, seeing as John McCutcheon's hands were too stiff to manage. She made as if she hadn't heard.

"Got one of my own she could work on," said Cousin Fletch, "if she needs to get herself up to speed."

"I swear to Christ, old son — you are a caution."

The Man from Decatur said this. He was sitting apart from the rest of them, by the ladder up to the loft. Rocking back in a wooden chair, taking from time to time a swallow from a bottle. It was colder there, away from the stove, but whiskey was a compensation.

65

Cousin Fletch chuckled, mistaking the tone for affability.

The Man from Decatur said: "You'd shame them in Gomorrah. You truly would. A leering old disgusting goat like yourself."

"Here, now," said Cousin Fletch.

"Those sinners in Gomorrah, lusting after God's own angels."

"*Angels?*"

"Read your Bible."

Still smiling as he said it. Almost playful. Leaning back in his chair and eyeing Cousin Fletch with a look of speculation. As if he found it a question of genuine interest, what the older outlaw would say next, or do—and what he might do about it in return.

Cousin Fletch chuckled again. It lacked conviction. "No call to bring goats into the discussion," he said.

"No?"

"Don't see no goats in here. Nor angels neither."

"You could be right."

"Just making a suggestion to the gal."

"Then give her a coin."

"What?"

"You heard me."

There was silence for another moment. From all of them, this time—Billie most of all.

Cousin Fletch rummaged inside his pocket and pulled out a silver coin.

"Now another," the Man from Decatur said.

"I ain't give her the first one yet."

"We already know what she'll do for a dollar. What we don't know yet is what she'll do for two."

He looked straight at Billie Skiffings as he said it.

Billie looked almost everywhere at first, excepting back at the Man from Decatur. At length she met his eye.

"Well," she said. "I s'pose I'd better show you."

*

Years later, looking back, it would seem to Gimp Tom that a bargain had been transacted in that moment, between his sister and the Man from Decatur. Tom had stood there slack-jawed, looking on — as we do, all the rest of humankind, whenever such bargains are made. In a moon-silvered clearing in the wood, say, or at a lonely crossroads with a gibbet, such locations being much-favoured by the devil. So the old tales would have it, though in fact a snowbound roadhouse will serve as well. Or anywhere.

Later still, it would occur to him that the moment might never have taken place at all, at least not in the manner that he recollected: the bloom of defiance on his sister's face, and his own instinct to cry out, "Don't you do it!" Perhaps such clarity had only been achieved through years of brooding; the telling and retelling of the story to himself. It would even cross his mind to wonder if he'd had it the wrong way around: that the soul being bartered had been the Man from Decatur's.

One way or another, Billie took the coins.

She would gladden their hearts, she said, with songs of the South. *Their hearts,* she said — but she sang to Dooley Sprewell. A Minstrel song first, "The Little Old Log Cabin in the Lane." She sang it so sweet that poor Dooley commenced misting at once. Gimp Tom might almost have misted himself, if he hadn't begun to glimpse what Billie intended.

Her own eyes misted as she sang of a home irretrievably lost, though Christ knows which home she might have had in mind. Not her father's home, with her step-mother in it — she had hated it there, as Tom could have testified, if anyone had asked him. And she hated their Uncle John's house even worse. But there was poor Dooley Sprewell from Alabama, wrapped in blankets and shivering by the stove as the north wind howled outside. When Billie sang "Old Folks at Home," there was pure desolation on Dooley's face. His eyes were orphaned, and tears as fat as late-spring lambs came trickling down his cheeks.

"He's a killer," Gimp Tom said to his sister, when they finally had a moment alone. "Like the others—all three of them." He'd guessed that from the start, but now he knew it.

It was deep in the night. He kept his voice to a whisper, confiding to Billie what Dooley had confided to him, and adding to it pieces of his own.

"A year or so ago, in a place called Santa Rosita. A shooting scrape. They killed three fellas—a Sheriff's Deputy was one. They shot some poor gal, too, who had no part in it at all."

"Then why'd they shoot her?"

"Spite."

They were in the back room where they slept. One cot on either side and a ragged sheet hung up for a divider. Gimp Tom heard Billie breathing on the other side, as she decided how much of this she could believe.

"Which one of them did the killing?" she said.

"Dooley Sprewell. I'm pretty sure of that. Or else the one you got your eye on."

"I don't have my eye on nobody."

"The one who says he's from Decatur."

"You're a liar."

"I'm not. I read about these fellas."

In his magazines and books, he meant. Billie knew that without asking. The dime stories he kept in his tin box of treasures.

"You never read no such book," Billie said, "'cause there isn't one."

"I read enough," he said. Enough to fit together with other things that Dooley Sprewell had let slip, and with news he himself had heard from travellers passing through along the Wagon Road, or scavenged on his bi-monthly journeys with his uncle to Yale. There the riverboats arrived three times each week with news from New Westminster on the West Coast, and the whole wide world beyond. This was an expertise of his, collecting up bits of news and squirrelling them away like nuts. You can learn a great deal from listening, if you have the knack and listen hard enough, and have as well a memory that locks up tighter than any tin box ever did. Billie knew that, too. He sensed her movement, on the other side of the divider.

"It was Dooley, then," she said at length, keeping her voice to a whisper. "He'd be the one to kill a gal. Him or Cousin fucking Fletch."

"Fletcher Quarles," Tom whispered back. "That's his name. Fletcher Quarles the outlaw, out of Missouri."

Time would prove this supposition correct, along with numerous others.

"The other one," Gimp Tom said. "I believe I know his real name, too. D'you want to hear it spoke?"

"No," said Billie. "Not by you—'cause you don't know it."

"Elijah Dillashay. From Carolina."

They heard the creak of footfalls, overhead. The Man from Decatur—Lige Dillashay, if Tom's supposing was correct—had claimed the sleeping loft for his own. The others were in the parlour, just beyond the blanket that hung in place of a door. They heard Dooley Sprewell out there, and Cousin Fletch: muttering in unquiet sleep, and farting evilly.

The Man from Decatur never slept. So it would seem from his pacing, all night long. Four steps from the ladder to the window, looking north. Six steps the other way across, west to east.

Billie was silent for a goodly while.

Sometimes she would light a lamp on an overturned apple-box she had for a bureau. She would do this late at night or first thing in the morning, before the dawn. By lamplight her silhouette would show clear through the ragged sheet, while she stretched like a cat scant inches away from her brother, or stood by the window all but naked.

"They done things to gals as well," Tom whispered. "Other than just killing them."

"What things?"

"Bad ones," he said. "The worst."

"You heard this said, or you know it?"

"It stands to reason. These are killers on the run, Billie. Outlaws with a price on their heads. These are men who'll stop at nothing. I know it, and so do you."

Right above their heads, the footfalls stopped. Tom heard a breath catch in Billie's throat; felt himself clench, supposing that their whispers had been heard. That the Man from Decatur had ears just as keen as Old Jehovah's, up on Sinai, and views on retribution no less stark. Tom did not let his breath out until the pacing resumed — away from them, toward the window. There the footsteps stopped again, and Tom could imagine him standing: stooped beneath the downslope of the rafters, staring out into the night.

Billie said at last: "How much, d'you reckon?"

"How much what?"

"The price on their heads. How much is it?"

*

Billie's Ma as a young gal had sung in music halls in London, England, where she was known as the Lanarkshire Lark. Later in her too-brief life she had appeared in concert saloons and melodeons in San Francisco, where she had ensorcelled men too numerous to tally, and ended in marrying one of them. This was Edward Skiffings, a sober and stalwart man whose offer she had accepted after auditing the hopes and dreams of her inmost heart and concluding that her modest talents as an artiste had taken her as far as they possibly could, and that the sands of her hour of maidenly bloom were dwindling.

Billie's Ma believed with all her heart that a gal must have faith in herself. She also knew what became of those as misevaluated their assets, or bungled the imperative to sell at the height of the market. She passed most tragically when her only child was just four years old, but in those four years she saw clearly and beyond all doubt: Billie Skiffings was her own true daughter.

And now, years later, Billie saw with clarity the nature of her own dilemma. The question was: how might she resolve it?

She turned first to her Uncle John, despite suspecting from the start that he would be no damned use. She found him at the creek below the roadhouse, chopping a hole through the ice with an axe. This was early morning on the third day. The snowfall had ceased, but the temperature continued to plunge. Twenty-five below in the shelter of the trees; ten degrees colder in the open. The wind continued to angle from the north: a cold incessant muttering, rising at moments to vicious gusts that scooped up snow already fallen and flung it.

"He keeps lookin' at me," Billie said. "The old one — 'Cousin Fletch.'"

She had brought two buckets down with her. Rags wrapping her hands against the cold, lurching through thigh-high drifts. Uncle John had broken a trail partway, but his footprints were spaced too wide.

"Looking ain't a crime," he said. He laboured red-faced, clinging precariously to his footing on the rocks. The ice on the creek had formed three inches thick. The water beneath splashed warm, so much colder was the air.

"It's the way he looks," Billie said.

"Which way is that?"

"You seen him. *Smiling.*"

"Nothing wrong with a smile," McCutcheon said. "Hell's bells."

"They put five hundred dollars on his head."

It made Uncle John break rhythm. He staggered, half-slipped. Cursed between his teeth.

"Five hundred at least," said Billie. "Could be more like a thousand."

"Your brother tell you this?"

"Between the three of them, could be three times that much. Could be *five* thousand."

"If pigs had wings, imagine how they'd fly."

"So this would be your last word on the subject?"

The question made him miss a second stroke. His breath came in painful wheezes. Cold this intense would hurt each time you drew it in; you'd feel it all down your breastbone.

"What exactly are you asking me?" he said.

"I'm asking: What am I supposed to do?"

He hadn't met her eye. Not once, since she came slip-staggering down through the trees with her buckets, the roadhouse behind her half-buried in the snow. The smoke from the chimney was swept sideways by that bastard wind; icicles hung like daggers from the eaves.

Uncle John had made his calculation. That was plain for any child to see, even one twice as young and half as clever as Billie Skiffings. Totting it up like numbers in his ledger-book, and arriving at the inexorability of arithmetic: three desperate outlaws under his roof, ten miles from Yale. No one leaving and no one coming for at least another day. Two children to look after, and one solitary uncle entrusted with the task. And what use would John McCutcheon be, in this regard or any other, if he ended up out back in the privy: upside down in the glory hole with his neck wrung like a chicken's?

"Hell's bells," he said. "A fella smiles. Couldja try smiling back?"

So Billie did a calculation of her own. Totted up the numbers. Separated them into two columns, the debit and the credit. Checking and rechecking the sums—as her Ma the Lanarkshire Lark would have done—to be certain that her totals were correct. That she had avoided the fatal blunders that undid so many gals and brought their best-laid plans to ruin.

She found that each calculation ended up with the identical result, and pointed her infallibly in the direction that she had known by intuition from the start: toward the loft.

Gimp Tom had resolved to stay awake that night. He secretly loaded three cartridges into his Deane-Adams five-shot, and slipped the pistol in between his mattress and pillow.

"I'll be here." He said this in a low voice to Billie's shape, on the other side of the hanging-sheet divider.

"Where else would you be?"

"I'm just saying. I'll be right here if you need me."

"Get some sleep, Tommy."

"Come what may."

He had read this latter phrase in a book and thought it particularly fine. But his sister made no reply. A methodical rasping came from her side of the divider. It took him a moment to make sense of it, against the moaning of the wind outside and the midnight creaks and protests of the timbers.

She was brushing her hair.

"Billie?"

"Go to sleep."

Her voice sounded strange and distant. There was a quiver in it. This he attributed to the cold, which was worst down low, by the bare floor. Gimp Tom cocooned more tightly in his blankets, redoubling his resolve to stay keen and sharp and watchful until daybreak. Some small while later his eyelids shuddered shut.

—

Cousin Fletch was slumbering as well, having swallowed sufficient whiskey to tamp down the hobgoblins of vigilance. His bedroll as before lay beside the woodstove, across from poor dying Dooley Sprewell. But he twitched awake as a small shape coalesced in the doorway to the back room. It was slender and insubstantial in the flickering spill of firelight, gliding straight toward him on soundless feet that never touched the floor. He levered himself up on one elbow, blinking against the evidence of his own two eyes: the slip of a gal with fine pale hair, shins stick-thin and bare above ravelled wooden socks, a blanket wrapped tight around her shoulders—as frail an angel as ever appeared to the hoariest old sinner in Gomorrah.

"Well, now," he began to say, baring his whole churchyard full of teeth.

The angel said, "Fuck off."

She continued right past him to the ladder, glancing just once to the lump stretched out by the front door. This was John McCutcheon, standing guard in such manner as seemed best to him: dead-drunk and horizontal. Cousin Fletch could only stare as the fog of slumber cleared and he watched his angel ascend.

It was almost warm in the loft, by the frigid standards of the road-house, provided you stayed close to the stovepipe in the middle. It glowed red in the darkness, hissing and crackling within.

A tatter of rug on rough planks. A low roof overhead, slanting sharply down to meet the outside wall, where a filthy window faced across the river. A bedroll and a mattress and a spindly wooden table with an oil-lamp, and the animal smell of the Man from Decatur. He was at the window, straddling a chair turned the wrong way around, his back to the ladder and Billie Skiffings. He stared out into the darkness.

"Think twice," he said, without turning. He wore boots and trousers and a grey undershirt that had probably been white to begin with. Suspenders dangled.

"I done that," Billie said.

"Then you're a fool."

He dangled a whiskey bottle by the neck. The smell of him was stale sweat and hickory smoke. Outside the night remained clear and bitterly cold; moonlight slanted across the snow.

It occurred to Billie that he could discern the shape of her, reflected in the filthy glass. Standing in the penumbra of the oil-light, in the red glare of heat from the stovepipe. A waif with stick legs, swaddled in a blanket.

"An' you're a son of a bitch," she said. "But I guess you're better'n he is."

"Fletcher? That's where you'd be wrong," said the Man from Decatur. "I'm worse."

"I expect he knows not to cross you, then. Or lay hands on what's yours."

Her breathing came shallow and quick, as if a band had tightened round her chest. She found herself shivering.

"Last chance," said the Man from Decatur. "Turn around and climb back down."

She unclenched her grip on the blanket instead. It slid from her narrow shoulders and whispered to the floor, and she stood in the teeth of the winter's night as naked as Eve in sagging woollen socks.

-FIVE-

The Accounting of Barry Weaver

San Francisco, 1892

GOD KNOWS what time it was when I lurched out of Mulvaney's Tavern that night.

Rain pissed down. A chill wind sliced. I fumbled for the buttons on my coat, and began reflexively to turn toward home—toward the flat on California Street, a ten-minute stagger from here. And it hit me, all over again: there *was* no home.

"Which way you headed?"

Tyree had emerged from the tavern, behind me. He stood in a dying spill of light, head cocked on that ridiculous neck.

I muttered something in reply. God knows what.

"I expect I'll see you around," he said, after a moment.

"You prob'ly will."

And still he hesitated. Rain spattered the thick round lenses of his spectacles; he looked like some species of small, bedraggled owl.

He must have a room, somewhere or other. I could ask him to let me stay there for the night. The thought occurred in one of those drunken shafts of illumination. It would be some dismal little crib, ripe with the odour of wet socks, but it would have a roof.

And he was waiting for me to ask. That came to me as well. He'd say yes—might even welcome the prospect of human companionship. The prospect of having—good Lord—a *friend?*

"So long," I muttered, and turned away.

"Good luck to you," he said.

When I looked back, he was receding into the darkness. Elbows pistoning, and oversized head bob-bobbing.

I might be homeless, but I still had my pride. So I told myself, anyway. Hunching against the slicing wind, I continued in the opposite direction.

Deadeye Ned was no stranger to homelessness.

Ned Hartland, I mean, the redoubtable scout and plainsman who was the hero of my three little novels, written in happier days under the pseudonym "B.W. Colton." All three were serialized across ten weekly editions of the *Five-Cent Boys' Own Library*, published by Messrs. Ferdinand & Nussey of New York, and subsequently released as individual volumes, beginning with *Deadeye Ned and the Call of the Plains* in 1885.

My books are long out of print, but from time to time a copy will turn up unexpectedly. Years after that dismal San Francisco night, I would chance across *Deadeye Ned and the Gallows Tree* in the five-for-a-penny box at a Methodist Church rummage sale in Coeur d'Alene, Idaho. It was battered and dog-eared and scourged by time, the cover half-severed and the pages rain-swollen. But it was nonetheless my little book. I picked it up and almost bought it, despite the flint-eyed scrutiny of the dour old Church Lady at the cash-box, who did not like the looks of me. And I'll grant that Young Weaver must have had an air of dereliction upon him, there amidst the gathering shadows of autumn. A waft of garments long unwashed, and the shakiness that discourages regular shaving. Still, they're supposed to take it seriously, these Methodists: the prospect that we meet the Son of Man each time we encounter suffering humanity.

I set the old book down again, leaving it for someone else to discover. I thought: *Who knows?* Some hopeful boy of ten or twelve sweet summers. He might pick it up of a rain-sodden afternoon when there was nothing in all this world for a boy to do, save sit on the porch with a mildewed book and discover a tale that would gallop off with him.

Or not. No, probably not. It probably went to some joyless elder who read nothing but the Bible and kept the pages of five-for-a-penny books on a spike in the jakes. Still and all, there's a chance it went to the Boy. One chance in ten—or ten thousand, even. And that's what we cling to, isn't it? That's all we ask. All of us, alive and drawing breath. Just a chance.

I'm drivelling.

Deadeye Ned.

The plainsman, as I say, would hardly have blinked at the prospect of a homeless night in April. But then, Deadeye Ned was possessed of every attribute pertaining to dime-novel heroism, beginning with (but not limited to) a remarkable prowess with the lariat, the sixgun, and the long rifle, not to mention a sublime indifference to physical suffering and the ability to fashion a snug dwelling out of three sticks and a copy of yesterday's newspaper.

I thought about Deadeye Ned's prowess as I reeled aimlessly through that particular night, with a rising sense of something that was very close to panic. I swear that the wind grew more bitter with each step. So did I.

Deadeye Ned was never a natural-born killer. But he would certainly kill, if you pushed him to it. I dwelt upon this, too.

There was nothing that Ned purely hated more than a bully. The oppression of the virtuous poor by the rich and the privileged and smug—oh, such behaviour would stir Ned Hartland to a smouldering choler. In fact, this had formed the very pith and substance of *Deadeye Ned and the Gallows Tree*.

In that adventure, Ned finds himself stranded temporarily in the

Kansas town of Good Hope, after his horse comes up lame. On the very first afternoon, he intervenes to prevent a young cowboy and his riotous companions from offering insult to a sodbuster's wife. Ned is required to deal out several brisk socks to the sneezer, after which he brings the ringleader and the worst of his henchmen to a deeper appreciation of their folly by dragging them to the horse-trough, one in either hand, and soaking their heads.

But Deadeye Ned has made a bad enemy. The ringleader turns out to have been no mere hired hand, but the heir to the largest cattle ranch in the territory. Lanky Staggars, the young man's name is. Prosecuting a deadly grudge against the plainsman, Lanky accuses him of rustling cattle, and proceeds to "discover" a branding-iron wrapped up in Ned's bedroll.

Our hero protests his innocence, but Lanky Staggars has the advantage of wealth and privilege. His father is Creed Staggars, whom Ned knows by reputation. Before settling in Kansas to build his empire, Creed Staggars had been a Captain of the Texas Rangers, known for his flint-eyed abhorrence of wrong-doers, and a man who had personally strung up horse thieves and cattle-rustlers the length and breadth of the Western badlands, wherever he could find a tall enough tree. Ned himself is to be hanged directly, regardless of his tersely worded denials, since he is after all just a plainsman with neither riches nor influential friends, despite his manly bearing and a frank and upright manner.

But Deadeye Ned does indeed have one friend in Good Hope, though he scarcely knows it yet: Chappie Gimbleton, the Deputy Sheriff. Chappie is lightly regarded by the locals — and flat-out scorned by the likes of Captain Staggars — as a lad whose heart may be capacious, but whose wits take their time before arriving at a destination. Besides, he is puny and bow-legged. But Chappie knows only too well how sodbusters have been treated by the haughty cattlemen. There is something that just sticks in his craw about Lanky's accusation. This is the phrase he uses himself: "It just sticks in my craw, and it won't be swallered down."

And it turns out that Chappie Gimbleton can rise to an occasion. While Deadeye Ned grinds his teeth in a jail cell, watching a blood-red prairie sun rise up through iron bars, the little Deputy has picked up the trail of the Truth. It leads him to an old blacksmith—a poor man, but honest as the day is long—who will swear on his Granddaddy's Bible that he fashioned that incriminating branding-iron *at the express command of Lanky Staggars.*

Chappie gallops back with the honest blacksmith's X on a sworn statement. Arriving in Good Hope, he discovers that Deadeye Ned has already busted out of the death cell, through coolness of head, firmness of resolve, and the unlooked-for assistance of another true-hearted American: the self-same sodbuster whose wife he had so stoutly defended. This leads in rapid succession to another escape, two chases, a near-lynching, a mighty gun-battle, and a chance encounter with an outlaw band led by none other than Jesse James in disguise. The narrative spans much of Kansas in its ten thrilling installments, culminating in a fist-fight between the redoubtable plainsman and Lanky Staggars, at the end of which the young hound can take no more and, grovelling in the dust, confesses his treachery. He did indeed plant the branding-iron in Ned's bedroll, seeking to frame the plainsman as a confederate of the cattle-rustlers, who are in fact in league with Lanky Staggars himself.

Hearing this, Lanky's father is, well, staggered. Grim as hoarfrost, Creed Staggars would hang his own son, save for the intervention of Deadeye Ned. In words few but manful and pithy, the plainsman reminds the old Ranger of a Higher Justice that ever is tempered with mercy, and asks whether Captain Staggars—or any man present—can assert that his own youth was unspotted by folly. Abashed, the old Ranger is reconciled to his son, and settles for hunting down like dogs the rustlers themselves. These are the Wild Monteiro Brothers, who deserve to suffer the full force of the laws of God and Kansas, being desperate and unrepentant killers. They are also—not to put too fine a point upon it—Mexicans. Meanwhile, an enduring bond is established between Deadeye Ned and Chappie Gimbleton, who observes, "That were a mouthful you spoke there, Nedward, right and proper," and recollects a favourite saying of his wise old Granny Hudgins: "Let the feller who'd be without sin shy rocks out his own glass winders."[3] You'd really have to read the book to appreciate the full effect. The point is, I brooded upon Deadeye Ned Hartland as I slogged homeless through the rain on that endless godalmighty San Francisco night, my gut twisting and sloshing with steam beer and grievance. As the wind grew colder and the darkness more intense, I brooded some more. Somewhere in the midst of this, a notion took shape: I needed a gun.

I was passing by a pawn-shop as this hardened into certainty. The shop was locked tight, the windows barred. But it occurred to me that there must be a back door in the alley—or a side-window that would yield to desperation—which there was. And I couldn't tell you, exactly, whom I intended to shoot. Ichabod Rourke was undoubtedly a prime candidate—the betting favourite, as the bookies would say. But I might just have settled for shooting Young Weaver first. Yes, Young Weaver was a dark horse, but we mustn't rule him out. I groped for a loose cobblestone and staggered, gathering myself to smash it through the glass.

"Hey! You—yes, you—stop right there!"

A blue coat with an Officer in it flat-footed out of the darkness.

---

3   For an extended discussion of Chappie Gimbleton, interested readers might consult "Hopalong and Harlequino: The Trope of the Comic Servant in Dime-Novel Tradition," by D.G. Brookmire (*The Journal of Western Folklore*, USWC Press, September, 1993).—*Brookmire.*

*

At this point, I should make a confession. I don't know that I discovered what kind of man I am—not on that particular night, or on any other night that came thereafter. It's harder than you'd think, to arrive at a moment of perfect self-definition. But I have come, over the years, to develop an alternative theory. In moments of extremity, we may at least discern our species of rodent.

Some rats will gibber and freeze when they're trapped. Others by savage instinct will go for the throat. Young Weaver turned out to be the third kind: the rat that drops its cobblestone and totters round to flee.

Fat lot of good it did me. Officers of the Law travel in pairs. A second had flat-footed up behind. "Whoa, there, Sonny-Jim," this one said. A fist like a cannon-ball came whistling.

When I swam back fully into consciousness, the rain had ceased and the wind no longer sliced. This was due to the fact that I was inside a cell.

Amongst San Francisco's most wretched malefactors may be counted those who find themselves on Alcatraz Island, twenty minutes by ferry-boat across the bay. There they may languish for months and years—for the rest of their lives—breaking rocks and gnashing teeth and hearing in the slamming of steel doors the death-knell of all earthly aspirations.

This cell, on the other hand, was just a stinking diverticulum in the bowels of the City Lock-Up, though its steel door slammed with a finality no less hideous. Cement walls and a spew-slick cement floor that sloped to a trough in the middle, with human hulks shipwrecked on either side. Two of them, besides myself: I'd glimpsed them in the shaft of light as the brawny arm of the Law slung me in. Then all light was gone from the world. A small barred grate high up in one wall opened only onto the deeper blackness of night.

PART ONE

The drunk cell.

Our hero lay stunned for a time.

I willed myself to cease my unmanly moaning, only to find that it continued anyway. Or not moaning, exactly: a faint, high-pitched burbling, expressive of woe beyond all bearing. The ragged, soggy sorrow that gives orphans a bad name.

It came from the largest hulk in the cell. So I realized, after another few moments. My eyes had adjusted a little, and I could start to make out shapes. A man roughly the size of a muskox, and the smell. He huddled against the wall to one side of the door, cradling in his lap something abject and broken. An image came to mind: a boy I had seen once, sobbing over a poor, dead kitten.

Oh, Lord, I thought. They wouldn't, surely—the bastard police. Lock up a drunk with a kitten?

"Fella had a knife," a second voice said. A ruined baritone, frogged with years of whiskey. "Bowie knife. In his boot. Pulled it out. Can't have that."

The weeping muskox was cradling his *wrist*. It sheared at a grotesque angle.

"The police did that?" I exclaimed. "Came in here and busted his arm?"

"'Course not."

"Then how did—?"

"Shout all you want—the Law won't come in here."

The muskox continued to weep, a woebegone burble from the distant shores of tragedy. And suddenly I had other concerns.

"Where is it now?" I said, feeling a certain scrotal tightening. "The knife."

"What knife?" said the ruined baritone.

"His knife."

"Never you mind."

83

There is a consoling belief—my father subscribed to it—that angels walk amongst us. We can always know them because angels say: "Fear not." Somehow, "never you mind" is not an exact equivalent. And when the seraphim confiscate knives, they don't snap wrists at right-angles and leave muskoxen blubbing in the blackness.

"He'll survive," said the ruined baritone.

"Oh, Lord," I said. "Oh, Christa'mighty."

Somehow this seemed to constitute a final straw. I commenced blubbing myself.

After a time, the ruined voice said: "Go ahead. Say it, if you need to. I'll listen."

"Say what?"

"Whatever it is you need to get off your chest. The whole damned story, if you have to. It's not like we're going anywhere."

So I told him. "I am a failure," I said. "I am a disgrace. I am homeless, and hopeless. If I was a man I'd just—God damn it, I'd hang myself."

Somehow, the option seemed almost a lifeline. "I should do it." I felt the thrill of despair, to say it right out loud. I savoured it, even—the way we may bite into the most appalling prospect as if it were a crisp red apple. "I should damned well just hang myself, and get it over with."

"Use my belt."

"What?"

"There's bars in the grate, yonder. Loop it round. That'll do the job, if you want it done. Or else don't."

I could almost see the shape of him: an old man, long and bent, sitting tattered against the wall, beneath that single barred grate. The first faint rumour of dawn came creeping through it.

"Your choice," he said. "I won't stop you. Did that once—now it's up to you."

"What are you talking about? Did *what* once?"

"Saved your life."

The accent came from somewhere in the South. There was some cultivation in it, too—down deep, beneath the ruination. The old man shifted his position, and a reek came off his rags. A mighty waft of unwashed humanity, both foul and eerily familiar.

And it came to me, where I'd seen him once before.

My Good Angel. The one who'd lifted me up on the night of my forty-fifth birthday. Dredged me out of the mud where I sprawled face-down and drowning.

"Be daylight in an hour," he said. "I'd do it soon, I was you, if it's to be done. Understand, I'm not recommending, one way or the other."

The boots that had tramped alongside mine. The tangled mane of white hair, and the face of a one-eyed Patriarch.

"It's no way to die, hanging. Not if there's a choice, though generally there isn't. I won't offer to help you with it. Not my place. Don't suppose it ever was. But for years I wasn't clear on that."

"You're telling me you were—what—a *hangman?*"

"Not as such."

"The hell is that supposed to mean?"

He made no reply for a considerable while. Then, at length: "I killed some folks."

"What folks?"

"A goodly few. Some as deserved it. Some as surely didn't. And my brother."

A few feet and a thousand miles away, the muskox kept up his sorrowing: the same lamentation that has echoed through the world since Eve first grasped the knack of being human. You don't even notice, after awhile. I surely didn't notice him now, poor bastard.

"Who are you?" I said to that terrible old man.

"Just leave it. Hang yourself, or don't. Or—hell if I care—take the knife and open up a vein. Be a Roman; that's what they did. All them Stoics, bleeding out in bathtubs. Just make a decision and leave me be."

He had turned his head away. His blind eye was toward me, milk-white and uncanny.

"No," I said. "Who *are* you?"

"I am what you see."

He drew in one long, weary breath, seeming to grow more ancient by the moment. At last, he said: "There used to be a boy, once. Long ago. I used to be that boy. Name of Strother Purcell."

PART TWO

– S I X –

From *The Sorrows of Miz Amanda and her Two Brave Boys*[4]

North Carolina, 1844 – 1848

1.

THE CHERRY TREES HAD BLOSSOMED on the third day of January, the winter that Strother was born. His little brother Lige was to hear all about this from their beautiful Mama, who so loved to tell him stories. She told him of all the Signs and Wonders that had accompanied Strother's birth, the comets and the camels and what-all else, and the old well behind the house, dry for many years, that had burbled up once again with water. Lige himself would grow to be a fine young man, strong-backed and reliable; so their Mama confidently predicted. "But Strother, now — Strother is extraordinary. He will be a scholar, as his Daddy was, Mr. Purcell. He will make us most astonishingly proud."

---

4   This lurid saga, concerning the genesis of the Collard-Dillashay-Purcell feud, may have existed in oral tradition as early as the mid-1860s, and is referenced by the folklorist Edgar "Punkinhead" Slocum in his seminal survey of Appalachian feud literature, *War in Them Thar Hills* (Antietam Press, 1909). The author of the Sturluson manuscript clearly possessed a written redaction of the saga, of which at least half a dozen variants are known to be extant. She — assuming Tilda Sturluson's to have been the sole authorial hand — seems to have quoted liberally from that text, while also making extensive and silent emendations, in order to incorporate independently sourced material, or more simply to shape it to her own narrative purposes.

Even more significantly, internal evidence strongly implies that the Sturluson author had access to at least one witness with first-hand knowledge of the brothers — including the tantalizing hint that Billie Skiffings may have served as a narrative conduit. But it is not possible to establish this conclusively, and so — here, and in subsequent sections — I will pass over this reshaping without specific editorial comment, as irrelevant to the general reader. — *Brookmire.*

They were in fact half-brothers. Lige understood this from infancy as well, believing at first that the "half" was by way of reference to his height. This was one of his deficiencies. Elijah was built blunt and square, in the manner of his own Daddy, who was a man of prodigious physical strength, though coarse. Mr. Dillashay owned the land farther up the hill, which though stony and rugged would combine to mutual advantage with the Purcell property. This he had pointed out to Lige's beautiful Mama some while subsequent to the sorrowful passing of poor Mr. Purcell. He had made himself indispensable in the meantime, taking on the oversight of the Purcell land without ever being asked; shortly thereafter he proposed the offer of a formal union, which the widow in due course accepted.

"I couldn't of made a well fill up just by getting myself dropped," he would confide some years later to young Lige. The boy was five or six at the time of this exchange. "But damned if the Purcells' only crik didn't start on my side of the property line." Mr. Dillashay had spoken with rough humour. In adulthood, it would occur to Lige that his Daddy had been trying in his way to reach out, in hopes that they might yet find themselves friends. But it was already too late for that. Far too much had already been done, and decided.

Strother had come into the world as easily as any first-born child might do, for all the high trepidation that had existed on his Mama's behalf. She was a willowy creature, fine-boned and narrow-hipped, not formed at all for the brutalities of bearing children. She had been a Beauchamp before her first marriage, and a notable debutante: Miss Amanda Beauchamp of Roanoke, Virginia. But Aunt Glory had been there to catch the baby — the old Negro woman who had caught Miss Amanda herself, and many others besides. Aunt Glory had accompanied the bride when she travelled to North Carolina with

Mr. Purcell to take up her new life at his side. Nine months later she had taken command at Miz Amanda's lying in, clucking reassurances and gentling the baby into the world amidst that midwinter riot of cherry blossoms.

With Lige it had been different. He had come truculent and terrible, with such violence that his Mama was never fully to recover, though she would live on for another fifteen years. Lige knew that too, from infancy. Knew the toll that he had taken, and the obligation that this had placed him under.

"Your Mama loves you," she would tell him, holding him with her gaze. "She loves you, but — O! — you came at such a cost. So you must always and ever be sturdy and true, and you must always — always — pay what you owe."

"Yes, 'm," Lige would murmur.

"Look to your elder brother," she told him. "Your brother will be as a beacon to light your way."

Lige's earliest memory was of his half-brother fetching him home again, one twilight when he'd wandered into the pinewood. It was late autumn, no time for a child to be losing its way. The mists hung low in ghostly tatters, and with darkness the cold came on. A child might blunder into a pond and be found there three days later, blue and bloated; it might lose its way and never be seen again, alive *or* dead.

There were known to be wolves in those woods. Panthers, as you went farther up the mountain. Not many, so close to a farm — just one in ten square miles, maybe. But then, it only took the one. Besides, you'd find in the woods other perils. Indians, coming and going when you least expected. White men who posed a peril all their own: men with dwellings deeper in the hills, who peered and festered.

And witches. There were witches in those woods and up those

mountains, beyond all question of a doubt. If you lived in these hills you'd seen witches, whether you even knew it. Lige understood this by instinct, as children do, and his Daddy never spoke a word to gainsay it.

But on that particular evening, Lige was to be spared all such terrors and tribulations. He saw a beacon come weaving through the murk: a lantern held up by his elder brother. Taking Lige by the hand, Strother walked him home. Carried him on his shoulder partway when his little brother flagged, which was the best and bravest vantage that Lige had ever known.

Mr. Dillashay stood stock-still at first when he saw them emerging from the twilight. He'd been labouring in the field with the hands. Now he straightened and lumbered the last few steps between them, wrenching Lige down from his brother's shoulder and thrashing the boy until he howled, as the enormity of this transgression required: this wandering off at such peril to his life. Then he wrapped the boy in a hug that near to stove his ribs in, unmanly tears leaking out both corners of his eyes.

"You," he said at length to Strother, straightening. "The hell took you so long?"

"He wasn't where I expected," Strother said.

Mr. Dillashay struck him a blow that sent him sprawling. "One job you were give," Mr. Dillashay said. "I said, 'Go find your brother — look after him.' Well, next time do it halfway competent."

There was between Strother and Mr. Dillashay a great contempt. Lige understood this from his earliest age, though he wouldn't have known to use that word, nor exactly where the great contempt arose. There was fear as well, though not in such proportion as you might expect, and not on the side of the step-son. For Strother was afraid of nothing in this world, and never would be. From this Lige began to understand something else: that there was something irredeemably low in his Daddy, whom he loved nonetheless, and something therefore low in himself that he never could rise above.

Strother himself said no such thing. Not out loud, and never within earshot of his younger brother, by whom he was worshipped in return. Squat, waddling Lige, as dark as his half-brother was tall and fair, with his brow habitually knitted even in childhood, and a left foot that was awkwardly clubbed: the legacy of his violent birth.

And Strother never called Lige half a brother, either. Not once.

But he thought it.

Lige began to understand this. Strother was never less than grave and kind, but in the privacy of his own mind he reduced his brother to half of what was rightly his. "Never mind that foot," Strother would say to him; "you can walk as tall as any man on earth." By which Lige knew he meant: *Your Daddy is small and mean and low, and you thereby are hopelessly diminished.* Or: "It's enough that you try your level best," by which Lige heard: *It will never be good enough.*

Lige would beam his gratitude and resolve to do better still, while knowing in his secret heart that his brother weighed him daily and found him wanting.

2.

Strother had been sent for help when his Mama's time with Lige came round, late in the autumn of 1844.

Aunt Glory had died two years previous, not long before Mr. Purcell had slipped away, and someone had to catch the baby. There was a young doctor in Asheville, but that was a full day's ride. Besides, Mr. Dillashay had no use for the man. They had quarrelled on some matter concerning the sale of a horse; the doctor had held himself cheated.

Doc Semmens, his name was. He would refuse to come, Mr. Dillashay said, and even if he came he could not be trusted. So he bade his step-son ride for the granny-woman, up Hanging Tree Ridge.

The boy, just eight years old, must have blenched at this, though he did not intend to show it. "Granny Smoak, you mean?"

Drusilla Smoak lived with the terrible Judge Collard and his clan; she was widely known to be a witch.

"Take the gelding," Mr. Dillashay said.

Hanging Tree Ridge was less than half as far as Asheville, in miles. But it lay in the opposite direction: northwest, higher and deeper into the mountains, where folks grew clannish and queer. The autumn rains had come early and violent that year, and snow had fallen once already at elevation; the road higher up would be uncertain. The journey could turn out longer than the ride to Asheville, and Strother said so.

"That's why I told you: Take the gelding. Not the mule."

Wayfarers in the previous century had set down accounts of the singular families they'd met living deep in the mountains. The travellers wrote admiringly of the independent spirit they encountered, and of the keen intelligence too, the hills having been settled by those who desired to live in their own way, on their own terms. But that time had been many decades past already. Three generations, or four, of living in isolation, and marrying closely. Folks in such circumstances began to turn inward, after a time; such a turning must some day come upon the Collards too. Such a turning had conceivably begun.

The Collard farm at Hanging Tree Ridge was in the notch between two peaks. The road was as parlous as Strother had expected. It was mid-afternoon when he reached the last turning of the trail, and he had left home at first light.

The dogs had his measure from a quarter-mile away. Three blueticks and a mastiff bitch. They'd have gone for him, too, except for Harris Collard's voice, cursing and calling them off. Harris Collard was the old Judge's swag-bellied son; he was in a clearing in front of the big house, boiling the bristles off of a newly slaughtered hog. It hung head-down in a cauldron of water, suspended by a rope from an oak-tree branch. Through the steam and the smoke, Harris Collard squinted Strother into view, demanding to know his purpose.

Strother told him.

The dogs slunk round him all this while, low-bellied and snarling. The gelding high-stepped, huge-eyed.

"You're Dillashay's boy," Harris Collard said. He spoke the name as if something had gone rancid.

"He's my step-daddy. He said, ride up and bid the granny-woman come quick. Otherwise my Mama could die."

He spoke with an eight-year-old's urgency, as you might to a man unclear on the relevant facts. As if Harris Collard might now exclaim: Well, why didn't you say so?

Harris Collard was a boar of a man, black-bristled and five-and-thirty, with a sagging paunch and pink watery eyes. He said: "An' why does your Daddy suppose I might care?"

Strother looked past Harris Collard to the others. "Please," he said.

The house was a ramshackle sprawl, a sagging veranda slung low across the front. An old man was there, in a chair with wooden wheels. A boy, four or five years old, stood by him.

The old man was Judge Zebulon Collard, of dire repute. Strother knew that without asking. Judge Collard was the man who had claimed this land in the first place, decades previous, clearing it by hand with an axe and a mule and building the house and outbuildings. He had come down the Great Wagon Road from Pennsylvania, trailing a wife and four children. Harris was the last son standing.

Judge Collard had not stood in Strother's lifetime. He slumped withered, the left side of his face slack and sagging, as if he had leaned too close to a fire and melted like candle-wax. A brilliant man in his time, or so it was commonly said: a man of wide learning and deep cogitation, as a Judge must needs be, though precisely where and when he had served on the Bench was never quite clear. The possibility remained that he had not been precisely a Judge at all, in the strict and formal sense of that office, but rather a man who passed cold-eyed judgement on such as came before him. He sat judging young Strother at this moment, his eyes in that slack face fixed and glittering.

The boy beside him had the self-same stare. A lifetime later, looking back, this would be Strother's indelible recollection: Meshach Collard, standing silent and uncanny, his britches rolled and sagging at the ass, as if he had prodigiously shat himself and bore the load. His stare was so black and unblinking that Strother supposed him at first to be defective.

Others began to appear. Ruth Collard, Harris's wife, wan and weary in the doorway. Bobby Collard, fourteen years old, as blithe as the others were grim.

"Please," Strother said, a second time.

Harris Collard hawked and spat. "Please what?"

"For Chrissake, Harris, just boil your hog," said Drusilla Smoak.

Strother jerked round. The granny-woman had come up behind him, so quiet he never heard it.

"You'll be the Purcell boy," she said, studying him closely, till she saw where he fit. "You've come a long, hard way."

This was hardly a feat of divination, though it almost seemed so to Strother. A child, eight years old, alone in this place, struggling to hold in the sweat-slick gelding. The slaughtered hog, suspended above the cauldron. Steam rising as if from the coals of the Place Below. The stench of flesh and the dogs and the snarls and those Collard eyes all about him.

"Tell me what you need," the granny-woman said.

She was not a Collard by blood, but the twenty-years-younger sister of Dorcas Smoak, who had married the old Judge. Drusilla had once been wed as well, to a man named Spivey from Tennessee, who had passed long ago and left her childless. After Dorcas's death she had taken up with her brother-in-law, the Judge, keeping his bones warm on mountain nights. So at least it was said. So it would inevitably be said, regardless of the truth: a widow who gathered herbs and built her own one-room cabin to live in, half a mile above the big house. Her late husband had been a drunkard who raised his hand, and in consequence withered and died — so it was reliably rumoured — just two years after the nuptials. She retained for an uncanny length of years an eldritch beauty, which had not faded entirely to this very day, though she was nut-brown and gnarled and old enough to be a crone.

"Will you come?" Strother asked.

"I will."

She sent Bobby Collard to fetch out her necessities: a cloak and a hempen sack tied with twine that was her granny-woman bag, containing the needful herbs and ointments.

"I'll take your horse," she said to Strother. "He'p me up."

He hesitated, fighting down an inexplicable shudder. This she noted with a dryness.

"If I was what you're notioning, I'd fly."

The old woman smelled of wood-smoke and of something else, dark and acrid underneath. Stepping into his hand-hold she was light as dry sticks bundled together. The gelding skittered but steadied. He was a good honest creature and would run himself to death, if his rider asked it.

"How am I to follow?" Strother said. Evening was already coming on.

"Give him the mule," the old woman said to Harris Collard.

"Can't be loaning out no mule," said Harris. "I might could trust him with the pig."

"Give him the damned mule."

Then she was gone, kicking the gelding into a trot and lurching with him down the trail. The dogs milled as she did, perplexed at whether to howl or let be. She clung with both fists in the gelding's mane, back bowed and skirts flapping like bat-wings.

It was midnight when Strother arrived home, numb with cold. The last ten miles he had ridden in utter blackness. But he knew the road, and the Collard mule was stolid and sure-footed. At last there was light from the house ahead, and the wink of a lantern as Solomon came out to meet him. Solomon was Aunt Glory's only son, old now himself.

The granny-woman had arrived hours previous, Solomon said. She'd ridden the gelding halfway to death, and lamed him.

"And my Mama?" Strother said.

"Bad."

Miz Amanda had been bad since Strother's leaving at dawn, and still the baby would not come. Solomon's loyalty to Strother's Mama was abiding, and his distress tonight was keen.

So was Mr. Dillashay's.

Strother might have understood this, had he been a few years older. Or had he been born other than he was, and more inclined to see the world from angles and obliquities. But he had from infancy stood square-on, staring straight at what presented itself before him, which tonight as he stepped through the door was his step-father at the table, pale with whiskey.

"The Prodigal, swanning home at last." Mr. Dillashay spoke through gritted teeth, looking blackly at his step-son. "Dawdling. Not caring if his Mama lived or died."

They were in the kitchen. Overhead was the bedroom. Strother heard his Mama's cries.

He said: "Is there something I can do?"

"Oh, you done enough, boy. Done quite sufficient for one day." Mr. Dillashay was in his way a handsome man, but just now in the candlelight he was a troll. "I give him one job," he said. Speaking to the whiskey, as men may do when the subject of their discourse won't bear naming. "One job, and he couldn't do it right. Fetch help, I said, and look after the horse."

Above, the cries went on and on. At length Drusilla Smoak came down the stairs.

"Well?" Mr. Dillashay demanded. He had lurched to his feet at her coming.

"Baby's turned the wrong way," she said.

"So turn it right."

The granny-woman was haggard with the fight. Her hands and forearms were streaked with blood.

Mr. Dillashay cried: "Get yourself back! The hell did you come down here for?"

"A decision."

Strother asked: "Will she die?"

"That choosing isn't mine." She was looking at Mr. Dillashay as she said it. "I might could still save one of them. Not both."

Strother knew at once what choice he would make, were the choosing to be his. Lige would spend his whole life knowing it, too. In later childhood he would picture making the same choice himself, and each time in these imaginings he chose self-sacrifice: the very choice that Jesus would have made, or Strother. "Take me, Lord," he would cry, this Elijah of his imagining. "Save my Mama, and let the club-foot die." But he knew he could never say it as instantly as Strother would have done, nor with such perfect nobility.

Lige's Daddy would have chosen to save the child. He would say so openly in later years, muttering it into his whiskey. On one terrible night, he hurled it in fury against his wife's bedroom door, which she had barricaded against him.

But in the moment, Mr. Dillashay stood stricken. He began to tremble, the brutal bulk of him quaking in such manner as his step-son would scarcely have credited.

"No," he said. "No, you can't just ... You'd ask a man — ?"

Then distress burst out of him the customary way and he began to rage, cursing Drusilla Smoak for a fraud and a witch. She had come in the guise of a Christian woman, and what had she done instead? She had tormented his wife to no purpose, and ruined his horse. The gelding, so lamed that it was doubtless past the saving.

The granny-woman's expression changed. "That horse is still alive?" she demanded.

Alive, cried Mr. Dillashay, but lamed beyond all mending, for which she would pay him cash money in recompense.

Drusilla Smoak said: "Kill it."

"Damned if I won't have to do just that," Mr. Dillashay cried. "First light, my best damned horse!"

A gleam had come upon the granny-woman. She said: "Kill the horse *now*."

What his step-daddy thought — how much he understood — Strother would never know for a certainty. But Solomon saw clearly. This understanding marbled him in the doorway, a statue of a Christian man aghast. Mr. Dillashay was already slamming past him. Seizing his rifle he stormed to the barn, where the gelding was moving gingerly. It lifted its head uneasily and nickered. Mr. Dillashay raised the gun and fired. The gelding's legs folded neatly and it fell, dead before it hit the ground.

A half-hour later Elijah Dillashay was born. He came squalling into the world, as red as if he'd been boiled. Drusilla Smoak noted with grim satisfaction that the baby was robust, with five fingers and five toes on each appendage, though twisted and clubbed in the left foot. The mother would live as well, and with time might even be hale again.

"You'll want payment, I expect," Mr. Dillashay said.

"A gift. Whatever seems right to you."

She had washed her face and arms at the trough, and taken some nourishment. Dawn had broken, and she waited for Strother to bring the mule. Mr. Dillashay stood in the doorway.

"I consider your service to be worth five dollars," he said. "The gelding was worth ten. We'll call it square."

"You do not want to say that, Jacob Dillashay. You want to think again."

"Get off my land."

Drusilla Smoak took his measure. "I'll come back," she said, "another day. When I do, I'll name my own gift. And you'll owe it."

-SEVEN-

The Accounting of Barry Weaver

San Francisco, 1892

THEY KNEW SOME TRUTHS, those old Greeks. Dire and gloomy truths, for the most part: the implacability of flint-eyed Nemesis, hunting each one of us down like the dogs we are; the awful irrevocability of deeds once done, and the certainty that we are trapped without hope of reprieve in the vast grinding cycles of Destiny and—worse yet—by our own nature. Truths without a speck of hopefulness in 'em, as opposed to the shiny new can-do truths that we peddle to each other in America.

But truths are truths; they don't ask us to like it. I would have cause to ponder this, long after the events of the spring and summer of 1892—events that I helped set in motion. At the time, of course—in April and May and June, right into July, when I was there in the midst of it all—this never occurred to me. I mainly thought that events were unfolding quite well, and that Young Weaver was a fine and clever fellow.

Just the way we always think.

Those old Greeks knew that, too.

I found Tyree at his street-corner newsstand on Market Street. This was a day or so after the night of my incarceration.

I was feeling much more like myself, by now. Tyree, on the other hand, looked poorly. His shoulders were hunched and his face was tinged with grey, but he sketched up the ghost of a wry grin as he saw me.

"Let you out, did they?"

So he'd heard.

"I hear a lotta things," he said. His chuckle gave way to a cough. It would seem he'd taken chill during his trudge home through the rain; it rattled in his narrow chest and came out wet and wheezing.

I said, "Are you all right? You sound halfway to dying, there."

The little man waved the concern aside. But his breath took a moment before returning, and he sat down abruptly on the wooden box he used for a stool. Another cough came rattling on. Pulling out a soiled excuse for a handkerchief, he hacked and wiped his mouth and glanced—a nervous, sidelong flicker—to ascertain what he'd produced. It was a gesture I recognized; my father had done that, during his long decline.

Passersby edged away.

It was mid-morning. Foot-traffic was brisk, coming and going— Tyree had a good location. His stand was a species of makeshift shed, with newspapers in stacks and a plank for a roof overhead, to keep off the worst of the weather. It was halfway sunny this morning, and almost warm—a San Francisco springtime day to fill the heart with optimism. Clouds scudded white across a pale blue sky, and a fresh salt breeze gusted in from the ocean.

I'd taken some steps since they'd turned me loose the previous morning. Small ones, admittedly—but all of them steps in the right direction. I'd pawned my father's pocket-watch. A gold-plated watch on a modest gold chain, passed down through three generations, father to son, and one of the only keepsakes I possessed. But it fetched enough to secure a coffin-sized room in a verminous rooming-house on the edge of Chinatown, with two weeks' spending money left over—enough to tide me through till the next remittance from my mother.

So. Homeless no more. Coat brushed, fresh shirt, clean-ish underwear. The jingle of a few coins in the pocket, and—most of all—the first glimmering of a sort of plan. I said, "What can you tell me about Strother Purcell?"

Tyree's fit of coughing had subsided. He looked up quickly at the name.

"You said you knew him, once upon a time," I said.

"I said I seen him. Once. He was riding by."

"And?"

"…And what, Mr. Weaver?"

"I have no idea. That's why I'm asking. How much do you know about him?"

Tyree's gaze had narrowed to a point. He said, "Why?"

"Because I'm a writer. There's nothing sinister, here—no ulterior motive. I'm just looking for a story to tell. And I'm wondering if Purcell's would be a good one."

"For—what—one of those dime novels, of yours?"

"Or else something I could peddle to the newspapers."

Tyree said, "No."

It perplexed me, I have to say—this queer reaction. I said, "Come again?"

"'S not a story you want to tell."

"Why not?"

"'Cause it's grim. Then it gets grimmer. Then it ends."

A customer arrived, interrupting us—a man in a fine frock coat, who wanted a cigar. Tyree hiked himself to his feet and obliged. His hand inexplicably shook as he counted out change.

"Tell me," I said, intrigued, as the man in the frock coat continued on his way.

Tyree hardly looked at me, now. "Purcell was a lawman," he said shortly. "From down South."

"Carolina," I said. "Yes, I know that much about him."

"I understand he killed some people there. Killed some others, elsewhere. Then he went after his own outlaw half-brother. Chased him all the way from New Mexico — up through the Oregon and Washington, into Canada. Kept on chasing, all to hell and gone, up North."

"And killed him?"

"They killed each other. Or some such. That's my understanding. The two of 'em rode up into the mountains, and neither one of 'em rode back."

"And this was ...?"

"Years ago."

"How many?"

"A goodly few. Fifteen or so. Sixteen."

"Sixteen years?"

"The winter of '76. According to accounts."

"You must have been a boy," I said. The realization was neither here nor there — but it startled me a little, nonetheless. "If Purcell disappeared sixteen years ago — you'd have been just a boy, when you saw him."

"We both started out as boys, Mr. Weaver. 'N look at us now." He sketched up a small, grim smile.

I said, "And neither Purcell nor his brother ...?"

"... Has been seen again, since. Not by me. Nor by anyone else, that I ever spoke to. And trust me, Mr. Weaver — I've asked."

It was a queer thing to have said. I thought so at the time — and continued to think so, afterward. "You've asked?" I said. "Why?"

"'Cause I like to know things. And maybe 'cause he left an impression. Sure, let's put it that way. I seen him once in my life. I was ten

105

years old, Mr. Weaver. But he was not a man like you and me — not a man you could forget."

"Describe him to me."

"Describe him?"

"Yes. What did he look like? That day when you were ten years old, and Strother Purcell rode by."

"He looked like Judgement Day, come to call."

The coughing took him over again. A fearsome bout of it this time, shaking his shoulders and curling his spine. He sat down hard, and it shook him some more, till it passed.

"You should probably go home," I suggested, gingerly. "Lie down — get some rest."

He hawked into that rag again. Flicked a nervous glance, as my father had done. My father's clean white handkerchief would be spotted with red.

At length, Tyree drew in a rattling breath, and looked up. "Forget about Strother Purcell, Mr. Weaver. That'd be my counsel. Find yourself another tale. One that has some hope in it, somewhere."

*

I had no intention of forgetting about Strother Purcell. But first I had to find him again.

I'd passed out, at some point subsequent to my derelict cellmate's astounding claim to be the wreck of the legendary gunman. I'd awakened hours later, face-down in an empty cell, with an Officer's boot prodding my ribs. "Off y'go, Sunshine," he grunted.

They'd set the old man loose already, along with the sorrowing muskox. They didn't know where the old man might have gone — and couldn't have cared less, either. They didn't even know he had a name.

"Old Cadaver, you mean?" the Officer demanded. "The hell d'you want with him?"

"What sort of a name is that?" I heard myself asking. "That's no sort of name for a human being."

"That's not so much of a human bein', neither."

We were at the exit door, at this point. The Officer elbowed it open. Outside, the skull-splitting sunlight of morning blazed down upon the alley.

"And you don't—?"

"No, I don't have no idea where you'd find him. But I got a suggestion for you. D'you want to hear my suggestion? Here it is: Fuck off."

Off I fucked.

But I didn't give up. After getting myself set up with a room, I went looking for Tyree. After that, I commenced searching through the sinks of San Francisco—the Barbary Coast dives and alleys, and the flea-pits down by the docks—looking for Old Cadaver, or for anyone who might have knowledge of him.

At the end of a day and a half, I was still looking. As mid-day rolled around, I found myself in the rough dockside area south of Market Street, with its jumble of match-stick buildings. The Salvationists had set up shop here a few years earlier—you'd see them on street-corners, banging drums and bugling Hallelujah. There was a Gospel Mission too, where indigents could get a free meal by yielding themselves up to a dose of preaching. That's where I encountered Brother Amos.

He was ladling out stew to derelicts at a makeshift dining-tent. These were the sorriest specimens of humanity you could imagine— shambling men in rags, missing arms and legs and ears and God only knows what else, men of sundry ages, and women too. Beggars too pathetic to be snatched up by the waterfront press-gangs, who'd shanghai damn near anyone who drew breath. They slunk in a line to a cauldron at the front, where Brother Amos presided with his ladle. Then they slank past to sit and slurp at long wooden tables underneath a canvas awning.

"Old Cadaver?" Brother Amos said, when I sidled up and introduced myself and asked him. "Friend o' mine, I do not recognize that name. But I recognize a soul in desperate need. Get yourself a plate, and get in line."

"*Me?*" I almost laughed. "No, pal, you've got the wrong fella. I'm not—"

"Sure you are," he said. "Maybe you just don't understand that, yet."

My heart sank as I recognized the type.

Brother Amos was my age, more or less. An emaciated man with burning eyes, so thin that his head was damned near just a skull, with skin and hair stretched over it. Oh, he was the strangest duck—but weirdly compelling.

"Break bread with us, friend o' mine. Or else don't—it's up to you."

"Look, all I want is—"

"Jesus sees you, just the same."

He reminded me of my mother. It was those damned eyes.

My father the Reverend Weaver was a man of abiding faith, but his was a religion of hope and comforting nostrums. Not that it kept him from dying, of course. No one's faith does that, and my father turned the trick before he was forty, coughing up blood and bits of lung.

My mother's religion ran more toward hellfire and torment. Her people had been Presbyterian—doughty Calvinists who foreswore all mirth on Sundays, and on the other days of the week just to be safe, and whose response to a glorious morning in spring was: "We'll pay for this." She thumped out hymns on the organ, quoted dire passages of Scripture with ominous satisfaction, and held out little hope for your immortal soul and—most especially—for mine. True, she had continued to send money, all these years, to her prodigal boy. This was Christian of her, I suppose, and possibly even evidence of some vestigial love. But there was an unspoken understanding in the arrangement: the remittance would keep coming, but on the whole she would prefer that the prodigal stayed lost, on grounds of being a grievous disappointment. So I did.

Now here was Brother Amos, with Mother Weaver's eyes in his head.

"Friend o' mine, I was a drunkard and a wastrel. I was given over to all manner of dissipation."

I told him that I didn't doubt it. He kept on going.

"I swindled and I stole. I lost every friend I had that was worth keeping, and I broke my mama's heart. But I was Saved, nonetheless."

"Hallelujah," muttered the derelict first in line. He was a man of middle years, managing to reek in the open air, and evidently hoping that a *praise the Lord* would earn him extra stew. It didn't. He scowled at the portion that Brother Amos had glooped onto his plate, then slouched away to find a place to sit, stink-eyeing Young Weaver as he did in a less-than-Christian fashion.

"Saved, friend o' mine," Brother Amos repeated. "And saved, if you'd believe it, by a fearsomer sinner than I had been myself. For I was called to the Lord by the Reverend Jacob Jacobson, one year and eight months and twelve days ago, in a hail-flattened cornfield in Ulysses, Kansas."

He clearly thought I ought to be impressed. He seemed to expect that I'd heard of the Reverend Jacob Jacobson, too. I hadn't, and had no interest in learning about him now.

"Well," I said to him. "My golly."

"Now, *who* did you say you're looking for?"

More stink-eyes were directed my way, as the indigents in line grew impatient. I felt a rising urgency to get away from here, truth be told. But I described the old man.

Brother Amos cocked his skull. "I do not know this man," he said. "But I have *seen* him."

"Seen him where?" I demanded. "How long ago?"

Brother Amos eyed me keenly. "Why?"

The same damned question that Tyree had asked. What was it, with these people?

"Because I want to find him, damn it," I exclaimed. "Because I want to *help* him, maybe."

"Do you?"

"Sure! What the devil is so strange about that?"

"The devil, friend o' mine? No. Oh, no. Let's not invite *him* into the conversation."

The lined-up indigents were muttering darkly, now. Much more of this delay and there'd be outright mutiny. There'd be pitchforks.

And still Brother Amos looked at me.

"Friend o' mine," he said, "we will make a bargain. If I do you this service, then you must do me one in return."

"Fine," I said.

"I have your word?"

"I just said so, didn't I?"

"And what is it worth?" said the man with my mother's eyes. "What is it worth, your word?"

– EIGHT –

From *The Sorrows of Miz Amanda and her Two Brave Boys*

North Carolina, 1848 – 1850

1.

THE AUTUMN OF THE YEAR that Lige turned four, Bobby Collard came down from Hanging Tree Ridge. It was Mr. Dillashay's custom to hire extra hands for the harvest and for planting in the spring, paying them with dollars that he squeezed out of his purse like rabbit-farts. Lige heard one of them say so once, though not within his Daddy's hearing. Reese Holcombe it was, the older of two brothers from up Black Mountain, who ran trap-lines in the winter. The farm was prosperous, by the standards of the time and place; some seasons Mr. Dillashay would take on half a dozen hands, and that autumn Bobby Collard was amongst them.

He was seventeen years old that year, a young man bubbling up with laughter who knew riddles and songs and abruptly out of nowhere would pitch himself forward and walk some distance on his hands, for sheer exuberance of being alive. He could be a good worker, though, when the mood was upon him. Mr. Dillashay admitted this himself in that particular manner of his, which was to scowl but not contradict when Lige's Mama made the observation. He even grew to like the boy, and paid him more fairly than he paid the others.

Thus, as all catastrophes do, it began in part with kindness.

—

Lige's Mama had never been the same, after giving birth. Lige heard this said by Solomon and others. Doc Semmens said it too. The young doctor had stopped by the farm a few months after Lige had been born. It was on his way to call on another patient, and he was prepared to set to one side his grudge against Mr. Dillashay. From time to time he would stop by again, to deliver the medicine he had prescribed to help Lige's Mama regain her strength. Each time she would profess herself to be more vital, and for the span of half an hour this might seem to be true. But the effort of such vivacity would wear on her. The doctor would frown to himself and shake his head, observing that Lige's Mama continued to languish, even as her boy grew sturdier by the season—almost as if one came at the cost of the other. Doc Semmens thought this privately, and once said so out loud to Solomon, who was greatly unsettled. Solomon held such statements to be pagan.

"So what if they are?" the doctor said. "Being pagan does not make a thing untrue." Doc Semmens was a young man with a young man's thoughts in his head.

Lige's Mama and his Daddy were still on terms of fondness, of a kind, though she continued to keep to her own bedroom at night, the room she had taken during her confinement. Mr. Dillashay was kindly in his way, asking awkwardly after his wife's health and from time to time bringing her bunches of wild flowers. These she would place in Mason jars by the window, and sometimes braid them into wreaths, which in playful moods she would wear about her forehead. The tincture from Doc Semmens would leave her languid, and one night in the tumult of a thunderstorm she was found to be walking barefoot in the pasture, drenched with rain and garlanded with petals, as if she were Persephone released from the Underworld. She fell gravely ill for a time thereafter, shaken by chills and wracked by fever. She recovered, but once again there was an infinitesimal loss, as if with each return she stopped another half-step short. She asked Doc Semmens for more of the tincture, which he with some misgiving brought to the farm at more regular intervals. This continued until the time of the Great Schism—such would be Miz Amanda's bitter term—which prompted Mr. Dillashay to ban the young doctor permanently from his property, on pain of being shot down like a dog. After this Strother would ride dutifully each month to an apothecary in Asheville; there and back again in one day, regardless of the season. "My Roman," his Mama would say on his return, opening her arms in benediction. The fever-glow had never entirely left her eyes, which in candlelight would shine.

Often of an evening she would have Strother read to her out loud. Her father, Mr. Beauchamp, had been a mighty scholar, as Mr. Purcell had been, in his less robust manner. She had a whole shelf of her father's books, which had come with her all the way from Virginia. *Pilgrim's Progress* and *Robinson Crusoe* and two volumes of Gibbon's *Decline and Fall*, and Mr. Dryden's *Aeneid* and tragedies by Shakespeare and a collection of stories from the Classical myths. There were as well books by Virgil and Plutarch written in Latin, and old Herodotus in Greek, which Mr. Beauchamp had been able to read just as easily as you parse nursery rhymes.

Strother was his mother's project. "You are my Roman and my scholar," she would say, and Strother would set himself to each task she put before him. "You have your grandfather's intellect," she would murmur—though the fact was that he plodded, working doggedly through a text with unbreakable resolve, looking neither left nor right as he did. Lige possessed the keener mind, much swifter and more nimble, though given to sudden swallow-darts and veerings. This occasioned frequent dismay to Solomon, to whom Miz Amanda had delegated the education of her youngest boy. Solomon's sole text was the Bible, from which Lige parsed his *begats* and *shalt nots* and began to glimpse the stain of mortal sinfulness that seeped down through the countless generations, all the way from Adam to his own small, squalid self.

—

The following spring Bobby Collard came again.

There was strife between Bobby and Harris Collard, who had cursed the boy for a wastrel. Lige was too young to understand, or to ask. But Strother learned the gist of it from Mama, who felt a protective instinct toward the outcast. A sort of friendship had grown between them; of an evening you might see them standing together, or even walking in the field. One evening, Lige came around the side of the barn to see them in close conference by the well.

"He is your Daddy, nonetheless," Miz Amanda was saying. "You understand? Whatever he said or did, nonetheless he is your Daddy."

Bobby Collard replied impatiently, and Miz Amanda grew more earnest still. "No," she said. "Bobby? *No.*" She touched her hand to his forearm, the better to communicate conviction. "There is duty—yes, there is—a duty owed by every child to his Daddy. And I believe you know it, too."

She spoke to Bobby Collard with the wisdom of long years, though in truth she was not so much older than he was. She'd been just seventeen years old when she married Mr. Purcell; even now she was not quite thirty. It was a fine May evening as they stood together by the well. Bobby Collard had been working all day in the field, and had stripped off his shirt to wash himself.

Mr. Dillashay stood watching from a distance. Lige scarcely noticed at the time, but in later years looking back he would see his Daddy clearly. His Daddy had been in the upper pasture that day, beyond the creek. Now halfway down the hillside he had stopped, and stood in stillness amongst the stones.

"Do you understand?" his wife was saying now, to Bobby Collard. "There is a bond—there is blood—and there is duty. You must always and ever be straight and true."

Bobby Collard drank water from the ladle, then poured what

remained over his head and shoulders. Arching back, he shook his head, the droplets flying.

"Yes, Ma'am," he said.

Doc Semmens had been in Mama's chamber the afternoon of his last visit, listening to her breathing with his stethoscope. Strother had afterward explained this to Lige, who had been the one to blunder in on them. In the confusion of the moment Lige had seen only a flustration of bodies separating, and his Mama snatching at a smock.

"A consultation, is what it was," Strother had told him. He was himself still flushed a little, and shaken by the outburst that had followed when Mr. Dillashay found out. Mr. Dillashay's swarthy face had been white with anger, and his voice had been taut as he said what would happen if Doc Semmens set foot on his property again.

2.

Kleobis and Biton had been straight and true. Lige knew this from a story.

The air seemed especially full of stories, that summer when Lige was four years old. Oh, there had always been stories in the world, and always would be. The world itself was woven from stories, as Lige in some manner had come to intuit already. But it would never be more alive with them than it had been in that year.

Kleobis and Biton were the two brave sons of Cydippe, a priestess of mighty Hera, queen of the gods. Greeks these were, from ancient times. Cydippe was beautiful, and at harvest time bedecked with flowers she would ride in an ox-cart up the winding mountain road to Hera's Temple. But when the day of the Festival dawned, not a single pair of oxen could be found to draw the cart, all beasts being occupied elsewhere with labour in the fields. So Kleobis and Biton said: "Let us take this task upon ourselves." And together they drew the heavy cart up the mountain, while beautiful Cydippe wept with happiness to have such sons.

Miz Amanda told the story as Lige sat with her on the front porch in the twilight. A breeze had begun to shift the oppression of August. Strother was with them, sitting on the step nearby. "Five miles," their Mama said. "Five miles up that mountainside — straight and true. Her two brave boys, not one single day older than the two of you, yoked to a task that was meant for two oxen together. Such was their love for their Mama."

Their strength gave out at last, but not until they had drawn the cart to the steps of the temple, where Cydippe was welcomed with all honour. Great Hera herself asked to hear the story told, twice through from beginning to end. So impressed was the goddess that Cydippe summoned all of her courage and asked Hera to grant her two brave boys a gift.

"And not just any gift," their Mama said to them on the porch, telling them the tale. "Cydippe asked: 'Grant them the greatest gift that any mortal may aspire to, in this world.' So Hera did. And can you imagine what that was?"

Strother said: "They died."

He spoke with solemnity, as was his way. Leaning back on his elbows, looking down the length of his outstretched legs. Strother was now twelve; his legs stretched prodigiously.

"Yes," their Mama said.

The two of them had shared this tale before. This was Lige's first thought, and it cut at him, though afterward it would seem to him more likely that Strother had read the story on his own in one of their grandfather's books. But now Lige saw with some confusion that tears were welling in his Mama's eyes.

"She went to wake them," Strother said. "But they were dead and cold."

"Yes."

"Now, there's a downright daisy of a gift," said Bobby Collard.

He had come up by the side of the house, where he stood listening. Lige startled at his voice, as did Strother. Their Mama alone seemed unsurprised. Perhaps her senses had been more keenly attuned, that evening at least, to the whisper of bare feet in the grass.

"Their time had come, you see," she said. Smiling at Bobby Collard through her tears. "Their time had come round, so they died in their sleep. But their hearts had stopped before they broke. And really, who could ask for more than that?"

Bobby Collard was full of stories too. But his were of a different nature, being tales he had learned from Drusilla Smoak. Tales of haints and hauntings, of tommy-knockers who lived down deep in mines, and of crossroads in the wood where Old Scratch might very well be waiting at this minute. Such tales as could make the blood run cold, though not always in the way that Bobby told them. He could describe the most harrowing haint with wide-eyed glee, and was apt to punctuate damnation by flipping straight over and walking on his hands: back bowed, shirttail slipping to expose his midriff, bare feet paddling at the sun.

He chuckled now to himself, and shook his head as he moved away through the gloaming toward the barn. There was a bunkhouse for the help, but Bobby Collard preferred to sleep in the hayloft, by himself. His hair, bleached by the summer sun, was the colour of straw.

Their Mama followed him with her gaze, tears still streaming.

Lige was left unsettled by the story. For a long time that night he was unable to close his eyes.

"They died of exhaustion, is all," Strother said in the darkness.

They slept in the same room, he and Lige, being brothers. "Their hearts blew out. Like a horse's will do, if you ask too much. Or else their lungs just ruptured. So go to sleep."

Strother lay on his back, staring up into the darkness; Lige could discern his profile, etched in moon-glow.

"That's where the old story started, Lige. Stories start somewhere, after all—that stands to reason. They don't turn strange till later, in the telling." Strother turned onto his side then, and soon settled into sleep. His breathing grew steady and measured.

Lige lay awake alone, willing his heart from one beat to the next.

3.

The look upon his brother's face: that would become Lige's most vivid recollection of the day Bobby Collard rode off with Dapple the mare. Lige would tell the tale in later years on numerous occasions, sometimes to others but most often to himself. It could cause him to laugh right out loud, though not in a manner that you would recognize as mirthful. And of all the recollections he might have carried forward from that day—the day the rat-gnawed timbers of the world gave way at last, and it all collapsed in ruination about them—the most enduring was the expression on Strother's face as he swung the scythe.

September. They had already begun the harvest, about which there was an unaccustomed urgency, the season giving signs of turning early. The days still sweltered, but the temperature at nights had plunged to the edge of frost; last evening dark clouds had massed beyond the line of mountains to the east. They'd start work well before sunrise, but instead the day began with the discovery that Bobby Collard had up and fled, riding on Mr. Dillashay's mare.

Mr. Dillashay uttered terrible oaths. Gathering up the hands, he rode off through the ghosts of dawn to fetch back the mare and to deal with Bobby Collard as such wretches are to be dealt with. The hands were a motley assortment that season: low and indifferent men, and not the sort you'd choose for a posse if choosings were to be had. But they entered into the spirit with some exuberance, as low men will do when licensed to despise. As the trail led them north they drew others into the hue and cry. The Holcombe boys were amongst these, keen trackers and hard dark men. They hated a horse-thief as much as any man in these hills, or did so at least on this occasion. They bore as well grudges unspecified but profound against the Collard clan.

Bobby Collard had stayed on right through the summer, sleeping in the loft and making himself more useful than Mr. Dillashay might have expected. He did not want to go home, though once he disappeared for a day and two nights without explanation, and Strother on another occasion glimpsed two distant figures standing together on the ridge just at sundown. One of these was surely Bobby Collard, and the other—so Strother was sure—was Drusilla Smoak.

It stood to reason that those two should have kept in contact. Blood is a powerful bond, and Bobby had always been his aunt's especial favourite. Like her he had eyes like a cat's, which changed their colour depending on the angle of the light, and knew more than was canny about the properties of plants and herbs, some of which were known to cause deadly harm.

"It is all the truth, what they rumour," Bobby said once to Lige, in a moment of fearsome confiding. "I am a witch-boy, and sold my soul." His eyes as he said this glowed green, and Lige felt his sphincter tighten its grip all the way up to his heart. But just as suddenly Bobby whooped with laughter to see the look on Lige's face, and was blithe and hazel-eyed again. This was another reason for Drusilla Smoak to love him best, Lige supposed: just being near Bobby Collard could bring you joy. He knew the best salves for cuts and wounds, and once when Mr. Dillashay was chalk-faced with megrim headache Bobby Collard brewed him a willow-bark tea that eased the pain.

Then in September darkness he rode off. Just up and galloped away, for no earthly reason — or none that a four-year-old boy could comprehend. The air had been roiling these past few days, ever since Lige's Daddy had spied his Mama lithe-stepping back from the barn in the shroud of night, and demanded to know what errand she'd been on. Last evening an argument had thundered beyond closed doors. But surely nothing to explicate why Bobby Collard should gallop away of a sudden on another man's mare, as if fleeing some impending retribution?

Lige recollected creeping down the stairs that dawn, into the knowledge that Bobby Collard was gone, and that his Daddy was already gone off after him. Gone off with all of the men excepting old Solomon, with the crop in the field and the weather commencing to turn. The last night had not been so cold, and by first light the air was grown sluggish and thick. Lige recollected the weight of it, sagging down. He recollected as well their beautiful Mama: the haggard dignity with which she saw what must be done.

"Mr. Dillashay has rode off," she said, "with his duty undischarged." Her hair was askew and her eyes were wild, but she spoke with great conviction. "Mr. Dillashay is derelict, but you will redeem the day — my two brave boys. You must bring in the harvest between you."

And so they did. Or at least, they tried. Long afterward, Lige would recollect that vast expanse of grain stretching out across the hillside; the rhythmic sweeps of his brother's scythe, and his own puny hackings. And their beautiful, mad Mama, exhorting them onward.

"Straight and true, boys — straight and true. And — O! — won't Mr. Dillashay be rebuked!"

She had about her a desperate energy, shards of it crackling and slivering like glass. Toward mid-morning she had gone up to the house; when she returned there was a languor upon her. She wore her burgundy frock with pearl brocade and wavered in the sullen light like the wraith of some departed debutante: the still-living ghost of Miss Amanda Beauchamp, late of Roanoke, Virginia.

"Straight and true, boys—straight and true. You must always and ever pull straight and true!"

The noon-day heat grew oppressive. Lige stumbled and flailed, and felt with sudden fear that his heart was about to explode. And he saw once again the look on Strother's face. An expression both exalted and terrifying: a sublime and appalling fixity of purpose, as if he could draw the whole world after him, straight and true.

Lige would say those exact words twenty-six years later, to a girl in the loft of her Uncle John's roadhouse near Hell's Gate. This was an account that she herself told, afterward. She lay in his bed, behind him, and the whole house shook in the teeth of a winter storm.

"What a godalmighty thing for a child to recollect," he said. "Can you imagine? Waiting for his heart to explode."

"Still and all," the girl replied. "It didn't." She sounded bored. This was a knack she had, to sound dead-bored by all of life, though she'd lived so little of it.

Lige knew he was duty-bound to hand her along to Cousin Fletch—at least as Cousin Fletch would define his duty. After that her well-being would be a question unresolved.

"Unless of course it did," she mused, by way of afterthought.

"Did what?" he said.

"Your heart. Exploded. And what you brung up that ladder tonight is a chest without a heart inside at all."

She was the strangest creature, he thought, pinched and watchful, though not without an eerie fascination.

"What would that make me, if I did?"

"Dunno," she said. "More int'resting than you might of been, otherwise."

"And it wasn't me come up that ladder," he said. "I was here in the first place. And no one invited you to climb up after."

"I don't recollect them asking me to climb back down, neither."

She had shifted her angle of perception, squinting out the small cracked window into the tumult of storm in the blackness. "Shitfuck filthy out there," she observed.

Lige said: "She'd've done it, though."

"What?"

"Kept the two of us working. Till our hearts *did* blow apart."

The bed was a mattress on the floor. He sat hunched on the side, the girl behind him, wrapped in her share of the blanket against the bitter cold. The ice-blasts searched through chinks in the walls and reached up beneath the blanket at his nethers.

"You don't care to offer a response?" he said.

"To what?"

"A Mama such as that, who'd wish her children dead."

She just shrugged her thin shoulders. This he found irksome.

She'd been a virgin. This had surprised him, though not in any way that would make a difference. Very much about this world is unexpected, and virginity unlooked-for does not rank high on the list. Especially not on such a night, trapped in a roadhouse while his brother came on through a cold that would kill any other man, and the haints of recollection squeaked like bats.

"Am I boring you, darlin'"? he said.

The blackness had been creeping over him for hours. It was surely the girl's own fault if she failed to see this, young as she was — and looking even younger, just at that moment. Looking secretly terrified, in fact, but getting on with what she'd set in motion.

"Boring?" she said. "No, I wouldn't say you're boring. I wouldn't guess that's one of your qualities."

"Then what would you say?"

"I'd say," she said, "that I have to admire it. When a man brings his Mama into my bed. I find it riveting."

There was silence again between them. The volleying of sparks inside the stovepipe, and the shriek of wind. He found himself beginning to think: This girl might be wasted on Cousin Fletch.

"So when did you start to understand?" she said.

"Understand?"

"What they'd done. Your Mama and the Collard boy."

*

The sky turned copper and drew low, and the men came riding back. Mr. Dillashay led the way, riding a cart-horse and leading Dapple. The Holcombe brothers were next, and then the hands, riding mules and whatever else would serve. A last few straggled behind on foot.

The mare was riderless.

Bobby Collard had gotten clean away: that was the first thought that came to Lige's mind. But there was something hard and haggard in his Daddy's face. His Mama saw it too; she made a sound in her throat, and stood unmoving.

"Where is the boy?" she said.

She knew already, looking past her husband to the others. They had been drinking corn whiskey since dawn; they had about them the slinking insouciance of men who have gone too far.

"What have you done?" she said to them.

Mr. Dillashay said: "His time come round."

Lige would recollect his Mama's cry—like a stricken bird—and his own bewilderment. He saw the lightning flash of loathing that his Daddy turned upon her, a hatred so pure and distilled that the devil himself might stopper it up in a bottle and measure it out three drops at a time. He saw his Daddy clench his fist and raise it to smite his Mama, and he heard his brother's voice say: "No, sir. You will not."

Strother stood ten paces behind. Slender, stone-still, holding his scythe.

Mr. Dillashay turned. "What did you say?"

"Touch her, sir, and I will kill you."

Lige saw that he would do it, too.

The same understanding had come upon Lige's Daddy. It bat-winged across his face.

He cursed, and snarled a laugh, but lowered his fist just the same. Lurching down from the cart-horse he went to Dapple instead. The mare skittered a step or two, but steadied. Her flanks were stained with sweat from the long day's journey. Bobby Collard had ridden her hard all the way to Chunky Gal Creek, which was fifteen miles; so Lige would afterward discover. His Daddy took her by the bridle and reached his right hand into his shirt, the mare nuzzling him in expectation of some delectable—a carrot or a bit of apple, for she was ever a favourite of Mr. Dillashay's. He drew out a pistol instead and in one smooth movement placed the muzzle between her eyes and pulled the trigger. Dapple's legs gave way and she subsided where she'd been standing, and Mr. Dillashay said to the world at large: "I will not abide a mare that was rode by Bobby Collard." Then looking neither left nor right he strode away, leaving the men to stand there open-mouthed like fools.

Lige stood, as stunned as any of the others. "See to Mama," Strother said to him. Her own legs had given way; she sat in alabaster shock, her burgundy dress tented about her.

Then Strother looked to the men, the hired hands who stood shuffling. "You're paid to do a job of work," he said. "Now let's do it."

—

A rattlesnake had done for Bobby Collard. They learned this afterward from Solomon, who heard it from one of the men. Bobby Collard might have ridden away clean, except the mare shied at a copperhead snake that raised up of a sudden on the trail, and threw him. The Holcombes came on Bobby after that, his left leg busted beyond all help of willow bark. They raised him up and then Mr. Dillashay raised him higher, with a rope thrown over the branch of a white oak tree.

The next evening Drusilla Smoak came.

"The devil do you want?" Mr. Dillashay demanded. He had locked himself in a room upon his return, drinking corn whiskey halfway through the night. With dawn he emerged, chalk-white but dogged, and set to work in the field. By afternoon his colour was back, though it drained away again as he faced the granny-woman.

She said. "I'm stopping to collect."

She was riding in a cart. It was drawn by a dun horse and there was someone sitting with her on the buckboard. Mr. Dillashay raised his arm against the glare, trying to squint out who it was. The storm had held off for one last day and the setting sun boiled red on the horizon.

"Collect? Collect what?"

"The debt you owe me. For catching your boy."

"I told you before—stay off my land."

"Your debt come due."

Meshach was sitting beside her. Shack Collard, now ten years old. Mr. Dillashay saw this now, as did Lige. He'd been working with Strother farther up the hill; they watched as the cart came wending.

In the back of the cart was burlap sacking. Some tools. Lige saw his Daddy see this too. Saw him hesitate. Squinting against the blood-red sun; trying to guess how much the granny-woman knew, and what it might take to be shed of her.

"You turn yourself around, and back you go," he said. "Same way you come."

"I come for Bobby Collard."

"Well, too bad. 'Cause you won't find Bobby Collard here."

"Will I find him at Chunky Gal Creek?"

"You go to the devil."

It shook him, though. Right down to the core. That twisted stick of a woman, and a silent boy beside her with his Granddaddy's merciless black stare.

"I caught your boy five years ago—alive. So you owe me my own boy back, the same way. That's the debt you owe me, Jacob Dillashay. Can you pay it?"

"Go back to hell, you old witch. D'you hear me? I charge you for a witch—I'll see you hang. I'll see you drownded in a pond!"

"Blood pays for blood." Her voice as harsh as a raven's. "Alive or dead, I'll have what I'm owed. If not today, then later. You owe me one living boy—twice over."

Looking straight at Lige as she said it. Then at Strother.

-NINE-

The Accounting of Barry Weaver

San Francisco, 1892

1.

"MEIGGS WHARF," Brother Amos had said. "He was sleeping rough out by Meiggs Wharf—two, three days ago. He may be still. That's my side of the bargain, friend o' mine. Now, don't forget yours."

And Brother Amos—give him credit—was true to his word. The old man was there, exactly as he'd said.

Meiggs Wharf was up at North Beach, at Francisco near Powell Street. It had once been quite the going concern, ships coming in from outlandish destinations, and going out again, and families thronging on weekends to the amusements at Abe Warner's Cobweb Palace, and businesses sprouting around it. These days, it was all slouching into decay. San Francisco had shiny new attractions elsewhere, and most of the ships had been drawn to other piers. The world had moved on, as the world will do, leaving Meiggs Wharf behind.

It was low tide when I arrived. Strother Purcell was sitting on a rock, staring out at the ocean. In the daylight, I saw that he wasn't as ancient as I'd supposed—at least, not in years. There was, rather, a quality of timelessness about him. He sat amidst wrack and seaweed like Moses shipwrecked and spewed ashore. He wore the same clothes as the other night in the cell—the same clothes he'd worn for weeks, presumably. I'd tell you that they'd been newly washed in sea-water, except that would be telling a lie.

"I've been looking for you," I said. "All over San Francisco."
He stared at me, bloodshot and blank. "The hell are you?"
"Your friend," I told him.
"*Friend?*"
"From the other night?"
The old man's stare stayed blank.
Shitbirds wheeled shrieking, overhead. Sea lions honked by the pier.
"Your cellmate," I said.
And he flinched. Some dismal recollection seemed to stir. "Yes,"
he said. "I drink." That ruined baritone. "I am a disgrace." He looked
back out to sea.
This wouldn't do, I was thinking to myself. The setting—the
stink—the abjection. I'd put him somewhere else, if ever I should
come to write his story. I'd give him a room, to begin with—some
human dignity. It would be small—sure it would—but clean. Spartan.
A bedroll and a basin and half a dozen books. A Bible, and somebody's
Collected Poems: Pope, maybe, or Dr. Johnson. The old man would
have occasion to say: These were once my Granddaddy's books. They
have been the companions of my lifetime.
"You're a man who's stumbled—that's all," I said. "A great man
fallen beneath himself."
"You got no idea who I am."
"Sure I do. You told me. Remember?"
He looked back to me, eye narrowing. He tilted his head and raised
one vast, gnarled hand to shade against the sun. That waft came off
him as he shifted. "I said my name?"
"You did."
"Then forget it." There was something in that rheumy look that
made the scrotum shrivel. "*Who* did you say you were?"
"Weaver," I told him. "Barrington Weaver. Barry. You gave me some

pointers on hanging myself. Remember? I never took you up on it, but still and all—"

"Go away."

"Sure. I can do that. But what I'm thinking—you should maybe try and put something on your stomach. D'you figure? A meal—or coffee, even. I've got some money..."

"I don't take charity."

"It's not charity."

"The hell is it, then?"

"I dunno. We could call it friendship?"

He wasn't sure what to make of that. To tell the truth, neither was I.

He had arrived in San Francisco a week or two previous. A month, possibly—he wasn't clear in his mind as to such details. He recollected it was cold his first night here, sleeping rough down by the docks. He'd intended to take ship, but had failed.

"Take ship?" I repeated. "What kind of ship?"

"Any kind. Whaling ship, maybe."

"*Whaling* ship?"

"Old Ahab. I read that book, once. Liked it."

He'd fallen in with sailors, he said, in a tavern. But then he'd gotten drunk and wandered off. Ships had come in and gone away again without him. "I missed my tide." He gazed out at the ocean as he said it. The water danced in a stiff spring wind; beyond, clouds massed low. Farther still, at the edge of the horizon, a ship was swallowed slowly by the mist.

We were in an eating-house by the docks. It was dank and filthy, as you'd expect—they were willing to serve the likes of my companion. "Old Cadaver," as they'd called him at the jail. Here—as

129

elsewhere—they didn't seem to call him much of anything, just gave him a wide and chary berth.

"Pork chop," he'd rumbled to the waiter.

He'd swallowed a mug of coffee, and kept it down. Now he was girding to challenge solid food. The waiter with gestures and fragments of English gave us to understand that this was a dockside establishment: look there, through the spiderwebbed window—ocean. Patrons were better advised to take their chances with fish.

"Pork chop," the old man said.

The chop when it arrived was vaguely porcine. Something that had at any rate been in a barnyard, at some unspecified point in its past. Now it lay grey and congealing amongst lumps of potato. The old man managed a few mouthfuls.

He'd been working at this and that for a good few years—that was the closest to a clear answer I could get from him. Working at that and the other, but travelling, mainly—drifting. "Where? Oh, here and there." He had ended in San Francisco because it was the farthest west you could drift, without a boat. Now his notion was to take ship, and go farther.

"Right off the edge of the earth?"

I said this as a sort of joke, but the old man gave it thought. "I don't expect that's possible," he said. It seemed to make him wistful.

Like Judgement Day, come to call. That had been Tyree's recollection. Jesus wept.

"What the hell happened?" I asked.

"To what?"

What had happened to *him*, of course. That's what I wanted to ask him. What manner of calamity had led from the one to the other—from the patriarch that Tyree had described, to the one-eyed ruin who sat across from me now? But you don't just blurt out a question like that, not to a fellow human sufferer. And most certainly not to a man who had once been Strother Purcell, and had filled more graves—if Rumour told true—than all of those doughty Earp boys put together.

"Talk about something else," he said.

"No, listen. I'm a writer. I told you that, didn't I?—two nights ago, in the cell. Well, I am. And that's why I'm thinking...see, I have this notion...I'd like to write something about you."

The old man looked at me.

I blundered ahead. "A book, maybe. Or an article, first, for a newspaper. Half a dozen of them, even. I'd write 'em, see, and sell 'em to someone—to Will Hearst, is what I'm thinking. And we'd split the money—fifty-fifty—right down the middle. Now, don't answer right away. Take a minute, and think about it. Because what I'm proposing—"

He stood.

It could be a disconcerting thing, to watch Strother Purcell stand up, while you were seated. He would rise, and then keep on rising. And just as you were certain that he'd risen to his full height, he'd rise some more—up to the totality of his six feet and five inches, with a shapeless crumpled hat like a dead opossum on top of that, from which vantage he would gaze one-eyed down upon you, wriggling in the muck of the earth far below.

"I'll thank you for the pork chop, Mr. Weaver."

"But—"

"We're done." He walked out the door, unsteadied by the ravages of Time and John Barleycorn, but managing somehow to conjure up a ruined dignity.

And there I sat. Startled, as you might expect. Somewhat squelched. But most of all, I felt unaccountably ashamed. That's the truth. I felt small, and mean, and grasping. I felt grubby, damn it, as if the wreckage of that man was still somehow finer than Young Weaver had ever been, even in those now-distant days when I *had* been young, and brim-full of promise and optimism, a lad whose father might swell up with pride, even as the consumption wasted him down to a stick in a cassock, the clerical collar around his neck grown as wide as a barrel-hoop.

I stood and hurried after him, strewing some coins onto the table to pay for the pork chop. He was ahead of me, tramping gaunt and resolute up one of San Francisco's sloping streets. It took awhile to catch up to him, in fact; I was halfway winded when I did.

"I misspoke," I said, huffing. "Sorry. We'll forget all that writing-about-you business."

He kept on tramping, giving no indication that he'd heard. I'd come up on his blind side, too, which didn't help in reading his expression. The milky eye was blank and unblinking.

"What I really want to say ... If you're looking for a place to stay— I've got one. It's not much, just a room. Hardly even big enough for me. But I'd share it, if you're so inclined."

"I'm not."

That came as a relief, tell the truth. But I was feeling distinctly better about myself, having made the offer. And a new idea had suddenly started to glimmer, as bright as a new silver dollar.

"I don't suppose you could use some work?" I said.

The old man slowed, a little. "Work? What kind of work?"

"The kind that calls for a man of your size," I told him. "And your skills, too, and experience."

He slowed just a little more.

"There's a woman and her sister," I told him. "They need help. It's a paying proposition."

*

Prairie Rose was surprised to hear it. "Help?" she demanded. "Who told you I need help?"

"No one did."

"That's right. 'Cause I don't need it."

"Yes, you do." I summoned my dead-earnest expression. "You just don't want to admit it."

"Barry?" said Rose. "Do me a favour, an' fuck off."

You recollect my friend Prairie Rose — the Mormon whore who slung drinks at the concert saloon on Dupont Street. The gal whose honour I had defended against Ichabod Rourke, on the ill-fated night of my forty-fifth birthday celebrations.

We were at the concert saloon now. It was mid-afternoon. This did not show the establishment — nor Prairie Rose herself — to best advantage. Too many windows, and through them daylight spilling without remorse. Items of human flotsam scattered about, and Prairie Rose wan and worn-out amongst them.

"What I'm proposing, see — he'd keep his eye out for you."

"His eye out for what?"

"For such men as might come up your stairs in the night, Rose. Men with grievance in their heart, and violent inclinations. I won't name names."

A shadow crossed her face. "And in return?" she said. "I mean, just assuming I'm still listening to you at all..."

"In return, you pay him two dollars a day."

"Chrissake, Barry. If I had two spare dollars, every day—"

"A dollar, then. Or fifty cents, even."

"Nope."

"A flat rate, then — three dollars a week. I can't say fairer than that."

"Barry..."

"...And I'll pay it myself."

That stopped her. Stopped me, too. I hadn't been intending to make any such offer—but there it was, burbling out of my mouth.

"Why the fuck would you do that?" Rose demanded.

"I don't know. I just know he needs some help. So let's just try it for a week or two—all right? Give him a chance to earn an honest dollar. Feel good about himself, or some damn thing."

"And what's your *real* reason?"

"That's it. I just told you."

Rose didn't believe me. I'm not sure I completely believed myself. But I kept talking. "He's a sort of a friend, Rose. I want to help him out. And maybe helping him can help you, too—you and your sister, both. Christ, you don't think I'm capable of one unselfish deed?"

She was looking at me closely, with a queer uncertain expression on her face. Then she looked across the room.

"Jesus, Barry. I dunno..."

We had chosen a quiet corner for our tête-à-tête. The old man was inside the door: the colossal wreck of him, standing ragged and one-eyed and half a head taller than anyone else in the place, like some derelict Lemuel Gulliver washed up amongst Lilliputians. A creature from an older dispensation, when men were taller and stronger and more terrible.

Such was my own impression. I am susceptible to a poetic cast of thought, as you will have noticed. Rose's gaze tended more to flat-out disbelief.

"I mean, look at him. Who *is* he?"

"A good man fallen," I said, "upon evil times."

"That's not a fucking answer."

And it wasn't. The problem was, what answer should I give? The old man had made it clear enough: he didn't want his real name to be known. And I didn't want that either—for his sake, and also because...well, you know. Because there was always a chance, wasn't there? That he might change his mind, and decide that he did want his life story told. The last great untold tale of the American Frontier, with all the elements that Deadeye Ned never had to offer—obsession and heartbreak and fratricide, by God, and a Retribution Ride across half a continent. And it would hardly serve anyone's best interests—the old man's least of all—to let on that Strother Purcell was still alive and here, right here, in San Francisco. A city full of hucksters and hustlers and snake-oil promoters, and two-bit scribblers who would swoop like crows to exploit the old man's saga in horrible and self-serving ways.

"He's a drifter," I said. "But I have reason to believe he was a lawman, years ago. He doesn't talk about it."

"A lawman? Where?"

"He doesn't talk about that either."

"Fucksake, Barry. Does he have a name?"

Another half-second of silence ticked past.

"His name," I told her, "is Lemuel. He calls himself Old Lem."

2.

Prairie Rose lived in a flat on Pacific Street. It was a long way down from Nob Hill, but neither was it some crib alley such as you'd find on Morton Street, where the lowest class of prostitutes clustered in shanties. On Morton Street you'd see them leaned out windows naked to the waist: a dime to touch a bubby, fifteen cents to touch 'em both—consecutively or both at once, strictly up to you and your personal preference, this being America and in America the customer being king. For two bits you could go right inside and follow where nature and inclination led.

Rose had been able to afford two rooms, on the third floor of a tenement. I can't say how she managed that, entirely. You'd hear wild speculation about Mormon gold, stolen from her husband the Utah Brute. Such talk never made sense to me—why would a Mormon gal with gold be whoring in a concert saloon to begin with?—though the rumours never left off swarming around poor Rose. I suspected the answer had more to do with an arrangement she'd made with the man who owned the tenement—or the bastard at least who came to collect the rent.

It was hardly uncommon for agreements to exist between Rent Collectors and women like Prairie Rose. Certain favours sought, and supplied; not an exclusive arrangement, exactly, for Rose still trudged to Dupont Street most evenings of the week. But she had agreed—wholeheartedly—that no trade of that nature would be transacted at the flat. The flat was for Prairie Rose to live in, with periodic visits from the Rent Collector. Three days in a row might pass between such visits—whole weeks, even—leaving Rose with entire afternoons to work with needle and thread. She had talent as a seamstress, and aspirations in that line. She was taking in piece-work for the present, but daring to take on outside employment in the back room of a shop, and beginning to imagine a time when she could support herself wholly in this manner.

But—life being life—complications had commenced.

Rose's Rent Collector had begun to chafe at the terms of their arrangement. A Sicilian, ape-shouldered and oleaginous, with a gold tooth front-and-centre in a predatory smile. Like all Sicilians of a certain demeanour he had been rumoured into *la maffia,* a secret brotherhood bound by dreadful oaths—like the Freemasons, with more garlic and less geometry—which had recently been much twittered about in the press. Whether or not this was true, he was exacting when it came to debts and obligations, and had formed the opinion that his friends had a right to Rose's favours on days when he himself was otherwise engaged. This had led to unpleasantness already, and tensions had only increased after Little Em'ly came to stay.

Little Em'ly was Rose's sister, more or less. She had turned up out of a rainstorm at the concert saloon a few weeks previous, half-dead in the dead of night, desperately seeking Prairie Rose, who duly took her home, where Em'ly collapsed of fever and exhaustion. For three days and nights thereafter she lay at death's dark portal, moaning to be let through. So I had learned from the quack who had been called to attend her. She was bad, he said, very bad indeed; as bad as a child can be and still recover.

But pull through she did, though she stayed in Rose's day-bed for another week straight, and scarcely set foot outside even after that. A tiny dark slip of a thing, with hollow cheeks and huge, dark, hunted eyes. The closest she'd come to the outside world was to sit in Rose's window. She'd do so for hours on end, sometimes, now that she'd come through the fever. Eerily composed, with her dark hair tied up tight in a bun and her face deep inside the shadows of a bonnet, so still that you could almost think she was sitting for a portrait. She never spoke, either—not even to Prairie Rose. I knew this because Rose told me. And I knew something else as well: the two of them were not exactly sisters. Little Em'ly was more as you might say a Sister-Wife, the youngest in the household of the Utah Brute, whom Rose herself had fled those three years previous.

Prairie Rose never said this, exactly. Not in so many words. She never would answer straight when asked about her past or that Mormon bastard. Her expression grew taut and she'd flinch away, as if that shadow was so long and so dark that she could not bear to let it touch her, even in recollection—and this was a gal who could cope with the clientele on Dupont Street. But from what little she did say, it was clear enough. Little Em'ly had arrived in that godforsaken household a few months before Rose herself had decamped. This had been long enough for the two of them to form a bond — and for Em'ly to have fled in search of Rose when she herself had reached the breaking point. Fled all the way to San Francisco, where she did not know another human soul and had no lantern to light her way, beyond a desperate hope that her sister-wife was in the city somewhere, and must surely take her in.

"She's terrified he'll follow," Rose said to me. "Terrified he's on his way this minute."

This had been some weeks previous, before the other events I've been telling you about. She was well into the gin that evening, and crept right up to the edge of speaking plain.

"What, the Mormon?" I said. "All the way from Utah?"

"Fucksake, Barry!" She hissed it through her teeth. We were in the back of the concert saloon. None of the rabble was glancing our way, but she'd gone five shades paler nonetheless. "I never said that word, all right? Never said Mormon, an' never said Utah. I never said fuck-all — so don't *you* fucking say it!" She peered round through the haze of smoke as if I might have conjured him already.

Em'ly was seventeen years old. She'd been married to that Mormon for three years. When you totted up the arithmetic, you began to see why the gal had stopped talking.

*

Em'ly would have to meet the old man first, Rose said, before anything could be decided. Rose herself was looking decidedly inclined just to say no. But I might bring him to the flat on Pacific Street that evening, she agreed, in order for a decision to be made.

So I did. We stopped at a stand-pipe in the street and he made ablutions: "Old Lem," as he was henceforth to be known. He had accepted the name without comment — had eyed me sidelong as I said it, but let the moment pass.

"Three dollars a week?" He'd asked this several times already.

"Three dollars," I confirmed. I hadn't mentioned that the money would come from me.

"Just to—what—keep a sort o' watch?"

"That's it."

The Utah Brute, I said to him. The Mormon who haunted poor Em'ly's nightmares—not to mention the Sicilian Rent Collector with his secret brothers. Here were two women beset; they needed him. "You'd be taking up your old calling. A sacred trust."

That was evidently a mistake.

"No," he said. "Don't you say that."

"Why shouldn't they trust you?" I protested. "*I* trust in you."

"D'you know who I am? Don't you know what I *done?*"

He began to shake his head. I'd come to recognize this already: a sure sign that Old Lem was in dispute with his inner demons. Now he commenced to shake more violently: back and forth, like some baited carnival bear. "Don't you see? There is nothing in me you can trust in!"

Passersby had begun to accelerate: giving us wide berth, eyeing us warily. I noticed a pair of constables on the corner, exchanging glances and reaching very casually for their truncheons. In one more moment this was liable to turn very sour, with the flat-feet commencing their ominous waddle toward us and all God only knows breaking out when they arrived.

"Let me ask you a question instead." I kept my voice as low as I could, and urgent. "Can *you* trust *me?*"

"The devil do I know?"

"Can you try? Just this once, and see what happens?"

And he hesitated. Just long enough for me to make one final attempt.

"We've come all this way," I said to him. "Look—there's Pacific Street, just ahead. So just take the last few steps, and meet her. Meet Rose's poor sister, and then decide."

It sufficed to set him in motion again. Through the leery stream of passersby; past those sidelong-scowling constables. Down the street and through the doors of Rose's tenement building. Up three rickety flights of stairs, with all the joy of a man ascending the gallows.

When I knocked at the door, Rose opened it. I stepped aside to clear the way for the old man, who was on the landing behind me.

Little Em'ly stood within. It was my first sight of her, up close—though "close" is not the word I want, exactly. A wisp of a creature, standing in the doorway to an inner chamber, across the expanse of an impossibly clean parlour—Em'ly's own doing, as we would learn. Prairie Rose was an indifferent housekeeper, but Little Em'ly was fanatical about it. She would scrub and straighten and sweep at all hours, as if by dint of unceasing exertion she might scour all stain and filth from the world around her, and set straight again all the pillars of order.

Rose cast a nervous look up—way up—at the old man in her doorway. She summoned something that resembled a smile. "Em'ly," she said, looking back over her shoulder. "This is Mr. Lem."

He'd taken off his hat. His grey hair hung in tangles. "'Evening, ma'am," he said.

Little Em'ly, neat as a pin, made no response. She was wearing a cloak and that incongruous Sunday bonnet. A thin, sharp face in shadow, peering out, like some sketch of a dread-filled Victorian orphan: Jane Eyre plucking up her nerve to step out of the study. Her hands were in front of her inside a lady's muff, God help us— a ragamuffin shabby thing that might have been skinned from a long-dead raccoon. It might also have concealed a knife, for use in an emergency; something sharp to stab with. This was something that only occurred to me later.

"Mr. Lem is offering his services," I said. I'd worked up a smile, and enunciated carefully, as you do to a child or a half-wit.

"I b'lieve the young lady knows that," the old man rumbled.

"Yes," I said. "Well, just in case—"

"I b'lieve she wants a moment to decide."

And still she made no response. But something had passed between the old man and that girl—I swear it must have done, though I had no idea what it was. A glimmer of nascent recognition, as when one lost soul sees another?

"I'll not come inside, ma'am," the old man rumbled. "But p'raps I'll sorta loiter, hereabouts. Hour or so—see how it goes. If you'll tolerate me? Lock the door, and I'll be outside it, for awhile. In case you need me."

Little Em'ly made no reply to this, either. But inside the bonnet— the damnedest thing—her head gave an infinitesimal nod.

The old man was there when Prairie Rose left again later that same evening, bound for Dupont Street and the concert saloon. She told me all about it, the following day. He was sitting on the stairs in front of her door, she said. As she came out, he stood and tipped his hat, then sat back down again as she went past.

This was not ideal, Rose thought. The neighbours, and all. But on balance she decided to think about it later.

He was still there when she straggled back in the first grey light of dawn. She felt soiled and soul-sick, as she often did. And she was trying to ignore the drunken badgerings of the two men who had been following her, the past quarter-mile or so. They were an aggravation, but harmless; so Rose had been telling herself. Just boys. Apprentices, reeling home at the end of a spree and egging each other on. But they'd followed her inside the tenement, which wasn't good. Followed her up three flights of stairs, which was worse. So all things considered she felt both startled and relieved to see that long shape in shadow on the landing.

He was no longer against the door, but right beside it. He sat slouched in slumber against the wall: knees up-jutting, the brim of his hat tugged low across his forehead.

"Lem," she exclaimed. "G'morning."

He was dead-drunk, or asleep. So she thought at first. The apprentices evidently thought so too.

"Fuck 'im," one of them muttered, behind her.

"Sooner fuck *her*," said the other.

"G'morning, ma'am," Strother said.

His solitary eye had slitted open. The apprentices stopped, three steps below.

"Got a dog there, eh?" said one of them to Rose. Trying to calculate how much he dared. "Got a filthy fuckin' mongrel on yer doorstep. Expect the thing has fleas."

"Expect it bites, too," Strother rumbled.

The apprentices shifted and muttered. They exchanged another look. Then the first one slunk back down the stairs, and the second one slank after.

Prairie Rose unlocked the door. She opened it, and stepped inside. A moment later, she poked her head back out.

"You know what?" she said to the old man. "You could prob'ly come in, for a minute, if you wanted. Cup of coffee?"

"Thank you, ma'am," he said. "But no. I'm tolerable right here."

*

Oh, I laughed out loud when Rose told me that story. I laughed with pure relief, and with something else too: the warm glow that comes of knowing you've done something *right*, for a change. Some deed that in its modest way has lit one tiny candle in this world.

Bring him here, Brother Amos had said to me. That had been his condition. *Bring him here, to the Mission, and come yourself. Break bread with us, and join us in fellowship with the Lord. That's all I'm asking of you, friend o' mine—but I'm asking for your word.*

I had given it, of course. But why the hell would I go to that Mission now? So I put that commitment where it belonged: clear out of my mind.

–TEN–

From *The Sorrows of Miz Amanda*
and her Two Brave Boys

North Carolina, 1850 – 1861

1.

THEY LOST MORE THAN HALF THE CROP in that autumn of 1850, the harvest-time when Bobby Collard was hanged and Drusilla Smoak pronounced her curse. Sheet lightning had shimmered as she spoke; in the hush that followed, thunder rolled like Judgement. Such at least was Lige's remembering, though he would afterward come to doubt the likelihood: lightning and thunder at that exact moment in time, and then rain lashing down with a fury unseen since Noah built a boat, as if the storm, so long delayed, had been conjured forth by the granny-woman herself.

But half the crop was lost. This much could be known for God's own truth, for the account was set down in the ledger book in old Solomon's hand: black ink on white pages. The storm raged through the night and came back the next afternoon, flinging hailstones the size of robin's eggs that flattened any grain still standing.

And their tribulations had only begun. Winter came early and cruel that year, and spring brought scant relief. A late frost thwarted the planting, and then in June incessant rains flooded the lower fields, rotting the corn in the ground. Three months later, in mid-September, the best mule died: a fine strong mule struck suddenly dead, as if it had been thunder-blasted. September 15, one year to the day after Bobby Collard was hung.

Mr. Dillashay understood beyond all doubt: this was the hand of Drusilla Smoak.

He said so to his wife, who laughed at him. "A witch so puissant she may thunder-blast mules in the field? Why, Mr. Dillashay, then you best run. To the tall grass, Mr. Dillashay—flee! flee!—before you are ensorcelled."

Miz Amanda looked not unlike a witch herself, dressed in mourning-black, as she had been since Bobby Collard's death. Strother asked her once when she might cease. "When Mr. Dillashay drops dead," she replied. On that day, she would cast off her weeds and array herself in brilliant colours, gay as are the lilies in the field.

The following summer drought set in.

"Boils, Mr. Dillashay," his wife predicted. "Boils will assuredly be next. Then locusts."

And—God help him—she was right. Purple sores boiled up on his back and shoulders, and grasshoppers descended in yellow clouds: multitudes of them with Biblical intent. Afterward swine sickness took hold amongst the pigs.

"Oh, Mr. Dillashay," his wife said to him, mocking. "Whatever shall you do?"

Such was his dilemma. Certainty is not proof, after all, at least not in the eyes of others; Mr. Dillashay's neighbours showed scant inclination to rally to his aid. And what could he achieve, a mortal man alone? Against a witch who rode the wind and commanded the storm, in league with the devil himself and his infernal powers, with whom she sported abominably on moonless nights—rising above Old Baldy on an eagle and yielding herself into the devil's embrace, his dingus as rough as a cob of corn? For of course she did; Mr. Dillashay knew it. And the farm slid steadily into ruin, despite the dogged exertions of his step-son.

So it continued until late summer of 1853, when on a warm dry night on the threshold of harvest-time Mr. Dillashay's barn unaccountably caught fire. Miz Amanda's cries awakened the others: *"Au secours!"* She did not sleep at night and thus was the first to discern the smoke. Strother did what he could to save the livestock and equipment, organizing Lige and Solomon into a bucket brigade while his beautiful, mad Mama fluttered on the periphery, crow-black in the glare of conflagration.

Mr. Dillashay took up his rifle and was gone before anyone thought to seek him.

It was the night of September 15.

He rode north toward Hanging Tree Ridge, bloody murder in his eye. So Cleve Hunsperger would afterward attest. Hunsperger had a farm five miles southwest of the Collard property; he was in his field just after dawn when Jacob Dillashay rode past, shouting that he was going to hang a witch, and urging Hunsperger to ride with him if he foreswore the devil and possessed a pair of testicles to swing together. Cleve Hunsperger desired no part of this, and that was the last he ever saw of Jacob Dillashay.

He saw the horse again, that afternoon. It was riderless, trotting sweat-streaked and flecked with foam back down the trail, which brought over Cleve Hunsperger a cold qualm of foreboding. It might very well have impelled him up that mountain road himself to investigate, were he the sort of man who intruded himself into the private affairs of others.

The County Sheriff in Asheville was a man of similar disinclination. Asheville lay thirty miles away, and he had more pressing priorities than to investigate why a farmer might ride up a mountain without riding down again. Especially one of the Great Smoky Mountains, where grievances went down so deep and tangled that Jehovah Himself preferred to keep to His own hilltop, up on Sinai. The Sheriff had prior acquaintance with this particular farmer besides, sufficient to persuade him that the aggregate total of misery in this world would not be increased by Jacob Dillashay's subtraction.

Strother might have ridden up himself, if only to find out what had actually happened. He promised his younger brother that they would do so—the two of them together—at the earliest opportunity. But first they must get the crop in, and then do what could be done to raise a new barn, with the weather turning and winter coming on.

"We can't just let this go," Lige said. Coming up on ten years old, he was understandably distressed. His own Daddy, after all. Despite his Daddy's failings, you only get the one. "It might could be he needs us."

"We'll go just as soon as we can," Strother said. "You have my word."

"He could be hurt, or lost—he could be anything."

Their Mama knew otherwise.

She had felt it in the air, she said: the very instant of her bereavement. It came at eight minutes before eleven o'clock on the morning of Sunday, September 16, with the ruins of the barn still smouldering and her two boys hobgoblined with sweat and smoke. They had spent the whole night battling the flames, with such neighbours as had come to assist. But during the morning the easterly wind had changed. It came now from out of the north, a bright brisk wind that carried with it a sudden waft of rot and decay: a carrion-stench wafting down from Hanging Tree Ridge. She knew this at once to be the earth's exhalation as it swallowed down the shade of her late husband.

"I am," she cried to Solomon, "a widow for the second time."

Going directly into her room she cast off her weeds and put on her yellow frock instead, which she wore as of old with such vivacity that the sunlight itself seemed to trip with her down the stairs.

A funeral service was never held. "I cannot in good conscience swear him dead," the widow stated. "I say merely that my husband burns in hell. There is a difference."

Eventually a memorial stone was placed in the upper field. Strother saw to this much, at least, believing that decorum required some gesture. On it a stone-mason had cut Jacob Dillashay's name and age and the inscription: *Not forgotten*. It was the early spring of 1855. Jacob Dillashay had been gone for nearly eighteen months; his step-son was entering into his twenty-first year. He had not yet gone up the mountain, despite his solemn vow to Lige, who did not forget this sort of thing—or anything else that savoured of grievance.

No corpse was ever to be discovered, though Cleve Hunsperger was in little doubt as to his neighbour's fate. "He got tooken up before Judge Collard," the farmer was heard to say. "Got tooken up that mountain and judged."

2.

In April of that year, at the widow's insistence, they let the farm go and moved to Asheville. It was at that time a hamlet of some two thousand souls, nestled on a plateau between the Blue Ridge Mountains to the east and the Smokies to the west. But it was beginning to bestir itself, now that the Great Drover's Road had been completed, stretching from Greenville, Tennessee, all the way to South Carolina, and connecting western North Carolina to the vast wide world. Asheville was, Miz Amanda proclaimed, a city on the rise. It must surely be the making of her eldest son, who would become a jurist and quite probably a Senator. Asheville was also home to Doc Semmens, the gallant young physician whose quondam solicitudes had been so earnest and so deeply appreciated.

Strother found employment at a feed lot, and a second position keeping the books for one of the hotels. They took up the lease on a small house, where Miz Amanda spent two hours each morning at her toilette and waited for Doc Semmens to call. He did not, being greatly burdened with other responsibilities. He was also losing his hair. The widow saw this with sorrow one evening while out taking

the air with Solomon. Doc Semmens, passing by on the other side of
the street, affected at first not to see them, then took off his hat and
offered the hurried formality of a bow, which laid bare both his shallow
nature and his bald spot. He had inclined already toward portliness,
Miz Amanda saw; in later life he would be florid and obese.

She herself did not age at all. She turned forty that year, but could
still fit into the frocks she had worn at seventeen. If anything these
had grown too large, a discovery she noted with inward joy, scoffing
at Solomon when he fretted at her to eat something more substantial.
Solomon had aged sadly, these past few years. His hair was white and
he walked with a stoop and a shuffle. She would tease him fondly:
"You are become the lean and slippered pantaloon." Solomon's loyalty
had never faltered, and never would. He remained at the widow's side
until the end of both their lives, which would come suddenly, three
years later, on the night of July 23, 1861. He walked out with her each
evening in the meantime, and undertook errands to the chemist and
Doc Semmens, who though shallow and balding continued to dispense
the medicine to Miz Amanda. She required it daily in a dosage that
by now had grown prodigious.

And she was still beautiful, though her loveliness was stretched ever
more thinly, with eyes that burned brighter with each passing year.
When she paced at night through the house, she might have been the
still-living ghost of Miss Amanda Beauchamp, the loveliest debutante
in Roanoke, Virginia.

Some nights she would encounter her younger son, coming in. On
one occasion in mid-summer she was startled badly, and shrieked out
in such alarm that Strother came stumbling from his room.

"Murder," she cried. "Oh, murder! — it is my husband, Mr.
Dillashay!"

"Where?" exclaimed Strother.

"There!"

She pointed in terror at Lige, who had halted halfway up the stairs, and stood dark and perplexed in the wavering light of his mother's candle. She carried a candle with her often in the night. Sometimes she left it unattended, a cause of some concern.

"It's me, Ma," Lige muttered. "Chrissakes."

Lige was now fifteen years old, and looked indeed more like his late father each passing day: the heavy dark good looks, and the wildness. His mother at length was calmed a little. She tried to summon a laugh. "Oh, my Lord," she said to Strother. "Oh dear Jesus Lord in heaven, I thought it was Mr. Dillashay, or the devil." Strother saw the look that crossed his brother's face, and reached out, heart-struck, toward him. But Lige hunched away and club-footed past the others on the landing. He stank of whiskey.

She had come unmoored in Time.

Solomon understood. The old man's wits were as keen as ever, despite the tremor in his gait. But he had seen this before, though seldom in someone as young as Miz Amanda.

"It's old folks, where you'll see it," he said. "One day something tugs loose."

Strother would not hear this. His Mama's nerves, he said; that was all. Her nerves were strung too tight with all the grievances life had brought upon her. This was bad nerves, and that tincture from Doc Semmens, which Strother ordered banished from the house.

"Yes, sir," Solomon said. His mouth turned down in a horseshoe of agreement, as in one who knew that withholding the medicine would just make matters worse. He may well have guessed that Strother knew it too. So possibly nothing was done to keep the medicine out of the house, except to bring it inside more discreetly.

The widow slept less and less as summer came on, which Strother set down to the heat. Who could sleep, after all, in the swelter of a Carolina summer; even here in Asheville, high up in the mountains? He was sleeping little enough himself, with his position at the feed-lot full-time and more bookkeeping work in the evenings. In her sleeplessness, his Mama grew steadily more peevish. Steadily more forgetful, too: forgetting what she'd said to you, and what you'd said back, five minutes previous. Forgetting whole conversations, and then denying that these had taken place at all. A look on her face halfway between queenly indignation and pure fear.

"Why will you torment me?" she burst out one evening to Strother, when his own frustration had left him frayed and short. "I swear, you never used to be so hard. Is this what they counsel, Louis, in those law books of yours — to be so hard and spiteful?"

"Strother," he said. He felt suddenly unmoored himself. "Your son."

"I know who you are, and you are horrid!"

She left the room in a choler. A few moments later she returned, sudued but anxious. "We mustn't quarrel," she said. "I can't bear it when we quarrel. Pax?"

"Yes. Pax."

He stood and she embraced him, laying her head against his chest. She was a bird in his arms. No weight to her at all; the bones were reeds, grown hollow.

"What's gone wrong with me?" she whispered.

"It's all right," he said, not knowing what else he might say. "It's fine. It's just — we're here together, so it's all going to be just fine."

"I hope you're telling me truthful, Lou. Oh, I do so hope. But I wonder if perhaps that's not quite right."

"Her eldest brother," Solomon said. Miz Amanda had gone back into her room; he and Strother were left alone.

"Yes," Strother said. "Louis Beauchamp."

"You favour him. The resemblance ... Well, I can surely see how

151

she'd make the confusion." He stood for a moment as awkward as Strother himself, looking for a way to make this better. "Her favourite of all the family."

"Yes."

"A fine gentleman. The very finest. Very much like yourself, in that way."

Strother said: "This can't go on."

Solomon grew absorbed in looking down between his feet at a knot in the floorboards. "But the thing of it is, Mr. Strother—it does. That's exactly what it does. It goes on."

Inch by inch Time lost its grip entirely. Miz Amanda asked after cousins long dead, fretting that they had not come around to take tea. She would rise to her feet in sudden agitation, recollecting that her Papa expected her home for dinner. She would hurry into the street if not attended, and on several occasions was found wandering in confusion a mile or more from the house.

After that she was kept to her room as much as possible, attended by Solomon. At night he would sleep on a cot outside her door; some nights when the agitation was worse than bad, Strother would turn the key in the lock. Her howls when she discovered this were piteous, and wrung his heart to hear.

Strother worked harder, leaving early in the morning and seldom coming back again until dark. Lige came home most nights later still, or not at all. Often one of the brothers would glimpse his Mama's face in the window, as he passed below: a chalk-white spectre with fevered eyes, half crone and half orphaned child. And so it might all have wound down of its own accord, the failing clockwork of this existence.

Then Lige found out about Sissy Baird.

3.

Lige had attended school for a time when they first relocated to Asheville. But he had long since abandoned even the pretense, maintaining that the schoolmaster was a droning fool with nothing whatever to teach him. This was in fairness substantially true; Lige was whip-smart, and knew it, and chafed.

He found employment instead, here and there: stocking shelves and making deliveries. He found himself often at Mackeson's Tavern at the foot of Third Street, where he made himself useful: clearing tables and running errands and sweeping up in the back room, where of an evening there might be a game of chance in progress. He learned how to calculate the odds of this outcome or that, and sundry means as well of influencing that outcome: reading tics and tells, and maintaining a stony visage of one's own, and dealing out a card that looks for all the world to have come from the top of the deck, but doesn't.

He discovered that he liked whiskey, very much. Women too. No, not that he *liked* them, necessarily; but he liked very much the possibilities they represented. And he discovered that women liked him back again: women at least of a certain caste and kind.

Sissy Baird was of the other kind. Not plain, exactly — that would not be fair to say — but not quite pretty either, at least not in a way that declared itself out loud. She was older, and a widow. She worked at a dry-goods store and on Sundays attended worship at the Presbyterian Church, where she'd been Saved with the minimum of to-do. She was in short the exact kind of woman whom Lige would scarcely have noticed at all. But Strother had set his cap. Strother had fallen earnestly in love, which Lige was bound to notice sooner or later, despite the gulf that had opened between them. Others had noticed, and tongues had begun to wag.

One such tongue was lodged in the mouth of Tess Thurmond.

Here it had direct access to the thoughts in Tess Thurmond's head, few of which went indefinitely unexpressed. She was married to Red Thurmond, the blacksmith, who had shoulders like an ape's and few illusions about the inclinations of his wife, which rendered Lige's aspirations to this particular hayloft perilous in the extreme. But Tess Thurmond had remarkable zest; her arms and legs were rubbery as pythons when wrapped about you and bouncing, and Lige Dillashay at fifteen years of age was much enamoured of risk-taking.

"She been seen with your brother, walkin' on the street," Tess informed him one afternoon, as flies drowsed and Lige lay contentedly on his back, chewing on a stalk of straw. She spoke a scandalized tone, tugging her dress back down and tucking one vast pap where it belonged. "I mean, don't your brother have no concern at all? Don't you?"

"Why would I care who my brother walks out with?"

Tess stared at him in frank incredulity. "You're sayin' to me that you don't know who she is?"

Strother could not have known it himself. This was Lige's conclusion, once past the first shock of learning.

After all, the brothers were still newcomers to Asheville, in all the practical ways that mattered. They'd come from away, and thirty miles could serve just as well as a thousand, in a place where everyone knew where everyone else had been born, and who their relations were, and what that signified. Besides, who could have guessed it just by looking?

"It's the truth," he said to Strother that same evening. "It kills me to be the one who tells you. But you got to know."

They were standing in the dust of Main Street.

Lige had gone first to the feed lot where Strother worked. Learning that his brother had left an hour previous, he had hurried directly home. But Strother was not there either, and it took no great leap of deduction to conclude where he must be: in the company of Sissy Baird. Lige's first overpowering impulse was to hunt them down.

But he told himself—once again—that Strother must have no idea who she was. This marked the pencil-thin line between blunder and betrayal. So Lige waited, pacing to the end of the street and then back. Carts and buggies trundled; dust rose in puffs about each hoof. The sun slid red behind the Smokies and the whisper of a cooling breeze began, and finally Strother's long shape appeared in the gloaming.

He was alone, thank God. And whistling. Decades later, Lige would recollect that sound: his brother's thin, tuneless whistling.

"She's played you for a fool," Lige said. "I heard this from someone who knows."

"What are you talking about?"

"Sissy Baird. She's a Collard."

A smile had kindled on Strother's face as he'd seen Lige loping toward him. Now it faded.

"She can call herself Baird all she wants," said Lige. "That's her dead husband's name. But she's a Collard. She's kin to that fucker Harris on her Mama's side. Her Mama was some manner of Collard cousin."

They'd come to a stop in front of the leased house, though neither particularly noticed this at the moment.

Strother sighed a little. He said: "Yes."

"Yes, what?" Lige demanded.

"I should have told you. It's just … Lige, it's hard to see how it matters much, in the end."

"How it *matters?*" Lige heard himself starting to laugh. It came out high and shrill. "They killed our Daddy, Strother. My Daddy, at least, though I accept he was never yours by blood. Just your step-daddy, if you want to make that distinction—just your Daddy by marrying your Mama, if you want to draw that line. Though it doesn't make one hair of difference, when it comes to what they done to him."

"We don't know even know what happened, Lige. Not for a fact."

"Of course we know!"

"You can hear all the rumours you like. But unless you were actually there…"

"All of Asheville knows what happened. All of western Carolina. He rode up that mountain to face them. He went up there alone, 'cause not one of us would ride with him. And they shot him off his horse, Strother — that's what happened! They had one of 'em laying in wait against his coming — Meshach, it was. It was fucking Meshach. Watching the trail, and shot him off his horse when he rode past. But the shooting didn't kill him, so they put my Daddy on trial. Dragged him up before Judge Collard, who called him guilty. That son of a bitch old man — he couldn't even say the words. Just sat there drooling in that chair of his — sat in the waft of his own shit, rising on up from his drawers — and Drusilla Smoak said the words instead."

Strother shook his head. He said, "Lige, you've got no way of—"

"Yes I do. I do so know it! And they didn't hang him, either. They drowned him in the pond — like you'd drown a dog. Hog-tied him, wrists and ankles. A millstone for good measure around his neck. That stinking pond, on the northwest boundary — all choked with weeds and rushes, but deep enough you can't see the bottom. They threw him in, and watched him sink. And that's what he saw, Strother. His last sight of this world. Not your face — not mine. Not a friend in the world. Just goddamned Collards, jeering him down. And that's what happened."

Still Strother shook his head. "Lige, even if some of that was true…"

"People know it, Strother! Everyone — the whole world! And when everyone knows a thing, then some of it has to be true. A story ain't just made up, if everyone knows it!"

"But Sissy Baird didn't do it. She wasn't there. So what could it have to do with—?"

"*'Cause Sissy Baird is a Christa'mighty Collard!*" God help him, Lige could have gladly shook his brother. Could have grabbed a plank and whaled him with it. "Sissy Baird's Daddy lay with Harris Collard's cousin! That's where he stuck that pecker of his. And left it there, which you're now proposing to do yourself. Your dick in the direct fruit of Harris Collard's cousin's steamy loins, to the gossip and disbelief of the whole town of Asheville and surrounding environs—that being a French word, Strother, as I'm sure you know, made up of French letters, one of which I pray to God you've got the sense to put on your own dick, before you—"

The twilight exploded into darkness. Lige had a sense of being flung, and falling.

Strother had never struck him before. Not once in fifteen years. Lige found himself on hands and knees, patting the dust for his fallen hat and Lord only knows what else, as if he might collect the sundered fragments of the last few moments and piece them back together. A hand reached into his narrow field of vision, which by concentrated effort he was able to associate with his brother. It helped him back onto his feet.

"I accept I should have told you, Lige. But I will not hear her spoke of in that manner. Not now—not ever. Understand?"

Strother had stepped away several paces, taking hard deep breaths to compose himself and clenching down the emotion. Strother had always hated his own passions; Lige knew this about his brother. He resented them in some essential way; dreaded them, even, lest once set loose they might thunder iron-shod and ungovernable, like all the horses of the Apocalypse.

Lige said: "What will you do now?"

"I don't know."

"I think you best decide." His own voice sounded unnaturally calm. It seemed to come from some goodly ways off. "I think you best tell me."

Strother said: "I might ask for her hand."

A great clarity was settling, despite the gathering darkness. Lige would ever afterwards recollect that clarity, and marvel: the world reflected back as if in the still, calm mirror of a lake.

There'd been others on the street when they began this conversation; no one was visible now. The neighbours had drawn back. Lige looked round at the silent houses. Looked up, and saw his mother looking down. His beautiful, mad Mama, framed by candlelight in the window of her room on the second floor. Her lovely long hair, now silvered, tumbled down, as if she were Rapunzel gone grey with yearning. Gazing down at God knows what.

"That's it?" Lige said to Strother. "That's all you propose to do?"

Strother said: "It's come time to let go of the past. Turn it loose."

Lige in that moment thought: *He's so young.* His older brother—six feet five inches, for he'd grown now to his full height—an inch taller still in boots with heels. Towering and spare and powerful, with a tumble of fair hair over his forehead. Strother Purcell in the first prime of his manhood, with all the gifts of his birth and a will that could move whole mountains. Lige thought: *In the ways of this world, he is a child.*

Out loud, he said: "I was never once good enough, was I?" And how calm the words came out. After fifteen years they might have come out howling. Ravening like wolves. "I was never going to be good enough—because *he* was never good enough. Not for her, not for you. He wasn't worth a half-day's ride up the mountain, when they killed him. You gave your word that you'd go look for him, but you never did. You broke your pledge, 'cause you didn't think he was worth it, nor me neither."

Strother's whole frame shuddered, just for an instant, as a man might do who has endured a physical blow. "Perhaps I did break my word," he began. His voice was thick, and not quite steady.

"Per*haps?*"

"And if that's so, then I was wrong. But I never once thought…
Lige, you've always been more than good enough for me. You're my
brother."

Lige said: "Half-brother."

"You need to see this clear."

But he was. Lige was seeing clearly for the first time. So it seemed
to him in that moment, and so it would seem for almost the rest of
his life. That evening in front of the house, he might have been Saul
on the Damascus Road.

"I wish you joy of your union," Lige said. "But you won't find it."

"Devil!" a shrill voice cried, above him. His beautiful mad Mama,
gazing down through the open window. "Devil! Dillashay! Get thee
hence!"

It cut right through him like a rusty blade. He found a freedom
in that.

"On my way, Ma," he said. "You enjoy the rest of your life."

He turned and strode away. A sullen figure, dark as a changeling,
club-footing into deepening shadow.

"Lige," Strother called. "Elijah!" On his face was pure distress.

Lige did not look back.

This would be Strother's last sight of him for thirteen years. He would
afterwards wonder how much might have been changed if he'd gone
after his brother right then and there. Run him down and wrapped
his arms around him, weeping and raging and professing his love, as
a brother might do if once he let those passions come welling out.

In the end, he decided that nothing would have changed. No
calamity averted, and nothing altered for the better. We are who we
are, each one of us on this earth, and there is nothing we can ever do
to escape that.

4.

Sissy Baird was twenty-nine years old in that spring of 1861, nearly five years Strother's senior and practically venerable by the standards of the mountains, where girls were women at fourteen and oftentimes crones before they turned forty. She had come to Asheville in the company of her husband, a weak-lunged and much older man, whose physician had thought that mountain air might help. It didn't. After burying him, the widow might well have left Asheville, but stayed.

She might conceivably have done so to be closer to kin, though Strother later said this was not so. The Collards were kin on her mother's side, but Sissy Baird never thought of herself that way: not as a Collard.

Perhaps it came about the way life's choices are often made: by the simple avoidance of choosing altogether. It just seemed less onerous to stay where she was. She had found a tolerable position as a clerk at the dry-goods store, and a one-room house on two acres at the south end of town, where she kept some mountain chickens and a shoat. She wore black for a time, but gave this up as impractical. The bachelors and widowers commenced to take an interest, unattached women being at a fair premium in the mountains, looks and age notwithstanding. But Sissy Baird soon made clear that she considered one marriage to have been sufficient for this lifetime. Mr. Baird had not set the strings of her heart to singing, but he was not a drunkard and had not raised his hand, being in general a man of good heart if deplorable lungs; all things considered, she thought it best to quit while she was ahead.

So she got on with her life. For amusement she sketched, and painted watercolours: not well, as she was the first to admit. But this was not the point of the endeavour. It was only drawing, after all; it was not like fixing the roof. Once the rains left off she set about doing precisely this—repairing the roof, which leaked. Often she might be glimpsed clambering up a ladder with her skirts hiked up and her ankles on display, or sitting at the apex with a bale of shakes beside her and an expression of fierce contentment, hammering like Thor. She was a woman well suited to such occupation, tall and sturdy with large capable hands. She had overlarge feet, as well, and a nose that reddened and dripped when she was heated.

There was a handsomeness, though, if you saw her from just the right perspective. Thus she was seen by Strother Purcell.

She came to see him in a like manner.

She made a sketch, which said exactly how she saw him. It was made in April or May of that year, well after they'd grown companionable, but prior to Lige's leaving and all that followed after. Sissy laboured to refine it, shading it this way and that and refusing to let him see it, until finally—with a sunburst of relief—she pronounced herself satisfied.

It was the face of someone much younger than himself: such was Strother's first impression. A long narrow face that was sober but unlined, young and impossibly earnest, on the cusp of startling into a smile. He said: "*That's* how I look?"

"It is to me."

As late as 1892 it was still in his possession, folded in quarters and pressed between the pages of a book. A young man squinting the future into focus: awkward and earnest and weirdly beautiful.

They often walked out together on Sunday afternoons. Sissy loved to go as well on rambles by herself. She had the gift of enjoying her own company—a gift that she and Strother held in common. Often she would walk for miles on the pretext of some errand.

She left the dry-goods store at six o'clock on the afternoon of Wednesday, June 27. In the normal course of events she would have been expected to arrive at home by a quarter of seven. But the evening was glorious and conceivably she chose the longest route accordingly:

a path that would take her up and along a steep wooded ridge, with a prospect overlooking the French Broad River. If so, she must have been light in spirit, though she would have felt misgivings as she heard a noise behind her: the crack of a twig, or a stirring in the undergrowth. The journey was not without its perils for a woman alone.

Hearing a noise, she'd have hurried, just a little. Hearing it for a second time, she'd have turned around.

"Who's there?" she might have demanded. "You-all can stop this right now, or else show yourself."

And perhaps there never had been anyone at all. Perhaps in turning so quick she just lost her footing. This was one explanation, and surely the most probable. A tragic accident, and nothing more; though a question remained as to why she would step so close to the edge, and whether indeed such a fall could be fatal in the first place. It wasn't so steep as all that, the slope that she tumbled down; not a fall that should take a strong woman's neck like Sissy Baird's, and snap it.

She never arrived at home that night. The bed was not slept in and the animals by all appearances had not been tended. She didn't arrive for work at the dry-goods store next morning, and when Strother went out to search he saw the spiral of carrion birds against the sky.

He found Sissy Baird at the bottom of the ridge. She was lying on her back in a tangle of undergrowth, one arm flung wide and the other bent beneath. Her head was cricked sideways and she looked at the world as she always had, from a most remarkable perspective.

*

There was of course suspicion at the time. The malice of Outsiders could never be discounted, and of late there'd been many more of these passing through Buncombe County: carters and herders traversing the Drover's Road, and commercial travellers from places beyond the mountains, bringing with them foreign lusts and alien inclinations.

God alone knew what might result from this—although Doc Semmens said no, it was no such thing; Sissy Baird had not been interfered with. Doc Semmens had examined the body.

She was interred in the graveyard by the church. Half the town turned out for the funeral. Strother stood alone throughout, gaunt and crow-black. Solomon had stayed at home to keep watch upon Miz Amanda, who had been took especially bad to wander and rave the past two nights. Lige had not been seen, hide nor hair, since storming away.

Strother went back to the churchyard in the shank of the following evening. He brought flowers for the grave, and had intended to say some words out loud to tell Sissy Baird how he felt. He stood instead for a goodly time in silence, head bowed. After another while he heard footsteps in the churchyard grass. He supposed that it might be the Preacher, come back to offer some platitude of solace. But the boots that stood across the mound of earth were old, and cracked with hard use, and when Strother raised his eyes he was looking across Sissy's grave at Meshach Collard.

They hadn't seen one another since that September more than ten years previous, when Drusilla Smoak had come with Meshach on the buckboard of the cart, bound for Chunky Gal Creek, where Bobby Collard's corpse still was hanging. Shack had been just a boy, then; a grown man stood in those boots this evening. Not nearly as tall as Strother, but solid. A man of twenty-one or -two years old, with a triangle face and cheekbones so sharp and high that shadows seemed to hang from them. He wore ragged working clothes and reeked with sweat and the beasts that he'd been driving.

"You had no right," Shack Collard said. "Not to touch her in the first place, nor let them bury her so quick."

His voice was flat and flint-hard. So were those eyes. He'd left the Collard farm a year previous and hired himself out to a business concern, for which he was driving pigs along the Drover's Road to market. "My Daddy's cousin's child," he said. "We'd of come for her, one of us. I'd of come myself, and took her home."

He had arrived in Asheville that afternoon and would be passing back through in another month or so. So it would prove out in subsequent events, though Shack Collard did not say so now. Just now he said: "Who had to do with this? The killing."

Strother shook his head. "She just fell."

"You believe that?"

"I was the one who found her."

"Where's Lige at?"

"My brother had nothing to do with this."

"Not saying he did. I just like to know where my friends are. And my enemies."

Strother straightened, aware as he did how much taller he was than Shack Collard. He felt his hands balling into fists, though he kept them at his sides. Kept his voice level, as well, though it cost him an effort.

"He's just a boy."

"Pups make hounds."

"Leave him be, Shack—wherever he is. Understand? He never had to do with Sissy's death. With anything else that happened. That was all in the past. It's gone, now."

"Gone?" Shack Collard said. "The *past?*" He looked at Strother in a kind of disbelief, that a grown man could hold to such a notion, much less say it. "My brother Bobby's eyes were gone. The crows had his eyes before we cut him down. My brother Bobby hanging from a tree, and Lige Dillashay's Daddy did that. Your Daddy too."

"He wasn't my father."

"Sleep in his house? Eat his food?"

"Never stole his horse. Which your brother Bobby did. Did more than that, too."

"With your Mama, you mean?"

There were replies that Strother could have made. By the time he had composed himself, Shack Collard was speaking again.

"You never come up that mountain," Shack said. He weighed Strother with Judge Collard's stare. His shoulders were sloped and his forearms were corded with muscle; they bunched and coiled as he twisted his hat between his hands. He had taken the hat off his head as he'd stepped up, out of respect one must suppose for the departed. "Not once, to pass the time of day—nor to ask what befell your Daddy in return. Shall I tell it to you now?"

"No, Shack. I don't want to hear it."

"He come up onto Collard land firing his rifle. That's where it started, though I don't expect there'd anyways have been a chance that—"

Strother raised his voice. "I said, I don't want to hear. Whatever happened that day, just leave it." He looked down at the plain white cross: Sissy's marker, and the flowers. He drew a breath, and forced emotion down. "Shack, there's been enough dying, already. More than enough, for two families. Let's you and me be the ones to let it go." Saying so, he extended his right hand—open—across the newly filled grave.

This stunned Shack Collard near to speechlessness.

"Put a stop to the *dying*, old son?" Shack said at last, with the ghost of a taut, thin smile. Around them the crosses stretched higgledy, from the church wall on one side and on down the hillside to the fence. "Why, the dying's just barely commenced. And I'd sooner take hold of a serpent, as that hand."

5.

Life carried on, and Strother rejoined it, after a fashion. He rose well before dawn each morning, as had always been his custom, and after making his ablutions he would read for an hour, studying his books of law or else translating a passage from Plutarch or Herodotus.

He found it difficult to concentrate his mental energies; most mornings it was onerous to last out the allotted hour. But he did: sixty minutes by the clock, however much his mind might balk and fret, brooding on recollections. Hearing in each creak of the house his prodigal brother's footfall on the porch, though it never was.

And always the shufflings of his beautiful, mad Mama, pacing and muttering above his head, in the stillness before dawn and at any hour at all of night or day. She would abruptly out of nowhere be lucid and clear—asking after Elijah, and exclaiming at the news that he was not yet home. Then just as she had it within her grasp—the reality of what had happened, and where she was—it would slip away again, sliding like minnows through the fingers. And off she would go, raving and lamenting, hunting for her Papa and her birthday frock, until Strother locked her up in her room again and hurried out of the house, certain that she must otherwise drag him into madness right behind her.

Strother came home in the early evening of July 23. She'd been docile that morning, but was agitated now. He couldn't bear it. Locking her in her chamber he went out again, leaving Solomon in the kitchen and taking the key with him.

He returned to his desk at the feedlot, where he worked at his ledger books for two more hours, lighting the whale-oil lamp as night came on. He left in the last glimmer of twilight at nine o'clock. But instead of trudging home again he went in the other direction, stopping at a shanty that served for a saloon. It was not his custom to take whiskey, but he did so on this occasion, sitting alone while the darkness deepened outside. This was a low establishment, with a dirt floor and a plank for a bar, sour with sweat and tobacco smoke and high with the reek of urine; the men would go around the back and piss against the outside wall. These were men from the nearby farms, in the main, but there were men from the town as well, several of whom nodded in guarded greeting when Strother came in, stooping low under the

overhang. There was sympathy for him, though he kept to himself;
Asheville knew of his tribulations.

A red-faced drunken man had been denouncing Mr. Lincoln, and
now he squinted oyster eyes at Strother, goading him to articulate his
views and taking insult when Strother remained silent. But someone
else muttered, "Leave the man be." It was a man called Hadley who
had taken Strother's part, a young farmer newly married to a Dutch
girl. Some while later he struck up a well-meaning conversation,
offering condolence for the death of Sissy Baird and mentioning—
as it occurred to him—that he had encountered her cousin earlier on
this very day. "Shack Collard," he said. This came as news to Strother.
"Shack Collard is back in Asheville?" he demanded. "Seems to be,"
Hadley said. "Or at least, he was here today." He made a wry expression
then, and added: "That boy does not care for you, Purcell. Not for
you, nor for any of yours." Strother shrugged and put this from his
mind. After taking another glass of whiskey, he reconciled himself to
the necessity of going home. Now the first exclamations were heard
outside. Someone's house up yonder was on fire.

The fire was a red ball against the night. Strother hurried up the
hill with a number of the others, for of course they would help out, as
neighbours. Besides, the month had been tinder-dry. In summer a house
fire could spread just like that, with hideous consequence. Before they
were halfway there, Strother knew with certainty which house it was.

He made three separate attempts to plunge into the inferno, drawn
by the screams of his Mama within. He was gathering himself to try
again, staggering blind in the cinder and smoke and flailing his arms
like a man drowning, when he was borne at last to the ground and
dragged away by half a dozen men, who saw that he must surely perish
else. Hadley was one of these, and the red-faced drunken man who
had inveighed against Lincoln.

Solomon had been in the kitchen when the fire broke out, as best as could afterwards be determined. He may have died mercifully from inhalation of smoke, though it appeared from the position of his charred remains that he attempted to climb up the stairs to his mistress's locked door. She remained alive until the end. Alive and shrieking, when the burning floor beneath her feet gave way and the structure collapsed inward upon itself.

Strother's last glimpse was of a flaming tatter at the window, just as the conflagration drew her down. She seemed to find his face at the final instant: huge white eyes locking onto her son's and a red mouth gaping impossibly wide.

Strother had not held a firearm since arriving in Asheville. But during his earlier life on the farm, he had earned a reputation for his skill with the long rifle. Some of this was inevitably exaggerated, given the wild reports that will attach to any man who comes to be known for his killing, not to mention the persistent myth that few men ever settled the mountains of Appalachia who could not snuff a candle at fifty paces. But Strother Purcell had indisputably been a capable marksman, and on July 28 of 1861 he walked into Klingbeil's Store in Asheville and stated his requirement for weaponry.

It was five days after the fire. Strother had washed and shaved; Klingbeil took note of this, and mentioned it subsequently to others.

"I need a rifle," Strother said.

Klingbeil replied: "We are all sorely grieved by your loss." Meaning the entire community. It was indeed much shaken by events, though of course not as shattered as Strother himself.

Strother had gone back to the ruin two evenings after. Had looked in a distracted manner through the rubble, as if to ascertain what personal effects might remain. Upturning a chair, he sat for a long while in the midst of it, drinking slowly but steadily from a pint bottle of whiskey. Observers spoke of a vast and unnatural stillness, as if he sat sorting it all into columns in a ledger: the immensity of the loss and the suffering, and the means by which the fire might have begun, and what—or who—might be held responsible. A funeral for Miz Amanda and for Solomon took place the day following. The coffins were clean white pine, and gave off a waft of smoke from the remains within.

Strother himself still smelled of smoke on the morning of July 28, despite having washed and changed his clothes. Klingbeil took note of this too, finding it inexplicably unsettling: the gaunt face looking down from its great height, and the faint smell of wood-smoke.

"A rifle," Strother said again. "I have money. I will pay you."

His hands had been burned as he battled the fire, but he seemed to take no notice. He chose out a lever-action Martini-Henry. Such was Klingbeil's recollection, although this would seem unlikely—a rifle of such design in the mountains of western North Carolina, as early as July of 1861. Asheville would boast a munitions factory in the latter years of the War, manufacturing firearms for the Confederate cause, but these were primarily Enfield-pattern muskets. More probably Strother chose out an 1853-model Enfield single-shot, which took .577-calibre cartridges and could be fired by a capable marksman at the rate of ten shots per minute.

"Cartridges," Strother said.

"How many?"

"How many do you have?"

He also purchased a pistol. An 1851 Colt's Navy model, by Klingbeil's account.

"That be all?" Klingbeil asked.

"A bowie knife."

Klingbeil hesitated, then. "You'd be leaving us?" he said uncertainly.

"I have a road to travel," Strother told him. "Debts to pay."

"Debts?"

"My family owes a debt to Drusilla Smoak. Five dollars, for the birthing of my brother. It was never paid, Mr. Klingbeil. If I pass by Hanging Tree Ridge, I will pay it. Along with other obligations."

He held a five-dollar gold half-eagle between his fingers, and as he spoke he placed it in his pocket. Klingbeil recalled this vividly, long after: the glint of the coin in a shaft of light through the window, and the glint in those cold blue eyes as well.

"Yes, I may very well find other debts to pay. A man must discharge all of his obligations, Mr. Klingbeil, as I am sure you will agree. Every payment that is owed in this life, whatever it may be, down to the last copper penny. I may have let myself forget that, for a time. I will not do so again."

He subsequently acquired a horse from McDavid, who ran the livery stable. It was a rangy dun hammerhead, leather-mouthed and vengeful of disposition. Klingbeil saw him for the last time some while later that morning, riding westward out of Asheville. There was something in the sight of it that chilled him; some intimation of fell purpose. So Klingbeil would say when he described the sight to others: a gaunt man astride a grey horse, riding stone-faced toward the Smoky Mountains. Low-hanging cloud soon swallowed them.

In later recountings, the horse was described as "pale."

PART THREE

-ELEVEN-

Tyree[5]

San Francisco, 1892

MESHACH COLLARD was not at Hanging Tree Ridge when Strother Purcell arrived there in his wrath on that summer day in 1861. Tyree knew this with a fair degree of certainty, along with other details. He'd scavenged these from sundry sources, according to his lifelong habit—newspapermen's gossip, some of it; random references in magazines; barroom tales told by travellers who could claim some connection to western North Carolina.

Shack Collard had not been there. But others had: several members of the Collard clan, including—possibly—women and children. Tyree was obscurely troubled by this thought, the possibility that women and children had been present when Strother Purcell arrived, since he'd not heard of there being survivors when Strother Purcell left. He'd heard tell of Collards lying dead in the woods, and Collards hanging dead from the branches of trees. But no one spoke of Collards drawing breath.

Tyree preferred to suppose that Rumour had erred, concerning women and children. Or, if Rumour told true, that they had somehow brought destruction upon themselves, and merited these just desserts. God knows, there are Innocents in this world who are anything but innocent, and deserve whatever comes their way. Often, Tyree in his secret heart thought that no survivors deserved to have been left behind

---

5   This chapter (among others) is apparently original to the Sturluson manuscript,
     and in point-of-view invites obvious comparison to the "Roadhouse Chronicles of
     Thomas Skiffings" segments. Readers may draw their own conclusions.—*Brookmire.*

when Strother Purcell rode on from McCutcheon's Roadhouse, either, in the winter of 1876. And most especially no children.

*

Tyree had been living in San Francisco for three years, nearly. His arrival had not been according to any design. At least, no design of his own making—Tyree did not discount the possibility that grander designs than our own might be at work in the world, possibly Providential but probably not, and that vast patterns might yet be discerned in the fullness of time, if only we could see them from this vantage. Which we wouldn't, Tyree thought, since we'd be dead.

He had been reared at a ghost-haunted inn faraway in the North, as you might reasonably expect of a crippled orphan destined for future greatness. This was an answer he gave, smiling wryly, when people asked about his origins, though mainly they didn't. Mainly they ignored him, which was fine. San Francisco was richly populated by freaks and curiosities, after all, and Tyree was hardly more freakish than most. He'd left the ghost-haunted inn six months after his sister had decamped. She had eloped with a man passing through on his way to Chicago, where he would help her make her fortune upon the stage. This had been the man's solemn vow, though Tyree saw no reason to believe him. Neither, he suspected, did his sister. But she was determined to get away from that goddamned inn, and was set upon becoming an actress. It had subsequently occurred to Tyree that she might end up in San Francisco, sooner or later—assuming she was still alive—which was one reason he had drifted there too. There were any number of stages in San Francisco, in theatres and taverns and concert saloons, and who was to say that his sister had not found her way onto one of them? She hadn't, though. This had been another of his life's disappointments.

He had a tiny, tidy room in a flat above a milliner's shop on Polk

Street, with a dentist's parlour next door to him and neighbours who nodded and murmured and left him alone. He had a window that looked out onto the street, and a shelf with books and a tin box full of treasures, including an old Deane-Adams five-shot that he'd carried about with him for sixteen years. He even had cartridges to go with it, though he'd only need one of those. Yes, one cartridge would suffice for the only job of shooting Tyree could imagine himself doing, when it all grew too wearisome to bear.

He had his newsstand, and his customers and acquaintances, and a certain undeniable standing amongst the local hacks who laughed at him but respected the information he kept stuffed away in that head. He even had a new name, since coming here: Tyree. He didn't mind. It was no worse than the old one.

As time went by, it occurred to him that he might never leave San Francisco at all. It occurred to him that he would probably die here.

That particular spring—the springtime of 1892—it seemed that dying might come sooner than he'd expected. A chill he'd taken had wormed down deep in the lungs. For several days he did not go outside at all, not even to tend his newsstand on Market Street. He began to wonder: Was this how the final illness felt, at its inception? The notion brought him a grim satisfaction, at first. There was in it a gallows drollery; he was impressed to discover how insouciant he was. But after awhile, he mainly felt desolate, instead.

Then two discoveries came upon him, one after the other.

The first was an article in a newspaper. He had returned to the newsstand, dragging himself out of his tiny room and into the open air, mainly from fear of what might come next if he didn't. It was a breezy article on a back page of one of the out-of-town dailies—the *Silver City Miner,* from Nevada—concerning the touring of a theatrical troupe.

One of the performers mentioned was an actress, who sang comic songs and sentimental ballads. She called herself Miss Arabella Skye.

Tyree read the article twice through, beginning to end. "No," he muttered to himself, out loud. "Not possible." He read it again. His hands, clutching onto the newspaper, commenced to shake.

That evening, he sat in the window on Polk Street, and tried to compose himself to write a letter. It did not go well. Words came, but in fits and starts, with blottings and cross-outs and crumplings of successive sheets of paper. He gave up after awhile, and dragged himself back outside, making his way toward a barroom that he frequented from time to time.

Night had fallen. Light from the windows spilled down as he passed, and pooled about the lampposts on the corners. A cable car trundled, one street over; closer by, someone played a concertina, badly. On the corner just ahead of him, two men stood. They were a mismatched pair—Tyree, deep in his thoughts, registered this vaguely. One of them was gaunt and towering, his companion trim and slight.

With a start, Tyree recognized the second man. It was Weaver, spruced and brushed and aspiring to be dapper, his hair centre-parted and his accents bright. Tyree flinched back before he could be recognized in turn, hunching into the deeper darkness against a building. He had no energy tonight for Barry Weaver.

The two men were talking. One of them, mainly—Weaver. Tyree heard cadences, but not words. Weaver's companion, towering in shadow, rumbled something in return. Tyree heard a gravelly baritone, and by lamplight glimpsed a one-eyed derelict.

That voice seemed to rumble ten feet up, from the hang of the scrotum.

Tyree's heart very nearly stopped.

–TWELVE–

From *High Crimes of the Outlaw Dillashay*[6]

Santa Rosita, New Mexico Territory, 1874

1.

THE BIG MAN gave his name as Strother Purcell. He had considerable experience in law enforcement, he said, having worked as a Sheriff's Deputy in sundry jurisdictions, these past years.

"Which places were these?" asked Sheriff Bob Lestander.

Jesus, the man was big, the Sheriff thought. Bob Lestander was no paltry specimen himself, bull-necked and broad athwart the beam as he sat behind the desk in his office. But Purcell towered over him.

"You want a list?"

Purcell produced a crinkled sheet of paper. The Sheriff counted seven different towns over the past eight years—tough rail-head cattle towns in Kansas and Wyoming. "Surely this ain't all of 'em?" he said.

Purcell appeared to miss the intended whimsy. He said: "Yep."

"You don't seem to stay in one place, for long," the Sheriff said.

---

6   As with chapters redacting "The Sorrows of Miz Amanda," the author (or authors) of the Sturluson manuscript is here drawing upon an existing source. *High Crimes of the Outlaw Dillashay* is a so-called "true-life novella" concerning Elijah Dillashay's depredations through the U.S. Southwest in the early 1870s. It was written in 1903 by Harley Carscadden, an ex-journalist and racetrack tout who was living at the time in St. Louis. An avid collector of Frontier lore, as well as a notorious dipsomaniac, Carscadden insisted that the account was "one hundred per cent by-golly certified Bible truth," being based in part on stories related to him by a man with a direct family connection to Santa Rosita c. 1874: the grand-nephew of Sheriff Bob Lestander. Even allowing for the vagaries of recollection and Harley Carscadden's own inclination to embellish, the account has served to provide a reliable superstructure for the Sturluson narrative, the author(s) of which in any case had supplementary information.—*Brookmire.*

"Not lately."

"Any reason for that?"

The big man gave a shrug. "It varies." His shoulders were wide and sloping. A scent of sage came off him as he shifted. "The time comes round," he said. "And I move on."

"How long would you be willing to stay here, d'you think?"

"I couldn't say."

"Because?"

"I just arrived."

The Sheriff leaned back in his chair, reflecting. It groaned a little, in protest. The chair was a new one, a swiveller with a padded seat, which he supplemented with a cushion. The office itself was newly built and gave off a fine, clean smell of new wood, which had been brought in by the wagon-load from the sawmill at Las Tablas.

Santa Rosita had been a sleepy town, not so long ago. A *nice* town. But it was changing, growing larger and more fractious, as were towns across the Territory. Hard men were slouching in amidst the jostling of moneyed interests; an outright war was brewing not far away in Lincoln County. So a Sheriff needed hard men of his own, deputies such as could hazard the rigours of law enforcement in New Mexico Territory, and would do so for the pittance that the County offered. This grew all the more vital if the Sheriff's hair was sparse and white, as was Bob Lestander's, who was no longer young.

He looked at the list. "Say I got in touch with these fellas—the Sheriffs who hired you in Kansas and Wyoming. "What d'you suppose they'd say about you?"

"You'd have to ask them."

Bob Lestander looked at the list some more. "Job pays a dollar a day," he said. "Plus a share of the revenue from fines. Still interested?"

"I'm still standing here."

"Any questions?"

Strother Purcell said: "Did you ever come across a man, name of Collard?"

"Collard?"

"Meshach Collard. Out of North Carolina."

The Sheriff knitted his brow. It seemed to him that a chill had crept into the room, despite the rising warmth of the spring day. Purcell's two eyes were icy and pale blue. Bob Lestander found himself unaccountably squirming in that gaze, which was peculiar and unsettling, here in his own damned office. He looked out the window instead, at the courthouse across the square, and the desert beyond. There was hardly a hint of green, even here in May.

"Collard," he repeated. "No, I can't say as I recognize the name."

"You're sure?"

"Why d'you ask?"

"Just someone I used to know. Someone I lost track of, awhile back. I wouldn't mind seeing him again."

It seemed to Bob Lestander that Purcell was not telling him the truth. Not all of it, at any rate. But it seemed to him, also, that this was not a man you questioned too closely.

"When could you start?" the Sheriff said. "Assuming I offered you the job."

"Could start right now."

Later that afternoon, the Sheriff sent a telegram of enquiry to an old colleague in Kansas, whose name Purcell had supplied as a reference. The reply was prompt: *HIRE HIM STOP THEN STAND CLEAR STOP GOOD LUCK*. Bob Lestander chose to interpret this recommendation as unequivocal.

He had, in any case, hired Strother Purcell already.

—

July came, and Purcell was still in Santa Rosita, serving as one of Sheriff Lestander's two Deputies. Deak Roby was the other.

Deputy Roby was eight-and-twenty in July of 1874, a decade younger than Strother Purcell. He was a man of goodly parts, sturdy and well-made, with a thatch of red hair and a bluff, amiable manner. Deak Roby lived a few miles from the town with a widow of a surly and independent disposition—his mother, in fact. But it is no necessary calumniation of a grown man to say that he lives with his Ma, although some might try to make it so; Deak Roby was, as it happened, popular amongst his friends—a man who was well enough liked, by those who liked him, with a ready laugh and a shoulder-slapping gift for ingratiation, although his eyes were perhaps too small. He also kept a room above the Gemstone Saloon, for use on nights when duty detained him.

"Collard," he said to his fellow Deputy.

Strother Purcell stopped. "What about him?"

"Collard was the name of the family—have I got that right? Folks you had some disputation with, up there in the piney-woods of Buttfuck Holler, or wherever it was you hail from."

The two of them were in the town square. Deak Roby had found a scrap of shade, where he stood in the stifling heat of the late afternoon, taking off his hat and swiping a sleeve across his brow. He had spoken as Purcell emerged from the courthouse.

"North Carolina, was it? Years ago—way back near the beginning of the War, when God knows what-all was being gotten up to, in them mountains. Or so I've heard."

"Where'd you hear this?"

"Oh, somewheres or other." Deak's grin was amiability itself. "I don't exactly recollect. Just one of those things a fella picks up."

The Deputy heard a good many things. He made it his business, as an officer of the law. It was also his vocation, Deak Roby being a noted hearer of barroom whispers, and a whisperer of them in return.

"So," Deak said, fishing a little. "Is it true?"

Purcell stared down, stone-eyed. "What else have you heard?"

Deputy Rectitude, Deak had come playfully to call him, though not to Strother's face. Deak Roby had a fondness for whimsical nicknames, with which he would amuse companions in the Gemstone. He had a gift for mimicry as well, and last evening had entertained them no end with an imitation of Deputy Rectitude's stiff-kneed walk and ramrod spine. "Tar-nay-shun," Deak had exclaimed in wicked approximation of his colleague's measured baritone, peering at the floor all about his feet; "Tar-NAY-shun, where-all did Ah mis-lay it, boys—the ten-foot Plank o' Rectitude Ah keep wedged up mah ass?" This had reduced them to gales of mirth; they begged him to stop.

"Whoo-ee," Deak Roby said now, fanning with his hat. "How 'bout this heat?"

"I asked what else you heard."

"I heard you been lookin' for him, ever since. Stopping here, and stopping there, but always looking. One of the Collards—assuming I heard correctly, about that name. The one who done you some particular wrong, even more than all them others. Whatever it was that happened to them, up Mount Wherever-it-was."

Deak had heard other rumours as well, though he didn't think it politic to mention these now. There were whispers of controversies in Kansas and Wyoming, at the stops Deputy Rectitude had made along his long, winding way from the piney-woods of Buttfuck to the stifling summer heat of Santa Rosita. Rumours of an implacability that went beyond the bare requirements of the Law, and had led to deaths that might have been avoided: the shootings-down of cowboys whose nature was wild, but not rotten; boys who were weak rather than wicked, or who lacked a head for strong liquor, or who had fallen — alas — amongst low companions, and from whom ought not to have been exacted, perhaps, the last pennies of the ultimate price. True, there was never a hint of back-shooting or treachery — not that Deak Roby had heard, at least, and Deak Roby could surely be relied upon to have asked. Those were all fair gunfights, as far as anybody knew. True as well that every young hellion has his defenders, and no lawman ever stood his ground without being impugned by someone. But still.

"Must of been a fearful wrong," Deak Roby said. "Whatever it was this fella done — to have you looking for him, all these years."

"Assuming what you heard was true."

"You're right. You're absolutely right. Assuming it was." Deak Roby smiled again. He smiled some more. Butter would not have melted, despite the heat of the afternoon. "So," he said. "… Was it?"

Deputy Purcell made no reply, nor did his stony expression alter. But Deak saw the muscles bunch, in his jaw.

"A good twelve, thirteen years — even longer, maybe," Deak said. "My, oh my. Such a long and onerous time, to be lookin' for a fella. An' I'll tell you what — if I ever hear that name again? You'll be the first to know."

The muscles in Purcell's jaw bunched some more. "Here's a question for you, Roby."

"Go ahead, friend — ask it."

"Do you have business of your own?"

"Why, yes indeed — I believe I do."

"Then you should mind it. And I'll attend to mine."

Strother Purcell started away. Deputy Rectitude, stalking stiff-kneed into the blaze of the sun.

"Purcell."

Deputy Rectitude looked back.

"Give my best to the gal, if you see her first. Miss Maria." Deak Roby continued to smile, though not so much. "You seen her the other evening, I understand."

"Why shouldn't I? She's a friend."

"'Course she is. An' friends are good—a man needs friends. God help the fella who's without 'em." Deak Roby's smile had faded some more. "She's half your age," he said.

"I know how old she is."

"And she's spoken for. I expect you know that, too?"

"Like I said. She's a friend."

"Well, that's good. That's fine and dandy. Long as we're clear." Deputy Rectitude stalked away.

Deak Roby, watching, no longer smiled at all.

*

The gal was Maria Teresa Lestander, the Sheriff's daughter. Strother Purcell did not in fact see her that evening, though he had half a mind to do so, just to spite Deputy Roby.

He knew that sort of man. He had dealt with sundry Deacon Robys in the long years since Hanging Tree Ridge. They were all of them the same, the Deacon Robys of this world, and it grated on him to see this one paying court to Maria Teresa, who was altogether a finer creature than Roby was equipped to appreciate.

But this evening, Strother Purcell had duties. He went first to the Sheriff's office to attend to paperwork. This fell to him when Sheriff Lestander was away from Santa Rosita, as he was on this occasion, having travelled to the outer reaches of the County to collect unpaid taxes from ranching concerns. After that, he looked in on the prisoners who were being kept in the courthouse cells. There were two of these, at present, both drifters. They had given their names as Smith and Miller, and had been locked here to await the Circuit Judge after allegations that a saloon gal had been menaced.

Shortly after nine p.m., Strother Purcell locked the courthouse tight and proceeded to the New Southwest Hotel, where he partook of a late dinner before conducting his nightly rounds. Finding nothing significantly amiss, he made his way to McMurtry Street, where he had taken a room on the second floor above a dry-goods shop. It was nearly eleven o'clock.

The room was accessed by a side door, up a set of stairs in the alley. The darkness here was profound. He set his foot to the bottom step and then stopped.

A horse. There'd been a horse, tethered to the rail a distance away, in the street. He had taken mental note of this as he'd turned toward the alley, and it came to him now: what it was in that image that seemed out of place. The horse in the spill of light from a window had been slick with sweat, as from hard riding, which was unusual for this time of night. He had just started to turn when he heard the click of a revolver cocked directly behind his head. A low voice advised: "Do not make the bad mistake of reaching for that iron."

The silence stretched, long enough for Strother Purcell to rebuke himself for careless inattention. Except he'd recognized that voice.

Jesus.

"Turn around, Strother."

The man in the darkness had been a boy to him, all through these long years. Such was the image he'd carried.

Jesus God.

"Are we friends, then?" Lige said.

Strother held in memory his fifteen-year-old brother, picking himself up from the Asheville dust. Lige had not lowered the sixgun.

Strother said at last: "You knew she died?"

"A fire."

"It was."

"Her and poor old Solomon. I heard. And I heard you went up the mountain, afterward. Up to Hanging Tree Ridge."

Strother did not reply.

"If I'd been around, I'd've come with you," Lige said.

"But you weren't."

"I understand my Daddy sleeps easier, ever since. Though he was never once good enough for the likes of yourself."

For an uncanny moment, it seemed to Strother that his step-father stood before him instead. Jacob Dillashay, swarthy and brutal and desperately uncertain.

"You can put the gun down," Strother said.

"Can I?" His brother seemed unconvinced.

"Why are you here?"

"Not to ask for your help. I can tell you that much. Not from the likes of you."

Lige was injured. Strother saw that now, despite the darkness. The clench of his brother's jaw; the way his mouth twisted in a grimace.

"What's happened, Lige?"

The front of his brother's shirt was caked with blood.

"Aw, Christ," said Strother, wearily.

He'd heard about Lige's activities, through the years—or some of them, at least. He'd seen a poster on a Sheriff's wall in Kansas.

"Trouble with the law, somewhere?" he said.

"You could say that."

"Posse on the way?"

"Not in New Mexico. Not yet, anyway. Unless you organize one."

"Aw, Christ, Lige."

"Will you help me?"

"Come up to the room," Strother said at last. "You can stay the night."

Lige's steps were heavy on the stairs, his left foot clubbed as ever. He leaned against the rail, but disdained any offer of assistance. Once inside, he sagged down onto the bed, sitting with his head hung low.

"There's a doctor," Strother said. "Not competent, but not the worst. I can fetch him."

"No doctor."

In lamplight, Lige's face was haggard. Someone had bandaged his right shoulder, but the dressing was makeshift and blood seeped through.

"You've took a bullet," Strother said.

"It went right through."

"At least let me change the dressing."

Lige suffered him to do so, using strips torn from the bedsheet. The wound was ugly, but seemed clean. "Don't waste good whiskey on it, then," Lige said. He took the bottle that Strother had fetched from the shelf, lifting it in an ironical toast. "Good health and long life to you, brother. May you live until I kill you."

"You intending on that?"

"Haven't decided. You'll be the first to know."

Lige's voice was slurred with exhaustion. Setting the bottle down, he eased himself to lie full length on the bed.

The room was small but immaculate in its neatness. The bed, a dresser, a nightstand with a basin. "The fuck," Lige said, "keeps his room this clean? You'd think a damned old woman lived here."

—

It was morning when he awakened. Strother sat on a wooden chair beside the door.

"Been there all night?" Lige said.

"Off and on."

Strother had in fact gone out twice, to the Sheriff's office and then to the telegraph office. He had sat quietly since returning, watching his little brother sleep. Lige looked in sleep as he'd always done, his left arm negligent across his face. He looked peaceful. Strother ached with that contemplation.

Wincing, Lige raised himself onto one elbow. Sunlight slanted through the curtains. "Time is it?" he said.

Strother said, "There's warrants outstanding in Tennessee, Kansas, and Arizona. I checked it out."

"Good thing I'm in New Mexico, then."

"There's a warrant in New Mexico, too. A shooting scrape near Lincoln, two days ago. The man they're looking for was wounded — rode off on a stolen horse."

Lige's gun belt when he went to sleep had been looped around the bedpost, near to hand. It was not there now. Strother, in shadow, held a sixgun in his lap.

There was stillness between them.

Lige said, "You've made your mind up — have you, brother? Passed your judgement."

"I've got no right to judge you, Lige. Nor any man."

"You do not."

"The Circuit Judge will have to do that, when he comes."

–THIRTEEN–

The Accounting of Barry Weaver

San Francisco, 1892

SOMETIMES WHEN PRAIRIE ROSE was out, Little Em'ly would watch for her protector through the keyhole. The old man might hear the faintest creaking of floorboards behind him; the whisper of muslin as she crouched. Sometimes he might hear nothing at all, which was deeply impressive to him. The walls in the tenement were wafer-thin—the rats themselves could not sneak along those floorboards. And even late in life his hearing was uncanny, a trait he of necessity shared with all of the great frontier man-killers. In his prime he could hear the click of a sixgun cocked at four hundred paces, and the breech-bolt of a Henry rifle at half a mile. Em'ly never opened the door or said a word, so at first he was unsure of her intent—whether she hoped to see him present, or to see him gone. But one morning when Rose was especially late returning, he was unaware of Em'ly's presence entirely, until he heard a single sigh one inch behind his head, and a gasp as Em'ly caught herself up out of slumber. She'd been there all along. It might have been hours; it might have been all night—just there, on the other side of the door.

He took heart from this. From here on he stayed at his post as much as was possible, save for unavoidable forays outside—to make ablutions at the stand-pipe or to avail himself of the courtyard jakes. These latter took longer than he would have wished; his bowels were not what they had been in youth. This affliction he held in common with Wild Bill Hickok, who late in life was much martyred by his digestion. He had in fact known Wild Bill, though not well enough to have discussed the gunman's bowels; had encountered Wild Bill while passing through Cheyenne in 1873, and was sorry to hear of it when Hickok was later murdered in Deadwood. Returning, the old man would announce himself by stamping his boots as he came back up the stairs, guessing that Em'ly might not settle in her mood until she knew he was back at his post. He would clear his throat with vehemence, or whistle; even hum some little snatch of melody, a thing he had not done in many years.

The attack, when it came, caught them horribly unawares.

It was shortly before eleven a.m. when the old man went outside. Prairie Rose had come home and gone back out again, that morning. Em'ly was inside, sweeping. Their own small corner of the world seemed to be in good order. Rose would be back soon herself, and so he decided he might safely stay away just a little bit longer than usual. He might walk in the warm spring sunshine, stretch his legs.

He walked a block or two along Pacific Street. Turning left, he continued on his way. In passing he failed to take note of the two men on the nearby corner.

In his prime, he would surely have seen them and made a mental note. Two scruffy men, unshaven and unwashed, though one of them wore a red silk vest and a fine gold watch on a chain. They fell silent as he drew near, and turned casually away. He would in his prime have marked that they seemed out of place, and desirous to avoid his eye. He would at the very least have intuited, at a level more profound than conscious thought, that something in the configuration was not quite right.

But we grow old. We fall upon evil times. Lost in his own thoughts he continued past, never seeing the two men exchange a look, nor hearing Red Silk Vest say: "See?" They let him reach the next corner before turning themselves and sloping up Pacific Street.

Little Em'ly was cleaning the bedroom—the back room—and was thus in no position to notice them either. Nor could she have noted their intersection with a third man, oleaginating around the corner from the opposite direction: Rose's gold-toothed Rent Collector. She could not have noticed their brief encounter in front of the tenement building, nor the hooded glance Red Silk Vest cast about, as if marking who might be watching. She did not see them at all until she started into the parlour a few moments later, just in time to see the knob turning on the front door.

The Rent Collector had no need to knock, of course. He had a key.

Just past eleven. A bank-clock had chimed the hour moments previous, startling Em'ly from her task and recollecting her intention to prepare a lunch for Prairie Rose. There was cheese wrapped up in paper on the shelf, and a loaf of pumpernickel, which Em'ly would slice into slabs with the bread knife. A fine knife of German make, one of Rose's few domestic luxuries: it lay gleaming on the cutting board, and Em'ly in just a few steps more would have reached it. But she emerged one heartbeat too late. The front door was opening at her; the doorway was filling with thug. For the span of that single heartbeat Em'ly froze.

The moment was lost. She darted for the knife, but Red Silk Vest was one step ahead, his accomplice moving to cut off her angle of retreat. An Irishman this second man was: Houlihan, though the name hardly matters. Now the third man, the Rent Collector, was closing the front door behind him and locking it with his key.

"*Buongiorno,*" the Rent Collector said.

Trapped. They had triangulated and hemmed her in. But she was not to fear; so the Rent Collector gave her to understand. They had not come here with malignancy of intention.

"No harm you. Yes? Come in, go out again."

The gold tooth gleamed in his smile. And that was their business here, wasn't it? They just wanted the gold. He explained this to her and Red Silk Vest said something else she did not understand, being as it was in Sicilian.

The Irishman translated: "Yer fecking husband."

The Utah Brute, he meant. The Utah Brute had been rich, as these Mormon bastards always were. Such was the rumour that had been festering for weeks. For months—longer, even—since Prairie Rose arrived in San Francisco. But then her sister-wife had arrived half-dead and storm-drenched at the concert saloon: a *second* wife fleeing, and now there could be no doubt. Little Em'ly had slit his throat and robbed him blind. She had fled Utah with a sack full of Mormon gold, and where else could it be hidden but in the flat?

This had attained to the status of incontrovertible fact in certain Barbary Coast taverns, frequented by men such as Houlihan. The Irishman had discussed possible initiatives with his colleague Red Silk Vest, who—as Fortune would have it—was not only game for burglary, and worse, but was a cousin of the very man who collected rent from Prairie Rose.

Em'ly knew none of this, of course. She just knew there was no way out. The Rent Collector turned to wedge a wooden chair against the door, as a further impediment to ingress; when he turned back his smile gleamed again. One last time he asked her nicely: *Dov'è l'oro?*

Little Em'ly screamed.

It was the first time anyone in San Francisco had heard her voice, except for Prairie Rose herself; the surprise made all of them jump.

Em'ly opened her mouth to scream again, although there was no point. No one in the building would come to help her, would dare to interrupt the Rent Collector. His countenance grew very dark indeed.

One last time she screamed.

And the door exploded from its hinges.

Such was Em'ly's experience of the moment. An explosion on the landing outside, and the door blown into pieces by the blast. Flinders of it, flying like shrapnel, and bits of the wooden chair.

There in the gaping doorway stood Old Lem.

See. The syllable that had been uttered some minutes previous, as he had passed without noticing the two men on the corner. Except he *had* noticed them; some ancient instinct in him had stirred, without his conscious awareness. And the syllable had not been *see* at all, but *si*.

The realization had brought him shambling to a stop, halfway down the block. He'd stood for a moment in vague perplexity, shaking his grey head as if to clear all those years of cobwebs, puzzling out what had troubled him. And clarity came. Those two men, so close to the tenement. The Rent Collector, and the single syllable. Sicilian.

He turned and saw them. Three of them — one, two, three — sloping through the front door of the building.

So he started back. Found himself moving more swiftly with each stride. Back up Pacific Street; through the door of the tenement and up the stairs. Paused to catch his breath on the first landing, then resumed. Took the second flight of stairs two at a time, and halfway up the third he heard Em'ly's scream.

The door burst apart before his boot heel.

"Exterminator, ma'am," he said. "Come to deal with the vermin."

Or so he would have said, if he'd had the wind. Something very much like it, or even pithier. But he was old, or seemed so to the world;

this must be borne in mind. A man with nearly three-score winters on his head, and cruelly aged by years of dissipation; two city blocks at an accelerating lurch and then those fucking stairs. What wind he had left was otherwise required.

Red Silk Vest came viper-quick, but the old man smote him. One sledging blow and down he flopped in a marionetting of limbs.

Houlihan took up a chair and struck him from behind. The old man staggered and nearly fell. He might yet have been finished right then and there — killed dead, had Houlihan reached for the bread knife and plunged it between his shoulder blades. But the Irishman went for his pistol instead. It was tucked in his belt and it snagged. The old man caught him by the wrist, and wrenched; as Houlihan fell with a shriek and a *feck!* the old man took the pistol for himself.

He had not held a gun in sixteen years. Not since he had cast aside the firearm with which he had brought his own outlaw brother to a reckoning. The Irishman's pistol was by contrast a risible thing: cheaply made, badly balanced, the sort of a gun to explode in your hand and take three fingers with it. But it fit into his grip. It belonged there. He lifted his gaze.

The Rent Collector remained. Three feet away: hunched and furtive, caught like a thief in lantern-light, his hand frozen partway to the derringer in his pocket.

Twenty years earlier, the old man might have given him his chance. He might have stepped back and put his own gun in his belt, rumbling: "Go ahead, then — make your play." If he'd been a younger man, more nearly in his prime. Or if his brother had been standing across from him instead; his brother, or Meshach Collard. If indeed he'd been able to speak at all — if the room had not commenced to spin, spots like dust-motes dancing before his eyes.

So instead he reached out with his left hand, as if to seize the Rent Collector's collar. Then, in that half-second of diversion, he swung the pistol in his right hand, bringing the barrel against the Sicilian's skull. This was a trick that Wyatt Earp had loved to use, in his days in Tombstone and Dodge. There was, as always, a satisfying *thock*. The Rent Collector wobbled and sprawled.

The Irishman was already out the door, clutching his broken wrist. Red Silk Vest was right behind, and the Rent Collector grovelled after. The old man stood swaying as they thudded down the stairs: stood swaying and magnificent. He turned at last to Little Em'ly. She crouched in the furthest corner of the room, staring huge-eyed back, as if gazing upon the Beast from the Pit, or some warrior archangel.

The old man took a breath. He gathered himself to utter reassurance. His legs gave way instead.

*

Prairie Rose returned ten minutes later. Pushing through the crowd on the landing, she found Little Em'ly amidst the shambles with Old Lem's head in her lap.

The old man had been murdered dead. So Rose had been reliably informed as she'd hurried up the stairs, by neighbours. They were appropriately sorrow-struck to Rose's face, although privately they had known no good could come of this, consorting with violent derelicts.

But Old Lem was alive and muttering, to Rose's great relief. Within a few minutes he was able to sit up, though he was much dishevelled and remained for some while not quite lucid. He had taken a fearsome knock to the back of the head. His hair was matted with blood and an ostrich egg was sprouting.

In lieu of a door that would shut against unwanted noses — Rose's front door, or what remained of it, being strewn in bits across the floor — she settled for begging privacy instead. When entreaties did not avail, she shouted for it, using language that caused some grievance but brought results. Duly offended, the noses withdrew. In a few more minutes Old Lem was attempting communication. He was able to articulate a few words, in roughly the order that he intended.

"What *happened?*" Rose demanded.

Young Weaver arrived at a lope some short while later.

I'd heard the news while taking lunch at a saloon, half a mile away —a shooting scrape, would you believe it, at a whore's lodgings on Pacific Street. Some old man with one eye blasting the hell out of Rent Collectors. *Oh, shit-fuck-pisspots,* I thought to myself, and sprinted.

So I hadn't—strictly speaking—been an eyewitness to the confrontation. The accounting I've given above is more what you'd call a dramatic re-creation, based on interviews and canny suppositions, honed by years of writing yarns for newspapers. But I think I come pretty close to the mark.

Rose's rooms, when I got there, were strewn with debris and spattered with blood. The door and two chairs were reduced to kindling, and three walls were cratered as if by cannon-fire.

"Fucksake, Barry!" Rose said to me. We were on the landing together, the two of us. Outside the gaping doorway, trying to have a private conversation. "Three of 'em—one old tramp. Jesus on a rented mule, who *is* he?" She was halfway giddy with relief, but she had me by the shirt front just the same: both hands clenched and nose-to-nose. "The truth, you bastard!"

So I told her. Or at least, I told a version thereof. It could hardly help the old man to start blabbing the *whole* truth, unvarnished and entire. Besides, I still knew only parts of it myself, despite having been busy for the past couple of days, scouring through newspaper archives in search of information. I'd written letters to old newspaper acquaintances, too, here and there about the country, casually asking for any information that fellows might have concerning the late gunman Strother Purcell.

There'd been no replies as yet—the letters had just gone out—but I had hopes. And in the meantime, my archival scouring had yielded up the broadest strokes of a biographical sketch.

Born in North Carolina. Left there as a young man, after a back-country blood-feud boiled over. Turned up a few years later as an itinerant lawman in tough, rail-head cattle-towns in Kansas and Wyoming. Turned up after that in New Mexico, where some manner of reunion with his outlaw brother led to a year-long pursuit all the way into Canada—the Retribution Ride—and a Reckoning sometime in the winter of 1876.

And there'd been corpses—by his own admission, that first night in the cell. Corpses left behind, at each stop along the way.

I didn't mention this to Prairie Rose. Not the details, and certainly not the name. Instead, I told her: "I believe Old Lem killed a man."

"He near to just killed three more!"

"No, hear me out. He shot a man dead, a few years back. In—in New Mexico, I think."

This was true. Almost certainly. Based on the research I had done to this point, it seemed clear that he had killed men in various States and Territories, not to mention Canada. So why should New Mexico be an exception?

"An' *now* you get around to telling me? Fucksake, Barry...!"

"Just keep your voice down. A gunfight—a fair fight—he was defending himself. But they called it murder. He's been on the run, ever since. And if word of this ever gets out—well, I don't know what will happen to him, Rose."

Searching does not do credit to Prairie Rose's gaze. "Is that the truth?"

"Rose, it's God's own truth."

Or if not God's own, then at least a version He might recognize as having loitered about the neighbourhood. A version that had a savour of God's own truth *in* it—and in the end, we can hardly do better than that.

"Jesus, Barry."

Rose's vulture-clutch on my shirt front eased. Shaking her head in weary wonderment, she looked back through the gaping doorway. The old man was inside. He lay stretched out on a day-bed that Little Em'ly had cobbled together. "Lord God Christ on a sway-backed mule—but all right. I'll keep this between the two of us."

"Your word?" I said.

"I swear. Nobody hears it from me."

The old man moved in with Rose and Em'ly after that—just as soon as a new front door had been installed. Old Lem did that himself, with a borrowed toolkit. He turned out to be a carpenter of no mean skill, having earned his crusts by such means through the long years of his self-exile. He fashioned a door that would withstand a bitter blast, and installed two heavy locks and a deadbolt inside, assuring the women that they should sleep soundly henceforward.

"The marvel is he didn't saw a finger off," I said drily to Prairie Rose. This was some days later. She eyed me asquint, as if to ask why he'd do such a damnfool thing. "John Barleycorn," I said. "The shakes."

"Old Lem don't drink," Rose said.

"The hell he doesn't."

She was serious. "That old man hasn't taken drink in days. You mean to say you haven't even noticed?"

I hadn't seen as much of him as I might have intended. He'd been lying low—which was good. Let him lie as low as possible, thought I. Meantime the hullabaloo concerning the battle with the Rent Collector had pretty much died down, which was even better. There'd been barroom speculation for a day or so, but then San Francisco had mercifully moved on.

"He quit drinking for Em'ly's sake," Rose confided. "I'm proud of him — an' so should you be, too."

I assured her that I *was* proud. Yes, you betcha. Proud as punch of that old man, now that I knew about it.

And I actually was.

It was early evening. Rose and I were walking together along Market Street, in the general direction of the concert saloon. Prairie Rose was working tonight. The evening was fine and fair, and Rose had taken my arm — just as if we were two ordinary friends, out for a springtime stroll.

Little Em'ly had a particular horror of bibulous men, Rose was confiding. "Owing to her Daddy was a drunkard. He was drunk for ten days straight, that time he sold her to the Mormon."

"Her father *sold* her?"

"She don't talk about it much. Or ever. The Mormon wasn't a drinking man, of course," Rose added. "He just had all the other vices. Every other sin God left with Adam — but sober as a fuckin' Judge as he sinned 'em."

Three sentences in a row. It was the most she'd ever said to me, about the Mormon.

"The Mormon we're talking about — he'd be your ex-husband?" I said, gingerly.

"He would. Except we *don't* talk about him." Rose's voice had grown terse and clipped. "Not now, an' not ever."

Rose walked a little quicker, for a time — almost as if she feared the Brute was behind us. It was an edginess so palpable that I nearly snuck a look back over my shoulder.

"Em'ly's fond of that old man, though," Rose was saying. "She don't take to anyone — but she's taken to Old Lem. An' I swear he's taken right back to her." Rose smiled a little, at that. Smiling was a good look for her. It lifted the shadow she carried with her. "Old Lem never had a child, I think," Rose said. "So Em'ly is kindly like that, for him, maybe—the daughter he wisht he could of had."

I said, "That's a blessing, then."

There must have been something in my voice, because Rose looked at me sidelong. "G'wan," she said, surprised. "*You?*"

"Sure," I said, and shrugged. It wasn't a secret, after all—just something I didn't tend to mention. "I have a daughter. Had one, anyway."

Rose's eyes softened. "I'm sorry. I didn't—"

"No, she's still alive. As far as I know. Somewhere. We've been—well, it's hard to stay in touch, sometimes. You know how it is. The years go by."

Rose's expression closed down, just a little. "Sure," she said.

"Things didn't work out," I said. "With her mother. So I moved on, and afterwards ... well, I guess that's just how it goes, sometimes. Look, you can think whatever you want, but—"

"*Me?*" Rose gave a small, bleak laugh. "Oh, sure—like I got the right to sit in judgement. On you, or on anyone else in this world."

-FOURTEEN-

From High Crimes of the Outlaw Dillashay

Santa Rosita, New Mexico Territory, 1874

1.

DEAK ROBY, RISING LATE, had watched it unfold. The Deputy had slept that night in the room he kept above the Gemstone Saloon — the second floor, with a window overlooking the main thoroughfare, by which he stood pissing into the thunder-mug as the procession of two came down the middle of the street. Deputy Purcell and his prisoner: Purcell keeping two paces behind, his sixgun in his hand. Stalking with those long, slow strides, his back ramrod straight with the Plank of Rectitude.

The prisoner was bare-headed, and walked with visible pain, club-footing with his wrists handcuffed behind. He glanced up as they processed underneath Deak Roby's vantage, meeting Deak's bleary gaze with pure defiance, then nodding a sardonic greeting to a clerk staring out from a shop doorway, opposite. "'Morning," the prisoner was heard to say. "Fine day, isn't it? And fuck you very much."

Deak Roby had no idea who the prisoner was, or how he had come to be apprehended — not yet, in the hungover fuddle of the morning, with John Percy in his palm and last night's taste in his mouth as if something furred and verminous had died there. But he found out soon enough.

"Your *brother?*" Deak demanded of Deputy Rectitude. Deak had pulled on pants and boots and made his way over to the courthouse.

A knot of gawkers had assembled outside, and from them Deak had heard this remarkable news. He shouldered through them, and clambered up the stairs to the second floor. The incumbent prisoners, Smith and Miller, were still locked in the makeshift cell downstairs. So Deputy Rectitude had placed this new prisoner in a separate room, above. It had one window, barred, and a heavy door that bolted on the outside.

The blacksmith had already been summoned. The prisoner sat in a straight-backed chair that constituted the room's sole furnishings, along with an iron cot and a wooden bucket. Deputy Rectitude stood guard at the open door, watching grimly as the blacksmith affixed leg-irons.

"That's your *brother?*" Deak Roby demanded.

"Only half," the prisoner said. His smile was sweet as Lucifer's, welcoming Judas Iscariot to hell. "The half that's Beauchamp is partway to a saint. It's the Dillashay side that brings such shame on our heads."

"Yes," Strother said to Deak Roby. "This man is my brother."

"He's gonna watch them hang me, too." The prisoner spoke as a man who savours the ironies of life. "That's exactly the sort of man he is, your Deputy Purcell. I always knew that about him. But somehow—all these years—I let the knowing of it slip my mind."

"The hell's he done?" Deak Roby demanded.

Deputy Rectitude's face was grey. "He's done nothing. Not unless a Judge says otherwise."

"*Then* we get to the hanging," the prisoner said.

"*Why?*"

This was Maria Teresa Lestander's question.

"I swore an oath," Strother said to her. "To your father. To the County. When I took up their badge." There was a look on his face that Maria Teresa had not seen before, not in such intensity.

"Well, good Lord," she said. "What did he do?"

201

"I don't know that, Maria. It's not up to me. All I know is what's alleged."

He'd missed the point. "No," she exclaimed, impatiently. "I'm asking—what did your brother do to *you?*"

They were walking by the river, just outside the town. It was evening. The river was low and brown in midsummer, and the heat of the day still slouched, oppressive. It would be intolerable in the makeshift cell on the second floor above the courthouse.

"My brother is a fugitive," Strother said. "He's wanted by the Law. What sort of a lawman would I be—?"

"A bad one. A bad lawman, derelict at best. But ... what sort of a *brother?*"

"Brothers don't come into it. The distinction is false."

She searched his face in some bewilderment. Maria Teresa had no brother of her own—no family at all, besides the sheriff. She would have liked, very much, to have had a brother.

Strother drew a breath. He said, "You need to understand—"

"*What?*" Maria Teresa demanded. "What is it that I need to understand?"

"The law." He spoke doggedly. "There's brothers, Miss Lestander, and then there's law. It tells us where we stand—what's right, what's wrong. Without the law ... It comes down to obligations. Obligations on either side—what's rightly ours to take, and what we owe. If those accounts get lost, or confused, or disregarded—then God help us. We lose our way, and then the devil only knows ..."

Strother's voice trailed away. He seemed to struggle for words. When he found them, his voice was unaccountably hoarse. "I lost my own way, once. I collected, maybe, more than what was owed. Well, I learned from that. I learned, never again. The *law.* What's due, and what's owed. If a man transgresses, then that man must stand trial, never mind whose brother he is."

It was the longest speech Maria Teresa had ever heard from him. His face was red when he finished, as if from some battle within.

And oh, the expression he wore.

Lige Dillashay had seen it once, though Maria Teresa could hardly have known that. It was the look Strother had worn on that terrible morning in childhood, when two boys had set forth to harvest forty acres of corn.

Maria Teresa was nineteen years old. She was not Sheriff Lestander's flesh and blood, although she had taken his name. She was more as you might say his adopted daughter, being the child of his late housekeeper. And she was a deep one. So her father had often reflected. A quiet gal, until a thought or an emotion should take hold. Then she would flash with it, and in that moment be remarkable. Devout, in the Popish way of her late mother: a gal for candles and Rosary beads, with uncanny Latin obsessions that would come fizzing up as unexpected as Vesuvius. Injustices could set her off entirely, sparking flames of indignation.

But she had never supposed that Strother Purcell could be heartless—not till that evening, by the river. This distressed her more than she let on.

The next morning, she carried the prisoners' breakfast to the courthouse. This was a chore she regularly undertook, though usually one of the men would relay it to the cells—one of the deputies, or else Woody McQuatt, who did odd jobs and served for a turnkey when required. Old Woody might also be entrusted to escort a shackled prisoner to the courtroom when the Circuit Judge arrived.

Today, she carried the basket up to the second-floor cell, while Woody McQuatt grumbled his way to the other prisoners, confined below. Lige Dillashay sat shackled on the cot, the leg-irons secured with a heavy chain to a metal ring in the floor. He'd been gazing out through the bars of the window, with its vantage overlooking the dusty street. "H'lo, darlin'," he said to her. "Miss Lestander, I should say."

She set the basket on the floor. The chain scraped against rough planks as he shifted.

"Like a chicken-killing dog," he said. "Mind you keep your distance." He summoned up a grin, but it seemed to her less devilish than wan. His face was pale, despite his natural colouration; he moved stiffly and with pain. The doctor had been by to dress his wounded shoulder. The bandage seemed almost shockingly white. "Thank you kindly," he said, meaning the food.

Maria Teresa thought: You heard the resemblance in their voices. The same slow accents of the South. "I know your brother," she said. "I'm a sort of... I'm a friend of his."

"So was I," the prisoner said. "But that was a long, long time ago."

*

There was a small table in the second-floor hallway, outside the door of the cell. Sometimes Sheriff Lestander sat there, when he was in town, doing paperwork while keeping one eye on whatever prisoner was within. This way the door might be left open, a mercy in the heat of summer. Other times it was Deputy Roby who sat at the table, though not so much in the interests of compassion.

He sat there for a time that afternoon, the Sheriff being still upon his tax-collecting rounds. "Next week," Deputy Roby said cheerfully.

"Next week what?" Lige said.

"Circuit Judge is comin'. Big week for you fellas. You, and them two in the cell downstairs. You acquainted with that particular pair? No? Well, you ain't missing much."

The Deputy did not do paperwork. Today he was preparing cartridges for his firearms. He liked to double the powder-load in a store-bought cartridge, and would carve as well an X on the tip of the bullet, working meticulously with his knife. Such loads had great destructive power, as oftentimes a lawman might require in the course of his duties. He had recently been called to dispatch a rabid, bat-bit dog. A disgusting cur, foaming at the end of a chain — not at all dissimilar to present company, Deak said affably. "No offense intended," he added.

"None taken."

"Well, what do you suppose? The bullet blew that dog's damned head off, and the muzzle-flash set fire to the carcass."

The Deputy laughed uproariously at this, being a big man who could enjoy a joke at his own expense. The prisoner looked away from him.

"If it's jail-time, you'll be shipped off to the territorial prison," Deak said.

"'Less I'm innocent."

"'Less you're innocent," Deak agreed. "Then pigs will fly."

The prisoner was looking out the window again, instead of at Deak Roby. The Deputy found this to be irksome.

"If it's hanging, they'll do it here. Right out that window, where you're lookin'." The lumber would be brought in from Las Tablas, he said, by wagon. Good, clean wood was needful, and then they'd nail it together. This was no doubt disconcerting to the condemned man, Deak Roby reflected — sawing and hammering dawn to dusk, the gallows going up right there, where he could see it. "Then again, you could of thought of that before you done 'em."

"Done what?"

"Your wicked deeds. Deeds so vile your own brother hates you."

The prisoner Dillashay was looking at him, now. Deputy Roby found that he liked this even less. It was a seething and a measuring look, despite the smile that went with it.

"I asked myself what she sees in you," Lige said. "The one you're sweet on — the Lestander gal."

"Take care how you speak of her," Deak Roby said.

"Then I realized — she don't see anything in you, at all. It's him she favours. And I believe you know it, don't you?"

Deak Roby gave this due consideration. A slow, red flush crept up his neck. "You might see certain benefits," he said, "in shutting your Got-damned mouth."

That evening, after dinner, Maria Teresa returned to the courthouse building. A hot desert wind had come up with the sun's decline, tumbling a solitary tumbleweed down the street. She found Woody McQuatt escorting the prisoner Dillashay down the outside stairs in the back, for his evening excursion to the jakes.

The outlaw shuffled like a man grown ancient, the short chain that linked the leg-irons clanking. His hands on the railing were cuffed, and when he lifted his head Maria Teresa saw that his face was battered on the one side, the eye and cheekbone swollen. He grinned most gallantly, though. "'Evening, darlin'."

Maria Teresa exclaimed in dismay, demanding to know what had happened. Woody McQuatt was following at a distance of two paces, clutching a shotgun against the possibility of escape. But there was an indignation about him.

"Couldn't say, Miss," the old man muttered. "Wasn't present at the time."

"Well, who *was* present?"

"Not sure, Miss. You might ask Deputy Roby."

"Deak did this?" she demanded.

"My own fault, darlin'," the outlaw said. "Fell down the stairs."

Maria Teresa looked back to Woody McQuatt. He scowled resolutely into the middle distance, as a man may do who keeps dark thoughts to himself. Woody was eighty-some years old by his own best estimation, leathered and shrivelled and spindly as a shrub, but he had been a top hand in his day, riding point on cattle-drives from Texas. He had broken every bone in his body, at one time or another — so it was said, and there was nothing in his posture to dispute it. But he was a man of freedom and the open range, and had no great fondness for the jackals of authority.

"My best regards to your intended, darlin'," Lige said, sardonic.

The wind had come up, with evening. A prowling mutter, gusting from time to time to sweep up grit from the street and fling it into the eye. In the desert beyond the outskirts of the town, it would be gathering force, howling with vengeance down the arroyos and setting the dust-devils spinning.

The air in Santa Rosita had changed, as well. Across the street, two townsmen glared sidelong at the shackled outlaw, before sloping in through the bat-wing doors of the Gemstone Saloon.

Deak Roby had been drinking there for several hours. The knuckles on his right fist were scraped and raw, a fact of which he was reminded each time he raised his glass. This lifted his mood, but only somewhat.

Shortly after seven p.m., a rider had come in from one of the ranches east of the County line. This was a man named Enoch Staunton, a drifter and gun-hand who was known to hire out his services to moneyed interests. He also had direct knowledge concerning the outlaw Dillashay. "He's a bottom-dealing gambler and a horse-thief," Enoch Staunton had said. "And that's just the start of it. He shot a man, two months ago, in Arizona. That fella lived — just barely — but them others didn't."

"What others?" Deak Roby said.

"Them others he shot, elsewhere. While robbing folks and terrorizing women."

Voices exclaimed, about them. Enoch Staunton had drawn an audience at the bar.

"Terrorizing *women?*" Deak Roby demanded.

"Countless of 'em. Widows and gals—he's famous for it, everywhere he's been."

"You're certain of this?"

"Hell, yes. 'Course I'm certain. Would I say it, otherwise?"

2.

"Look at me," Strother said. "No, let me see you." He lifted up his lantern. "Turn your face."

By lantern-light, the bruises were purple.

"Deacon Roby did this?" he demanded.

Lige did not reply.

Strother said grimly, "That man's time will come. A time always comes, for men like Deacon Roby."

It was later that same evening. Strother had gone to the courthouse to relieve Woody McQuatt from sentry duty. In the makeshift cell on the second floor, Lige sat on the cot, leg-irons chained once again to the iron ring.

Setting the lantern down, Strother stood by the window, looking out into the night. Light spilled from the Gemstone Saloon across the street. Dark voices spilled with it.

"Why?" Strother said at last. He spoke with great weariness. "Why did you have to come here, Lige? Of all places?"

"'My Roman,'" Lige said. "That's what she called you. Remember? The priestess Cydippe, our beautiful, brain-cracked Mama. My fucking Roman."

Strother very nearly smiled. So it seemed to Lige, though this could have been a trick of shadow.

"I'm tired," Lige said. "That's why I came. I fought with you, then I fought with the whole damned world. I'm just worn out."

Very slightly, Strother nodded.

"You could speak for me, big brother. You could do that. Take my side."

Strother said, "All right."

"You mean that?"

"Yes."

Hope kindled. "You can fix this, Strother. I know you can. Talk to the Sheriff, when he gets back — tell him to put a word in with the Governor."

"Can't do that. But I'll speak up at your trial."

"My *trial?* No, see, that's not what I'm—"

"I'll stand as a character witness. Do my best."

"Jesus Christ!" Lige's distress was keen, almost startling.

Strother said, doggedly: "What more could you expect? I swore an oath."

There was silence. When Lige spoke again, his voice was wormwood. "Straight and true, eh? Straight and true. Always and ever, pulling straight and true."

"I swore to uphold the law. You knew that, Lige — before you came here."

"And what about Hanging Tree Ridge, brother? What law were you upholding, when you rode up to kill the Collards?"

A change had come upon Strother, subtle but profound. The whole of him stiffened: all that great height, the slope-shouldered power.

"I went there to find *one* Collard," he said. "I was looking for Meshach."

"And you couldn't find him, could you? So you killed all the rest instead."

"State your proof."

"Proof? I've got none. No one has. But I heard what they found there, afterward." Lige leaned forward, just a little. The chain scuffed against the floor and rattled. "They found Harris Collard hanging from a tree, with old Judge Zebulon next to him. That hideous old man. Someone hauled him out of that wheeled contraption, where he sat on the porch in his prune-shat drawers, and hung him up right next to his fat fucking son."

Strother stared out the window, into the night.

"Don't misunderstand me, brother," Lige said. "I don't criticize. I'd've cheered you on, if I'd been there. I'd've whooped in celebration. We'd've done it together—the two of us, united in joyful purpose. I believe we might have lifted our voices in song."

Lige's voice could be beautiful, when he wished. There was dark music in it. His smile was sweet and serene and insinuating. "But the rest of it," he said. "The rest of the killing that was done that afternoon—well, some of the rest was not such cause for singing, maybe."

The smile began to grow reflective. Sorrowful, even. "The house was burnt to the ground, and there were two more bodies in the woods. That's according to Cleve Hunsperger. You recollect Cleve? Lived a few miles from the Collard place. He rode up when he saw the birds, circling and circling over the ridge. Animals had been at the bodies in the woods. Cleve supposed it must have been the youngest Collard boys—Joey and Sam. Right little sons of bitches, the both of them. Just the kind to open fire on a rider coming up the trail. They'd have tried to back-shoot him—that'd be my guess. And they'd get what was coming to them, in return. Still and all, it's not like they were grown men, really.

"And Ruth Collard? Fat Harris's poor wife? Cleve found her inside the burnt-out house. The body was so badly burned that Cleve couldn't say what had happened—whether she'd been shot first, or whether she'd just been inside that house when it caught fire. Hell, maybe she set the fire herself. Burnt herself to a cinder out of grief, or else—who can say?—out of pure relief to be finished with this life. All those years of toil and tribulation—labouring in the house and the fields all day, and all night in bed with old fat Harris grunting away on top. Yes, I can see how she'd set that fire and then weep with joy at her own deliverance. Melancholy prospect, nonetheless—poor Ruth, making such an end."

Strother stared out the window some more, into the night.

Lige said, "'Course, Cleve Hunsperger never saw the deeds being done. The killer could have been anyone at all. Hell, the killings that went on in those mountains? Back then, under cover of the War? Scores being settled and people being and hung and God only knows what-all else." Lige leaned forward some more. The chain rattled again. "But it wasn't anyone, brother. It was you."

Strother's face in the lantern-light was grey.

Lige said: "The granny-woman, though—Drusilla Smoak. She wasn't there, was she? Shame. She's no doubt drawing breath to this very day. And so is Meshach Collard. He was in Tennessee, when he heard the news. You knew that already, since you went after him."

Imperceptibly, Strother nodded. "I went after him." His voice was very low.

"Shack Collard enlisted," Lige said. "Or so I heard."

Strother nodded again. "Early in '62. A Tennessee unit—the Confederate side. Then he deserted. He was with Quantrill's Raiders in '63—I know that for a fact. He rode with Bloody Bill in the raid on Lawrence, Kansas, where they slaughtered two hundred Lincolnite civilians. He was in Missouri for a time, just after the War ended. But he was gone again before I got there."

Lige widened his eyes, as a man may do in admiration. "You've made quite the study of that bastard. I declare, brother—you are a mighty scholar on the subject. Our beautiful, brain-cracked Mama would be proud. Still and all—you never did find him, did you?"

"Not yet."

"Any notion where he is?"

"Not as of this moment."

"Well, I do."

Strother stood stone-still. "Is that the truth?"

"It is." Lige leaned forward, even closer. "And I could help you."

"Don't you lie to me. You know where I could find him?"

"Where *we* could find him. We could do this together."

Strother turned. "Tell me where he is," he said.

"First turn me loose."

"Can't do that, Lige."

"I'm your *brother,* you son of a bitch!"

And something wavered in Strother's eyes. Lige saw it; he was sure of that. And it wasn't just a trick of shadow in the lantern-light.

"I'll tell you if you turn me loose, big brother. We'll do this together. You have my word."

"Purcell!"

The shout came from the street, outside the window. Deak Roby's voice, thick with whiskey. "You in there, Purcell? With that brother of yours? Well, then fetch that bastard out—or we're comin' in!"

Other voices bayed in approbation.

-FIFTEEN-

The Accounting of Barry Weaver

San Francisco, 1892

1.

THE OLD MAN did not take to the bottle again, even as time went by. And he didn't move back out of Rose's flat. He'd be there, inside, with Em'ly, when you arrived at the door.

Sometimes they'd venture outside together: his long slow strides, and Little Em'ly sheltering in the lee. He'd taken to washing on a daily basis; had brushed off his coat and trimmed his hair and beard. Or else Em'ly had done this for him: combing out such tangles as would yield, and cutting out the worst of what remained, the brambles and locusts, so that he looked less with each passing day like a Bible Prophet gone to ruin.

Mainly, though, they stayed close to home. Little Em'ly was very far from shedding her terror, regardless of her faith in Mr. Lem. And the old man for his part seemed strongly disposed to avoid the public eye, having no desire to be sidelonged and queried, and still less to be flat-out asked his name and whence he hailed. Oh, his past was as a haunted wood, writhing with serpents; such deeds had been done there, far from sunlight. I knew that for a fact, and knew as well that I'd hardly glimpsed the tenth part of it.

In the night he would cry out. He'd wake up moaning and slick with sweat. Prairie Rose confided that to me. "What does he say?" I asked her one afternoon. Because I was curious—of course I was. "When he cries out, are there names?"

"I expect there prob'ly are," Rose said.

"Such as?"

"I try my best not to listen. And if I did hear names, I wouldn't tell you, Barry—you, nor anybody else."

"Lige," I said.

We were standing on the street, outside the tenement. It was late May. The air was warm and birds were singing.

"Elijah," I repeated. "Does he say that name?"

Rose hesitated. Then scowled. "Why don't you ask him, Barry? I expect he might tell you all about his nightmares, if he reckoned it to be your business."

The old man was inside, sitting on the stairs with Em'ly. I found them after Rose had trudged on her way.

He was on the half-landing between floors, and the gal crouched at his back. They were both of them in shadow. The stairway stank of dogshit and old urine and whatever the tenants down below had been boiling, cabbage and onions and God knows what-all else. But it was quiet here, and cool in the rising warmth of the afternoon. Light slanted across them from one small window, but only a little of it.

"Hello, there," I called up to them, arriving.

She'd been whispering something in his ear, as a child might do, confiding in her dear old Granddad. Or else possibly like a fledgling Fury—though that particular analogy did not occur to me at the time. She broke off as she saw me.

"It's just Weaver," I added, amiably. In case they couldn't see clearly in the gloom.

"'Afternoon," the old man said.

Em'ly shrank more closely against him, and whispered something else.

"What's that she's saying?" I asked cheerfully, thinking maybe the observation had been meant for all three of us to share.

"Em'ly says, she don't believe she likes you much."

"Ah," said I. Feeling just that tich wrong-footed—as one does, when answers come back more blunt than one had expected. "Well, then."

I waited a moment for the gal to grin shyly, or for the old man to chuckle and confess that he'd made this up. But they didn't. The look Em'ly angled down at me was fraught with unease. After a moment, she detached herself and withdrew up the stairs, reticulating into deeper shadow and letting herself into the triple-bolted flat.

The old man watched till she was safely inside. Then he looked back to me. "It's your look," he said.

"My look?"

"She thinks there's something shifty in it. Maybe she's right— I couldn't say, just yet. I expect we'll see."

I worked up a little chuckle of my own. "Well, I can hardly blame the child."

"Blame her? Blame her for what?"

"Well, for—"

"What cause have you to be attaching blame?"

"I only meant—"

"Who *are* you, anyway?"

He'd leaned suddenly forward, his one eye gun-barrelling.

"It's me," I said. "It's just—it's Weaver. I'm your friend."

It was the strangest thing. But for just a moment, it was possible to think that the old man didn't know me—that the look on his face was plain confusion. It passed, though. He blinked me into clearer perspective.

"Weaver," he said. "So you are."

"I'm just saying, the gal has a right to be fearful," I said. "Of men in general—of anyone. Considering all she's been through."

"True enough."

"I mean, my God, the brutality..."

"'Course, she didn't say 'men in general.' What she said was, specifically you."

But he leavened it with a wintry grin.

Other times, though, he was friendly, even warm. Once or twice we went out walking, in the evening. He moved gingerly still, not fully recovered as yet from his set-to with the Rent Collector and his thugs, and was reluctant to venture too far afield, with Em'ly alone in the flat. But he'd stretch his legs.

And you know what? I liked the old man. The realization startled me. It seemed almost an impertinence, to *like* such a man — the shambling one-eyed revenant of Strother Purcell. It seemed damned close to presumption. You'd as well presume to like the second cousin of Odin, or Goliath's less loquacious nephew, or the shade of grim old Abraham himself, creaking sandal-shod down Sinai after his latest disputation with Jehovah. But I did — I liked him. And I guess I wanted him to like me back.

"You're something," I said to him. "That's the truth. And that poor child thinks the moon and the stars of you."

"Hmm," he said, sounding gruff. But he wasn't displeased. After another while, he said: "It would've been a fine thing, to have a daughter. I do think that, sometimes."

"Well, who can say?" I winked as I said it, man to man. "It might turn out you do."

"My time of life? Not likely."

"No," I said. "What I meant... All those years, travelling from one place to the next. A man never knows..." I probably waggled an eyebrow, as a stimulus to comprehension.

"I know what you meant, Mr. Weaver. I was preferring to let it pass."

"Ah."

Walking next to him, you felt easily abashed.

He didn't care for insinuating humour; I was coming to understand that. I was coming to understand a few things about him, though he was hardly—as you might say—an open book. When he was asked about his past, the answers did not leap forth in sparkling streams.

"And you never married?" I said to him.

"Nope."

"Never fell in love?"

"Don't remember."

"Oh, come on, now—everybody falls in love. There must have been *someone*. All those years?"

"Maybe," he said. "Once. Long time ago. We won't talk about that."

We'd come to a turning in the street. The evening sun was low in front of us. The old man flinched away from it, lifting an arm to shade his face. He was still troubled by bright light—that blow he'd taken, in the melee. Terrible headaches would come upon him; he was laid low by one of them for a full day and a half. So I'd been told by Prairie Rose. He had lain on the day-bed with a wet rag over his eyes. His face beneath the Bible-prophet's beard had been chalk-white, Rose said, and beaded with perspiration; it was no better than parchment-grey thirty-six hours later.

"And there isn't going to be any book, Mr. Weaver. So you can leave off with such questions."

I thought to myself: *We shall see about that*. Because the book I would write about him would be respectful. More than that, it would be *mighty*. It would be nothing at all like anything I had written before—if he'd just learn to trust me.

"You've been married, though," he said.

A statement, not a question. Evidently Rose had told him.

"I was," I admitted. "Still am, I guess. Assuming she's alive. She probably is. That was a long time ago, out East."

"And a daughter?"

Ahead of us, across the street, there were children playing—a rabble of boys, trying their utmost to seem rough and ready, the better to impress a fair-haired girl in a dress looking out of a window. It was one of those wide bay windows they had in San Francisco houses, on the second floor, with lace curtains pulled open on either side. I looked in that direction for awhile.

"She'd've been—oh—two, three years old, last time I saw her," I said. "Turns out I had to leave."

He one-eyed me the question, looking down. "Had to?"

"Well, sometimes things don't work out, exactly."

"Sometimes things get hard, you mean."

I might have dignified that with a reply, if I could have thought of one. The fair-haired girl in the dress had receded, leaving the boys on the street to show off for the benefit of an empty window.

"I guess we make mistakes," I said at length, "from time to time."

"I guess we do."

He started forward again, veering eastward, away from the sunset. I kept pace and we found ourselves trudging in silence, for awhile. The past will do that, if you let it creep up on you. It'll spread out its shadow like the wings of oncoming night, and there you are, in gathering darkness.

I said: "Tell me about your brother."

"I don't have a brother."

"You do, though. At least, you did."

The old man said shortly, "I don't talk about him."

–SIXTEEN–

From *High Crimes of the Outlaw Dillashay*

Santa Rosita, New Mexico, 1874

THERE WERE TWENTY MEN on the street in the night, milling about Deputy Deak Roby. Strother saw this, through the small barred window. So did Lige, behind him.

"D'you hear me, Purcell? Fetch that fucker forth!" Deak Roby roared.

They'd all been drinking, most of them for hours. They had firearms, and torches.

Lige had seen such men before, and such a mood upon them. That long-ago day when Bobby Collard rode off with the mare, and Jacob Dillashay raised the hue and cry and the Holcombes. He said: "Strike the leg-irons off me, brother. Do it now."

Strother called out through the window: "You go on home, boys. Go home, and sleep it off."

More men were hurrying down the street, to join. Someone had fetched a rope.

"Strike the damned leg-irons off." Lige's face was pale. "Give me a gun. We can stand them off together."

"I can't do that," Strother said.

"You son of a bitch. You'd let them hang me?"

*

Hanging was too good for the likes of a horse-thief, and most especially for this one. Such was the epiphany that had come to Deak Roby at the Gemstone, drunk on whiskey and resentment and surrounded by good men and true.

Now here they were, in the street. Two dozen, now — and more still coming. It was Deak Roby's finest hour. Deak knew this, even as he lived it. Ballads would be composed about him, in this hour. Statues would be erected.

"Ten seconds, Purcell! Then we're comin'!"

Torchlight snaked and flickered in the night. The mob was coiled about him, a single living entity, and Deak Roby was its beating heart.

"D'you hear me? One … two … three …"

Deputy Rectitude appeared without warning at the count of seven, more suddenly than Deak had anticipated. And he came around the side of the courthouse building, not out the front door.

Deak was startled. He lurched just a little, in turning. He stumbled for an instant, tangle-footed, reaching for his sixgun. It was a fine one, too: a Colt's .45-calibre Frontier 1871 model — the Peacemaker — purchased at considerable expense, and loaded with the very cartridges that had recently set fire to the rabid, bat-bit dog. Strother Purcell in the glow of torchlight had an eight-gauge shotgun, which he pointed at Deak directly.

"If I was you, Deak, I don't b'lieve I'd move."

The mob gave a wrathful exclamation. It came out somewhat strangled. Deak Roby stood almost as still as the statue that might otherwise have been commissioned.

Strother Purcell stood statue-still himself. His voice was cold. "First thing you can do for me, Deak, you can leave off reaching for that Colt. Then you can tell that fella behind me to set down the rifle."

Deak licked his lips, discovering they'd gone dry. "What fella?"

"The one with back-shooting on his mind."

Strother spoke without looking around. Enoch Staunton stood on a rooftop alongside the courthouse, dramatically backlit by the moon.

PART THREE

He had taken careful aim with his rifle at a spot midway between Purcell's shoulder blades.

"Go ahead and try it, Purcell," Enoch Staunton said. "You're a dead man if your finger twitches."

"An' you're next," wheezed an ancient voice.

It was Woody McQuatt. The old cowboy had crabbed his way out of the shadows beside the Gemstone. His rifle was nearly as tall as he was, but he aimed it remarkably steady, and had Enoch Staunton dead to rights.

Woody's initiative came as a surprise to Strother, as well as to the others. Strother did not complain, though.

"You carry on, Cap'n," Woody McQuatt called to him. "I'll shoot this one if'n he blinks."

"I thank you," said Strother Purcell.

It seemed to Deak Roby that he might yet seize back the advantage. He had thirty men about him, after all. Most of them armed, and all of them primed with righteous wrath.

"What are you waiting for?" Deak demanded of them. "Rush 'im!"

No one seemed in quite such a hurry.

"It's a shotgun," Deak exclaimed. "The bastard's only got two loads!"

"First load's for you, Deak," Strother said. "Leaves one for someone else. Any takers, or do I choose the volunteer?"

Looks were exchanged. Imprecations were muttered, and fearsome oaths. There did not appear to be takers.

"G'wan home, fellas," Strother said. "Fun's over."

He continued to stand guard for some goodly while, after the last of them had sloped away into darkness. At length he was satisfied that the threat had passed.

Lantern-light still glowed in the window of Lige's cell, above him on

221

the second floor. Strother saw this as he turned to go back inside; the sight brought both reassurance and a melancholy ache. The courthouse building was otherwise dark as he made his way up the stairs. Reaching the top he found the cell door ajar, light bleeding out through the gap and pooling on the floorboards.

This gave him pause. He had shut the door behind him when he'd left; surely he had bolted it, as well.

"Lige?"

His voice echoed, hollow, in the stillness.

"Elijah," he said, more loudly.

No reply.

Strother kicked the door wide, raising the eight-gauge as he entered. The lantern, set by the window, lit an empty room. The chain and shackles lay strewn on the floor, as ineffectual as shed snake-skin.

It would remain for many years unclear who'd been responsible.

Strother's first, sick certainty was: the gal. She must have done it—his friend, Maria Teresa Lestander. But old Woody McQuatt's whereabouts had gone unaccounted for also, after he'd stood down the gunman Enoch Staunton. This occurred to Strother afterward.

Just now, wheeling out of the makeshift cell, Strother glimpsed his brother's face. It was grim in the half-light of the hallway. Strother levelled the eight-gauge; too late.

Instinct saved his life. He ducked back just as Lige's bullet shivered the doorframe, driving shards and splinters into his eye. The pain was blinding and the world was black and Strother dropped like a sack.

—

Whoever had set Lige Dillashay free, it was Lige who subsequently freed the others, the pair of prisoners in the cell downstairs—the ones who had given their names as Smith and Miller. "Smith" was a lean, leering man in middle age with a cornpone voice and a grin like a tumbledown churchyard. "Miller" was hardly more than a boy, with dirty yellow hair and a straggle of unsuccessful beard and the sweet, slow smile of a dead-eyed cherub. They had not previously known the outlaw Dillashay, but were pleased as all get-out to be making his acquaintance now. "Whoo-ee, Fletch," the cherub was heard to crow, as the mayhem commenced. "Nothin' stopping us now!"

These two were the authors of the worst carnage that night, though Lige was hardly blameless. So Strother came to understand in the interminable darkness that followed, lying in a curtained room with both eyes tightly wrapped. The outlaws had burst out of the courthouse together. Deak Roby chose this exact moment to lurch back through the doors of the Gemstone Saloon, which he had ordered to remain open until Deputy Goddamned Roby said it could close. The first shot struck him exactly between the eyes, enabling the Deputy for one last instant to stand like the statue he had so aspired to. Then down went Deak, to the very great sorrow of no one in particular.

Maria Teresa Lestander would have been secretly relieved. Such was Strother Purcell's conviction, and he carried it with him ever after. Wherever she had been ten minutes previous, the gal was at her father's house now. She stepped out onto the front porch, drawn by the commotion on the street: the outlaws wheeling on stolen horses, men shouting and flailing their arms and shooting wildly. No one could even be sure who had fired the shot. But it left her huddled and horribly still, the night wind plucking at the hem of her frock and her eyes wide open and unblinking.

Strother Purcell's bandages were unwrapped on the morning of the third day. Rising from the bed, he demanded to know how many men would ride with him, to hunt down his brother and the outlaws he had freed.

Few men would meet his one remaining eye.

He rode out regardless.

–SEVENTEEN–

From *The Roadhouse Chroniclesof Thomas Skiffings*

Near Hell's Gate
Winter, 1876

IT WAS ALMOST DAWN when Billie climbed back down the ladder, her legs white and bare beneath the blanket she'd wrapped round herself, padding on sagging woollen socks into the grievance of Cousin Fletch's stare and the desolation of her younger brother.

With daylight the wind came up again. Billie had taken on a new role, it seemed. She dared to essay the Pirate King's Consort, bantering with the Man from Decatur and brazenly ignoring the sidelong looks of the others. Finding himself beside her, Gimp Tom essayed an insolent look of his own. "Well, aren't we the Queen of Spain," he said, not loud enough for anyone else to hear.

"Not 'we,'" she replied. There was an archness about her, but also a desolation of her own. "Just one of us."

It must surely drive them all mad.

So Gimp Tom thought, as one day degenerated into the next, and still the wind would not stop. On and on, that godalmighty wind: shrieking and moaning and shaking the house, reaching down deep inside your skull where the rodents gnaw and chitter.

It had already driven his sister batshit.

"Go comfort the boy," the Man from Decatur would tell her. So she would.

She'd sit by Dooley Sprewell, who had taken a turn from poorly to ominous. His wound, when Cousin Fletch inspected it, was angry with discolouration. The sick-sweet waft had become a stench that pushed the older outlaw back, and disinclined him to look at it again. So Billie conjured for Dooley images of the Cariboo.

She had not been nearly so far north herself. She had never in fact been north of John McCutcheon's roadhouse. But she'd heard tales from travellers who had, teamsters and packers who trudged the Wagon Road all the way to Quesnellemouth and the Barkerville goldfields. She conjured for Dooley's benefit the intensity of a cold that split pine trees in half, from the sap freezing solid inside—tall trees shattering with a sound like rifle-fire. The rumble and groan of ice blocks ten feet thick, shifting in the frozen lakes. Cold that would freeze the spray from river rapids, so's it would fall one second later as crystals of ice; cold that would freeze up your fingers, black as spruce.

"Oh, Lordy-gawd," said Dooley Sprewell, wanly. He lay haggard by the stove as she told him tales, a shipwrecked boy who would never reach the sea.

At night Tom lay shipwrecked himself as his sister climbed up the ladder to the loft. Blocking his ears as the wind told tales of how it ended, and always would, for the likes of two orphan children and their Uncle John, trapped in a roadhouse with men such as Cousin Fletch and the Man from Decatur.

The man who came hunting them was worse. Billie had this on excellent authority, and confided it in Gimp Tom. "The brother," she said. "He claims to be a lawman—but he's got no jurisdiction. That makes him no better'n a bounty hunter."

Gimp Tom could think of men much worse than any bounty

hunter. Outlaws themselves were five times worse: killers and fugitives, such as those they had amongst them right this minute.

"I call it low," Billie said. "I call it lower than dirt—to hunt down your own blood, for the sake of filthy lucre."

She'd rehearsed this in her head. Billie was like that. Essaying declarations, trying on roles. Seeing what would fit.

It occurred to him that his sister had been batshit to begin with, long before the outlaws came. Batshit deranged, as we all of us are deranged, and always were, and always will be, awaiting only the time and the place and the circumstance, and above all that most special companion, to license us in every batshit derangement that we've secretly yearned to indulge since the day we first drew breath.

The Man from Decatur's moods grew more extreme. He would lapse for an hour into seething stillness, then lurch to his feet and pace, stopping at each window to stoop and peer.

"He won't be comin'," Cousin Fletch said. "Not today—not in this. I misbelieve he even crossed the Line."

At first they'd avoided the use of names and specifics, from which Gimp Tom had drawn a degree of reassurance. You don't take such care around hosts who won't survive your departure. This was logic. Gimp Tom had faith in logic.

"He crossed," the Man from Decatur said. "A week ago—not twelve hours after we did." As if the Canada boundary had been drawn in black ink, and he'd had secret reports as to its crossing. Borne to him by ravens, battling their way north against the wind.

Cousin Fletch shook his head. He was in his way another man of logic. "Posse wouldn't follow him, Lige. Whole 'nother country."

"Suppose he cares about that? He crossed alone."

"He's a man. Men got limits."

"My brother don't."

At first, Cousin Fletch had lived in hope that the gal might yet be shared amongst the outlaws. This hope having curdled, his notioning turned instead to defective boys. At such times he would take out his bowie knife.

It had a blade one foot long. An instrument of fearsome precision, ideally suited to all duties relating to vivisection. Useful as well for shaving down corns, which task Cousin Fletch would perform after peeling off his woollen socks and hanging them over the woodstove, the ripe-cheese odour of foot-rot and the reek of soggy sheep overwhelming for a time all other stenches of six human souls confined too closely together.

"Go see t' them poor beasts," he would say abruptly to Uncle John. McCutcheon might be slinking past with a bucket; trying in general to remain as invisible as a tall, spare, gangling man can be. Uncle John would stand for a moment paralyzed, all movement suspended save for a spasmodic bob-bobbing of his Adam's apple, thinking of all the reasons why he should stay right here with his poor, dead sister's son.

"The horses, you fucking eejit."

"Right you are," Uncle John would agree. Bundling on his greatcoat and boots he would slope out into the teeth of that wind, telling himself that in preserving the horses he was preserving the children as well: if those horses should perish, the outlaws would never ride off at all.

Cousin Fletch would recommence carving his corns. He would suck his teeth, studying Gimp Tom with slantways malevolence, as if considering all the sundry ways that a man with a knife and a boy and time on his hands might while away the hours.

"So what if he crossed that Line?" Cousin Fletch said abruptly, the fourth afternoon. "Let the bastard come."

The Man from Decatur had been stooped by the west-facing window. It offered a prospect across storm-blasted pines, with a churn of rapids snaking through the river ice below.

"If he's out there, Lige, then the cold's kilt the fucker already. They's a thousand ways to die in cold like that. Take my word."

Cousin Fletch spoke as a man who had devoted a lifetime to avoiding such cold. A man who had never for one moment forgotten the lesson that his own late Daddy had taught him: avoid such cold. His Daddy had illustrated this lesson in dramatic fashion, by blundering into a Kansas winter while relocating in haste from more southerly climes, where law enforcement authorities had placed a jaundiced interpretation upon his recent activities. Ambushed by a January blizzard, he froze solid as a block of ice in circumstances of great anguish, leaving his kinfolk no consolation beyond the certainty that the son of a bitch was dead.

"And even if the cold don't kill your brother," Cousin Fletch continued, "for some reason contrary to all good sense, then he's still a dead man when he gets here. That solitary bastard, on his own, against the both of us? Two compadres, Lige."

"Three," whispered Dooley Sprewell. He was still huddled by the stove. "Three compadres, Fletch. Don't you be forgetting your friend Dooley."

His face had taken on a tinge of grey, as you see in old wasp's nests and in dying men.

"I stand corrected," Cousin Fletch said, "in my arithmetic. They is at this moment three compadres."

—

But they were wasting their sympathy, if they gave a second thought to Dooley's suffering. This was the opinion of the Man from Decatur, as passed on by Billie to Gimp Tom.

"That boy is the worst he ever rode with," she said.

They were at the creek fetching water. The fifth day had dawned more bitter with cold than any of the days before. Wind scythed down from the hills, whipping ice-hard crystals.

Dooley Sprewell had forced himself on gals, she said. Three separate times in the New Mexico Territory alone. "White gals, not even counting hoors. Two of 'em he left for dead. And those are just the ones as can be ascertained."

The Man from Decatur would not abide such usage of women, Billie said. He had told her so himself.

"And you believe him?"

"What reason would he have to lie?"

Tom thought, but did not say: *The same reason he has to lie to you about every other godalmighty thing.*

Or perhaps he didn't think that: not exactly, or not at the time. Perhaps he only thought of it years afterwards, when looking back on his young self he saw more clearly what a boy could not have been expected to understand, about the ways of this world and the men and women who are in it. Perhaps on that childhood morning by the creek, he thought only of how cruel the cold was and how bitter the wind, and how much he would give to have his sister back, the way she was before the outlaws came.

"Oh, I believe him," Billie said, in a tone of righteousness. "He does not abide that sort of a man."

The Man from Decatur misliked Dooley Sprewell for other causes also. There was a quality in Dooley that reminded him of someone

else, Billie said—some other fair-haired, laughing boy who'd taken
liberties. This galled the Man from Decatur most ferociously.

"So I reckon," she said, "that Dooley Sprewell deserves just as bad
as he gets."

She stood blade-thin against the winter wind as she passed this
judgement. Her lips were blue and her teeth as sharp as icicles. Returning to the roadhouse, she sat beside the stove by Dooley Sprewell, who
shuddered at the cold she brought in with her.

"Lordy-Gawd," he moaned, "it's perishing."

"Not like up North," she replied. "Where you're going."

It was a mighty thing, this power she had. Her brother could only
watch, and marvel. She sat for hours with young Dooley Sprewell, as
consoling as a mermaid on the rocks.

"Some day you'll pay three dollars just to see me," she told him.
"When I'm an actress on the stage, somewhere faraway from here.
Chicago, maybe, or New York. San Francisco. Three dollars just to
stand at the very back. But of course, you won't never be going to San
Francisco, will you? You won't be going south again. You'll be going
the other direction entirely."

So she conjured the North for him. In the names of those gals in
New Mexico, or wherever else it was, whatever the hell their names
might have been. And in judgement of all the bastards just like him.
All the men who ever made her terrified and small, from her Ma's
admirers right on down to her Uncle John, who would have loomed
in her doorway that same night if he'd durst.

"It can't be that cold," Dooley whispered. "There's nowheres on this
earth as cold as that. If there was, no one could ever know—they'd
be no one to survive."

"They don't, mainly," Billie assured him. "For the most part, it mainly kills 'em. The weak ones, anyway—the ones who aren't cut out to survive in cold like that. But who knows, Dooley? Maybe you'll get your strength back. You'll be strong."

Dooley Sprewell had taken no sustenance for days. His face was a skull with skin on.

"Miss Billie?" he said. "I done bad deeds."

"We all done bad things, Dooley. At one time or another."

"Not like me. I done such deeds, you couldn't even know."

It was late in the afternoon. The men had gone outside, Uncle John to batter through the ice and the outlaws to see to the horses in the barn. The wind had come up as the last light died away. That left Billie and Dooley alone by the stove—all alone in the world, and free to speak plain—with only Gimp Tom looking on from the shadows. So quiet and still they'd forgotten he existed.

"D'you b'lieve in the Lord?" Dooley said to Billie.

"'Course I do."

This was news to Gimp Tom.

"I b'lieve the Lord is watching, right this minute," Billie said. "Watching us and judging, the way He does."

Dooley had commenced to weep. "So do I," he whispered. "Oh, so do I. An' I swear—I'd hang myself sooner than freeze to death, if it wasn't for the thought I'd have to face Him."

"Oh, now," said Billie. "There, now. Maybe the Lord's forgiven you already."

"No," said Dooley. "If I b'lieved that, I'd go hang myself in the barn. If I had my strength."

—

Billie left him, a little time after that. Dooley lay weeping, alone. There was silence, except for the howling of that wind, and the hissing of smoke in the stovepipe.

Gimp Tom had looked on all this while, watching Dooley Sprewell. Now he sidled close. "Dooley?" he said. "God loves you. I believe that— I do. He's got a place in His heart for you, and it's warm." He leaned in even closer. "And I could help you, Dooley. If it ever come to that."

His sister could make her voice as soft as silk, when she chose. A way she had of pitching it low in the throat. Tom lacked this gift, as he did so many others. But he did his best to mimic it now.

"There's a rope out there in the barn," he whispered to Dooley Sprewell. "There's rafters and a bucket to stand on. If you truly saw the need, then I could help you."

–EIGHTEEN–

The Accounting of Barry Weaver

San Francisco, 1892

I BELIEVE IT WENT LIKE THIS:

The old man and the gal were venturing outside frequently, by that time. In the evening, you might see them strolling half a mile afield, or even more, the girl in the lee of her protector. They might even be seen in broad daylight on a public thoroughfare. Little Em'ly grew bolder with the old man beside her, though crowds would still unsettle. From to time she would stop stone-dead and shrink deeper into herself, as if some profile glimpsed in the crowd, or the timbre of a voice, had conjured dread.

From this the old man understood: Em'ly lived still in mortal terror of the Utah Brute. The Mormon's arm stretched out like Judgement, and the fist at the end of it was huge and hard.

"I'll be here," Old Lem said grimly, one night. "Whoever comes to call." He was speaking to Prairie Rose, Little Em'ly having retired to bed with the megrim. "Let me sort out any Mormons as need sorting."

Prairie Rose flushed at this. Her voice was brittle as glass. He would do no such thing, she said, nor even think it. "Chrissake, Lem — this isn't no Rent Collector."

"Nor am I."

"You don't know him. I do!"

She was at her needlework as they spoke, glasses perched on her nose. But her hands grew so unsteady that she had to set the work aside.

The Mormon feared no man at all, she said. The Mormon feared none but the devil—as well a sinner might who lived so steeped in wickedness. "And the devil might stand a chance," she said, "if ever it come to a mortal fight, between them." But Old Lem would stand no chance at all. He'd be broke and ground to bone-meal, bless his heart. "So let's have no more talk of this—not ever."

"Well," said Lem. He had grown very dark in his expression.

He likewise said no more, keeping to himself what thoughts he may have harboured, concerning the Brutes of this world. He did not say, not to Rose or to Em'ly, nor anyone else: there once was a man called Strother Purcell who might pay this Brute back what was coming to him, down to the penny.

Sometimes in twilight he would walk out alone.

He would stay strong. Stay keen. You never could be sure, what might be coming.

-NINETEEN-

Tyree

San Francisco, 1892

DEAR BILLIE, he wrote. *I see from the newspaper that you are in Silver City, Nevada. I hope and trust that you are well. I have thought of you often, these past 16 years. I have thought of you every day. Perhaps you have thought of me, also. Perhaps in your heart you have kept a small corner, where memories of a brother may still—*

Pathetic. Maundering and soggy and pathetic.

He crumpled the sheet of paper, and started again.

Dear Billie.

He crossed this out.

Billie. So you are alive. Well, I am, too. I'm in San Francisco. Your feelings as you read this will be mixed. But there is something that you need to know. It is important, and—

The bitterness welled up, catching him off guard with its intensity. Yes, he thought—his information was important. Crucial, even. But Christ on a crutch, after sixteen years? After all they had meant to each other, once?

His vision had blurred behind the huge, round spectacles, thick as the bottoms of Mason jars. His reflection in the window pane was woebegone and absurd. Rain streamed in turn down the outside of the window, obscuring the figures who hurried through the darkness along the street.

The night was unseasonably cold. Tyree shivered, despite the closeness of his room, which would be stuffy beyond bearing in high summer. He sat at his table by the window, with a bottle of cheap whiskey and a glass and an oil-lamp and his ink and pen and paper.

He tried again.

You just left, and you never once looked back. Not once. I could have come with you. Or you could have sent for me afterward. Well, I hope you've been happy with the path you chose, and I hope you found joy along the way—except I don't, Billie, I really don't. I hope you trod in desolation, every step, and wept bitter tears in the night. Why should you be better off than me? We did it together, that thing we done.

Billie, this is what I think, so I'll just say it. I think you are the worst person I ever knew, excepting only for myself. I think you are heartless and faithless and cold as ice. I wish I could see you one more time. I wish that very much.

He signed this with a bitter flourish. Then he crumpled it up.

But she needed to know. Not so much that he was here, in San Francisco. No, what she truly needed to know was that Strother Purcell was here as well, still alive—through some miracle of God or of the devil—though dreadfully altered, in case this should resolve her to stay far, far away herself, for the rest of her life. Or else prompt her to come here directly, in hope of making some manner of peace with the past, and all that had been so irrevocably done.

He reached for one final sheet of paper.

*To the actress as calls herself Miss Arabella Skye: I am alive. I am in San Francisco. So is **he**.*

He signed it: *T. (your brother).*

237

–TWENTY–

The Accounting of Barry Weaver

San Francisco, 1892

1.

WYATT EARP had seen him walking along Sutton Street. I learned this from Josephine Sarah "Sadie" Marcus, and it gave me an awful turn.

"Not half the turn," she assured me, "as it give my husband."

Wyatt had been stepping out the front door of a gentlemen's club, she said. He had been meeting with certain Leading Men of Enterprise to discuss Unspecified Investment Opportunities, the details of which Sadie was not at liberty to disclose. "'Cause then they wouldn't be Unspecified, would they?" But she gave me to understand that these were remarkable in scope and dimension.

This might or might not contain a grain of truth. Facts were malleable in the hands of Missus Earp, who was assiduous as ever in polishing them into Legend. But to hell with Unspecified Investment Opportunities — this was hardly a concern of mine.

"*The* Strother Purcell?" I exclaimed, working up a show of astonishment. "The shootist?"

Oh, yes, she said. Just a glimpse, but it was him. Years older, but the very man. Strother Purcell himself, gone gaunt and grey, and possessing one ocular orb fewer than he had done in days of yore — although she would not personally say it was "*the* Strother Purcell." It was more to her mind a case of "*the* Wyatt Earp," glimpsing for half a second the profile of a lesser lawman entirely. But yes, it was without a doubt *that* Strother Purcell.

"But—it can't have been," I said.

And to myself, I thought: *Oh, Christ. My poor, old, one-eyed friend does not need such rumours to commence. And neither does the man who might yet become his biographer; to wit, the Reverend Weaver's astonished-seeming boy.*

"It can't have been Strother Purcell," I repeated. "Why, Strother Purcell is dead."

"Or so it's been *presumed,*" said Wyatt Earp, without looking up from his newspaper.

We were in the café at the Plaza Hotel, amidst breakfast smells and the clink of cutlery. Here Wyatt was wont to take his toast and eggs. It was a decent class of café, much favoured by Elite Persons of the Business World and halfway up Nob Hill, though surprisingly reasonable in price. So Sadie had confided, in the note she'd sent inviting me to join them.

The note had not come out of the blue. I'd made intermittent efforts to re-establish diplomatic relations, following the Ichabod fiasco. Sadie and I had bumped into each other on the street, once or twice. Purely by accident, you understand—and because I'd made a point of lingering near their house from time to time, just for the chance to tip my hat. A writer relies on his contacts, and it could surely do no harm to re-cultivate the Earps.

Sadie was a political creature herself, and apparently saw no need to alienate a man who might eventually stumble into success in the scribbling dodge. Stranger things had happened, after all. And I began to suspect that the Earps had their own motive for inviting me to breakfast—though it had nothing to do with this sighting of Strother Purcell. That had been a random bit of gossip, to them. I was the one who'd been riveted by it.

"Purcell has been *presumed* dead," the future Lion of Tombstone said now. "By others."

"But not by you?"

"My husband," Sadie Marcus said, "was a lawman. And lawmen don't presume."

"Yes they do," said her husband.

"Some of 'em do indeed," Sadie amended. She executed this reversal with shining eyes and vast integrity. "Some lawmen presume in shocking ways, Mr. Weaver. It would curl your hair, the way some lawmen presume. But not my husband."

"I never seen the corpse myself," said Wyatt. "So I couldn't be prepared to say one way or t'other." He eyed me impressively, then receded behind his newspaper, giving it a shake for punctuation.

The future Lion was sitting by himself at an adjacent table, as he had been when I arrived ten minutes previous. Several papers were spread out before him, and Earp pored sagely over each one in turn. "My husband must keep himself abreast of business developments," Sadie Marcus had confided, leading me to a smaller table of our own. It was getting past the breakfast hour, and the café was half-empty. I had of course been gracious.

"But you have no doubt that you'd recognize Strother Purcell?" I hazarded now, lifting my voice just a little and addressing the great man.

"No doubt at all."

"So . . . you actually *knew* him? In the old days?"

"I met him. Once. A lawman don't forget a face like that."

"Some might," Sadie Marcus said. "But not my husband."

"In Dodge," said Wyatt Earp. "July of 1873. I'd of shook his hand that day, if he stuck it out. Wouldn't shake it now."

"Alive *or* dead," said Sadie. "Neither way." Her gaze was luminescent in its integrity, her lovely eyes at full-wide for my benefit.

I'll confess that I hardly noticed. "Why not?" I asked the future Lion. "What did he do?"

Wyatt eyed me portentously. "That man hunted down his brother.

Rode fifteen hunnerd miles, for a chance to kill him. That was never Law—that was plain vengeance."

"But—you did the exact same thing," I exclaimed—or almost did. I caught myself just in time. "What I mean to say is, you rode out yourself, when your brother was shot."

Wyatt Earp said: "That was different."

"It was not the same, Mr. Weaver," said Sadie Marcus. A quiver of reproach now sounded in her voice: that I could be so wrong about her husband. "It was entirely the opposite. My husband was never vengeful. He was resolute. And any man who seeks t'know my husband, must understand that. And especially any writer who might write about him, some day."

So there it was—the reason I'd been invited to breakfast. They hadn't given up on my proposal, after all. My heart ought to have leapt, I suppose—except somehow it didn't.

The future Lion was leaning forward, setting his newspaper aside. "I rode with heavy heart, Mr. Weaver. To bring my brother's murderers to book. Purcell rode *against* his brother." He tapped with his forefinger upon the tabletop, for emphasis. The famous mustache walrused indignation. "I do not stand with them as turn against their kin."

It was of course rehearsed. I was watching a performance. In his way, Wyatt Earp was as consummate an actor as his consort, who sat swelling now with tremulous admiration. If Sadie were to swell one half-inch farther, buttons would burst. They would ping from the front of her frock like bullets; bosoms would come bounding free in celebration of Wyatt Earp.

This was my cue to murmur something duly reverent, and drivel some allusion to what an honour it would be to write about Wyatt Earp. I'd have done it, too—God knows, Young Weaver had never scrupled to grovel. But that's when the realization truly settled: I didn't give a damn about Wyatt Earp or his deeds or his insufferable mustache.

"Tell me about Strother Purcell," I said.

"He told you already," Sadie exclaimed. "My husband does not stand with such men. And more than that, he don't *abide* 'em."

"I do not," Earp said.

"If my husband encountered him on the street again, he would say so to his face."

"Now, Sadie," Earp murmured, with dignity. "The man ain't here to defend himself, and we won't speak ill of—"

"No, Wyatt, I will *not* be still. It's the truth of the matter, and I'll say it. Mr. Weaver? If Strother Purcell walked through that door right now, my husband would offer to thrash him."

Earp looked.

Oh, yes he did. His eyes went swiftly to the door. It was the reflex of an instant—but it happened. I saw something else, too: a flicker in those famous eyes that was actual apprehension.

"How good was he?" I asked.

"What?"

"Purcell. How good was he, in a gunfight?"

Earp shifted in his chair. "Couldn't say," he said. "Never saw him throw down."

"But based on reputation. How would he have done—against John Ringo, say, or even Hickok?"

"Do you truly suppose," Sadie Marcus said, "that my husband cares?"

But Wyatt was looking oddly reflective. He cleared his throat. He smoothed that damned mustache with the knuckle of his right index finger. His trigger finger. "Doc said: 'If you see him comin', walk away.'"

"Doc Holliday, you mean?"

"Doc said he seen Purcell fight once, down South. Said it left an impression. You couldn't always be sure, with Doc. But I halfway think he may have been telling truth."

Another thought occurred to me, then. "Down South ..." I began.

"In Georgia, or some such. Where Doc was from"

"Did he ever mention seeing the brother?"

"What, Dillashay?" Earp gave a low, brief laugh. "Doc said, 'If you see *that* bastard comin', don't walk at all. Just run.' Purcell was fast — but that brother of his was faster, and meaner, and altogether worse. According to Doc."

"And yet Purcell killed him," I said.

Wyatt arched one leonine eyebrow.

"When he finally caught up with his brother," I said. "There was a gunfight, or some such. And Strother Purcell shot Lige Dillashay dead."

"Dead?" said the future Lion of Tombstone. "What makes you so sure that Lige Dillashay is dead?"

2.

"Because I shot him," the old man said. "And I watched him fall."

We were outside the tenement on Pacific Street, that evening. They'd been out when I'd come earlier, the old man and the girl — the door he'd rebuilt with his own hands was shut tight and bolted. I'd come back twice, and then waited outside on the street, till at last the old man's long shadow had reached out of the westering sun, the girl's slight and wavering beside him. He'd been holding Em'ly by the hand, her hand swallowed up in his and her sharp little face peering out from the shadows of her bonnet. He'd sent her inside when he saw that I needed to talk.

"You g'wan ahead," he said to her. "I'll be coming up directly." His voice when he spoke to her rumbled fond and gruff; it grew hoarse as he learned what I'd come to ask him.

"We won't talk about this. I don't talk about my brother," he said. "Why would you be laying in wait, to ask me such a question?"

"I thought —"

"Well, you thought wrong. I'm grateful to you, Mr. Weaver—you been a friend. But we're not going to do this book you want to write. Leave it lay. Or write some damned thing once I'm dead. But I've got a job to do, right here—it's looking out for that poor gal. And I'll thank you to let me get on with it."

He raised two fingers to the brim of his hat, in a gesture of seeing me off. It was a damned straw boater, of all things, in place of the shapeless monstrosity he'd been wearing when we met, the one that sat on his head like a possum squashed flat in the road. He and Em'ly had been all the way out to Meiggs Wharf that afternoon, where I do not doubt that they both ate ice cream.

"But are you *sure?*" I said.

"My brother is dead."

The setting sun was directly behind him. I lifted a hand to shade my eyes, squinting to discern his face. There was silence for a moment, and then his voice again, rumbling hoarsely out of the dying light.

"I went after him, up into those mountains. We fought. I tried to carry him back down. But I couldn't, Mr. Weaver. Couldn't do it."

"Carry him down ... still living, you mean? He was still alive?"

"At first. But then I lost him. I watched him fall."

"So you didn't—forgive me, but I have to ask—you didn't actually see him die?"

There was silence again. Then that voice again, from out of the dying light. "What have you heard, Mr. Weaver?"

"Nothing, really. Nothing certain. A kind of rumour."

"Where did you hear it?"

"Just something that was said by someone. A fella. I don't know him all that well. And I couldn't say where he heard it."

This was true, pretty much. Wyatt Earp had gone all sage and mysterious when I'd asked him for elucidation. He'd raised one eyebrow and uttered cryptic murmurs, before disappearing behind his newspaper once again: the future Lion of Tombstone becoming a Sphinx. He'd said just enough to make me suspect that he'd heard some sort of rumour himself, but had no actual first-hand knowledge. And why would Earp have followed up a rumour, after all? He wasn't a lawman anymore; it had nothing to do with him.

"My brother is dead, Mr. Weaver." Strother Purcell was a thousand years old, as he stepped stiff-legged past me. He was older than Methuselah, and carried more weight of sorrow. "Never speak of this again."

It took me three days to find Tyree.

He'd disappeared from his corner on Market Street, and no one seemed to know where he might have gone. No one seemed to care overwhelmingly, either, which struck me as a melancholy thing. It crossed my mind that the poor bastard could have died — that he lay undiscovered in his room, wherever it was, lying glass-eyed on his back with his legs in the air, like a dead budgerigar. So few of us leave a trace when we depart this world, though we prefer not to be reminded of the fact. Besides, I needed the little man.

I'd sent out a letter or two to fellas I knew on newspapers here and there about the country, fishing for anything they might have heard about Elijah Dillashay. But Tyree, now — if anyone in San Francisco had heard whispers concerning Dillashay, then Tyree was the little fella who would have done so. And if he hadn't heard anything yet, then he'd be amongst the first to hear in future. Tyree had keen ears, and kept both of them close to the ground. There's an anatomical unlikelihood in that image, but let it pass. The point being, if the brother was still alive somewhere, then this was something the old man needed to know — for any number of highly obvious reasons, quite apart from any biography that might still get written. And he needed a friend to track this down, on his behalf.

When I found Tyree at last, he was in a tavern near Polk Street. It was a dingy little bolthole, around the corner from the building where — so I'd discovered — he had his digs.

"Christ on a cracker," I said. "You look like hell."

He'd fallen ill again, it seemed — had relapsed, or been gripped by some new affliction, worse than before. He was perched on a stool at a small round table in a corner — wearing a coat, despite the warmth of the day, his huge eyes lit with the residue of fever, behind those lenses.

"H'lo, Weaver," he muttered.

"I need your help, my friend," I told him.

"*My* help?" A sound gurgled up that may have been a laugh. "God help you, then."

About us malingered such a clientele as you'd expect, in a place like this. Layabouts and chancers, and stick-armed drunkards lifting glasses with shaking hands. Tyree's hands were shaking too, and his face was more pinched than ever.

He looked hunted.

That was the thought that came to me, of a sudden. He looked like a man who was harried and hunted down.

"Strother Purcell, eh?" he said.

That stopped me. "What about him?"

"It's him — that old man. I saw you with him. That's Strother Purcell himself. You found him — still alive. Or what's left."

I might have tried to deny it. But really, what was the point?

Tyree sketched up a little smile. He was trying to look arch and knowing, I think, but mainly he just looked sickly. Then abruptly, the smile collapsed. "Jesus, Weaver — I thought he was dead. But ... what happened to him?"

I answered truthfully. "I don't know — not exactly. In fact, I don't hardly know at all. He fell to pieces after that business—whatever it was—with his brother. Up there in the mountains of the North."

"Jesus," Tyree said again. He was drinking whiskey. Lifting his glass, his hand shook worse than ever; he used the second hand to steady it. "Still alive—but a wreck. I would never have believed ... *that* man, of all the men I ever saw."

He seemed genuinely distressed about it—that's what seemed so curious. A man he'd seen once in his life, assuming the story he'd told me was true. And yet he was shaken by *that* man's fall, as if Strother Purcell in tumbling had brought the very roof-beams down.

I was touched somewhere close to the heart—I truly was.

I thought, as well: *Oh, this story must be told. It truly must, somehow, some way.*

"He told me he tried to carry his brother down," I said, leaning closer and keeping my voice down low. "Back down from the mountain, after they fought—up in Canada, that winter of ... whenever it was."

"It was 1876," Tyree said. "They rode through Hell's Gate and the Black Canyon, along the Wagon Road. Then north, up into the Cariboo. Dead of winter."

"The brother was still alive—that's what he told me. After they fought. He tried to carry him, but he failed. Is that what happened?"

"It was a travois," Tyree said. "Like the Indians make. That's what I heard, anyway. He tried to lug him down the mountain on a travois. But the mountainside gave way. An avalanche, or some such—it took both of them down."

"How does that even make sense?" I said. "He hunted his brother for fifteen hundred miles. He shot him. And then, he—what—he tried to *rescue* him?"

Tyree shuddered a little, all over, as if with cold. As if the ice of that faraway mountain had come creeping all the way down to San Francisco, and his breath when he spoke might billow white. "I expect he wanted to take him back for trial," he said. "Down South, to a Judge who could hang him. No, I don't know that for a fact. But if it came down to the guessing, then that'd be mine. It'd be rightful, y'see — as he'd've seen it. The right thing to do. That's how he thought."

I'd begun to feel a smidgen shivery myself, as I sat there listening to this. As if the Arctic frost had inched its way to my side of the table.

"You saw him just that one time," I said.

Tyree nodded. "Ten years old."

"And based on that, you can claim to know how he thought?"

"That's all it took. You'd know it, if you'd seen him back then. If you'd seen him the way he was."

"And … what about the other one? The brother. If Purcell survived, then maybe Dillashay did too?"

The little man hunched tighter. The pony glass of whiskey was on the table before him, clenched between both of his hands. The knuckles were white. "No." He stared down into the glass. The light from the window shimmered on the whiskey. "Lige Dillashay is dead."

"That's what you heard?"

"Lige Dillashay could not have survived. Not possible. Once the devil caught that man's ankle, he'd not let go."

I leaned forward. "Anything you hear — any leads, any information. And I'm not asking for a favour — I'll pay you for it. Cash on the nail. All right?"

Tyree lifted his head. His eyes were lamps and he shuddered again, all over. "Weaver, listen to me," he said. "Whatever you heard, or think you know — forget it. Lige Dillashay is dead, and burning. If he isn't, then he should be. Just leave it."   *

It was, all in all, one of the more singular conversations I'd experienced of late. And Christ knows, this had been quite the season for those.

Extricating myself, I left Tyree huddled and shuddering on his bar stool and went outside, into light and life, giving one valedictory shudder of my own. I had it in mind to slope down to Mulvaney's, to see if any of the newsmen I knew had stopped by. I could troll them for information, I thought—subtly, so as not to give anything away.

But I didn't get there. The afternoon was lying in wait with its strangest turn yet: one that could make you think those old Greeks really were on to something, about Fate and what-all else.

I was making toward Geary Street when I saw the drunken man on the corner just ahead, exhorting sinners. He was shambling and slurring, and passersby veered to give him a wide berth—except for those who paused to jeer instead. "Mock—oh, yes, mock!" he cried. A clutch of young fellows were happy to comply; the catcalls flew. He was undeterred. "I am as you see—a sinner, jus' like you. Yes, jus' exactly like each of you!" ("No!" a young wag interjected. "We smell better!" General merriment, and an apple-core chucked.) "I am lower than the muck—oh, I am, I am, and I know it." ("So do we!") "But I shall be raised up, despite of my unworthiness. 'Cause I stand before you, river-baptized, by Brother Jacob Jacobson himself!"

It was Brother Amos, from the Gospel Mission by the dockside south of Market Street. The strange duck who'd been ladling out stew to indigents—the one so thin that his head was just a skull with hair and skin, who had stared at me with Mother Weaver's eyes.

And recognized me.

"You!" he cried. "Oath-breaker!"

Christ.

The catcallers had started to move on, leaving me momentarily exposed. Brother Amos lurched toward me.

He'd fallen from the wagon, quite obviously. Fallen abject and headlong—but he was strangely undismayed. Possibly this was just something that happened to him, every few months—hell, on alternate Tuesdays, for all I knew—after which he'd clamber back up again, once the binge had run its course. Or else possibly this was the tumble that would wreck him, once and for all.

"Friend o' mine, you see a wretch before you. But friend? I see an even worse one, before *me*."

He stank of gin and urine. But he still had my mother's come-to-Jesus eyes. They were bloodshot and they burned.

"Friend o' mine, it's not too late. No, never too late — not ever — whatever you may be thinking."

In fact, I was thinking how very much I would like to be elsewhere, just at the moment. But Brother Amos had me by the sleeve.

"You can still make amends," he said, eyes burning bright. "Friend o' mine, you can be the man you yearn to be, in your heart. But it's getting late — oh, it is — I b'lieve you know it. 'S late, and time to be bringing in the sheaves. We can pray together, friend — right here — if you wish it. And you do — oh, you do, friend o' mine, you do, you do — even if you don't understand that yet."

This was getting out of hand. We'd caught the eye of passersby; smirks were kindling, and elbows were a-nudge.

"Let go of me," I muttered, wrenching free. I shoved him to emphasize the point — a little harder than I'd actually intended. He staggered back, and one of the smirkers stopped smirking, to call out a protest instead. "Easy, fella — there's no call to *hit* 'im."

Damn.

I dug into my pocket, fishing out a coin. "Here," I said gruffly. "Buy yourself something to eat. Or — hell if I care — go get another drink."

Brother Amos looked wounded. Mother Weaver's eyes had a flair for that look, too. But he took the coin.

"I am a wretch," he lamented.

"So you said."

"But I been Saved. By a greater sinner than I will ever be. A greater sinner than you can even imagine."

"Sure," I said, beginning to edge away. "The Reverend Jacob What-Not."

"Jacob Jacobson."

"In a patch of potatoes, was it?"

"A hail-flattened cornfield."

"That's the one."

"In Ulysses, Kansas."

"Sure. Well, you take care of yourself, and—"

He had my sleeve, again. "The Reverend Jacob Jacobson was the worst man, once, who ever lived. He told me that himself—an' it was true. But even *he* was Saved. So there's hope. Hope for me, an' hope for you too, friend o' mine."

I had heard enough of the Reverend Jacob Jacobson for one afternoon. For one lifetime, in fact. I tried to tug my sleeve free again, but Brother Amos held fast. The man was like a limpet.

"Look, I don't care about Jacob Jacobson," I said through clenched teeth. "Whatever he did—or whoever the hell he was. Let me go, damn you, or I swear to God—"

"Dillashay," said Brother Amos.

He'd pulled himself right up against me. Whispered the name into my ear—as if this was the secret that would seal a compact between us, making us friends in Jesus ever after.

"That was his name," Brother Amos said. "He never tol' it to me—but I found out. The Reverend Jacob Jacobson was once the fearsomest outlaw of them all, Elijah Dillashay."

PART FOUR

-TWENTY-ONE-

From *The Testament of Rebekah*[7]

The Southwest, 1892

1.

"I HAVE BEEN SCORNED and scourged," Brother Jacob would cry. "I have been well-nigh broke on the wheel of retribution."

Yes, he spoke like that. Rebekah would marvel to hear him.

"I have been lost, my friends, and I have been betrayed. I have been beaten and left for dead, and nailed to hang on the tree of my own transgressions. But I give thanks for every torment I endured—for I deserved each one of them. Oh, my friends, I am the worst man that ever walked."

("No," they would exclaim, though they loved to hear him say it. "No, never—you are not!")

---

7   There is controversy concerning the provenance and authenticity of this remarkable document, which has not elsewhere been published. It turned up at a Salvation Army hostel in Philadelphia in 1933, amongst the personal effects of an elderly indigent known as "Crazy Becky." A street preacher with an eschatological perspective, she was often sighted on Skid Row street corners, where for several years she prophesied the imminent arrival of the End of Days, whenever the Spirit so moved. The End came at last—or at least, it did for "Crazy Becky"—on December 28, 1932, when the Spirit moved her in front of an oncoming trolley. The document passed from hand to hand, before coming into the possession of a collector of Frontier memorabilia in Kansas City named Archie Dozier. Private correspondence confirms that Mr. Dozier was contacted in the summer of 1983 by Tilda Sturluson, with whom an exchange of several letters ensued.

   We cannot state with certainty that "The Testament of Rebekah" is accurate and reliable, given that it is the accounting of a woman who was by all reports—and not to put too fine a point upon it—crazy. But the existence of a tent revivalist calling himself Brother Jacob Jacobson can in fact be independently documented, and his movements across the U.S. Southwest in 1891 and 1892 correspond remarkably to such specifics as are provided in the "Testament."—*Brookmire.*

"Oh, it's true."

("No!")

"I stand here in the Sight of God, a sinner ten times worse than any one of you. Yet I am washed clean again in the Blood of my Redeemer."

They loved him all the more for this, though they were afraid of him as well. Even Rebekah was afraid, just a little, and she feared few men, excepting her Daddy and her brothers. Brother Jacob's eyes were dark as coals, and there was coiled power in the way he moved, despite the maiming of his body. And that voice of his. It would simmer low and quiet, to draw you in: "And I'll tell you something, friends. I'll share with you a secret. Shall I do that?"

("Yes!" they'd exclaim, and lean in close.)

"The scourging I endured—the torment and betrayal? It made me strong. Oh, yes it did. It made me ten times stronger than before—stronger than ever I was in the days of my youth and wickedness. And there's someone who will pay a price for that. Shall I say his name to you, friends?"

("Yes, say it!" they'd reply, though they knew already.)

"That someone, friends—" And suddenly his voice would rise. It would soar and roar and ring out like the mightiest church-organ: "That someone is the devil!"

("Hallelujah!")

"I never seen a godly man with such a deal of danger in him."

Esther said that once. She was standing beside Rebekah by a sludge-brown meander of river where Brother Jacob was preaching.

"D'you s'p-p-pose," Rebekah began to say in reply. "D'you s'p-p-p—" But the words wouldn't come, so she gave up making the attempt. She was stirred by Brother Jacob's preaching—that was the problem. She was exalted by it. When Rebekah was exalted, the syllables jammed themselves unbearably. She would otherwise have said: "D'you s'pose there was no danger in Moses? Or the Lord God

Jesus Himself?" This had been a saying of her Mamaw Plovis, back home. "There was no Man ever walked this earth more perilous than the holy Lamb of God."

On an evening in May they were inside a barn in the Prescott Valley. The sun sank low and dust-motes danced in shafts of light. Only a dozen souls had come out to hear Brother Jacob's preaching, but that was all right. It was their first time in this part of Arizona, and now word would spread. A few days earlier, near Tempe, whole multitudes had come. They stayed right where they were for six days straight, Brother Jacob and his closest followers—a real Crusade, with a write-up in the newspaper and any number saved. Other times, other places, Brother Jacob would preach to Rebekah and Esther and the birds. But that would be all right too.

"It was g-good enough for Jesus."

Rebekah had said this to him once, when no one came out at all. It really had been just Rebekah and Esther that time, along with the poor simple boy from Nebraska who had tagged along with them for a bit. Brother Jacob had been sunk in brooding, afterward; a darkness had come upon him, which Rebekah did not like to see.

"'Wh-whenever two or three are gathered in m-my Name,'" Rebekah had said on this occasion, quoting the Bible. She spoke slowly and with great care, so that the stammering might not take hold.

"Huh," said Esther, unimpressed.

But Brother Jacob lifted his head. "No," he said. "She's right. Rebekah rebukes me with the truth." He looked at her and smiled.

It changed him wholly; darkness lifted.

"Rebekah is my good angel," he said, "recollecting me to my best self." This made her happier than you could imagine.

"Reb-b-b-b-bekah," muttered Esther.

—

On they went.

Brother Jacob would preach the Gospel and call souls to the Lord. Often he would lay on healing hands in prayer—his own right hand so horribly maimed, though the left hand was still whole. Sometimes he would cast out unclean spirits. Rebekah had never witnessed this, but Esther claimed to have seen it. Esther had travelled with Brother Jacob in a time before Rebekah knew him. It was thrilling and terrible, Esther said: standing like Samson with his two hands clasped to the head of an afflicted child, contending against the unclean spirit.

"Did it yield?" Rebekah asked her. They were kneeling by a stream, she and Esther, washing clothes.

"Oh, one of them devils might of did." Esther took on a particular look, sidelong and knowing. The devil inside the afflicted child, said Esther—that devil might very well have yielded up. For the child gave out a shriek, then went limp as rags. "But as regarding to the other devil, I wouldn't assume to say."

Rebekah asked: "What other devil?"

"Oh-ho," said Esther.

Esther said a good many things without quite saying them at all. Rebekah took such pronouncements for what they were worth. Esther was a red-haired woman on the far slope of thirty, with a certain kind of eye and two titties that swayed together. She had left a husband behind her when she went off to follow Brother Jacob, and two children as well. Such at least Rebekah had come to conclude, from things Esther said and other things she didn't. This might have seemed unnatural and worthy of Rebekah's condemnation, except that would have been judging, and Rebekah knew that she must not judge, as a Christian. She must pray for folks instead, even Esther.

She prayed for Esther every morning, in private. Rebekah had great red hands, which she clasped together as she prayed. Her Mamaw Plovis had been the same way. "God gave us fine strong hands for wringing chicken-necks," Mamaw Plovis said once, perceiving that Rebekah had grown ashamed of those hands, as of so much else about herself. Esther had laughed out loud, when Rebekah shared that confidence. "Chicken-necks?" said Esther. "Rebekah, them hands you got could wring a goat."

So Rebekah prayed. "Lord, help Esther mend the error of her ways. If she don't, I leave the judging to you. You will know what is best and needful to be done, Lord, and by golly you will do it."

Brother Jacob had been a drunkard and a thief. He said so every time he preached. He had laid violent hands about him, for which he was rightly locked in jail. And they should have thrown away the key, he said — this was the mistake they made, when they had him locked inside. They should have put him down like a rabid dog.

One time, Esther said to Rebekah: "Brother Jacob done outright murder."

Rebekah did not want to believe this. Brother Jacob had never said that word himself, in preaching nor in private.

"But then," Esther said, "he don't spend time in private, does he? Not with you."

They were setting together in the evening shade, the two of them. This was in the early days, when Rebekah first began to travel with Brother Jacob and his followers. Back then, she had harboured hopes that Esther might turn out to be her friend.

"Outright murder," Esther repeated. She spoke with relish, savouring the words. "There was five thousand dollars on his head. Then a one-eyed lawman hunted him — fifteen hundred miles, all the way into the mountains of the North. Oh, yes. It come to a reckoning at last, and that lawman shot him down. You might see the scars to this day,

Rebekah—the white scars from the bullets—if he'd show them. But he won't. Not to a gal such as yourself. A great ungainly gal, as I say in a spirit of kindliness."

Esther leaned in closer, then. "Will I tell you something else?"

"N-no," Rebekah said. "I don't b-b-believe I want to hear it."

Esther said it anyway. "The one-eyed lawman who hunted him down? That lawman was his brother." Then she lowered her voice to a whisper. "And if they ever meet again, on this earth? Brother Jacob will kill him. Oh, yes he will. You'd like to s'pose that Brother Jacob would Save him, instead. Brother Jacob would like to s'pose that himself. But he won't. Brother Jacob done outright murder before. And if he ever lays eyes on that brother of his—you mark my words, Rebekah—he'll do outright murder one more time."

Those bullets hadn't killed him, though. Brother Jacob had been left for dead, but he hadn't died. He had risen.

He didn't rightly understand it, at all—the hows and the wherefores of this rising. Why he should have been lifted up again, of all the wretched sinners in this sadly Fallen world. He confided this in Rebekah, one evening as they broke bread together.

"I think p'raps the Lord was not done with me, Rebekah. I think he had some task in mind, which I have yet to accomplish. I don't know. I can only s'pose. And carry on."

It had been away up in the North, this rising of his; it had been some years ago. So he confided, though he did not offer up specifics. He had gone by another name in those times, too. Jacob was not the name he was born with, he said—it was his Daddy's. He took the name to honour his Daddy, whom he never honoured while alive.

"And that could have been the worst of all my sins," he said. This startled Rebekah, but he meant it. "Yes, of all the sins that are writ down on my ledger—and that list is long and black, as you well know—the blackest of all might could have been the shame I felt to be my Daddy's son, and the doubly shameful way I let him see it."

So: Brother Jacob. If anyone needed a second name to go with it, then he was proud to be Jacob Jacobson. His Daddy was long since gone—had grown old and died in torment, he said, a ten-years-younger man than his own son on this day.

"And Lord knows, I am halfways old myself. I am maimed and lame and I know that my time grows short. I suspect that yours does, too—whatever age you may be." He said this on that final night near Tempe: a hundred sinners gazing back at him. "My friends, I suspect that Time itself grows short. A Reckoning is on the way. And my friends—oh, my friends—you had best be ready."

Brother Jacob was dark in his eyes and complexion. His hair was silvering and his face had grown gaunt. There was scarring all down one side, from the corner of his eye to his jawbone; it showed white against his colouration, as if bitter tears had carved their way. Three fingers on his right hand were gone, and the hand that remained was clawed. His fingers had frozen black that long-ago winter in the North; they had subsequently been cut away, along with the toes on his left foot, which was already clubbed from birth. He had this maiming as a gift from God; in his ugliness, Brother Jacob was beautiful.

But he'd grown darker than ever, that final night near Tempe. A shadow had stolen across him, long and black, despite the triumph of the Crusade: more coming out each night to hear him. There had even been a telegram. It was sent to him at the telegraph office, two days after the newspaper wrote that Brother Jacob was in Tempe saving souls. A messenger boy brought it out to the field, where the tent had been set up for his preaching.

Rebekah had been nearby, as she almost always was, or tried to be. The messenger boy had arrived just prior to the service, in the first long shadows of the evening. Rebekah saw Brother Jacob take the telegram, and read it. She saw the look that came upon him. He stood stone-still, in deepening shadow.

"Did someone p-pass?" she asked him, working up her nerve.

He gave no sign that he heard the question, or noticed Rebekah looming there.

"The t-telegram," Rebekah said again. "Did someone d-d-die?"

"No," Brother Jacob said at last. "Someone didn't."

His face was darker than she had ever seen.

He crumpled the note and slung it aside. The wind blew it into some bushes. It was still there later, when Rebekah went back to retrieve it.

2.

It was early in the planting season, the first time Rebekah heard him preaching. This was in Arkansas, where Rebekah had been raised.

She had been working here and there, ever since she'd left her Daddy's farm. Wherever they'd take her on. For a time she worked at a slaughter-yard, swinging the mallet that brought down the steers as they reached the end of the chute, but she did not find this congenial. Rebekah liked much better to work in the fields: wide-open places under the sky, where she could breathe.

Then Brother Jacob came through those parts, as if he'd been conjured out of air. Rebekah went to listen. His text was Jesus saying to Peter, on the shore by Galilee: "Put down your nets and follow Me."

Well, Rebekah thought; she had a hoe. She could put that down instead.

Esther was with him already, at that time. The simple boy from Nebraska was tagging as well, and one or two others. They were a rag-tag little band, but they had a spirit about them, and Rebekah set down that hoe and followed after.

A few miles down the road, it grew clear to Brother Jacob that

Rebekah did not intend on turning back. So he fell into step with her, limping alongside.

"Do not mistake me for the Lord," he said. He might have suspicioned that she was simple herself, from the earnest way he spoke. "D'you understand, Rebekah, what I'm saying?"

Yes, Rebekah said to him. She understood. And she hoped he wouldn't mistake her for someone as could sail a fishing boat.

He blinked his eyes at that. Began to chuckle. "I believe," he said, "we have an understanding."

Brother Jacob had been a wayfarer too, which gave them something else in common. He had worked on farms and slept under hedges, enduring such privations as could hardly be imagined, except by someone who'd done the same.

He'd begun his wayfaring as a boy, fifteen years old. His family had cast him out, he told Rebekah. This was no worse than he deserved, being a boy much given to wicked inclination. But once cast out, his sinfulness ran riot. He fell amongst low companions, and dragged them lower still. He committed such deeds as he could not bear to countenance in himself, until at last he grew so soul-sick that he confessed his wickedness and sought out help, turning to the one man in all this world who might redeem him.

But here, he said, he made his worst Error of all, turning not to the Lord but to a mortal creature just like himself. "Just like *you*, Rebekah," he said to her—to Rebekah alone, for the two of them were walking together as they spoke, along a hard and dusty road— "a mortal creature such as yourself, but lacking the friendship that shines in your true heart." A man he had once looked up to, Brother Jacob said. "A man I put up on an altar, like unto a god."

She said to him: "Your b-brother."

He made no reply.

"Your b-b-brother who locked you in jail," she said. Knowing the danger she took in speaking so free. "Then hunted you like an animal."

"What else did Esther say to you?"

"N-nothing that I believe. Not unless you say it too."

They walked in silence then.

It was this brother who was spoken of in the telegram — the message that had arrived before the final night of the preaching near Tempe, Arizona. Rebekah had read it while no one was watching.

Your brother is alive, it said. Still living, but in great need. Can you come to him?

Weaver was the name of the man who sent it.

A few days later, the widow came out to hear him.

They had been travelling in the meantime, but not with intent — not as far as Rebekah could determine. Just letting the Spirit move them, as they always had before. It was just the two of them now, Brother Jacob and herself. Esther had left them a week previous, taking her smirk and those titties along with her.

The widow had two grown sons. But only one of them was with her, on the evening when she came out to hear: a great silent creature who stood staring. A simpleton, as was clear. When Brother Jacob called out to know if anyone here present knew of a soul in need of saving, the widow said: "My boy." A wiry twist of a woman, nut-brown from toiling in the field. "My boy is in peril of his soul. He needs your prayer," she said.

Brother Jacob reached out his hand and asked the simpleton to come forward. But the widow shook her head. No, she said — the other son. This one, the simpleton, was a mighty comfort to her, strong as a horse and good as gold. It was his brother's soul that was in such peril; a boy born into this world with every advantage in his person and demeanour, but he ran riot and reckless.

She was prideful in the way some people are, who have nothing but their own two feet to stand on. Rebekah could see how it twisted her heart to ask for help, right out loud in front of others. But the widow besought Jacob's prayers nonetheless. And Brother Jacob said to her: "No." He would not pray nor intercede, he said.

He stood in shadow as he said it. He spoke as if from the darkness of a wood.

"No," he said again. He would not pray for the likes of her son — nor would such prayers avail. For some are set beyond the pale of salvation. "Two thieves were crucified beside our Lord, but only one of them was saved."

This was not his own choosing, he said, but the judgement of Almighty God. And there was nothing that could ever be done for that second thief, not through prayer nor deeds nor tearful contrition. We are some of us marked out before we are ever born.

Well, this shocked the widow. Shocked all of them, there assembled, Rebekah not least. Looks were exchanged; uneasy murmurs. The widow's chin began to tremble.

"Your son standing here has been marked by the Lord for His own," said Brother Jacob. "But that other bears the mark of Cain, and all the tears of the world won't wash him."

"Have I been marked?"

Rebekah asked this of him afterward. The others had gone and the two of them were alone.

He said: "Oh, yes."

"Which way?"

"You've been marked out as my friend."

He smiled just a little as he said it. This pushed the shadow back, but only by an inch.

They had a barn to sleep in that night. The man who owned it was a Christian and offered it for lodging, which Jacob accepted in the ravelled way he often had after preaching. It took time for him to settle, and this evening he seemed more ragged than ever. Rebekah could see the age on him, nights like this. The scars and lines on his face were furrowed deep.

"Did you have to break her heart?" she said. Meaning that widow.

"Her boy did that. He broke his Mama's heart." His voice had gone harsh. "The devil are you, Rebekah, to say such things to me?"

"Your friend. You said it yourself. Don't that give me the right?"

"Take care, Rebekah."

Rebekah did not take care. She said: "What call have you to break that widow's heart, just 'cause of what your brother done to you?"

The look he gave her could have forked out lightning. And Rebekah felt suddenly sorry to have said one single word, seeing how it was costing her this friendship. Her one friend in this world, she thought — the only man who ever smiled at a creature such as herself, a gal who'd hulked away from children shying stones, on account of her face and the size of her.

But in the morning, he rose up with first light, and went to find out where that widow was living. Rebekah followed.

A clapboard shack on a scrap of land, it turned out to be, huddled beneath the vast blue dome of sky, with a trickle of sludge for a creek. The widow was working in a patch of corn, alongside her simpleton son. They watched him coming from a mile away, Brother Jacob limping sorely on his clubbed foot and dust rising up with each step till at last he stood before her. He was a man himself in grievous need of Grace, he said, and would pray for the redemption of her boy.

The widow stood straight-backed, as tall as she could muster.

"I do not deserve your thanks," Brother Jacob said. "But I will ask of your forgiveness."

The widow nodded, very stiff.

He led them in prayer, and afterward the widow asked would he stop for a time, to rest and break bread. He would gladly accept a drink of water, Brother Jacob replied, but could not stop. "I have a journey ahead of me."

He did not look at Rebekah as he said it. But right then she knew what decision he had made, and her heart sank like a stone.

Afterward they walked some miles in silence. They had taken the road west, their shadows stretching out behind as the sun crossed over, long and black and thin as blades. At last he said: "I thought him dead, Rebekah. All these years." As if some explanation was needful, between them. "Whatever it was that happened between us—whatever was done, on either side—he's my brother."

She shrugged by way of reply.

"California is a long road, Rebekah. I don't ask you to come with me."

"Are you sending me away?"

"I'm saying, the choice is yours."

"Then I come with you."

He put his hand on her shoulder, then, as the two of them walked together. It was the nearest he would ever come to touching her as a woman.

"Rebekah," he said, "you are my one true friend."

3.

Brother Jacob continued to save souls along the way, stopping to preach and heal, as was his custom. But always they were travelling into the West.

Often they walked, but accepted with gratitude a ride on a wagon, if such was offered. Other times they would travel by train, covering many miles in a single night. They stowed themselves away in freight cars, having few enough coins as it was without squandering them on railway tickets. Besides, Rebekah suspected, Brother Jacob plain liked the adventure of it. When someone would stop them and demand to know their business—some switchyard worker or railroad policeman, very stern at first and then perplexed, seeing the preacher's flat black hat and the Bible underneath his arm—Brother Jacob would smile with merriment, like a boy caught out in mischief.

"Where you headed, Reverend?" the railroad man might say.

"Bound for Glory. Is this my train?"

Sometimes, though, the railroad man would startle at the sight of him. Hold up a lantern and eye him keener, aslant. It happened once in a railroad yard as they crossed into Nevada.

"Do I know you from somewheres, Reverend?" It was an older man, in a Conductor's uniform.

"I don't know," Brother Jacob said. "Do you?"

"I seen you on some other train. Years ago, this would of been. A younger man, but he had your cast of feature."

"I don't believe we know each other, friend."

The Conductor asked to know his name.

"My name is Jacobson." Brother Jacob was still smiling, but had gone quieter, a little.

"Dillashay," the Conductor said. "There used to been an outlaw by that name. This Dillashay ran riot in New Mexico, and other places."

"Yes," Brother Jacob said. "I believe I once heard something of that man. But I never saw him."

"You're sure?"

"And I misdoubt that you saw him either, friend. Not up close. Because you wouldn't be standing here, if you did. From what I heard."

"That might be," the Conductor said. "I did once meet the brother, years ago."

Brother Jacob went still.

"Dillashay had an older brother," the railroad man continued. "He served as a Sheriff's Deputy, place called Santa Rosita. A fine tall fellow — righteous in his dealings. It perplexes the mind, how two brothers could be so different — don't it, Reverend? The one of them such a credit, and the other worth nothing at all."

In the desert, the night can grow cold all of a sudden.

"God go with you, friend," said Brother Jacob. "Watch out for the devil."

When the Conductor left, they climbed onto the train. It carried them many miles deeper into the desert.

The devil was waiting for them, when they got off.

-TWENTY-TWO-

The Actress Arabella Skye[8]

San Francisco, 1892

MISS ARABELLA SKYE, the actress, arrived in San Francisco at five minutes before noon by the platform clock on the morning of June 30, 1892. "At last," she whispered to herself.

She had imagined many times her arrival here, under sundry names, dating all the way back to the name she had been born with. She had hugged the image close in her thoughts: the heave of the ship upon blue water and the city rising up through the mist to meet her. She had arrived by sea in these imaginings, almost always: hands gripping the rail and her face upturned to the rapture of possibility. Her brother was with her, perched monkey-nimble in the rigging high above; pointing from this exalted vantage and then climbing higher still, in defiance of the sea-slick hemp and his own deformities — her younger brother, who had sailed with her on so many voyages of the mind, especially in the early days.

This defied the evolution of nautical transport too, considering that riggings belonged to sailing ships, which had vanished from the whale-roads by the heyday of Arabella's imaginings. And as it turned

---

8   This is unlikely to be the personal statement of "Arabella Skye," for reasons that will in due course become more clear. In terms of authorship, the chapter should more probably be included in a sub-group with the "Roadhouse Chronicles" segments, and certain other chapters as well, including (but not limited to) those headed "Old Lem" and "The Death of Strother Purcell" — i.e., as imaginative reconstructions by an author (or authors) with independent sources of information and/or a close personal connection to the protagonist. — *Brookmire.*

out, her actual arrival in San Francisco was not achieved via ship at all, but on the train. She was gritted with cinder and tooth-rattled by the journey: thirty-six hours of bony-assed jouncing on bench seats, steam belching from the locomotive as it shuddered at last to a halt at the platform, and—praise be to the God who hates us all, but ordains nonetheless finite terms for most torments—disgorged.

The platform was crowded, of course. There had always been a crowd. In the halcyon days of her shipboard arrivals of the mind, there had been streamers and cheers as well, and a banner stretching overhead that proclaimed: *WELCOME MISS ARABELLA SKYE!* Frequently in her imaginings there had been a band, which would strike up joyfully as she came down the gangplank, one white calfskin boot before the other. "Look!" someone would cry, as she was recognized. "Is it—? Oh, it *is*—it's her!"

No one recognized her today. For one disorienting moment on the train, last night, she had failed to recognize herself. Arabella, looking out into the darkness, glimpsed a face in the window, reflected back. It was eerily familiar to her, except older and harder and haggard-seeming—a thin, sharp face with small, sharp eyes, all angles and calculations.

Christ, she had thought. *I have left this almost too long.*

It was taking an hour and a half, these mornings, just to recover her bloom.

But now here she was, at long last. Noon, by the platform clock, which she glimpsed through the torsos jostling past. Stanley grumbled behind her, dragging the trunk. "Fucksake," he muttered, straightening up to glare at a man who had bumped against him in passing. The man was large, so Stanley took care to wait half a moment, so as to evil-eye the back of his receding head. "Fuckin' wotcherself, eh? Fucker. Or someone gets a fuckin' clout."

Stanley was an actor. He was nineteen years old, a sleek young thing with flaxen curls and ears that tucked flat against his skull, like an otter's. He was pretty rather than handsome, and defensive about this. Stanley couldn't really act much, either. But he was biddable, and kept Arabella warm at night. Her bed-warmers had grown progressively younger over the years, as Arabella herself had aged.

"All right," Stanley said, looking around. "We're here. So *now* what?" He was attempting an attitude of rugged insouciance, which was not the most convincing of his poses. Taking off his hat, he swiped his brow with his bicep. "San Fran-fuckin'-cisco," he said.

Her brother was here, somewhere. Arabella tried to decide how she felt about that.

And according to the letter, *he* was here, too.

Arabella felt her breath catch, and quicken. "Follow me," she said.

Stanley followed.

I am alive. In San Francisco. So is he.

The message had been delivered to the theatre in Silver City where Arabella and the Troupe were playing; someone redirected it to the rooming-house where they were lodged, so that Arabella did not receive it until later. The theatre was just a hall, with miners sardined on wooden benches: the sort of audience you'd expect at a silver town in Nevada, in the last convulsions of its heyday. The show itself was music hall fare. Clog-dancers and contortionists and comic songs; a wiry Swiss who performed a version of the Big Boots routine made famous by Little Tich, except with smaller footwear.

The tour had been interminable already — eight months since leaving St. Louis. The past sixteen years of Arabella's life often seemed as one unending tour, through camps and whistle-stops and the occasional third-rate city, ever since she had left her uncle's roadhouse with the man who had promised to take her to Chicago, but didn't. Still, the miners in Silver City had been appreciative. Miss Arabella Skye had been accorded second billing, right after the wiry Swiss, which wasn't bad. Besides, they had let her keep her clothes on. This marked a blessed change from the early days of tableaux in filthy clubs without her drawers.

On this tour, she dressed up as a swell and sang patter-songs like Dan Leno, all of them with lyrics that could be taken in two different ways, depending on your turn of mind. Arabella had a gift for this, delivering with perfect innocence such innuendo as would give your old granny the vapors. She also appeared a second time to perform a dramatic recitation. This would usually be a passage from some brooding Romantic in torment; the choice would vary, depending on Arabella's mood. That particular night in Silver City she had chosen a tragic one, concerning a maiden left pining unto death by her Demon Lover.

Any number of the miners would have been pleased as by-golly to squire her afterwards. But she had been morose, and sat for a considerable while in the dressing-room by herself with a bottle of whiskey, long after the others had left. Of late, such moods had been coming upon her with increasing frequency. In the depths of them, she would ask herself what reason there was to keep going; sometimes she could not think of a likely answer. She thought often of her mother, who had been tragic and thwarted and died four years younger than Arabella was herself, which was sad and a great waste but possibly not the worst outcome, all things considered.

It was long past midnight when she went back to the rooming-house. Someone had stuck the letter in her door. She glanced at it blearily, then recognized the writing on the envelope: that tiny, cramped, spidering hand. The recognition left her rigid.

Her brother had delivered it himself—this was the thought that came to her in that first moment, lightning-struck, even though the words said otherwise: *in San Francisco*. She ran back outside, clutching the note and the unfinished bottle.

"Tommy?"

Light from the doorway spilled about her. She gazed around wildly, into the desert darkness.

"Tom? Are you out there? Tommy!"

But he wasn't.

The rooming-house slouched at the edge of what passed for civilization. Points of light still flickered from the town: saloons. Distant laughter rose in bursts, but out here on the edge there was only silence.

Arabella felt unaccountably bereft. She might almost have felt tears coming on, except Miss Arabella Skye never wept. Not ever.

"Fuck you, then," she said to the night. "You mangy fucker."

Someone had opened a window, behind her. Stanley's voice came querulously down. "'Bella? The fuck is—?"

"Fuck you too," she advised him.

But she took Stanley with her, nonetheless—two days later, when she made the decision. Breaking her contract, she left Silver City, by stagecoach first and then by train. She arrived in San Francisco in a belch of steam to the indifference of multitudes, with Stanley behind her dragging the steamer-trunk. They stopped outside the station and gazed about them.

"Now what?" Stanley said. He was tired and feeling overwhelmed, which made him cranky.

"First we find someplace to stay."

"Then what?"

There was the question. A quarter of a million souls in San Francisco—Arabella could trudge from door to door, and it might take years. She'd be a crone by the time she found either one of them.

I am alive. In San Francisco. So is he.

The solution was to draw him to her.

"I need," Arabella said, "to find us a theatre."

–TWENTY-THREE–

From *The Testament of Rebekah*

The Southwest, 1892

WHEN THE DEVIL resolved to overthrow our Lord, he did so in the desert.

The fiend is sly, and will always choose such wilderness. Rebekah knew this from her Mamaw Plovis. It is not the devil who is stronger in wilderness places, Rebekah's Mamaw had counselled; it is we who are weaker, and the devil knows it.

Rebekah said this once to Brother Jacob. "Yes," he replied, growing grave. He knew this for a truth himself.

In the desert a man cannot fix himself into perspective. There is nothing by which he can measure his true size. In the desert a man might be nothing at all, or he might could be Goliath. He begins to suppose he might stand as tall as the shinbone of Jehovah.

"The worst mistakes of my own life were always in the desert," Brother Jacob said. "The desert of one kind or another."

So it only stood to reason: the devil would be waiting for that train.

The train took them only partway, before stopping to decouple freight cars. Rousted out, they walked half a day down a road, before the sun was too hot and too high and they rested in a scrap of shade. There were trees here by the roadside, and a river, and some arable land. A little town, just ahead, where they stayed that night. In the morning, Brother Jacob was moved to preach Christ Crucified and Risen to such folks as had gathered. One of these was a man who had come to seek help for his child.

She was six years old, he said. A beautiful child with golden hair, the light and life of her whole family, excepting an unclean spirit had possessed her. Her Daddy broke down and wept as he related this, a fine strong man in his prime.

Brother Jacob said: "You lead the way."

The farm was miles in the wrong direction, but Jacob was set in his mind upon helping that child. When at last they arrived, it was worse than he'd feared.

The spirit was a paralytic one. Such was the outward sign of its uncleanness. The child lay rigid on a bed; still living, but in mortal distress, staring wildly up toward the ceiling, as if the dust-motes dancing in a shaft of light were every one of them the shade of some poor child who'd died unsaved.

Brother Jacob saw at once what he was up against.

"Can you help her?" the Daddy asked.

Esther claimed once to have seen such a battle. Ever after, Rebekah had longed in her heart to see for herself, to witness Brother Jacob contending against the devil. But Esther had never confided how terrible it was. Or how it could end.

Stepping into the slant of light from the window, Brother Jacob placed his hands to the poor child's head, one on either side. Clenched faces looked on: the child's Daddy and her Mama, and one other—the Mama's younger sister, in the doorway. A room in a small white house on a ragged-ass farm, with desert stretching out on every side and the dome of desert sky overhead. And up beyond it all the Lord looked down in vague distraction, as if tugged from mighty works by the thought that somewhere in the world below a little sparrow had fallen.

But the world is wide. It has many sparrows in it.

Brother Jacob called that spirit to come out. It was a strong one, lodged down deep, and clinging as fierce as a mandrake root. The child's eyes rolled as he called again. Foam flecked the corners of her mouth and she juddered, spine arching.

The women were gasping and praying now. The Daddy was chalk-white.

Jacob called that unclean spirit again: "Come out!"

The afflicted child commenced to flail.

"Hold her!" Brother Jacob cried.

Rebekah caught the child's wrists in her hands. But the gal very nearly wrenched free, before Rebekah could brace—and Rebekah was the strongest one in the room. It was all the farmer could do to clamp one ankle, the Mama clinging with her whole weight to the other. Four grown adults to hold down that little child, while a fifth one—the Mama's sister, Dolly-Ann her name was—gawped in the doorway.

"Unclean spirit, come out!"

The little girl was now thrashing and howling, as if that spirit would shake the bed into slats. Dolly-Ann fetched a razor strop to wedge between the poor child's jaws. She went out again to fetch drink for Brother Jacob, who was flagging sorely. An earthenware jug. She held it to his lips and he gulped it down. It half-choked him first, before he swallowed.

"More."

Brother Jacob seemed revived. He gave his head a violent shake, and sweat-drops flew.

"Unclean spirit—*COME OUT!*"

And at last it did. It issued with a shriek straight out of hell, shuddering from the afflicted child like a steam-train bursting from a tunnel. The little girl lay limp and foul with the stench of that spirit's uprooting. But she looked around with her own blue eyes at last, to the almighty joy of her poor family.

Rebekah was joyful too. She wrapped both arms around Brother Jacob, who began to sag and shake with a rumble of laughter. That's when Rebekah understood what Dolly-Ann had done—when she was right up close, and could smell it.

The earthenware jug. Dolly-Ann had not brought water.

Rebekah was not sure, at first, what might follow, having never before seen Jacob take strong drink. But she could guess, from things he'd said and hadn't said. From the manner of the darkness that would come creeping, with nothing worse than pure spring-water to drink.

Dolly-Ann brought the jug back again, and he drank some more. There was nothing that Rebekah could have done to stop him now. He slit-eyed her a look when she tried to caution, and then turned his attentions back to Dolly-Ann. Growing giddy and gay he danced a jig; Dolly-Ann took drink herself and shrieked with happiness.

And the devil was not done yet. Late that night, he whispered blandishments to Dolly-Ann, urging her out to the barn where Brother Jacob lay down his head. A shawl was wrapped round her shoulders, and she carried a blanket. In case he should be cold, she said.

"You should go back inside," Brother Jacob said to her.

"Yes," said Dolly-Ann. "I 'spect I should."

He was afterward sick with what he'd done. In the purple dawn, at cockcrow. Dolly-Ann had slipped away long since, gathering her garments about her. Brother Jacob sat doleful and disgusted, his head hung low.

"Is this the way it must always be, with me?" he said. "There is not one decent act I do not defile."

Rebekah would not look at him.

Gathering up their few possessions, they left in haste and travelled with grim purpose. Ten miles covered by mid-morning; another ten by late afternoon. Finally he allowed they should stop and rest, by a gully with the trickle of a stream. Now he discovered another loss: his Bible had been left behind, a keepsake from his Daddy.

Brother Jacob gave out a woeful exclamation. He would have turned around right then, and walked all the way back to the farmhouse to retrieve it—twenty miles, despite the suffering he endured already, from his lameness. Walking any miles at all was a trial to him, though he'd never say it.

"You go on," Rebekah said. "I'll f-fetch it."

At first, he would not hear of this.

She said again: "Go on ahead. Set here, or else keep going—please yourself. I'll catch up. And I don't want to hear no more about it."

She was thinking to herself that no good could come of his returning to that place. She was thinking also that she would burn in fire before he laid eyes on that Dolly-Ann again. Before he could say more, she turned and started back.

*

When she caught up to him again, night was falling on the second day. He'd been travelling for most of it, trudging west into California. Now, in gathering darkness, he sat on a hillside by the road. Rebekah nearly hurried right on by, except he'd seen her first.

"Did you find it?"

His voice was thick and heavy in the darkness. A bottle was in his hand.

She took the Bible from her pack.

He stood. "Rebekah. You are my good angel."

"You said yourself. M-marked out for your friend."

280

The Bible had been right where he left it last, on an overturned bucket. Rebekah had seen it straightaway, as soon as she'd stepped into the barn. They were setting down by a fire as she told him this. They wouldn't be travelling again till morning: not on such a lonely road in the dark, and Rebekah so worn out already.

He asked: Had she seen them? The family.

No, she said; not hardly. She'd come and gone that quick.

"And the gal?"

Rebekah said she hadn't seen the child. But of course he hadn't meant the little girl. He meant the other one, that Dolly-Ann.

"Yes," Rebekah said. "I seen her."

"And?"

"And what? Just what I said—I s-seen her."

It had been early that same morning. Rebekah had come upon Dolly-Ann fetching water from the river, the one that ran beyond the hill on the far side of the barn. There had been lively words on either side, though Rebekah saw no point in relating these to Brother Jacob. "You are a h-hoo-er," Rebekah had said to Dolly-Ann. "You are l-lower than the dirt beneath his feet." Dolly-Ann flung back at her: "You'd be lower than that yourself, if he'd have you. You'd be on your knees in one half-second."

She and Brother Jacob sat in silence for awhile, by the roadside. He held the Bible in his hands, the smell of whiskey upon him. Firelight flickering, and darkness.

He said: "My Daddy was never good enough for the two of them. Under his own roof, he could never be good enough—nor me neither. How is it, Rebekah? You tell me that. How is it I can never be good enough?"

His face was closed and harrowed.

"I could have killed him at the end." He said this suddenly, out of nowhere. "We came finally face to face. In the North — such cold you never imagined. But I couldn't shoot my own damned brother." He lifted the bottle, and took down a long, slow swallow. "He could kill me, though. Oh, yes he could. Now, isn't that a puzzle to reflect on?"

That morning, the river had been slow and sluggish behind the farm. Such waters are a special peril, as Dolly-Ann ought to have known.

Eddies and pools along the bank, wherever the water is murky and thick with reeds — that's where you must be mindful. Because Jenny Greenteeth lives in such places. She'll sink down deep, deep, deep, will Jenny Greenteeth, just waiting for gals who won't listen to their Mamaw Plovis, or neglect their chores. Ungainly gals with strawberry birthmarks stained across their faces, too ugly to be taken by anyone else — those are the gals she loves best, because nobody else will have them. And wayward gals. Jenny Greenteeth loves wayward gals beyond all measure. She'll seize 'em and drag 'em down with her again, lank hair streaming back and fingers like talons reaching.

Yes, Dolly-Ann should have been mindful. And she should never have flung herself at Rebekah, the way she did.

She would have been found, within an hour or two. Someone would have gone out looking for her — the farmer, probably, or his wife, Dolly-Ann's older sister. Rebekah hoped it had been one of them, and not the little girl, who might have been considerably upset to discover her aunt floating in such an unnatural manner, face-down with her arms and legs out-splayed. But this was out of Rebekah's hands. And sometimes there's no other way but to drown the devil.

—

"It all goes wrong for me," Brother Jacob was saying, "where my brother is involved." His voice was dark as pitch. "I want to rise up tall, but it all goes wrong. It always will, I think. It will always go wrong for me, with my brother."

–TWENTY-FOUR–

Old Lem[9]

Afternoon

IT HAD BEEN A GRAND DAY for the pair of them, the old man and Em'ly both. They'd journeyed all the way to Golden Gate Park, at the end of the farthest cable-car line, where a fair was in progress, with carnival booths and a band striking up and more delights than you could imagine. They mingled with the crowds and Little Em'ly bought spun candy: a wondrous sweet confection, evanescent as a cloud. Afterwards they walked all along the row, listening to the shouts and the laughter until they came to a shooting booth. A nickel bought you three shots, and a bullseye won you a stuffed toy animal.

The Barker saw the two of them coming. As he would. Saw how Em'ly's eye had been caught by a toy bear with a wonderfully woebegone smile.

"C'mon, then, Grampa," the Barker called. "Make the little lady's afternoon."

He winked at Little Em'ly, in the depths of her bonnet. Chuckled as the old one-eyed man fished about in his pocket for a coin. "Here," the Barker said, and handed over the sidearm. "Have the first shot for free."

It seemed more a play-thing than a weapon. A .22 pistol. It all but disappeared into the old man's hand. But a curious change occurred, as he took it. His hand ceased to tremble. With one smooth

---

9   See note on the authorship of Chapter 22. —*Brookmire.*

movement—scarcely pausing to aim—the old man snapped off a shot to the heart of the bullseye.

The Barker blinked, and reached for the woebegone toy bear. A Barker must ever be good-natured about such lucky outcomes. "Like to see you do that again," he said.

The old man did.

Other punters began to cluster, pulling out nickels and urging the old man to have a go on their behalf. He seemed to enjoy this, firing off bullseyes as the crowd around them swelled, until the Barker's rack of animal toys grew alarmingly depleted, a reduction unmatched since the slaughter of the buffalo herds. The Barker's face grew hot and red. He invoked an ancient fairground rule that all punters must take their own damned shots, excepting Grampa, who should take himself to another booth entirely.

They laughed like children, the two of them. Little Em'ly had her woebegone bear and four other toys besides. The old man had a giraffe under either arm. It was the best afternoon that either of them could remember.

Later, walking home after the cable-car let them off, Little Em'ly fairly glowed in the depths of her bonnet. She had turned to the old man, about to exclaim right out loud in appreciation, when she discovered that he had stopped suddenly dead, staring at a poster stuck to a wooden hoarding. His one eye was wide in disbelief.

Miss Arabella Skye, the poster said. The celebrated actress, appearing at the Barbary Theatre. And below her name was the title of the play: *The Death of Strother Purcell.*

–TWENTY-FIVE–

The Death of Strother Purcell[10]

THE BARBARY THEATRE was a dingy nook on the second floor of a building on Jackson Street, above a dance hall. An alley door led up a set of wooden stairs to a stage and benches where eighty or ninety might wedge themselves. It was an actual theatre, though, reputed even to have its own resident ghost, as any true theatre must: in this case the spectral remains of a jilted clog-dancer who had lost in love and hung himself in protest. On moonless nights when the wind came up he might yet be heard, clomping dolefully.

Arabella had found the theatre on her second day of searching for a venue. It had been vacant for several weeks, which aided her in negotiations with the proprietor, a weary man much martyred by his digestion, who just wanted to get something signed. Arabella had a sharp head for business and had always enjoyed the bargaining process, right up to the point at which she ended on her knees—which didn't turn out to be necessary, in this instance. The proprietor had been beaten down already by the vicissitudes of life; once Arabella had beaten him down some more, he capitulated and they shook hands. So Stanley lugged the costumes and such up the stairs, and they commenced their preparations.

The play itself— *The Death of Strother Purcell*—was the goddamnedest thing. This was the consensus of those who saw it in San Francisco, as it had been of those who had seen it elsewhere. It was simply the goddamnedest play.

---

10   See note on the authorship of Chapters 22 and 24.—*Brookmire*.

Arabella Skye had written it herself. There was a starring role for
her, and several other parts to be played by a second actor: in this case,
Stanley. He had never performed in the play before. It was not entirely
clear to him why he should be performing in it now, apart from the
fact that Arabella told him to.

"But why *this* one?" he had asked her on the train.

"'Cause this is the one we're doing," she had said. She sat coiled
and practically quivering, staring out at the night as it rattled past
the window.

It occurred to Stanley that much was involved here that Arabella
had not told him. This left him uneasy. "'Bella," he said, "I gotta
think—"

"No, Stanley," she interrupted. "No, you don't gotta think at all.
Stick to something you're good at."

"But—"

"You couldn't outthink a lukewarm bowl of soup."

Stanley grew sullen.

"And for Chrissake, don't sulk," Arabella said. "We're doing the
play—doing *that* play—and that's all you need to think about."

The play was narrated by Arabella. She took as well the role
of a young woman whose heart had been captured by a dark and
smouldering outlaw on the run, who fled through the teeth of the
Canadian winter, pursued by a one-eyed lawman who was his brother.
Stanley essayed the outlaw, with insipid results. He subsequently
appeared as the lawman, in which role he was somewhat more
successful, since it afforded him the opportunity to glower and gnash
his teeth. Stanley's glower was not half-bad, all things considered; at
least it was better than his smoulder. The eye-patch was quite good, too.

As the drama escalated, Arabella narrated the lawman's obsessive
pursuit of his quarry into the frozen hell of the North. There was a
gun-battle, at the culmination of which the outlaw spared the life of

his brother through sheer magnanimity of spirit, and was foully back-shot in recompense. Vaunting, the lawman proclaimed his triumph, only to have Nature itself recoil. An avalanche was triggered by his laughter. The mountainside gave way beneath his feet, sweeping him down—one strangled shriek from Stanley, and a descending wail—to his demolition.

Out of a dreadful silence, Arabella's voice arose. Clad in black weeds, framed by a single light, she delivered a savage Jeremiad upon the iniquitous lawman, and a heartfelt lamentation for his brother. The text was overwrought and purple, but it had a certain force. Arabella's performance—as several audience members would comment later—was eerily compelling. And here at the climax, the play achieved an actual *coup de théâtre*. Stanley had fallen to his well-deserved death as the one-eyed lawman. But as a pool of light seeped across the stage, Stanley rose again—as the outlaw brother. He tottered—steadied—stood: as if conjured back to life again by the sheer intensity of Arabella's longing.

And then—around 9:45 p.m. on July 9, 1892, in the dingy confines of the Barbary Theatre—all hell broke loose.

-TWENTY-SIX-

Tyree

Evening

THE OLD MAN had gone to the performance. He went alone, on the pretext of having some personal business to attend to, leaving Em'ly back at the flat. The name of the actress was unfamiliar to him, and he was not someone who went often to the theatre. But few men could ignore a play that had their own death in the title.

Tyree knew about the play, as well. He had seen the self-same poster, and—lightning-struck—had girded himself to attend. In the late afternoon, he betook himself to a barber around the corner and paid four bits for a shave. His hands were shaking too violently to hazard straight-razoring himself. "You okay there, fella?" the barber asked him, in the chair. "You seem kinda tense."

"Tense?" Tyree might have replied. "*Tense?* I'm going to see my sister on the stage—first time I've laid eyes on her in sixteen years. I wrote a note and now here she is. Didn't even look me up. Didn't even try. The sister I would've died for. The sister I goddamn *killed* for. And you ask me, do I seem kinda *TENSE?*"

He did not say any of this, however. Instead, he said to the barber: "Fine. I'm fine, all right? Just, fine."

The barber raised one eyebrow, slightly. He'd been shaving San Franciscans for twenty-eight years, and very little fazed him. "*Eau de cologne?*" he said, when he'd finished.

"What's that?"

"Got *eau de cologne*. From Paris. Slap 'er on?"

"Slap 'er," Tyree said.

The barber did so, charging an extra quarter. "There y'go," he said, sweeping off the bib. "Smelling like roses."

Tyree did smell like roses, too—at least a little. It was a welcome change from smelling like death, as he suspected he'd begun to do, up there in his tiny room. He'd put on his cleanest shirt for the play, and in a moment of abandon had purchased an actual rose from a street-seller, as a *boutonnière*.

But in the end, he couldn't will himself all the way to the Barbary Theatre.

He tried. He made it as far as Mulvaney's saloon, half a mile away. Arriving there at seven o'clock, he bought a pony of whiskey, in a bid to steady himself. His heart was thudding with great intemperance, and his breath came quick and shallow. Tossing back the shot, he had another. Then he ordered a third.

When eight o'clock came, he was on his fifth. Half a mile away, the curtain was rising. Around nine, he left Mulvaney's, dragging himself down the road to one or two other establishments. He ended back at the Spyglass, just around the corner from his own room on Polk Street.

Weaver found him there just shy of midnight. Tyree hunched, wretched, in a blue pall of smoke, feeling as low as he had done for years.

"Tyree! Oh, for Chrissake—*here* you are."

Barry Weaver was in a state. He had been looking for Tyree all over. "The old man," he exclaimed. "Have you seen him?"

"No," Tyree muttered.

He wished Barry Weaver would go somewhere else and hang himself. A down-the-hall neighbour at Polk Street had done just that a few months earlier. He had been discovered in his room after three days, when he started to smell—just inside his door, hanging from a bootlace tied to the knob. Tyree had been thinking about his old neighbour while he drank whiskey. He had bootlaces of his own, he reflected. And a doorknob.

"Christ!" Barry Weaver was exclaiming. "The theatre—he went to the goddamned Barbary Theatre. I was there. I need to find him!"

"The Barbary?" Tyree felt a constricting in his guts. "What's happened?"

Calamity had happened. So Weaver gave him to understand. Disaster on a monumental scale, or at least the thwarting of Barry Weaver, which came out to the next worst thing, in Weaver's own reckoning of the universe.

"That damned play," Weaver said. "That goddamned play."

Tyree said: "Tell me."

So Weaver did. In rising dread and disbelief, Tyree listened.

Weaver had gone to the theatre, having seen a poster with the title—*The Death of Strother Purcell*. Weaver and two dozen others, scattered here and there. The old man had arrived just as the lights were brought down. He came in high-collared and desperately starched, said Weaver, his face chalk-white and his one eye wild, as a man might do who ascended the steps to the gallows. And then that goddamned play had begun.

"It was hardly a play at all," Weaver said. "It was—hell, I hardly know what the damned thing was. A tale, told half in darkness, by that March-mad actress." He reached for a stool and sat on it, much harried. He signalled for someone to bring him a goddamned drink. "Alone on the stage, half the time—some fence-post of a boy up there with her. But damn it, Tyree—somehow, she drew you in. The goddamnedest uncanny creature—eyes like lamps. Eyes like *yours* are, right this minute—Chrissake, Tyree, you look like death on a stick. And who the hell knows how *she* knows the story, or how much of it is even true. But I could almost believe she was there, when it all took place."

"She was. She was there at the roadhouse, where it began."

He'd spoken so low that Weaver didn't hear him. Weaver kept talking, and Tyree listened some more.

"...And off they rode, fleeing north through a winter storm," Weaver was saying. "At least, according to her telling of it. Lige Dillashay, and another outlaw with him."

"Quarles," Tyree said, louder.

"What's that?"

"Fletcher Quarles, out of Missouri. The third one was a boy called Dooley Sprewell."

"He wasn't in the play."

"They killed him."

"Wait. What? *Who* killed him?"

"Doesn't matter," Tyree said. "Just tell me what happened at the theatre."

Weaver's drink had come. He slurped, eyeing the little man askance. But he told the rest of the story. He grew caught up in it, even—the cold, and the chase, and the showdown; the shot foully fired by Strother Purcell, and the gods of ice and earth passing judgement. "Then she called to him."

"Him?" Tyree demanded.

"To Dillashay."

That March-mad actress. Like some pagan priestess—like a witch. A flea-pit theatre on the second floor above a dance hall: she lifted her arms and conjured with his name. And he rose—that fence-post of a boy who was on the stage with her. He rose up, in counterfeit of the outlaw. There was a look on the actress's face like holy dread and rapture—and then it happened.

"The old man," Weaver said. "*He* rose. Strother Purcell."

Weaver had all but forgotten about him, so rapt had he been in the goddamned play. Jesus Christ, what Purcell must have been thinking—to have sat there in that theatre all along. But now he was on his feet, in the back row: "It is infernal!"

She had seen him, then—the actress. She spied him past the glare of the footlights, Weaver said, as the rest of the audience craned and peered. That one-eyed old man, six foot five inches of him, as distressed as ever Lear was on the heath. "It is not the truth," he cried. "I never intended... And *he* did not... It is infernal!" And she recognized him, Weaver said—in that first stunned instant, she seemed surely to recognize him. She gave a cry like a stricken bird, and exclaimed: "Not you. Oh, no, no, no—not *you*. I don't want you—you are the wrong one! Where is your brother?"

Well, that was it, Weaver said. The Barbary Theatre was in chaos. That actress let out such a shriek as would make a banshee quake. The fence-post of a boy stood stupidly beside her, squinting and exclaiming, while the audience milled and by-golly'd and Barry Weaver bee-lined for the old man, thinking to intercede before God-help-us-all had a chance to happen next. "Well, you know what that did? It nearly got me killed!" The old man laid violent hands upon Weaver himself, when Barry tried to impede him. He seized Weaver up and flung him bodily.

Tyree sought to keep his voice steady. "Is she hurt?"

"Is *she* hurt?"

"The actress."

"To hell with her—she's fine. He never went near. *I'm* the one—flung clear across three rows of seats! I swear to God—the grip on that old man. And before I could get up again, he was gone. Barged right on out of the theatre. I've been looking ever since, but I can't find him."

The hand that had seized Tyree's heart eased its grip, just a little.

"...And you hear things, Tyree," Weaver was saying. "So anything you pick up, about the old man — I need to know it. Understand? And there's something else, too." Weaver leaned in closer, desperately confidential. "The outlaw brother."

"What about him?"

"He's alive. And as far as I know, he's on his way."

"The hell are you — ?"

"I sent him a telegram."

Tyree felt his jaw sagging open. It was an extraordinary sensation — a weirdly detached disbelief.

"Jacobson," said Weaver. "He'll be using the name Jacob Jacobson. He may arrive any day, now. And I need to know it, just as soon as he does. Anything you see, or hear — I'll pay you. Cash money. D'you understand?"

Tyree said, numbly: "Dillashay."

"Yes. He's alive. Have you been listening to a word I've — "

"You called Lige Dillashay *here?*"

"I told him about his brother."

"Why in Chrissake would you — ?"

"Because I'm the old man's *friend*." Barry Weaver was earnestness itself. He spoke as a man might do if he actually believed what he was saying. "He thinks he caused his brother's death, you see. I thought: What a gift this would be — as a friend — to give him his brother back. To effect a — a joyful reconciliation."

"*Joyful?*"

"And it would bring my story to a mighty culmination. *His* story. The life-saga of Strother Purcell — it can't finish until he comes face to face with the brother, at long last. There's no Third Act without that, you see. For better, or else for — no, for *better*. Of course it'll be for the better. For the *best*. I mean, I'd never try to engineer a tragedy — even though Tragedy is the highest form of... Speaking strictly as a writer, you understand."

Weaver had grown unaccountably shifty. It was something about the eyes, though his shit-eating earnestness notched up another three degrees.

"And there's nothing *I* stand to gain, here," Weaver assured him. "You understand that, yes? It's just … I need to stay on top of this."

Tyree looked at him. When he spoke, his voice was remarkably calm. Cold, even. "I understand," he said.

"So anything you manage to find out…"

"You'll be the first to know."

"Good man."

Weaver clapped him on the shoulder. He looked desperately hopeful, despite the travails and dishevelments of the night. And Tyree found that he'd come to a decision. "I don't know of any Jacobson," he said. "But I know just the man who might help us."

"What man?" Weaver exclaimed.

"I could take you to him."

"*When?*"

"I'll take you now."

A filthy summer squall had broken out. The night sky opened and rain pelted down as Tyree set forth with Weaver. They were undeterred.

"I love that old one-eyed man." Weaver raised his voice above the deluge. "I actually do." He hunched his shoulders and held one arm up overhead, as if this might ward off the downpour. Here and there about them, figures ghosted. "And I only want what's best for him — truly. You understand that, don't you? But by golly — to bring the two of them back together. To *be* there — and to write about it — whatever happens. Oh, Tyree — now there's a tale to make a man's career. There's a saga to make up for everything!"

Tyree limped, implacable, leading the way. He veered into an alleyway, which took them to the back entrance of another tavern, the Blackstone. "Wait here," he said to Weaver.

"He's inside? This man you know?" Weaver practically quivered with expectation.

"He is."

Or had been a couple of hours earlier, the last time Tyree had seen him.

"Wait here," Tyree said again. "I'll fetch him out."

Inside, the barroom was thick with smoke and the sour yeast-waft of all such places. The tang of sweat and horse-shit and spilled beer, and the clamouring of drunken men. Amongst them was young William "Ichabod" Rourke, still here, slumming amongst low companions.

"He's outside," Tyree told him.

"Who?" demanded Ichabod Rourke.

"The one who chipped you with a beer-mug. Remember? Your good friend Barry Weaver. You told me once the score was only halfway settled."

Ichabod was flanked on either side by brutes. Their eyes—all six of them—went simultaneously wide, then narrowed to feral slits.

"No charge for the information," Tyree said. "Call it a public service."

He continued on his way through the smoke and din, leaving through the front door. Behind him, Ichabod and his companions were already sloping out the back. Into the alley, where Barry Weaver waited in such anxious anticipation, sheltering from the squall beneath his arm and a canvas awning. Shielding himself from the eyes of the Almighty.

God had perhaps seen enough of Barry Weaver, thought Tyree. Christ knows Tyree was sick to death of him.

–TWENTY-SEVEN–

The Leland Hotel[11]

Midnight, and thereafter

THE THEATRE ARTISTE Miss Arabella Skye had taken a room on the fifth floor of the Leland Hotel. This was a hostelry on Mission Street, much faded from whatever grandeur it had formerly aspired to, which never had been much. But it would still lie beyond the limited means of Miss Skye, were it not for Lyndon Ackerman.

He was the night manager. Unmarried, intense, Romantic. Not a theatre artiste himself, but a man who held strong views on the human spirit. In addition, a man much inclined — by instinct and passionate conviction — to the side of the scorned and neglected. Prone to elevating Unappreciated Artistes into a personal pantheon of the mighty: often instantaneously, on the basis of slight evidence. Lyndon Ackerman would have wept with fierce joy to have met Sarah Bernhardt. In the meantime, he had Miss Arabella Skye. On principle he reduced the rate that would otherwise have applied to the room; when that was too much, he reduced it further. He was zealous as well in guarding Miss Skye's privacy. In Lyndon Ackerman, Miss Skye would always have a friend, regardless of the world's opinion.

So he took a dim view at first of the little man who came shivering in well after midnight, to stand hunched and dripping on the Leland's faded carpet, asking after Miss Arabella Skye.

Lyndon Ackerman said, archly: "Who?"

"I know she stays here. I found that out. Just tell me what room."

---

11   See note on the authorship of Chapter 22. — *Brookmire*.

Lyndon Ackerman pursed his lips, considering. "Miss Skye is not receiving visitors," he said. Certainly not at this time of night, he might have added; possibly not at all, depending on the reason for asking. Miss Skye was an actress, but not *that* sort.

The little man did not seem that sort of visitor, either. He was small and drenched and wretched, his lank hair plastered against his head. "I need to see her," the little man said, blinking owl-eyed and desperate behind misted lenses.

Lyndon Ackerman hesitated again. "Will she want to see you?"

"Prob'ly not."

"Then why should—?"

"She's my sister."

"Good God," Lyndon Ackerman said. He peered. "Is that the truth?"

"If I wanted to lie, I'd do it better."

"Fifth floor," Lyndon said at length. "Room 501."

"Thank you."

"Except... the lift is broken."

The little man looked to the stairs. "I'll manage."

It didn't seem certain that he would, though. Not to Lyndon Ackerman, who had a kind heart. He watched as the little man limped his slow way to the stairwell door: as if he was climbing already, well before the stairs had even started.

"Friend?" Lyndon Ackerman called. "You should see to that cough. Before it sees to you."

At each landing, Tyree stopped to catch his breath. He found it would not easily come. He hadn't expected to feel so close to panic.

He climbed on.

The carpet on the fifth-floor hallway was threadbare. Cracked plaster walls, the smell of damp and mildew, and the murk of lamps at infrequent embrasures. He stopped at the door to Room 501 and composed himself to knock. Smoothed back dank wisps of hair. His hands were shaking.

There were voices inside. A young man's, querulous. And his sister's, slurred and bristling.

When he knocked, her voice abjured him: Go away! Whoever the hell he was.

He knocked again. At last the door was wrenched open.

Arabella Skye, dishevelled and unsteady, stood framed against the shambles of the room. Seeing him, she took one half-step back.

"Oh, Jesus," she said.

"H'lo, Billie."

"Oh, Jesus Christ."

Her eyes were red-rimmed and her hair was wild. A glass of whiskey in her hand, angled at forty-five degrees, and a cotton shift. Clothes were strewn over sticks of furniture behind her; a naked young man sprawled amidst tangled sheets on the bed.

"The fuck do you want?" she demanded.

Tyree said, without thinking: "You've changed."

"You haven't. Not in any way that matters. Still the same little lying swine."

The naked young man on the bed squinted the intruder into focus. It would seem this was his dangerous look. "'Bella? D'you want I should—?"

"Shut," she said, "the fuck up, Stanley."

The young man commenced to look aggrieved. He was better at this expression.

"You never looked for me," Tyree said.

"I'm looking at you now."

"Sixteen years."

"And *you* couldn't even write a proper note."

"I heard what happened at the theatre," Tyree said.

"Your note said *he* was in San Francisco. Not the brother!"

And he should have known, shouldn't he? Should have guessed what she'd be thinking—the wild hope she'd leap to. He had always made it his calling to know such things, about other people—and above all to know them about his sister. What else could the likes of him be good for, after all?

He heard himself sigh. "I'm sorry," he said dismally.

"Yes, you are. The sorriest little fucker I ever seen."

"I should've stayed away."

It was the truth. Whatever he'd hoped for in coming, it wasn't here. He understood that now. Whatever bond of loyalty they'd shared had died long years ago, at the Roadhouse. It had passed with poor Dooley Sprewell.

"I suppose we shouldn't see each other again," he said. "It's no good for us to be together. Bad things happen, don't they? Look what happened the last time."

"That was never my fault. That was you."

She flung it instantly back at him, as if it were the truth. And who knows? Maybe it was.

"Whatever I done," he said, "I did it for your sake."

"You're a liar."

"I'm not, though. I'm lots of things, most of 'em foul, but whatever was done..."

"*You* did it, Tommy. Not me."

She had never been so cold, he thought, in the old days. She'd always been the sort who would coarsen with the years, and here in the glare of unforgiving light she looked ten years older and harder than she ever was on the stage. But surely she had never been so cold.

She said: "It should of been you, Tommy—the one who ended

up dead, instead of Dooley Sprewell. You should of died before that winter, even. They should of drowned you in a sack, like they do with defective kittens."

There is a kind of peace that comes of desolation. "Well," he said. "Be that as it may."

For a moment, it seemed to him that something had wavered, in her face. That she'd rather take back what she'd just said, or some part of it at least. But of course, we don't have that choice. When things are said and done, they stay that way.

"I'd send the boy away, if I were you," he said. Meaning Stanley, on the bed. "If you ask my advice."

"Nobody asked it."

"For his sake."

In the background, Stanley commenced to huff.

"He's alive," Tyree said. "And he's coming."

That's what he'd come here to tell her. So she'd be warned. One last consideration, for old times' sake—blood being thicker, after all.

"I can tend to my *own* sake," Stanley huffed, "an' I don't need—"

"Stanley, shut your potato-trap," said Arabella. To her brother she said: "Who's coming? The hell are you talking about?"

"Lige Dillashay."

Arabella stood very still. "So he *is* alive?"

"He goes now by the name of Jacobson."

"How do you know this?"

"I know a man. He told me."

"What man?"

"A man named Barry Weaver. But you don't need to concern yourself with him. I don't guess anyone does, anymore. Just—look out for yourself, would you? Dillashay—Jacobson—he may be on his way this minute, to San Francisco. And whatever you've been imagining, all these years, to make some peace with what was done

301

to you … Whatever you need to pretend, about who you are, and what he is, and what the two of you could've become …"

"He *loved* me," Arabella said.

Tyree glimpsed it, then, in her face, both shining and constricted: the immensity of the tale she'd been telling herself, for all these years. His poor, wild, vengeful, broken, batshit sister.

"He's a stone-cold killer, Billie. For God's sake, run — 'cause the devil only knows what'll happen when he gets here. Just … run. That's all I came to say."

–TWENTY-EIGHT–

Em'ly

Dawn

THE OLD MAN did not return to Rose's flat at all, that night. Em'ly waited for hours in rising agitation: pacing and fretting inside the door, listening and listening for his boots on the stair. At last, unable to bear it, she wrapped herself tightly in a shawl and slipped outside to go searching, all alone in the first grey light. She took with her Rose's sharpest knife, clenched tightly in one fist, because you just couldn't know what might come lunging at you, out of the dawn with unspeakable intent.

The old man took shape instead, coalescing at the bottom of the street. Em'ly cried out in almighty relief. He trudged, crepuscular, toward her, looming longer with each stride.

"It was lies," he said, as he reached her. "Nothing but lies, what the gal said on that stage."

He'd been lumbering through the streets all night, fighting to compose himself—so it would come out later. Clenching those two great hands of his and working his jaw, such that other night-dwellers shrank back to clear his way. Rain had lashed for a time and then stopped; puddled water splashed knee-high in the vehemence of his passing.

"Lie upon lie, Miss Em'ly—except it wasn't. There was truth in it too, which made it even worse. But twisted and maimed in ways you could hardly recognize. I hardly recognized myself—except I did. And I recognized her too."

"Hush," Em'ly whispered. She'd hurried toward him and now she clung on tightly, pressing her cheek against the rain-sodden shirt.

"It was the child, from outside the roadhouse," he said. "That gal from so long ago—ruined and wrapped in a blanket, knee-deep in snow."

His voice was a rumble against her ear. "Hush, now," she whispered again. "It's all right."

She discovered that she'd dropped Rose's knife, in the tumult of reaching him. She stooped for it, laughing aloud and swiping at tears with the back of one hand.

"I owe you the truth," he told her.

"First come inside."

She reached to take his hand, but he stood fast. He'd come to a resolution, and would not be deterred.

"Strother Purcell," he said. "My true name is Strother Purcell. That's who I am."

"Of course it is." Did he take her for a fool? She'd seen the poster for the play, just the same as he had. She'd seen the title written there, and the look on his face as he'd read it. So who else could he be? "Strother Purcell," she whispered. "I knew already, that's who you are."

"But you don't know what I've done."

"I know enough. I've heard you spoke of. *He* spoke of you—my husband."

This took the old man aback. He blinked his one eye. "That Mormon, you mean? What did he say?"

"Just come inside." Em'ly tugged at his arm, feeling suddenly naked and exposed, here on the street. It was stirring to inchoate life. The bruise of the sky was shading toward light; somewhere, not far off, a dog was barking.

"Tell me what he said," the old man demanded.

She told him. "He said Strother Purcell was the devil."

"How would your husband—?"

"He knew Strother Purcell. That's what he said. He met the devil, here on earth. That devil was called Purcell."

The old man stood for a very long moment, confounded. "Tell me *his* name," he said.

So Em'ly told it—so faint and fluttering that he didn't seem certain that he'd heard.

"Say it again," he said hoarsely.

She beckoned him closer. He knelt, and she whispered in his ear.

His face grew pale, and then very dark. A sound came out of his throat: a groan, but suffused with rage.

"Ohhhhhhhhh," said Strother Purcell.

A long and dreadful syllable. It rattled like a cable in a mineshaft.

-TWENTY-NINE-

The Accounting of Barry Weaver

San Francisco
July 10, 1892, and Thereafter

FATE—FORTUNE—call her what you will—had been an almighty bitch to Barry Weaver.

We must consider Weaver in the third person, for a time. We have entered upon days and weeks that are dark to our wretched narrator, owing to the drubbing that was dealt him. Such details as he can muster were related to him afterward, by others. But Fortune, that harridan goddess, had done herself proud. In later years, during his lengthy twilight, Barry Weaver would tell you so himself. "I had fancied myself Fortune's Darling, friend—but, nope. Turns out I was Fate's Fool." He would utter this pronouncement in barrooms, hoping that someone would stand him a drink and listen to his tale. Sometimes they did, though more often they didn't. Weaver in latter days was a shadow of himself, his left leg palsied and weak and his left arm as well; his mouth drooped on the left side, and he slurred his words even when stone-cold sober, which he wasn't very often, admittedly.

"Wait here," Tyree had bid him on that fatal night, outside the back entrance to the Blackstone Saloon. So Weaver had waited. He had paced a few expectant steps, unable to keep still. Rain lashed the alleyway, drumming violently down on the rooftops on either side. A distant ship's horn sounded out at sea, and the din from the tavern itself seemed muffled and faraway. *On such nights we are all wayfaring strangers,* Weaver thought; *we are orphans abandoned far from home.*

This was a melancholy reflection, but Weaver liked it. It was trenchant; he might work it into his book about Strother Purcell.

The din from the tavern was briefly more distinct. The door banged open; light spilled sluggish and yellow.

"Tyree?" demanded Weaver, peering.

It had crossed his mind to wonder, right at the last: *What cause have I to suppose that Tyree should keep his word? What have I done, after all, to earn his friendship and fidelity, or the friendship indeed of any other man?*

"Tyree, you dog—is that you?"

It was not. Three men were moving, not one of them less than two feet taller than Tyree. The tallest bore a sheen of triumph.

"Barry Weaver, in the flesh. Ain't you a sight for these sore eyes?"

A figure of speech. Ichabod's eyes weren't literally sore, just glinting most alarmingly. Weaver's heart leaped up into his throat in response. His testicles shrivelled northward in pursuit.

"Aw, fuck," he squawked. He tried to flee, but they had him.

Afterward, it would seem, they dragged him out to the mouth of the alley, and left him there. This might pass for consideration, under the circumstances. In the alley, he might have lain unnoticed for hours. But here he was stumbled over in due course by a pair of passing constables, who cussed him irritably for a drunken lump and kicked him to get up. But only once or twice, and without any real zest of application, before one of them peered more closely and realized that this lump had been beaten three-quarters dead already. So they took him round to the Sisters of Mercy on Stockton Street.

Prairie Rose found him there two days later, apparently, amongst the indigents at St. Mary's Hospital. He was one in a long row of stick-men on cots, on a reeking ward patrolled by nuns.

"Fucksake, Barry—look at you," she said.

He made no reply, being still a good two-thirds dead. They'd cracked his skull and cheekbone, and fractured several ribs. Rose may have leaked out a single tear of empathy. Then she let him have it, for the calamity he had wrought by refusing to tell the truth. Her passion was—by all reports—untrammelled, her language such as to shame the attendant nuns, and Christ knows most of them could swear like sailors.

"If you'd just *told* me, Barry—fucksake! Just told me who that old man was. If you'd said the name, then I could've told *you* what would happen if poor Em'ly ever found it out. And she did! She did find out, you fucker, and now they've gone—the two of 'em together, God help 'em both. I found out too late to stop it, Barry. They've cleared out already—they've left San Francisco. They've run off to kill the Mormon Brute!"

Rose knew, because they'd left a note. Em'ly had scribbled it in haste, and left it on the table for Rose to find when she dragged herself home at last from the concert saloon. Rose had the note with her. "Here!" She thrust it at our narrator. "Go ahead—fucking read it."

Weaver did not take the note, owing to his general state of health. He was—so he was later assured—just two haunted eyes staring bloodshot, out of a mass of purple. Accordingly, Rose in her distress offered to leave the note with him, for him to peruse when more coherent. She would pin it to the bedsheet, or else to some item that would not be stripped away and laundered. His scrotum would serve, she suggested. Here—would he like her to pin it to his scrotum?

Weaver's gaze seemed to Rose both woebegone and vacant. It did not indicate a preference.

"Do you understand?" Rose burst out bitterly. "They're already gone, the two of 'em. They've gone to hunt down that Mormon Brute."

"In Ooh-ah?" Weaver is reported to have said. He was evidently following the gist, but slurring badly.

"What did you say?" Rose demanded.

"*Ooh*-ah."

"Utah?" Rose exclaimed. "Who the hell ever said it was Utah?"

Weaver looked abject, and bewildered.

"*I* never said it was Utah," Rose cried. "*You* decided it must be Utah, all on your own. You never did listen to a goddamned word, not when it actually mattered. They're bound for *Oregon,* Barry. That's where they're bound—the two of 'em, on their own. And God help them when they get there!"

–THIRTY–

Tyree

San Francisco
July 10, 1892

THE OLD MAN and Em'ly had gone directly to the railroad station. Em'ly had some money put away, concealed in a biscuit tin beneath a floorboard in the flat. She fetched it out, hands trembling like linden leaves, and the old man said to her: "Good girl."

A vast and terrible resolution had settled upon him. Em'ly had never seen the like. She must surely have lost her nerve — must have stuffed the money away again, and slid straight under the bed, and stayed there — except for the old man's resolution. It did not seem possible to contradict such certainty.

"Say it one more time," he said. "Say his name."

Em'ly whispered it.

"There can be no mistake about this?"

She shook her head.

"So it's him," the old man said. "After all these years. And *he's* the villain who done such vileness to you?"

Em'ly nodded.

"Well, then," said Strother Purcell.

A gleam was upon him. He had stuffed his few possessions into a battered valise. His razor and a change of shirt; the sixgun, as well — the one he had taken from the Irishman, Houlihan, the day the Rent Collector and his thugs had menaced Em'ly. He'd need to arm himself more formidably for the task that lay ahead, but first things first. First they needed to be on their way.

Em'ly scribbled her note for Rose, and gathered her own possessions, and then they left. They were at the railway station before it was properly light.

*

Tyree had dragged himself back to his room on Polk Street, after leaving his sister at the Leland Hotel. But once he was back inside, he could not abide it—not the room, nor his own existence.

He had left his sister without another word on either side, limping along the corridor and back down the stairs as she slammed the door shut behind him; past Lyndon Ackerman at the front desk in the lobby, who had cleared his throat before asking, was he all right? Tyree thought: No, he was not all right at all, and never would be—not that it mattered.

"She turned it into a tale. She's been telling it to herself, ever since." Tyree heard bleak wonderment in his own voice. "All these years."

"Excuse me?" said Lyndon Ackerman.

"The gal and her demon lover. Like—I don't know—like Catherine and goddamned Heathcliff, in that book. That's how she coped with it all, I guess. That's how she's kept herself going. Jesus wept."

Lyndon Ackerman hesitated some more. He seemed to entertain the notion that Tyree might be addled with fever. "Is there something I could do for you, friend?" he said.

At the door, Tyree paused, one last time. Looking back, he said: "Yes. Yes, there is."

"What is it?"

"Look out for her."

"I'm sorry?"

"My sister," Tyree said. "Look out for her, if you can. It won't save her, if he comes. But you could try."

Back at Polk Street, he sat on the edge of his cot for some long while, as the rain outside subsided and darkness leavened. He thought about doorknobs and bootlaces, and his trusty old Deane-Adams pistol. But after another time, it occurred to him that there was something he needed to do before he died. There was someone else he needed to speak to.

Struggling to his feet, he fed the laces back into his boots, and tied them. Then he used the doorknob in the conventional way, to open the door with. He went down the stairs and onto the sidewalk and set his face toward Pacific Street.

That was where the old man stayed. Tyree had discovered that weeks ago, by following Barry Weaver. The old man cribbed with those Mormon women in a flat on Pacific Street.

Tyree arrived there in the haze of a San Francisco sunrise, footsore and heartsore and aching in every limb. An old woman beating a rug on the tenement steps advised him that he'd come too late. The one-eyed old man and that queer little gal? They'd just left, the old woman said. They seemed bound for the railway station. Well, good luck to 'em, and good riddance.

*

The two of them were on the platform.

The old man towered, one-eyeing the other travellers. The gal huddled on a bench beside him, clutching a valise. Reaching them, Tyree stood head bowed, wheezing for breath. When at last he looked up, the old man was squinting one-eyed down at him. "I seen you before," the old man said.

Tyree found the breath to speak. "Yes, sir. You have."

"By God," the old man said. He'd realized. "You were the boy."

"I was."

"The boy, at the roadhouse. I'll be damned. The girl, last night —and now the boy. Doesn't that beat all?"

"I couldn't say how much it beats, exactly," Tyree said. "But I expect it's probably something."

Little Em'ly, tucked in the old man's lee, peered out from the depths of her bonnet. It occurred to Tyree that he should tip his hat. Lacking one, he touched his fingers to his forehead.

"Ma'am," he said.

About them, the platform thronged. A bout of coughing took Tyree, bowing him more than he was already and shaking him painfully. When it passed, they were still looking at him.

"'S there something you want?" the old man said.

"You judged me, once."

"Did I?"

"Yes, sir. You did. You looked down from that horse, and you judged me in one second. You judged that I was low, and vile, and would never amount to one thing worth being, on this earth. So I just come here to tell you ... I just want to say, you were right."

"And that's it?"

"Yes, sir," Tyree said. "I'd say that's about all of it. I never done a thing to prove you wrong. I never will."

"Why not?"

"'S too late."

The old man considered this. "Are you dead yet?"

"Pretty near it," Tyree said. "Not quite."

"Well, then?"

Tyree found himself starting to squirm, under the intensity of that eye. Em'ly was staring at him too, from the depths of her bonnet. He touched his fingers to his forehead once again, signifying that he was about to take his leave. But somehow he just kept on standing there some more.

"Where you bound?" he said to the old man.

"'S that your business?"

"No, sir."

But then the old man answered anyway. "I'm riding to pay out the treatment that was done to this child Em'ly," he said, "who is my most particular friend. I intend to pay it out in full, one hundred copper pennies on the dollar. And I will settle an old ledger of my own, at one and the same time."

"Is that a fact?"

"Why else would I say it?"

Tyree allowed as he did not know.

"My family owes this man's aunt five dollars." The old man's demeanour had grown remarkably grim. "I propose to discharge the obligation."

"Well," Tyree said, after a moment, feeling as though he ought to say something. "This is honourable in you."

"And then I'll collect the debt that is owed to me and mine."

Tyree said, after another moment: "Will you do this alone?"

The train's whistle sounded. A porter commenced bellowing travellers aboard. The old man picked up the valise as Em'ly stood.

"You g'wan, now," he said to Tyree. "Go about your business."

"I've got no business," Tyree said. "None that matters."

"Find some."

The porter called out some more. Travellers jostled, steam from the engine chuffing up about them.

"I've got cash." Tyree had intended to bid the old man farewell, but found himself saying this instead. "Cash," he repeated. "Enough for a ticket, I think—wherever you're going."

And it wasn't Tyree who was speaking at all. Tyree had opened his mouth, but someone else's voice came out—a voice that hadn't spoken in sixteen years.

"I've got an iron," said Wild Gimp Tom.

"You what?"

"A shooting iron. A Deane-Adams five-shot. I can use it."

-THIRTY-ONE-

From The Roadhouse Chronicles of Thomas Skiffings

Near Hell's Gate
Winter, 1876

"DON'T GO UP TO HIM AGAIN," he said to his sister. "Just don't. Not tonight."

She replied to him, in a withering tone: "An' then what—ask him *nicely* not to kill us?"

They were at the creek, the two of them, fetching water. It was early morning of the sixth day since the outlaws' coming. The morning was grey and brutally cold, but there had been the barest shifting in the wind. Gimp Tom was certain of that.

"No, listen," he said. "Billie? Listen."

She had climbed down haggard from the loft, just at dawn. He had glimpsed her face through the edge of the hanging divide as she had crept into their back room.

"*We* can kill *them*."

She very nearly laughed in his face. Then she saw—by God—that he meant it. "Tommy…" she began.

"Not three of them at once," he said. "But one by one. We can."

He started to tell her, then, the plan he had made. He'd thought it all through in the night, while she'd been in the loft with the Man from Decatur. He'd had nothing but time to think it all through.

"I'm your brother," he said to her, fiercely. "Billie, I swear, I will not stand by no longer, while low and wicked men abuse you."

He had rehearsed this proclamation in his head, and said it now out loud. It sounded in his ears less grand than he might have hoped, owing to the treble pitch of his own small voice. But the words themselves were very fine indeed. They warmed him, and a thrill of desperate resolution fluttered inside his chest.

His sister had actually been moved by his fervour. Seeing this, he thrilled more than ever. She touched his arm with her hand — the first time she had touched him since the outlaws' coming. "Tommy," she said, "I know you think…"

She broke off as the door of the roadhouse opened. Cousin Fletch stepped outside, peering evilly into the morning. Billie flinched, as his eyes found her. She said to Gimp Tom, very earnest and low: "If a heart was all it took, you'd be a lion." Then she squared her thin shoulders and straightened her back, and waded through the snow like the Queen of Spain with water buckets, or possibly Joan of Arc.

It would occur to him, much later, that Billie was just playing a role of her own; that all of this, however dire, was not quite *real* to his sister. She had heard that utterance about lions and hearts in a play — spoken by her mother, perhaps, in tones no less tremulous than Billie's own. But in the brutal cold of that grey morning, with Uncle Fletch seething in the roadhouse doorway and Billie struggling bravely away, Tom heard only how desperately she needed him.

So he waited.

His chance came late that afternoon.

Cousin Fletch had gone out to the barn with the Man from Decatur, anxious to see to the horses. They took Uncle John with them. Billie had gone outside as well, back down to the creek, leaving Gimp Tom all alone with Dooley Sprewell.

The young outlaw lay huddled by the stove, as he'd done ever since his arrival. He'd been very bad all day, dozing fitfully and moaning to himself. Now, with the coming of nightfall, he stirred.

"Fletch?" he said, and tried to look around.

"They've gone," Tom told him.

Dooley's face was sunken like an old man's, dying. Fever burned in his eyes. "Gone?" he said.

"Both of those friends of yours," Tom told him. "They rode off."

"Rode off?" The concept seemed difficult for Dooley to grasp. "Rode off where? When they coming back?"

The men would likely be back in ten or fifteen minutes. That was Tom's estimation, though Dooley Sprewell couldn't know it.

"They've left you here, Dooley."

"No, they never," the outlaw said. "They wouldn't."

But they would, too. Of course they would, and Dooley knew it. If not today, then tomorrow, or the day after.

He said: "Billie?"

"She left too," Tom replied.

Dooley gazed at him, seeking to comprehend. The darkness of evening was closing about them. He began to moan. "Oh, Lord," he said. "Oh, Lordy-gawd, there's a stench in here."

"It's all right," Tom told him.

"It's like death."

"It's just you, Dooley. It's just your wound."

"I can't die like this." Two fat tears carved their way down Dooley's face. "Not this way."

"There's a rope," Tom told him.

"A rope?"

"From the barn. I brought a rope inside. Will I tie it for you, Dooley? Help you to stand?"

—

Gimp Tom knew all about the crimes young Sprewell had committed. He could guess what further evils the outlaw would surely wreak, if he were somehow restored to health, through the intervention of some wrong-headed saint in heaven—crimes too heinous to contemplate, no doubt commencing with the desecration of Billie.

Even so, Tom had not been able to stand it, right to the end. He discovered that there is something stark and ghastly in the workings-out of justice—however poetic it might seem in the abstract—which the nickel magazines in his collection failed to mention. So partway through Dooley's dying Tom fled and hid himself in the room at the back, squeezing his eyes tight shut and covering his ears, despite knowing that this was done for Billie's sake, entirely for the sake of protecting his sister, and nothing else.

Billie was the first to return, after it was over. Tom heard the rattling of the front door, as it opened. Creeping out of the back room, he saw her in the doorway. Billie stood in the red spill of light from the dying sun, staring in disbelief at the puppetry between them: the overturned stool and the feet six inches above it, toes strangely juxtaposed and inward-turning.

"Just two outlaws now." Somehow, Gimp Tom found his voice. "Just two more, Billie. Then you'll be safe." He tried, and failed, to sound plucky and undaunted.

Billie looked at him. He would never forget the expression on her face—like the back door to hell opened up right by the roadhouse, and he had just come spidering out of it.

PART FIVE

–THIRTY-TWO–

Arabella[12]

July 12, 1892

SHE HAD SENSED IT on awakening that morning: a perception that the air itself had altered, in an elemental way. From this she knew that some vast apotheosis was at hand.

So at least she was to remember. This became the tale as she told it to herself.

Thus she picked a fight with young Stanley, and sent him packing. The boy had grown insufferable, and was in any case no longer needed for the play, which had closed after two more performances, due to lack of an audience and the ill-health of the star, "ill-health" signifying—as it often did, amongst theatre artistes—that Miss Skye was too drunk to perform. She had been able to keep her room at the Leland Hotel through the good offices of Lyndon Ackerman, who guarded her privacy more zealously than ever and warded off visitations by such riff-raff as the landlord at the Barbary Theatre, who had come by on four separate occasions to seek payment for use of the venue. It is arduous to be the lone defender of an artiste in crisis, but Lyndon Ackerman stood fiercely by Miss Skye, though he was glad enough to see the back of Stanley.

Early that afternoon, however, Lyndon Ackerman left his post for an hour or two's sleep, delegating the front desk to an assistant who

---

12   As with Chapter 22, this would seem to be an imaginative reconstruction by an author (or authors) with close knowledge of the actress, rather than a statement set down by her own hand. Its veracity thus remains an open question. — *Brookmire.*

lacked Lyndon's own fortitude. This would explain how the hotel's defenses should come to be breached.

Miss Skye had been much unsettled all morning—had been agitated, even. She had changed her frock three times and took unaccustomed care at her toilette. Ninety minutes, longer than she'd spend preparing herself for the stage.

And such a shock it had been, nonetheless. That first sight of him, standing in shadow in the fifth-floor hallway when she answered the knock at her door: a preacher, God help us. He stood in a flat-brimmed preacher's hat and a long black coat, despite the summer swelter. And so much older.

"Miss Skiffings," he said. "So it *is* you."

"Oh, Lord," said Arabella. Her legs very nearly gave way beneath her.

Even in shadow, his face was scarred and lined. One hand was maimed, as well; she saw this as he lifted it to touch the brim of his hat.

"A preacher?" she said. "A fucking *preacher?*" Her brother's visit had braced Miss Skye against surprises. But nothing could have prepared her for this. "You come about sixteen years too late," she said, "if you're looking for a likely soul to save."

"Miss Skiffings..." he said again.

"And the fuck is that—'Miss Skiffings'? I wasn't Miss Anyone, the last time you saw me. I was nothing but the gal who warmed your bed."

"Billie, then."

"It's Arabella, now. Miss Arabella Skye. You turn up, after sixteen years—you call me Billie?"

"I'm looking for my brother."

"You're a son of a bitch."

Her voice very nearly broke, and betrayed her. She drew in a steadying breath, and essayed the blade-thin smile of a woman whose indifference is colossal.

"Why would I give a damn," she said, "about either one of you?"

"They told me—someone said—my brother's still alive." His voice was exactly the same. Oh, she remembered that voice: husky and dark and suffused with the South. "If that's true," he said, "I want to find him."

"And kill him?"

"You mistake me. I'm not that same man, anymore."

He was, though. Arabella began to see that. The knowledge brought a flutter of fear, and exaltation.

"I expect you think I'll invite you in," she said. "Well, think again."

Behind him, in the shadows, something shifted. Arabella saw that he'd brought some manner of companion.

"Who's your friend?" she said.

"This is Rebekah."

Arabella saw a great ungainly gal, with fists like hams and a strawberry birthmark stained across her face. She wore coveralls and vast clod-hopping boots, and glowered judgement down at Arabella from a towering height, as if she'd laid eyes upon the Witch of Endor from the Bible, who'd brought low mighty King Saul.

"H'lo, Rebekah," Arabella said.

Rebekah glowered some more.

Arabella thought: They'd need to be shed of this one.

"I heard there was some play," he said. "I thought to myself... I wondered if it was you. I need to start somewhere, you see. So I thought—"

"Yes," Arabella said, abruptly. "I seen your brother."

"When?"

"Three nights ago. We never spoke. But it was him."

He had taken the preacher's hat off. He stood squinting down at it, turning it slowly in his hands, round and round. Arabella saw that his hands were shaking.

"How was…" he began, then trailed off. Tried again: "How did he look?"

"Old."

"But was he… Would you say he was all right?"

"It would prob'ly depend. On what the fuck that even means."

Behind him, the ungainly gal clenched those hands. Rebekah seemed to be deciding that she had been in error, in supposing Arabella to be a mere witch, and not the Whore of Babylon herself.

"Do you know where he is?" Lige Dillashay said.

"I do not," said Arabella. "Nor do I give one solitary shit."

"I should go, then."

"*No.*"

The syllable burst out before she could stop it, like a cork from an over-agitated bottle. Lige Dillashay blinked, and Arabella wrestled emotion down. She lacquered a veneer of boredom over top and managed to recover her drawl.

"You *are* going to kill him, aren't you?" she said. "Your brother."

He shook his head, and said tersely: "I already told you—"

"Now tell me the truth."

"I want to talk to him. Sort things. Settle with him."

"Settle?"

"Certain issues. From the past. And then move on."

"Well," Arabella said. "I wish you luck."

There was silence for a moment.

"I should go," he said again. "Don't want to take up any more of your time."

Arabella might have shrieked at him, then, and clawed him with her nails. She might have cried out: You took the last sixteen years of my life, God damn you—why scruple at taking the rest? Instead, she replied with desperate sang-froid: "Go, then. Don't let me stop you."

He stood there some more, turning that hat slowly round and round, staring down as if secrets had been inscribed in mystic lettering—in Greek, maybe, or Aramaic—along the brim.

The smell of him was exactly as she remembered: wood-smoke and the sweetness of whiskey and something deadly feral underneath it. Arabella placed one hand against the door-frame, to demonstrate perfect nonchalance and also to steady herself.

"You look well," he said to her.

"Do I?"

"Considering. We've all of us aged."

"Sixteen years. And he comes here strewing compliments."

"Have you been happy, at all?"

Christa'mighty, Arabella thought; *what a fucking question.*

"I expect you'll want me to pour you a goddamned drink," she said.

"No," he said. "I don't use it anymore."

But he did, though. It was on his breath, thick and sweet.

She began to see how this might go.

–THIRTY-THREE–

Em'ly [13]

SHE HAD BEEN BORN Emily Braxton, to a Mama who died when her only child was four years old and a Daddy who drank thereafter. She'd lived with her Daddy for ten more years, and then she was taken up the mountain to stand before Judge Shackleford. That was the name the Judge called himself, though Em'ly guessed soon enough that he'd had another name, once—down South, where he came from, in Tennessee or Carolina. And that was the nub of how she came to be Em'ly Shackleford, the youngest of the Judge's Mormon wives; she whispered the story out in bits and bobs to the old man, over the course of their journey into Oregon.

She whispered some of it to Tyree, as well—Mr. Tom, as she preferred to call him, once he'd confided his true and proper name. The rest of it he overheard, and afterward recollected, as was his way.

They travelled by train at first. Mountains bulked before them, the Sierra Nevadas and the Cascade Range beyond, sheering skyward. As evening came on, the shadows stretched out across them, as if the Judge had loomed in front of the sun.

"He's up on his mountain right this minute," Em'ly whispered.

"Hush, now," the old man said.

---

[13] Emily Braxton's birth is verified by County Records, though the date of her death cannot be so clearly ascertained, and her presence on the Ride of Reckoning into Oregon in late summer of 1892 would seem to be unquestioned. On its own internal evidence, this chapter would clearly seem to have been composed by "Em'ly" herself, or at least with her active collaboration. This in turn may be taken as speaking—loudly —to larger questions pertaining to the sourcing and authorship of the Sturluson manuscript. —*Brookmire.*

From time to time, the old man would stand, unfolding himself from the hard bench. "Look after the gal," he would say to Mr. Tom, as if he might be days or weeks returning. The carriage could scarcely contain him when he rose to his full height; stooping, he would stalk along the aisle, swaying from side to side in his progression.

His pretext was to stretch his legs, but he would hawk-eye in turn each of their fellow travellers, as if malefactors might be pocketed amongst them: concealed inside the red suspenders of the pot-bellied drummer, who had boarded the train in Sacramento, or under the bonnet of the harried young mother who sat several rows ahead, with three apple-cheeked children huddled about her. She had a weary prettiness that attracted unwanted looks from other passengers, most particularly a young man sitting on the other side of the train, facing toward her. He possessed, it would seem, a high opinion of himself; it emboldened him to eye the young mother with frank appraisal, until it occurred to him that one ice-blue eye was fixed upon him in return, looking down from a height.

"Son, this is the land of liberty," the old man said. "But mind how many liberties you take."

The bold young man said: "What?"

"I'm sitting just back there." The old man pointed with his chin. "Got a view of the entire carriage. Just so's you know."

The bold young man sputtered briefly, as if working himself up to take umbrage. But that ice-blue stare grew unsettling. After another moment or two, the young man discovered some item in the passing landscape that caught his eye, and required his full attention. He scowled and scrunched lower in his seat.

"Ma'am," the old man said to the young mother. He inclined his head in respectful greeting.

He said the same to her each time he passed. She smiled shyly in return. The eldest of the apple-cheeks — a tow-headed boy of three or four years old—grew so bold as to poke his head up from time to time above the back of the bench, grinning milk-toothed at the old man. He shrieked in delight when the old man stared right back at him, and winked.

More often, though, the old man's face was grim. He stayed deep in his thoughts. Sometimes you'd be sure he was asleep, only to have him open his eye abruptly.

"Jesse was fast and cold as ice," he said once, out of nowhere at all, after a lengthy silence. "But that didn't help Jesse, did it? Not in the end."

Em'ly looked around quickly, wondering who the old man was addressing. A man sitting opposite seemed to wonder the same. His face was chipped from granite, in the manner of Frank James in tintype images, although this man was reedier than Frank James ever was, and much less certain of anything at all.

"What matters," the old man told him, "is you keep coming. A man in the wrong cannot prevail—not against a man in the right who keeps on coming."

"By golly," said the man who was not Frank James. He twitched up a nervous smile. "I expect that's the God's own truth."

"God don't come into it. Not at the end. You know that—same as me. It comes down at the end like it always does. Just two men, and a Reckoning."

The man who was not Frank James cast about for another smile. "Well," he said, "I been told, so I know it now."

Em'ly would hunch smaller when the old man spoke like this. She would recede ever deeper into her bonnet, until she was just two sharp eyes, panic-bright, peering out. *Oh, Lordy-God,* she would think, *what have I begun?*

Mr. Tom knew what she was thinking, because she whispered it to him. It was the deep blue darkness before dawn on their first night of travel, the passengers slumbering as best they could, the train crawling slowly up an incline. "Don't you worry," Mr. Tom whispered back. "That old man beside you? That's Strother Purcell. Whatever's begun, he'll finish it."

Em'ly tried to convince herself this was true. She didn't entirely succeed. "You never saw him — Judge Shackleford," she whispered. "You don't know what he's like."

A sound came from her other side, like water gurgling in an ancient pipe. The old man had not been asleep, it seemed; he had given a laugh. "A Judge? No, he was never a Judge — not when I knew him. No more than his grandfather was, though that old devil claimed to be one too." His one eye was open. It gleamed. After another moment, he said: "Tell me, though. Is he as bad as I suppose him to be?"

The old man had asked this several times before. He seemed to require particular reassurance on this point.

Em'ly whispered: "He is."

"Is he, though?" He seemed to have grown uneasy in his mind. "Because I suppose him to be very bad indeed."

"He is," whispered Em'ly.

"I suppose him to be among the worst men as ever walked, and deserving of neither mercy nor quarter."

"As bad as you can suppose? Judge Shackleford is worse," Em'ly whispered.

"And deserving of no quarter?"

"None."

"Well, then," the old man said. He settled back on the bench, seeming very grim and wholly satisfied. "Then there's no question about right and wrong. No question at all. It's clear as clear what needs to be done. And I'm the man to do it."

—

Em'ly had been still a child when she'd been taken up before Judge Shackleford.

This was not due to any crime she had committed. It was due to her Daddy. Mr. Braxton was a fearful man for drinking, and had acquired debts he could never hope to settle. Compounded together they made up a prodigious sum, and all of it came out in the end as a debt that her Daddy owed to Judge Shackleford, as debt in that district had a way of doing.

"How do you propose to pay what you owe?" the Judge said.

Mr. Braxton said: "I got the gal. She's all I got, and all the world to me."

Judge Shackleford said: "Then you better fetch her forth."

So Em'ly had been taken up the mountain. Judge Shackleford was at the top of it, in the room where he did his calculations, tallying up the figures in his Ledger. Nobody kept accounts the way he could do, and with such cold clarity: revenues received and payments made; everything set down in long black columns. There was no one in Oregon who could calculate more exactly, nor hold out less prospect of hope for you at the end. When word was brought to him that the Braxton gal had been fetched, he came outside.

Em'ly was fourteen years old that summer, though she knew she looked much younger, on account of her size. She saw a man of some forty-five or fifty years step out onto the porch, in dungarees and suspenders and a shirt that was soiled and frayed, and boots near as shabby as Mr. Braxton's own, despite his wealth and holdings. He was square and hard and cold and unshaven, and he looked Em'ly slowly up and down. His eyes were black and his hair so fair that he seemed to have no lashes.

"Turn around," he said to Em'ly.

When she came full-circle, he was frowning.

"Puny," he said.

"She'll grow," said Em'ly's Daddy.

Judge Shackleford grunted, unimpressed. "Does she talk?"

"Not much," Mr. Braxton admitted. "But she's got good teeth. All her limbs, too—fingers, toes, you name it."

Two or three of the wives peered out of windows. There was a horrible old woman, too—a hundred years old, at the very least, twisted and shrivelled and glittering with malice. Such was Em'ly's first impression, and nothing would subsequently cause her to revise it. The old woman was some manner of relation to Judge Shackleford; she had come with him all the way from the Smoky Mountains, long years before.

The Judge looked Em'ly up and down some more. "All right," he said at last. He spit into his hand, and Mr. Braxton did likewise, to seal the bargain.

"Here's what we'll do," Em'ly's Daddy said. "I'll keep her for the present time, and bring her back when she's older." He was not an evil man at heart, and loved his daughter dearly, in his way. "When she's fifteen, maybe. Sixteen, even."

The Judge said: "No. You'll leave her here right now, and go on home."

Mr. Braxton was white with drunkenness. He'd have left her one way or the other—Em'ly knew that—drunk or sober. But the drink made it easier for him to bear.

He looked to his daughter, and would have said something, if only he could think what it might be. Em'ly saw that his eyes were moist and red. Then he turned and shambled back down the trail: a small man, growing smaller with each step.

*

They travelled by train for the first day and a half, and by stagecoach after that. It would take them as far as a town called Mears Lake, where the old man would acquire a horse and ride the last leg of the journey.

"You'll stay with the gal, at the town," the old man said to Tom. They had reached the final posting-stop before Mears Lake. The passengers had been set free to creak and stretch while the driver changed horses. The mountain air was sharp with the scent of pine, and the dust rose in puffs where they stepped. Tom stood with the old man in a scrap of shade; Em'ly was nearby at the pump, drinking water from a ladle. "I'll ride the last leg myself," the old man said.

"No, sir," Tom said. "I'll be riding with you."

The old man allowed himself one-sixteenth of a smile. "You? Astride a horse?"

"I've been on horses before," Tom said stoutly. "Plenty of them."

"Sure you have."

"I know one end of a horse from the other."

Tom could scarcely move at the moment, truth be told — the stagecoach had no springs, and the lurchings up the mountain road were all but unbearable. But he did his best to conceal this fact, and swung his arms to demonstrate how much better he was feeling, up here in the dry mountain air.

This was true, actually. His lungs had cleared considerably, despite the aggravation of the dust. His colour was much better, even — he knew this because Em'ly had told him so, earlier that day. "Another few days, and — by golly — I may start to grow," he had said to her, hoping to make her smile. She almost did, which egged him on. "I'll be cutting a caper next — you watch," he had said. "After that? Why, it might be handsprings."

"I can ride," he insisted now, cricking his neck to look up at the old man. "I'll ride with you, against that Mormon bastard."

"I don't believe he's a Mormon, either," the old man rumbled. "No more than he's a damned Judge."

"Whatever he is, I'm riding."

"It's not just him," Em'ly whispered.

She had come up silently, and took shelter now behind the old man. Em'ly seemed more fearful than ever of straying from him, with each mile that brought them closer to her husband.

"It's more than just Judge Shackleford," she repeated. "He's got sons."

It was the first they'd heard of sons. Tom shot a quick look up at Strother Purcell; the old man had been taken off his guard.

"How many?" the old man demanded.

"Two are full-grown men."

"Are there others?"

Em'ly, deep in her bonnet, looked hunted. "Zebulon is the oldest," she said. "Then Uriah. The others are younger."

"How many others?"

"The others are boys. Robbie—he's the youngest."

"You should have told me this," the old man said.

"'S there one of yours, too?" Tom blurted out this question. He felt obscurely relieved when Em'ly shook her head.

"No," she whispered. "I never had a child."

Tom said, "That's a blessing."

The old man did not appear to perceive any blessings. He moved away from them, squinting up toward the mountains and seeming much unsettled by Em'ly's disclosure, which Tom set down to the altered arithmetic, and the necessity to recalculate his angle of attack.

Em'ly stood, wretched. "I should've said," she whispered to Tom.

"You did," he told her. "You said it now."

"Zebulon's nearly as bad as his Daddy."

"And Strother Purcell never lost a gunfight. He never once backed down."

Mr. Tom was the man who would know it, if he had. Em'ly knew this to be true. That head of his was stuffed over-large with all the names and dates and facts he'd crammed inside. The old man was steadier than Wild Bill ever was, Mr. Tom assured her now; he was more resolute than Wyatt Earp, and altogether more dangerous than any man she would ever meet, even if she lived to be a hundred.

"He's old," she whispered.

"Doesn't signify."

But she wouldn't be comforted. Not now, with the stagecoach driver calling out that they'd be on their way to Mears Lake in ten more minutes, and the Judge on his mountainside just two days' ride beyond.

"He took a blow," Em'ly whispered.

The old man, she meant—that day when he had kicked Rose's door into flinders, and then stood against the Rent Collector and his ruffians. She saw clear as day how he'd beaten them, one against three; but then she'd recollect the way he had fallen afterward.

"A fearful blow, to the head. Afterward, he was … there's been something not quite right, ever since. You see that too, don't you?"

"No, ma'am," Mr. Tom said instantly. "No, I don't."

But he did.

"That old man is Strother Purcell," he insisted. "And he's right as rain."

But he thought of an old neighbour woman he'd known as a little boy, whose thoughts had come unmoored. Her wanderings grew steadily more unpredictable, until she went out one morning naked as a jay and squatted pissing in the road, her grey-haired son trotting shamefaced to retrieve her.

"Family," the old man muttered, out of nowhere. "I did not stop to suppose there might be family."

He was standing a few paces away, still staring grimly into the distance. Now he looked over his shoulder. "How many sons?" he said to Em'ly. A shadow had fallen across him.

Em'ly held up six fingers.

"Six sons," the old man said. "Are there daughters?"

She held up a single finger.

"God's teeth," the old man said. "The devil has he been up to, in those mountains? Breeding himself a damned army?"

Em'ly stood small and mute and wretched. Then she nodded.

-THIRTY-FOUR-

Missus Mann[14]

THE REVEREND MANN and his bride had been drinking steadily since leaving San Francisco.

They were newlyweds, or nearly so. This was almost as you might say their honeymoon. Such at least was the missus's version. Arabella, her name was—Arabella Mann, née Skye, the bride of the Reverend Mann from Decatur. This was the name she signed in hotel registers, and it gave her visible delight to do so. Missus Mann hailed from somewhere farther north—she was apt to be sliding when pressed for specifics—though her accent would migrate to meet her husband's. It was almost possible to suppose that she might not be a clergyman's wife at all, but an actress playing the part of one with a wonderful intensity of conviction.

Reverend Mann's mood was more turbulent altogether. A dark man, scarred and brooding, his eyes and his coat both Bible-black. He would be silent for considerable stretches, his bride coaxing him into brief simulacra of jollity, after which he would lapse into shadow again. As they travelled, he would ask railway porters and ticket agents if they had by chance encountered a tall, old, one-eyed man. He had information that such a man might be travelling in this direction, having left San Francisco by train on the morning of 12 July.

A ticket agent in San Francisco had supplied this information to

---

14   See note to Chapter 32, as regards probable authorship. It is worth remarking that the rough contours of the journey herein described can be independently documented, with startling precision. And a "Rev. & Missus Mann" do indeed appear in the Guest Register of the Historic Ross House Lodge, as it is now designated, on a date that corresponds exactly.—*Brookmire.*

Reverend Mann, when the clergyman asked him. Yes, he had said, he recollected such a traveller: a towering man, ramrod straight and with a singular demeanour, like Moses *en route* to the Red Sea.

Reverend Mann had exclaimed to hear it. "Did he say where he was bound?"

The ticket agent recollected: Oregon.

"You're sure of this? What else can you tell me?"

He'd been travelling with two companions, the agent said: a gal and a cripple.

"A cripple?" Missus Mann demanded. She'd seemed unsettled by that word, and sought clarification: An ambulatory cripple, upright and walking?

"Yes, 'm," the ticket agent confirmed. Upright, more or less, and walking, if such was the term that best described his means of locomotion.

Reverend Mann was eager to know what intention the old man might have expressed, and what his final destination might have been. The ticket agent could not elucidate further; but curious, he asked to know: "Is he someone of particular significance to you, then, Reverend?"

"We have a discussion to conclude, between the two of us," said Reverend Mann. "It got interrupted, temporarily, in 1876."

Missus Mann had grown oddly agitated, or so it seemed to the ticket agent, for reasons he did not of course comprehend. "Let him go," she urged the Reverend.

He would not.

The ticket agent was a man named Walter Perkins. He had a wife and three daughters, all of whom thought well of him, and of an evening would fashion little wooden models of ships, being wonderfully clever with his hands. This is mentioned for interest's sake, none of it being germane to the present narrative, into which Walter Perkins will not reappear, except just once.

The day after his odd encounter with the Reverend and his wife, Walter Perkins arrived for work at his usual place in the line of wickets at the railway station. As he did, he could not help but notice that a small contretemps had broken out to his left, two wickets over. A fellow ticket agent was having a difficult conversation with a customer in line: a great, ungainly, agitated gal in coveralls and clod-hopping boots. She had a strawberry birthmark stained across her face, which turned redder and redder as she tried to force out syllables.

Walter Perkins took it upon himself to intercede. His middle daughter was afflicted with just such a stammer, which only grew worse if you badgered; after a few patient moments, he was able to explicate what the young woman wanted.

A p-preacher. She was seeking a p-p-preacher, name of Ja-Ja-Jacobson.

Walter Perkins did not recognize that name. But he mentioned having sold a ticket just yesterday to a preacher named Mann. Two tickets, in fact; Reverend Mann was travelling with his wife. He described the two of them, as the great ungainly gal seemed to wish: the Reverend dark and limping, one hand maimed; the wife small, sharp, and animated.

"Wh-who-whore," the young woman managed. Her face was now bright crimson, and her fists were clenched like hams. "Of B-b-b-b-b—"

"Babylon?" he hazarded.

This seemed harsh, though Walter Perkins did not say so. The ungainly gal seemed to want a ticket of her own; he helped her get sorted with this, then returned to his own wicket. When he looked to his left again a few minutes later, the gal was gone.

He never did know what became of her, or of the Manns, or of that towering, old, one-eyed fellow. There was something lurid in the newspapers a week or two later, but the names were different, and he didn't make a connection.

×

A porter remembered the old man clearly. From him, Reverend Mann learned that the name of a town had been mentioned: Mears Lake. It was accessible by stagecoach, so they went there.

Mears Lake was a settlement of some five hundred souls, on a plateau beneath tall mountains. It existed as a centre for supplies for the ranches in the area, and was a hub of sorts for travellers as well. There were three or four lodging-houses, some of which were notorious for fleas, and the Ross House Lodge, which mainly wasn't.

Arriving at the Ross House Lodge, Missus Mann signed their names in the Register. They were much grimed with travel; Missus Mann expressed high hopes for a bath. Reverend Mann seemed much preoccupied instead with a party he was seeking, and described him to the woman at the desk, who shook her head. No, she did not recollect such an old man, with or without two singular companions. Privately, she thought: She would not have let rooms to such travellers, regardless. She was having qualms enough about Reverend Mann and his bride.

The woman behind the desk was Missus Ross. She was the widowed daughter-in-law of old Major Ross, who had built the Lodge, and she had strong views concerning propriety. The Lodge was a Christian house, and the Reverend Mann and his wife were dishevelled and considerably drunker than a man of the cloth had any business being, in the Widow Ross's opinion.

"Just let him go," Missus Mann said to her husband, when his repeated description had drawn a curt shake of the Widow Ross's head. "We're here in ... where the hell are we?"

"Mears Lake," said the Widow Ross.

"It's the mountains. There's a lake. We're on our honeymoon. We'll take a bath!"

Her husband would not listen. He went back out again to search for news, and his wife with a bitter exclamation trailed after him.

Reverend Mann found the news he was seeking at the livery stable. The man who owned it was named Emmett Hoddle, and he nodded immediately at hearing the description. Yes, Emmett Hoddle said; he had seen such a party as the Reverend described. He had in fact sold them two horses and a mule.

"When?" the Reverend demanded.

"Two days ago," Emmett Hoddle said.

The beasts had not been young, he added, but they were sound in wind and able to bear up over distances. Honest creatures at an honest price.

Emmett Hoddle had been a blacksmith. He was a plain-speaking slab of a fellow, unlettered and unlovely, which in itself is no guarantee of honest intention. But sometimes men are indeed what they seem, and Emmett Hoddle may have been an instance.

The travellers paid in cash money, Emmett Hoddle said, which the girl produced from out of a leather pouch. No, he could not say where they were bound. The old man had about him a manner that discouraged inquisition. "He seemed settled," Emmett Hoddle said, when pressed.

"Settled?" repeated Reverend Mann.

"In his own mind," Emmett Hoddle said. "On whatever it was he decided. That's how he seemed."

It had also seemed to Emmett Hoddle that he was standing just then in the old man's way. This did not seem the wisest place to be.

"And you never saw which way they went?" Reverend Mann demanded.

Emmet Hoddle shook his head.

"And he never said a word about where he was bound—or what he wanted—or why the devil he was travelling in the first place?"

Emmet Hoddle shook his head again.

"Well, then which way *could* they have gone?"

Emmett Hoddle cocked his head. After a moment, he scratched it. Then he shrugged his massive shoulders. "Truthfully, Reverend? I expect they could of gone pretty much any way," he said.

"Let him go," Missus Mann urged her husband yet again.

It was later that same evening. Reverend Mann had come very close to purchasing a horse from Emmett Hoddle, with the last dregs of his financial resources, and riding bull-headed some way—any way—after his brother. But his wife had prevailed upon him to take just one more drink, and think it through. Then she prevailed upon him to take another. This led him to take a third and then a fourth, as she had hoped it might. And after all, he was worn out; he was weary in every bone; he just wanted to sleep.

"Yes, you could track him down, sooner or later. I believe you could do that, I truly do," said Missus Mann. "But even if you did, what would it serve?"

They were sitting outside the Lodge in gathering darkness, on wooden chairs on the veranda. Soft light spilled through the windows behind them, and occasionally a passerby would ghost along the street. Sometimes one of these nodded a greeting, but mainly they kept their eyes averted. Reverend Mann held a whiskey bottle, which infrequently his wife took from his hand. After sipping she gave it back.

"You'd confront him, I suppose. Demand some justification—

if he'd give it. Maybe kill him, if he didn't. Or else—what—*save* him? Oh, my love." Missus Mann ached with solicitude. She cupped a hand to his stubbled cheek. "He's long past saving, even if you tried. God knows that, too. If there's a God at all in heaven, looking down—and who knows? It's possible there is. If there is, He gave up on your brother, long ago."

Her husband would not look at her.

"Oh, my love," she said again. She said it with such sadness, there amidst the soughing of the night. "Your brother's gone. You're with me, now. Just let him go."

He laughed harshly. "You know what the truth is?" he said. "The truth of it is, we long since ruined the best part of ourselves. The only part of either one that might have been worth saving."

"You and your brother, you mean?"

"No. You and me."

This cut her. It did. Still, she gave it her due consideration.

"Well," she said, "then I'd say what's done is done. I'd say, in the light of that, we should go upstairs."

After another while they went inside. She led him up the stairs, the two of them ruined and reeling, to the silent disgust of the Widow Ross at the desk, who pruned her lips at the spectacle of a preacher carrying on in such a manner, and most especially with such a woman as Missus Mann most plainly was, no matter whether he'd married her or not.

As it happened, though, he could not perform his duties. For the first time in his recollection, he could not discharge the debt a husband owes a wife. At length, he gave up and rolled soddenly out of the bed. Leaving her tangled in grievance and bedsheets, he shambled back outside again.

He was sitting alone on the front steps some while later, despising the world and all those in it and himself beyond them all. Moths batted against the porch light; frogs chorused in the distance, down by the lake.

A throat was cleared.

He looked up to see a stranger standing, hat uncomfortably in hand.

"You'd be the Reverend?" the stranger said.

"What of it?"

The stranger's name was Nickerson. A traveller, he said, passing through from the north. His errand was private in nature, which he did not divulge; Mr. Nickerson believed in tending his own affairs, and leaving others unmolested to tend theirs. This in part explained the awkwardness with which he stood now, looking more at his own hat than at the preacher.

Mr. Nickerson cleared his throat again. He'd arrived in Mears Lake a short while previous, and had fallen into discourse with the man at the livery stable: Emmett Hoddle, who was as you might say an old friend. From Hoddle he learned that a preacher had been by that morning, asking after an old man travelling with a gal.

"And?"

"I seen 'em."

There was a change in the tenor of the night, subtle but unmistakable. So it seemed to Mr. Nickerson.

"When?" the Reverend said.

"Earlier."

"Where?"

"Oh, thirty miles or so—northeast, up the Old County Road. The old man, the gal, and a little fella."

"A one-eyed man," the Reverend said.

"That's him."

"Name of Purcell?"

The old man didn't give a name, Mr. Nickerson said. But one-eyed, yes. And he'd recognized the gal. Emily Braxton, as she had been once — Harley Braxton's child, who'd been married off to the Mormon up at Deadman Creek, in settlement of debt.

"In settlement of *debt?*"

"Not my bidness," Mr. Nickerson said. "Never was. But not a wholesome situation, neither."

"Sit down," the preacher said.

Mr. Nickerson hesitated. It unsettled him to speak so plainly of another man's private affair. Nor did it set easily that a preacher should be so sodden with drink as this one manifestly was: pale and sour and stinking with it.

But the preacher's stare had levelled with dark intensity. "Sit down."

Mr. Nickerson sat, choosing a lower step than Reverend Mann was on. By this expedient he avoided that stare and could address himself more generally to the night, which by comparison seemed less black and perilous. A breeze had come up, stirring their habiliments. An owl hooted.

Mr. Nickerson twisted his hat between his hands.

He'd always felt sorry for that gal. There was the nub of it, and he said so now. She had been dealt with shamefully by her Daddy, whom Mr. Nickerson had known in a general way. Harley Braxton farmed a scrap of land near Juniper Plateau, where Mr. Nickerson himself owned property. Braxton was a feckless man who had fallen on evil times — dissipation and debt, compounding weekly. Nickerson was not a man to judge, nor to intervene. But when the daughter was as good as sold to the Mormon — well, it had crossed Mr. Nickerson's mind to wonder if a man might go too far, in respecting the business of others. That question had come to his mind again, upon seeing the gal that same afternoon.

"First time I seen her in months," he said. "She'd run off, y'understand. Left her husband and disappeared."

She had fled with a pouch stuffed full of her Mormon husband's coin, dug up from a hole in the ground behind the barn. That was the story that went around, at least; Mr. Nickerson could not say, one way or the other. But there she was again, that same afternoon: Missus Emily Shackleford, née Braxton — travelling with those two companions right back up toward Deadman Creek.

"And you spoke?" Reverend Mann demanded.

"Yes."

"Tell me."

The encounter had been odd and unsettling, as Mr. Nickerson told it. He had come around a bend in the road, to see the trio riding up toward him. It was just a wagon road, but it widened at this turning, making room for two parties to pass one another. Tufts of scrub-grass grew along the sides, despite the drought of summer; pine trees rose up on either side.

"G'day," Mr. Nickerson had said, reining in his horse.

The old man one-eyed him with appraisal. He was forked on a horse of improbable size — a draft horse, half Clydesdale by the look; not a saddle horse at all, but of a size required to bear that old man up a mountain. The little man sat suffering astride a mule, while the gal on a small white horse hung back a little. Mr. Nickerson had recognized her almost at once; she had recognized him too, turning her face away right quick, in hopes that the bonnet would shield her features.

"What news from up the mountain?" the one-eyed old man had said, on learning that Mr. Nickerson had come from that direction.

"The world goes on as it will," Mr. Nickerson said. "Up the mountain and down it as well, I expect."

"How go our friends, the Latter-Day Saints?"

This had unsettled Mr. Nickerson a little further, knowing as he did the gal's history. He would have spoken to her directly, except that she manifestly did not want to be recognized, which left him feeling uncertain where to look. Such uncertainty is awkward at a bend on a mountain road, with nothing but trees below or on either side; Mr. Nickerson felt it keenly, but did his best to make amiable conversation.

"I believe," he said, "that the Mormons are as they were, pretty much."

"There's no more of 'em than there used to be, a year or so ago?"

"No, sir."

"Nor no less neither, I suppose?"

"Pretty much the same," Mr. Nickerson confirmed.

"Seven of 'em, then. If I'm not mistaken. The Judge and six sons. Eight Mormons in all, including the daughter, according to my reckoning."

"Ten Mormons, including the wives," Mr. Nickerson said. "There used to be two others, of course. Two other wives. But they left, first one and then t'other." He sidelonged a glance to the gal as he said it, wondering if she'd make some reaction. She kept her face averted.

"Yes," the old man said. "So I am given to understand."

"Ten Mormons, at present," Mr. Nickerson repeated. "Eleven of them, actually — if you're including the old woman."

The old man had sat very stolid all this while, forked upon that improbable horse. Now he stiffened, all but imperceptibly. An instant's silence ticked past, and then another.

"Oh, yes," the old man said. "I include the old woman in my reckoning."

He leaned himself forward a little, one elbow resting on the pommel, his one eye trained intently upon Mr. Nickerson — as if holding him in the cross-hairs, Mr. Nickerson thought, till he should be satisfied with all the answers that had been given. The notion made Mr. Nickerson uneasy.

"Eleven Mormons up there, in sum total," the old man said. "Eleven of 'em, as might bear arms. Is that correct? Supposing they should make certain choices, and it ever came to a fight."

This left Mr. Nickerson flat-out unnerved. "Why should it ever come to a fight?" he said.

The old man said, "Just supposing."

On the steps of the Ross House Lodge, in the night, Reverend Mann had remained in stillness all this while. Now, perplexed, he demanded: "Why?"

Mr. Nickerson did not follow.

"Why would he care?" the Reverend said. "What's this Mormon to him, to travel all the way from San Francisco?"

"Well ... the gal?" Mr. Nickerson suggested, lamely. None of it made any sense at all, as far as Mr. Nickerson was concerned. But the Reverend very clearly required an answer.

"Shackleford," the Reverend said. "You said the Mormon's name was Shackleford?"

"Judge Shackleford. Yes." Such was at any rate the name he used, though Mr. Nickerson had once heard another. The Mormon had come to Oregon some years ago, he explained, with two wives and several sons already, and set about acquiring more of each. He was a man with a window-pane beard and an uncanny stillness about him. A way of watching like something coiled in a cave — him and that old woman who'd come with him. A twisted old stick of a female relation, Mr. Nickerson said. Some manner of granny-woman.

Reverend Mann had taken on an uncanny stillness himself. "You said you once heard another name."

"I did."

"Say it to me."

Mr. Nickerson said: "Collard."

"Judas Priest," the Reverend said.

*

It was mid-morning when Missus Mann woke up. She found herself alone in the bed, and in the room. Sunlight pooled.

She saw the note almost at once. It was propped on the washstand, beside the basin:

> *I won't be back. It's better like this. I'm sorry. It could never have been what you wanted to imagine, whatever the hell that was. Hate me like you'd hate the devil, if you find that helps.*
> *—Lige*

She howled, instead.

The Widow Ross heard this unmistakably: a howl of such desolation that she looked up from the front desk, two floors below. Moments later, Missus Mann flew down the stairs, demanding to know if her husband had been seen. Her face was unmade and her hair was wild. A less righteous woman than the Widow Ross might have been moved almost to compassion.

Finding no one here with news of the preacher, Missus Mann rushed out in search of him. But he was gone. He was lost to her, irretrievably, though she importuned each passerby with desperate intensity and ran nearly a mile up the northbound road in wild hope that she might yet glimpse him.

At last, she returned. She was worse than merely inconsolable—so it seemed to Widow Ross at the Lodge, as Missus Mann limped back in. She seemed withered, as if she had aged half a century just that

morning. She seemed as a woman might who had come to glimpse
a towering delusion, and who saw her whole life — all at once — as
ridiculous.

But against all hope, Widow Ross had information. Some person
had been here, in Missus Mann's absence.

"Who?" Missus Mann said.

Some person asking after the Reverend's whereabouts. Failing in this
quest, the person had asked after the woman who travelled with him.

A desperate light rekindled in Missus Mann's eyes. "Where is this
person?" she demanded.

The Widow pruned her lips and pointed: out the back.

The person hulked outside in the dust of the morning. It was quiet here
at the back door of the Lodge: almost secluded. This might under less
frantic circumstances have seemed ominous to Missus Mann. Instead,
she exclaimed in disbelief: "Oh, Jeezus!"

Blaspheming in her wicked way and wounding our Redeemer anew.
Her face whittled down to a sharp point, like it was a stick she would
stab with.

"The devil are you doing here?" she cried. "Have you seen him?"

Rebekah had not. But she had already pieced it together: what had
transpired, and what she must do in consequence. For Rebekah was
not simple, as many had supposed. Sundry persons had made this
supposition, to their cost. No, you could not be easily shed of Rebekah.
You could slip away from Babylon Francisco like a thief in the night,
having ensorcelled Brother Jacob. But Rebekah would pick up your
trail. She would follow you all the way to the Ross House Lodge, in
Mears Lake, Oregon.

"I've not s-seen him, no," Rebekah said. "But there's a w-woman
who could help us."

She stammered scarcely at all. This was often the case when Rebekah saw clear—very clear—the path ahead.

"What woman?" Arabella demanded. She almost managed to sound imperious. Yes, despite her wild distress, she was almost splendid. "Has she seen him? Has she information?"

"She s-seen him."

"*Where?*"

"By the l-lake," Rebekah said. She pointed. "I'll take you."

"What woman?" Arabella cried again. "What is her name?"

Rebekah told her: "J-Jenny Greenteeth."

–THIRTY-FIVE–

Beyond Hell's Gate

STROTHER PURCELL had ridden in grim certainty through the Black Canyon in the midwinter of 1876, following his outlaw brother's trail. He passed through Hell's Gate, where the ravine plunged down into the boil of the ice-choked Fraser River, then followed the trail along the Wagon Road to Hat Creek and then north into the mountains beyond the Cariboo. The outlaws had begun with a two-day head-start, but slowly, inexorably, he closed it.

This was inevitable. No man in the wrong can outlast a man in the right, who keeps on coming.

Strother Purcell kept on coming. He arrived at the Hat Creek roadhouse in bitter twilight. All around was bleak desert landscape, snow-swept and brutally cold; the Secwepemc hereabouts still wintered in the old way, some of them, in *kekulis*—pit-houses dug into the ground. He learned that two men matching the description had stayed at the roadhouse the previous night; they had left again, heading north, with first light.

As darkness closed he negotiated the trade of the iron-grey hammer-head for two fresh horses, with a man who operated the local office of Barnard's stage-line. The man's eyes widened as he saw the sixgun that Purcell kept in a holster slung round one shoulder, and the Sharps rifle in a saddle-scabbard, and most of all the sawed-off eight-gauge shotgun that he was wrapping at this moment in a bed-roll.

"The devil wouldja call that thing?" the man exclaimed. "By golly, that's one Hell Bitch of an implement."

Strother Purcell did not reply.

"By golly," the Barnard's man said again. He ventured the observation that such an implement was not exactly lawful here in Canada, strictly speaking. You couldn't just carry a sixgun here, either.

"I can," Strother said.

"But, see, the law says—"

"I am the Law."

The Barnard's man blinked. The temperature was dropping by the moment, it seemed to him, and not only because of the oncoming night. He stamped his feet awkwardly and stuck his hands in his armpits. His breath came in white billows. "Where's this, then?" the Barnard's man said. He meant, in which jurisdiction had Purcell been duly authorized.

"Right here," Strother said. "I'm the Law standing right here. A few hours' sleep, I'll be the Law heading north. I carry it with me."

At daybreak he rode out again, through a lashing wind that lasted for six days. When one horse broke down, he left it and rode the other. On the seventh night, snow fell prodigiously over the mountains. The morning dawned cold and unbearably bright. Strother wrapped his horse's eyes against snow-blindness and forged on, leading it by the reins and clambering on foot through thigh-high drifts.

He never lost the outlaws' trail. He kept on coming.

He caught up to them at last in a cleft between two hills. It was late morning. The sun rose high in a pale blue sky—a dazzling winter sun that brought no warmth. He'd have waited till nightfall, or else worked his way in behind them, except they'd seen him.

Lige's voice floated down, lilting and sardonic. "'Morning to you, big brother."

They were ahead of him, and above. His brother was, at least. He had yet to pick out the other one, Fletcher Quarles. Lige was behind a snow-covered outcrop of rock.

"So this is where it ends," Lige called. "That about the size of it, big brother?"

"Unless you throw your guns down," Strother called back. "You and that partner of yours."

His brother laughed. "And why d'you suppose we'd do a thing like that?"

He glimpsed Lige, now—a shadow shifting. But still he could not locate Fletcher Quarles. This was a concern, as was the fact that the outlaws had the sun behind them. But Strother had right on his side. He knew this, with certainty. He eased the Sharps out of the saddle-scabbard, keeping the snow-blind horse between him and the outcrop above.

The horse snorted, skittering. "Easy, now," Strother murmured. To Lige, he called: "Last chance."

Still he couldn't locate Fletcher Quarles.

Then something changed. Something had gone badly amiss. Strother heard it first in Lige's sudden exclamation: "No, God damn it—he's mine!"

Lige reared, wrathful, directly into his line of sight. The sun remained behind him, though; Strother could scarcely make him out against the glare. Strother had half a heartbeat to aim and fire, and he did so.

Lige fired first. Strother heard the shot, an instant before his own. His horse trumpeted and wrenched away, leaving him nakedly exposed. But no bullet struck him, which was welcome, albeit odd. In that moment of perplexity, he had time to register the fact: this was undeniably odd. In the next moment, though, all certainties began to slip away.

There was a scrabbling in the rocks behind him. Strother turned his head to see the second outlaw pitching forward. Cousin Fletch wore the trout-faced look that may dawn on a man in the first indignity of knowing that he's dead. While Fletch had been taking languid aim to back-shoot Strother Purcell, some son of a bitch had gone and shot *him*, instead. His own compadre had done this—Lige Dillashay, no less. Cousin Fletch for an instant seemed poised to launch a protest—to say, "Aw, here now, Lige, there was no damned call," or, "Well, ain't this just the fucking-est how-d'you-do." Then he thudded down head-first and lay there in a heap, stone-dead before his sphincter had time to unclench.

Lige stood upright, framed against the lemon glare. But he began to slip. He reached one hand to brace himself against the rock, but this didn't seem to help. He subsided, slowly, to sit splay-legged in the snow, wearing an expression of unmistakable irritation. He began to utter something—some pithy irony, no doubt, on the theme of brothers who shoot you dead while you're trying to ward off a bushwacker. Blood gurgled out of his mouth instead.

Strother said to him: "Lige? Hang on. Gonna get you out of here."

Because that was only right. That was Law. He'd left New Mexico to take three outlaws, dead or alive. Two of them were now deceased. The third, being still amongst the living, deserved all considerations pertaining to that estate: medical care till he should recover sufficient health to travel, then a fair trial in New Mexico, with benefit of able counsel and the right to due process under the law, and three square meals and a clean cell, unless and until the Territory saw fit to hang him.

Lige's eyes met his. Strother read a look of pure disgust. Then Lige toppled sideways.

"Lige!"

Strother heard his own voice, grown ragged. He saw that the horses had spooked and fled. It occurred to him that he might fashion a travois, some conveyance by which he might transport his brother. It occurred to him that he'd best act in haste, before the cold and the loss of blood should kill him.

"Aw, God damn it, Lige. Goddamn!"

He lifted his brother in his arms. It could not be more than ten or fifteen miles, he thought, till they should come upon some manner of habitation—a trapper's cabin with a fire, or a Native village, where there'd be warmth and sustenance and someone who might know how to help. With Lige in his arms, Strother set off down the mountainside, essaying with great sliding strides to make up those ten or fifteen miles by nightfall—gigantic strides like the boy with seven-league boots, in a tale their beautiful, mad Mama had told to them long ago. "Hang on, brother," he urged. "I'll get you out of here."

He'd have done it, too. He'd have carried Lige out of those mountains. His first stride was strong and his second even stronger. But with his third, the mountainside gave way. With the fourth he was tumbling headlong. There was a roaring in his ears, and the mountainside swept him down into the darkness and left him.

He was found by an old Ts'ilquot'in man and his grandson, who dug him out. Such was Strother's understanding of events, when he was able to piece them back together, though it was never clear to him exactly how it happened, or why they'd have bothered. No trace of Lige was found.

The Ts'ilquot'in man had been confounded to learn of Strother's intent—that he should risk his life to carry an outlaw down the mountain to a Judge with a rope. Strother told him, "He was my brother." This did not appear to clarify the situation.

Strother lay shuddering by the fire in a pit-house. It was some days after the avalanche; a month, possibly, or a week. Time had lost its linearity. Strother's left leg was splinted and his ribs had been caved in and dark eyes regarded him through the pall of smoke with grave perplexity. The old man murmured something sorrowful, which the grandson, possessing some English, translated. "He says you are disordered in your head."

It seemed to Strother that there was some reply he ought to make to this. But just when he thought he had it, it slipped away.

*

Such was the tale as it was told to Tom Skiffings, on the final night on the trail to Deadman Creek. Blackness was shading toward indigo when at last the old man finished: that time of not-yet-light when the world takes inchoate shape.

"That's God's truth," the old man said. His face was an ancient mask. "I figured someone should know it. In case they kill me, today."

The two of them sat by the embers of a fire. Behind them, Em'ly lay in unquiet slumber.

"What am I supposed to do with this?" Tom said.

"Whatever seems right to you."

Tom considered, bleakly. "'Course," he said, "odds are they're going to kill me, too. You figure?"

The old man considered this in turn. "Probably," he agreed.

"I mean, if they can kill you, how fucked am I?"

"There you go," the old man said. "All your problems, solved."

There was the barest glint of a bleak grin as he said it. Tom Skiffings was certain of that. It brought a feeling welling up that was almost damned near love.

They rode out with the sunrise, the three of them.

-THIRTY-SIX-

Deadman Creek [15]

August 3 and 4, 1892

EM'LY KNEW OF AN OLDER TRAIL up the mountain: longer and narrow and rugged, infrequently used. There was less risk of unwelcome encounters with other travellers, and they'd be less exposed to someone high above them, looking down.

"With a spyglass, you mean?" Tom asked her.

"That's one way," Em'ly whispered.

She had withdrawn ever deeper into herself, as they drew nearer. She believed her Mormon husband, the Judge, to be possessed of eyesight so keen as to be scarcely human; that he stood on his mountaintop for hours on end—whole days, from first light to last—staring down. The granny-woman might have at her disposal other means entirely.

"She'd see us first," Em'ly said. "I believe she's seen us already."

"That's not possible," Tom said.

"You don't know her."

Em'ly did. She'd lived with that old woman for three terrible years. The granny-woman might lack her puissance of old, being far removed from the Great Smoky Mountains of her prime, where she knew how to read each portent. And she was ancient, shrivelled down

---

15   This climactic sequence is clearly the product of composite authorship. It is not possible to make categorical distinctions, although I have my own opinion; you, the reader, may well have your own.

    We may recall that Tilda Sturluson had appended to the manuscript a hand-written note. "To whosoever may be reading this: it's true. All of it. Every damned word, more or less, except for the bits that maybe aren't, so much. But the rest you can take to the godalmighty bank." It hangs on the wall of my study.—*Brookmire*.

to nut-brown sinew. Her joints were gnarled and her mind would cloud with cobwebs; she'd sit at the end of her nephew's table like a bundle of sticks knit together by nothing but malice, with yellow egg-yolk dripping down her chin. But she'd know that enemies were coming.

The old man nodded, grimly. "She'll know."

It unsettled Tom, that Em'ly might place belief in such eldritch possibility. It unsettled him worse that Strother Purcell agreed.

"She'll know *I'm* coming," the old man said. "She's been waiting for thirty years."

They left Em'ly at mid-day, despite her protestations, half a day's ride below Deadman Creek. She could use a gun, she exclaimed; she desired to be with them at the end, whatever it might be.

"No," said Strother Purcell. She would stay below, in a hollow, sheltered. She had water and a horse. If he and Tom did not return, then she must flee back down the trail, taking whatever refuge might seem best to her. If worse came to the very worst, she would have at least her choosing in how she would die.

"My choosing is to die with you," she said.

He shook his head. He must be focused on the task at hand, he said, and not be thinking of her safety. She must describe to him one last time how the Big House was situated: where the windows were, and what firearms were possessed, and whose nerve was steadiest, beside Shack Collard's. These and sundry other details, right down to which son might carry a bowie knife, and if any one of them preferred to shoot left-handed. He needed to see it plainly in his mind. Then—once he had it clear—he would put Little Em'ly from his thoughts.

It seemed to Tom that the old man was narrowing, right there before his eyes. Shedding any thought or inclination, excepting what he would need to kill Shack Collard. This seemed dreadful, and a mighty reassurance.

"Do as he says," Tom said to Em'ly. "Please."

She stood in the hollow, orphan-eyed, clutching the pistol that the old man had left with her. It was part of the small armoury they had obtained at a gun shop in Mears Lake, and paid for with money from Em'ly's secret cache: an old Smith & Wesson No. 2—the very model that Wild Bill had been carrying on his person when he had been shot dead in Nuttal & Mann's Saloon in Deadwood, Dakota Territory, while holding a poker hand of Aces over Eights, by the coward Jack McCall. Tom knew this interesting historical fact, but did not confide it, suspecting that it would not contribute materially to Em'ly's peace of mind.

"You've fired a sixgun before?" he said instead.

"Damn you to hell," Em'ly whispered in reply.

Under the circumstances, Tom chose to interpret this as yes.

Behind him, the old man was riding off already. Tom stood for one last aching moment.

"Go, then," Em'ly said.

"I'll be back."

He said this with scant conviction. But he sketched up a little smile to go with it, nonetheless, and hoped that it might seem carefree in the looming face of death, as were the smiles that heroes sketched up in books.

"You are low and false and I hate you," Em'ly said.

"I know it," Tom agreed.

"Don't get killed."

*

Through his spyglass, Purcell could discern three of the sons, working in the field below the Big House. The others he guessed might be inside.

He had this vantage from a rocky mesa, half a mile distant. It was nearly level with the lower field itself, but there was no way straight across. The trail led down into a wooded ravine, then back up through the trees on the other side, exactly as Em'ly had described it. There would be tree cover till the last eighth of a mile, which would require a desperate charge across exposed terrain.

"Someone could work his way on up behind," Tom said, pointing. The house was set against the slope of the mountain, which rose steeply up behind it, rugged and well-treed except for bare precipitous strips of loose shale. "Someone could work on up, and then open fire from above. Give you cover."

"Someone would have to get there first," the old man said. "Someone would get his head shot off his shoulders. If he was lucky."

"What, then?" Tom said.

Purcell gauged the height of the sun in the sky. A few hours' daylight yet, though half the ridge was already in shadow. Beyond, to the north, thunderheads were massing; the air was oppressive with the portent of a storm.

They'd work their way closer, he said. Then decide.

*

Five o'clock p.m.

On the other side of the ravine, meanwhile, it had probably gone very much like this:

A watch had been set the previous night, owing to the agitation of the granny-woman, who was ancient and addled but uncanny in her convictions. The sons had been posted in rotating shifts near the top of the old road; the second son, Uriah, was now on duty, after a fashion. The heat was oppressive in late afternoon, and Uriah nodded with it. He was twenty-two years old: a weak man at his essence, striving but insufficient.

Young Robbie had just gone down to his brother from the house, no doubt with something to offer as sustenance, such as bread and cheese. Robbie was just eight years old, the Judge's youngest and the favourite of all his sons. He had the keenest eyes, as well, and saw, before Uriah did, a shadow move.

"Lookit!"

The devil, eight-foot-tall with one eye, leading a monstrous horse. Thus he must have seemed to young Robbie. Behind the devil was a twisted imp.

At the Big House, they'd have heard the distant cry of warning. Robbie's shrill exclamation—the first hint that much had gone amiss. Then the crack of Uriah's rifle, and an answering shot, and then Uriah's voice, feebly wailing.

Zeb might well have been at work by the barn. Zeb was the eldest son, a lean, dour man of six-and-twenty; he'd been sired in Missouri near the end of the War, before his father had taken the name of Shackleford, or commenced calling himself a Mormon—the days when Meshach Collard was still raiding with Bloody Bill Quantrill. At the sound of gunfire, Zeb would have hurried round the front of the house to see Robbie pelting across the field toward him. Robbie rode on Uriah's horse, galloping as if the fiend himself had risen in pursuit.

"The devil happened?" Zeb would have shouted. Others would be spilling from the house behind him.

"He come up the old trail," Robbie shouted back. "The one-eyed devil! He kilt Uriah!"

Or had not killed him yet; not quite. A feeble wailing continued, rising from the ravine, as if from some lost soul at the gates of hell, which had not yet slammed shut.

Judge Shackleford had emerged from the house. Meshach Collard, as he had been in the long-ago: a man in the last brutality of his prime, with his Granddaddy's fearsome black stare. He was shirtless, suspenders hanging like raptor's wings.

They heard the flat, dry crack of another shot. Uriah's wailing ceased.

"See to your Mamas and your sister," Shack Collard told the boy. "Go inside."

"But—"

"Do as I say. Inside. Stay there."

Around him, the sons were in motion. Zebulon and three others: Bendigo, Brigham, and Joseph, all of them grown men, or nearly so.

"Wasn't your fault," Shack Collard said to Robbie. So at least he might well have said, had some witness been standing by to record the moment. A father, speaking to his boy: "You are not to be blamed." He might even have put his hand on Robbie's shoulder, despite the urgency of the moment.

*

Uriah had fallen asleep while keeping watch, awakening befuddled at his young brother's exclamation. Seeing the old man, he had lurched upright and fired the first shot, without ascertaining who had come or on what errand. He would immediately have fired again, almost certainly to greater effect; Uriah was a capable marksman, as were all of the sons. But before he could adjust his aim a blow from nowhere spun him sideways, furrowing him in bewilderment and leaving him aghast that his rifle would clatter from him.

Strother Purcell would not have fired at all, had circumstances been other than they were. He would not have announced his own coming in so peremptory a manner, with daylight still remaining. Nor would he have finished the sentry off, necessarily: taken slow aim and fired the *coup de grâce,* had Uriah left off his wailing, or ceased his crawling, gut-shot, back up the trail. But the killing was clean. One bullet to the base of the skull, as Uriah groped toward sunlight. It was a kindness, even, in its way: greater kindness than Uriah had come to expect from men of his Daddy's generation.

Shack's second son juddered, slid one coffin's length back down the slope, and there subsided.

Tom stood very still. He had not been accustomed to death's coming in such a manner, dealt out with such economy of purpose.

"I do not say this boy will be sorely missed," the old man said. He took off his hat, believing that some eulogy was owed. "But he was some mother's son, which in itself is worthy to be noted."

He put his hat back on.

"What now?" said Tom.

"No choice. He's forced our hand."

Taking his horse by the bridle, the old man started up the trail again, moving fast and keeping low — as fast and low as a man may keep, who is six feet and five inches tall and old beyond his years. Above him, the trail wound upward for another hundred yards, through thickets and outcroppings of rock. Then it opened onto the wagon road. He was halfway there when the first barrage of rifle fire rang out.

Tom, right behind him, flinched back. A hornet snarled past his ear, through the space of this world that his head had occupied one half-a-heartbeat since.

The ravine was rugged and steeply sloped, which saved them. Shack Collard had the high ground, he and his remaining sons. But they couldn't find a clear shot, not without coming down themselves.

The old man had flattened against the slope, shielded by a ledge above and by an outcropping on one side. Tom had managed to secure the horses, leading them further down the slope. When he hitched himself back up again, he brought with him water and ammunition.

Two cartridge belts and the Sharps, which had been scabbarded behind the saddle.

"Good boy," the old man said.

Strother Purcell had been hit, but not badly. So it appeared to Tom. The old man did not reply when he framed the question.

"Purcell!" a voice called from above. "That you down there?"

A cold, dry, nasal voice, curiously flat. The old man stiffened as he heard it.

There was silence for a moment. Then came that voice again, insinuating itself through the tinder-dry pines. "You killed my boy, Purcell. My second-born son, Uriah—after all the other crimes you done."

The old man neither moved nor spoke, for a moment. He remained in perfect stillness, peering up through deepening shadow.

"Purcell? You hearing this? You still alive?"

"Your boy fired first," Strother Purcell called up. "He brought it on himself."

There was silence then, from atop the ridge. At last, Shack Collard's voice said: "I never wanted this day."

"I know it," said Strother Purcell. "That's why you ran. Thirty years, across half the country. Hid yourself under another name—a whole 'nother religion. But here I am."

"You're a son of a bitch," Shack Collard said. "But here's my offer. We'll call it square. Set this killing of my boy against whatever grievance you got left—and walk away. You asked for that yourself, one time. Remember? Standing by the grave of my kinswoman, Sissy Baird. 'Stop the dyin',' you said to me, 'and move on.' Well, I'll do that now, if you will. Just let me fetch up the body of my son."

The corpse lay where it had been, all along: one coffin's length from the top of the ravine. But it was on the trail. It was visible from below. Whoever fetched it would expose himself to the Sharps.

"Are you hearing me, Purcell? I'm saying, let a Daddy see to his poor butchered boy. Let Christian honour be done to the dead."

"Come on, then," said Strother Purcell.

The shadows were deepening, now. Tom heard—or imagined—the quick rustling of birds in the trees along the ridge-line. Or else the hoarse susurration of human voices.

"You give your word on that?" Shack Collard's flat, cold voice again, out of the twilight. It seemed to Tom uncannily remote, uninflected by human emotion.

The old man said: "Come on down."

The old man's eye was fixed on a gap in the trees at the top of the trail, one coffin's-length above the corpse. An opening onto the sky above, into which Shack Collard would have to appear, like a tragedian stepping out onto the stage.

The sky stayed empty. The grey of twilight and the purpling bruise of storm clouds, pressing down. The air was grown electric with dire potentiality; somewhere in the distance thunder muttered.

"I never did aught to deserve such persecution," said Shack Collard. An ugly note of murder had crept in.

"You burned my Mama alive," the old man replied. "Her and poor Solomon, both."

"Did I?"

"Yes, you did. You killed my step-father Jacob Dillashay."

"And you killed my whole damned family!"

"Not all of them, Shack. You're still alive."

Still no glimpse of Shack Collard, through the trees. But the evening seethed with him.

"So this is what it's come to, has it?" Shack Collard said.

"I've come to pay what I owe," said Strother Purcell. "And collect what's owed in return. Tell the granny-woman: I've brought the five dollars."

"Five *dollars?* The devil does five dollars—?"

"Come on down, and I'll hand it over. Then we're square—no more debts owed between our families, on either side. Except for one, Shack. And that's yours."

"You're insane."

The sky stayed empty. It seemed to Tom, though, that the voice had shifted. It came from a distance to the left of where it had been.

"Send the women and children up into the hills," Strother said, "while there's still time. I cannot guarantee their safety, else. You hear me, Shack?"

The evening exploded into gunfire, instead: a fusillade from above, but from different angles. They'd spread out—found new vantages—now that they'd ascertained the old man's position. Bullets snarled and rang and ricocheted, kicking dust and splintering rock. Tom could only cower and cover his head, taking as little space in this world as he might, which was still far more than he wanted. Below them, the horses trumpeted consternation.

When at last the barrage ended, the trees themselves had been singed of foliage. A pall of gun smoke hung over the ridge, above them. There was silence, then Shack Collard's voice. "You still living, Purcell?

The old man did not stir.

"If you're living, then you'll rue it. You'd be better off dead already. We know every tree and trail on this mountain. How to find our way down, in the dark—and back up again from below. We'll come on you like haints, old man, and hang you. We'll fire the woods and burn you alive, you and that rat you brung along. If he's any friend of yours, then you best kill him. Best slit his windpipe now, Purcell—before we find him."

*

Nine o'clock p.m.

Em'ly had heard that terrible fusillade, hours earlier. It was five miles off, at the least, up the steep mountain road—so distant that it might not have been gunfire at all, just a rumour of faraway thunder, muttering across the evening sky. She told herself: That's all it was. How could it be gunfire, after all?—not when it rolled on and on and on, as if a whole regiment had opened fire.

It was silent, after that. Em'ly waited for thunder to resume—closer, maybe, and louder, with the reassurance that it had been thunder all along. But it didn't. Thus she knew that the old man had failed. He'd been pinned down—in the ravine, most like—she could see in her mind where it must have happened. They'd shot him to tatters, and Mr. Tom beside him. And now they'd be coming for her.

Knowing that, she couldn't move. She huddled in her hollow by the trail as darkness deepened, knowing that the Mormon's eye would find her. They'd be ravening down the trails, the Mormon and his misbegotten sons; they'd be in the trees on every side, like wolves. And just when she couldn't breathe at all, so sure was she that someone must be there in the darkness—or there—or *there*—there was a sound and a shifting of shadow and someone was.

*

Eleven o'clock p.m.

It seemed to Tom the worst night he had ever known.

He was himself unharmed. But the old man had been badly hit in that last barrage, or else the wound he had taken earlier was much worse than Tom had supposed. As the darkness deepened around them, it grew plain that Purcell was dying.

A pale moon had arisen, above the trees. A wind had come up with it, and the tinder-dry woods about them muttered.

The old man moaned in reply. He was haunted by ghosts of the past.

His Mama was here. So Tom was to gather. The ghost of mad Miss Amanda Beauchamp, late of Roanoke, Virginia. Strother's own Daddy came also, and Sissy Baird; poor Solomon as well, who had been nothing else but loyal all his life, and perished horribly nonetheless. They didn't rise as haints would do in the Great Smoky Mountains of Strother's youth, curling amongst the tree-trunks in tatters of bluejon mist. Here they rattled as dead branches, pine-sharp with recrimination.

The old man's brother was the final haunting.

"What should I have done, Lige?" the old man said. "Tell me what I could have done, and I'll still do it."

"Should've killed me when you had the chance," Lige Dillashay replied. It seemed to Tom he could hear that voice in the wind, as plain as if the outlaw had come up the trail behind them. "That was the mistake you made."

"You came to finish it?" the old man said.

"I did."

"Go on and do it, then."

"Let me see your face."

"You know what I am. I'm what I've always been."

"Show me your face."

The old man struggled to lift his head. He shifted himself onto one elbow, despite the pain. His face showed in the moonlight, ruined and haggard.

"Aren't we the pair?" Lige Dillashay said at last.

Tom looked round.

In moonlight, the outlaw stood. He was tattered and bramble-torn; stinking with long travel and bad whiskey. Older and maimed and wearing that preacher's hat, but still Dionysus when he chose.

"Well, fuck," he said to his brother. "Look at you."

"What will we do, Lige?" Strother said. "Tell me, and we'll get on with 'er."

"I expect we better kill someone. Shack Collard, to start with. Then that old witch."

Behind him, Em'ly stood shaking. Her bonnet was shapeless and her eyes were vast and she clutched the Smith & Wesson in both hands.

Lige said: "The gal can patch you up a little, maybe."

"I believe I'm past patching," Strother said.

"At least we can plug a few holes. H'lo, there, Tommy," the outlaw added. "Long time. You look like desolation on a stick."

*

Eleven-thirty p.m.

Up in the Big House, it might have gone like this:

The granny-woman could not settle. She shuffled and seethed and muttered, peering out into the night. "But did you kill him?" she demanded. Not for the first time, or the twenty-first, which grated sorely upon the others.

"He's dead," said Zebulon.

He had come back up with his father, after the final barrage, leaving Bendigo and Brigham posted down by the ravine, just in case. They were young and had keen eyes.

Rachel, the eldest of the sister-wives, sat still as stone at the long table. She was Uriah's mother. Hannah, three years younger, sat with her, clutching her hand. The boy's body, once recovered, would be laid out here for washing.

"Nobody could've survived," Zebulon said. "We must've fired a hundred rounds. And I hit him — once, at least. I know that for a fact."

"But did you kill him? Is that one-eyed bastard *dead?*"

Shack Collard said: "No. I don't believe it."

"Nor I don't, neither!" said the granny-woman.

Thunder rumbled.

Shack Collard had sat silent all this while, adding greatly to the miasma of unease. He'd been working through all the steps he must take, with no margin for blunder, now that it had come to this: the day he had avoided for thirty years, come to call on him at last. When Shack Collard fell so silent, you held your breath. You did not say one word that might provoke him. Not even Robbie, his favourite, would dare do that.

But now he made his decision. "Zebulon," he said. "Take Joseph. Double round behind the bastards, in the ravine. Come up on 'em from below."

"Now?"

"While there's moonlight. Set fire to the woods."

"Lord-a-mercy," Sarah exclaimed. The daughter. She could expect to pay a price for this interruption later, when her Daddy had more leisure at his disposal.

Shack was intent on his planning. "Storm's on the way," he said to Zeb. "Wind's coming up, from the south. Fire will flush him, if he can walk. Burn him to cinders if he can't. We'll have rifles on the ridge, while we wait to find out."

"There's fire already," Sarah said.

"Quiet."

"But it's true!" young Robbie exclaimed. He'd moved to stand by his sister, at the window. They stared out, across the porch and into the night.

"Look." Robbie pointed. "Look-look. They's fire along the ridge!"

—

The fire had been Lige's doing, to create a diversion. In this, he was assisted by Em'ly, who revealed herself to be an incendiary of no mean talent.

And the suddenness of it had taken the sentries off their guard. A precipitate kindling of flame amongst the pines, swept abruptly forward by the wind—as if, while they'd been nodding at their posts, the ancient gods of gorge and ravine had been breeding dragons.

Smoke billowed up, and Strother Purcell boiled out of it: one-eyed as Odin, forked upon that godalmighty Clydesdale. The draft horse heaved, ungainly, up the last steep slope of trail; staggered, stumbled, found its footing, surged into a shambling gallop. The old man raised his sixgun. The bullet shattered Brigham's sternum; the boy pitched from the knoll where he'd been posted.

Bendigo turned to flee. But he'd fired his own shot first, thus settling any question that might linger, concerning his fitness to draw further breath. Besides, he was a Collard. A shot spun him, flailing herk-a-jerk; another slammed him face-down, sprawling, a hundred yards short of the house.

The draft horse thundered over him.

The old man had been tied in place. A rope around his waist bound him to the saddle-horn. Another, round his ankles, secured his legs. Bendigo might have seen this: a last glimpse vouchsafed, as light died from his eyes. He might even have found in it a source of wonderment, if dying seventeen-year-old boys are inclined to wonder.

Lige had done the binding, after lifting his brother astride the horse.

"Make 'em tighter," Strother had said.

Lige did so, ensuring as well that the cinch-strap would hold. "That strap busts, and you're dead," he warned. "No way for you to clear the saddle."

"This is one hell of a thing," Strother said, "to say to a dying man." He summoned up a wintry smile to go with it.

Yes, it would have gone very much like that: the final words between the two of them, there at the end of the world. Tom was not standing with them at that moment, but afterward he knew it nonetheless. This is how such exchanges go.

Lige had one half-bottle of whiskey remaining, which he now proffered. "One last drink, with your brother?"

Strother shook his head. "Waste of good whiskey."

"You're sure?"

"It'd just leak out."

Lige drank for both of them. "Can we count on the cripple?" he asked.

"Tom Skiffings has never once let me down."

"I should've laid on healing hands, before he went."

"Mite late for that," Strother said.

"I suppose. And relations being strained, just now, between myself and the Lord."

Lige took one final swallow, and slung the bottle aside.

Strother looked down at him. "Lige? I would ride against Satan himself in hell, with all his infernal legions, knowing I had such a brother to ride with me."

Yes, he would certainly have spoken thus, at the end. All the heroes have done so, in books. Lige, for his part, found that words unaccountably failed him.

"Well, then," he managed. "For my Daddy's sake. And for Mama. And ... oh, fuck, let's just do 'er."

Strother reached out one hand in benediction. "Straight and true, brother. Straight and true. Ever and always, straight and true."

Lightning forked as he said it.

—

They'd have watched from the Big House in disbelief. Young Robbie and his sister gawping out windows, and their father bellowing, "Get away from there!"

Strother Purcell came on.

It must have seemed to young Robbie that Time itself had slowed down. A one-man cavalry charge, but at a fraction of the customary speed, as if that godalmighty horse came galloping through fire and treacle—a *Clydesdale,* save our souls, eighteen hands at the withers and hooves as wide as pie-plates. Slow, slow, impossibly slow, but unstoppable as an oncoming locomotive.

"Jayzus Godfrey," Robbie'd have squawked, ducking for cover one instant before a bullet shattered the window. His sister went inexplicably legless, dropping down beside him. Robbie's hoot of laughter trailed into perplexity; it occurred to him that Sarah's eyes were wide and blank and staring, owing to the fact that she was dead.

Zeb now took matters in hand. The eldest son, and all. He smashed the butt of a rifle through the window nearest to him, and rising into the aperture he commenced to blaze away.

His first shot struck the old man in the shoulder, wrenching him halfway around. But it didn't kill him. Righting himself in the saddle, Strother fired. The bullet took Zeb through the throat and he gurgled on down; sat dumbly, as if at a loss to explicate why such indignity should be visited upon him—and in his Daddy's front room, no less. Then he toppled.

Shack Collard must have seen his eldest die. Saw Strother Purcell sling the sixgun aside, and reach for another. Saw the crimson totems of trees ablaze, and a second rider galloping out of the smoke: Lige Dillashay, with a Winchester rifle and a rebel yell.

Shack understood, then, how desperate this had become.

But there would still have been a way. Four sons were dead already, and one daughter. But two sons remained to him. Both sister-wives could shoot, and Shack Collard himself did not want for coolness of head, nor for murderous efficiency in the snuffing out of life. This was a man, after all, who had raided with Quantrill—had hung whole families from trees, from white-bearded grandfathers right on down to blue-eyed gals in ringlets, cordially inviting some sobbing wretch to choose which sibling should die first. Or so at least the story went. And who would wish to dispute a legend such as that? Yes, Shack Collard would still have had every chance to defend the house—to barricade the windows and pick off the assailants, one after the other.

Except now he saw his youngest son, bolting out the door.

"Robbie!"

The boy had endured quite enough of this. He resolved to shoot that old one-eyed bastard dead, and reckoned he'd best get as close as he could to do it. Or possibly he wasn't thinking at all, just rushing outside and firing a pistol, clutching it in both his hands and spraying bullets.

In all likelihood, the old man never saw him. The draft horse lurched, spooked by flames and din and confounded by the old man's sawing at the reins. He was hauling to pull a gun from the saddle-scabbard: an eight-gauge, acquired at Mears Lake, and sawed off to approximate the Hell Bitch of old. As it came free at last, the draft horse lurched again, trampling over the onrushing boy. Robbie cried out—or would have done, had one vast hoof not borne down, iron-shod, blotting out the Oregon sky.

"What stops us?" Lige cried, as he reached his brother.

"Nothing!" the old man replied. His voice was thick with dying.

Shack Collard tried. He came out the door, a pistol in either hand. His first shot ripped through Lige, and two more struck Strother, before the eight-gauge boomed.

The blast disassembled the Mormon. His legs struggled on, impelled by his previous momentum, but his torso would not come with them.

His face turned skyward, eyes rolling. Then the legs gave way and the weight of him crumbled down, and Meshach Collard passed from this weary world, unlamented.

The force of the recoil set Strother back as well. It left him reeling and swaying, and wrenched a woeful trumpeting from that godalmighty horse.

The house was now on fire.

It had started by misfortune, as nearly as could ever be determined. A paraffin-lamp knocked over, or blasted apart. A lick of flame against fabric—lace curtains, or a muslin dress—and then with a whoosh the whole of it going up.

The godalmighty Clydesdale reared, shying from this new conflagration. O, what fresh equine hell? And the old man saw, as through a red mist, a figure on the roof. It was the twisted stick of an old woman, untouched as yet by the tongues of flame, pointing him out for eternal obloquy.

He shouted something at her, then. The old woman couldn't make out what it was, amidst the roar of conflagration. But she saw him reach into his shirt, and between his fingers was a glint that might almost be—though what devil should account for this, she could not say—a gold coin.

Drusilla Smoak took dead aim with her rifle. She had him, after all these years. But just as she squeezed the trigger there came—from somewhere behind her—a muted but unmistakable *Pop!* Something struck her, directly between the shoulder blades. She felt herself totter—half-turned, obscurely swatted, as one might do in warding off a wasp. Then that sound again, that muted plosive: *Pop! Pop!*

It occurred to her, vaguely, right there at the end: *This might not be wasps at all.*

—

It was, in fact, Tom Skiffings.

Of course it was. You could have guessed that, without having to be told. You could hardly have a tale at all, without the likes of Tom Skiffings to save the day—assuming that any part of that day or night was receptive still to salvation.

Tom had worked his solitary way behind the Big House, exactly as he had pledged himself to do. While the frontal assault had been conceived and launched, he had hirpled himself under cover of night through the trees that skirted the edge of the field, thinking to make himself invaluable in some manner—by drawing off fire, say, or distracting savage dogs, neither of which opportunity had presented itself, thank God.

But once he had succeeded in his quest—had crept all the way around, to crouch quaking and exultant in a copse of trees, with the light of the Big House's back windows directly before him, no more than fifteen paces off—it dawned on Tom that he had not accomplished anything at all, except to secure for himself a unique prospect onto the end of the world. The woods before him were ablaze. Fire was crowning in the trees. The house was on fire, and Lige Dillashay was down, along with assorted Collards. Strother Purcell was riddled with bullets, and dying. And suddenly—there on the rooftop before him, standing crabbed and horrid amidst spouts of flame—was a witch with an Enfield rifle.

God knows how she'd managed to climb up there, a woman as old as Methuselah's great-aunt. In certain later retellings of the tale, God would have nothing to do with this at all; it was the devil who raised her to such a height of unholy exaltation, according to a bargain sealed in the Smoky Mountains half a century before. But she was set to finish Strother Purcell, one way or the other. And in that fateful half-second Wild Gimp Tom rose up, with his trusty Deane-Adams five-shot.

Under different circumstances, he'd have called out some pithy utterance. He'd come up with a list of these many years ago, when as a boy he'd carried out in his head many feats of valour. But none of them would come to mind in this particular half-second. Most had in any case applied to shoot-outs with brooding desperados—throw-downs on dusty main streets of Dodge, and such—and did not transfer, exactly, to the back-shooting of granny-women on rooftops.

But the first *Pop!* staggered her, by golly. The next two—*Pop! Pop!*—staggered her some more. The fourth slung her forward, and the fifth and final was not a *Pop!* exactly, but more of a *BOOF!* as the trusty Deane-Adams exploded in Wild Gimp Tom's hand and blew off two of his fingers. But she fell. He saw it. A tattered black rag, wreathed in flame, as the rooftop collapsed beneath her.

In front of the house, Strother Purcell fired one last blast with the eight-gauge. It bowed him backward, and this time the cinch-strap broke. The saddle swung sideways with the old man still tightly bound, pitching him under the hooves of the plunging Clydesdale.

— EPILOGUE[16]—

BARRINGTON WEAVER recovered from his injuries, after a fashion, though he was never the same man afterward. He left San Francisco early in 1893, and over the ensuing years made a meandering progress northward, picking up odd jobs here and there in Oregon and Idaho, but never staying for long in one place. He was never to see Tom Skiffings again, or Prairie Rose, or anyone else from his San Francisco days. He never learned for a certainty what had happened to Strother Purcell, either, though he made haphazard efforts to find out.

By 1907, he was panhandling in Vancouver's Gastown district, where he would tell a version of Purcell's saga in barrooms, to anyone who would stand him the price of a drink. This came to be known as Weaver's Yarn. The story would seem to have had a certain narrative force, though its provenance was murky and no one was certain how much of it to believe. Weaver had latched onto the notion that Strother Purcell and his outlaw brother had reunited to hunt down their old archenemy from Smoky Mountain days, which was close enough to the truth. This he would presumably have gleaned from barroom tales that he himself had heard, in Oregon. But he had also formed the conviction that neither of the brothers had perished at Deadman Creek.

Weaver's Yarn grew cryptic at this point, and the storyteller himself would turn mysterious if pressed for details. There would seem, in fact, to have been shifting versions of this culminating sequence. These

---

16   The authorship of this final segment cannot be categorically established. But it seems clear to me that we hear Tilda Sturluson, speaking directly to us. I will admit that I wish, very much, that I might speak back to her: as a scholar in the last twilight of a long career—and as an old man who might, had circumstances been otherwise, have become her friend. —*Brookmire*.

evolved over time—possibly due to research breakthroughs, but on the whole more probably not. By 1909, Weaver was hinting that the reunited siblings had escaped to Bolivia, where Lige Dillashay robbed trains and banks while his older brother strongly disapproved.

Weaver's mother continued to send her son quarterly remittances until her death in 1910. Late the following year, he was interviewed by a young newspaper reporter who had been assigned to write an article about outlandish local characters. Weaver is quoted as telling the young man: "I met giants in my day. Truly. Oh, I met men of the most remarkable courage and achievement. I wasn't one of 'em, myself. I was never much of anything, really. But I *met* 'em."

Two days later, Barry Weaver was found dead in a rooming-house on Powell Street. It is reported that he looked wistful.

*

Tom Skiffings—"Three-Fingered Tom"—survived the events at Deadman Creek, much to his own surprise. He and Em'ly left Oregon together, making their way eventually to the Okanagan Valley of British Columbia, where in 1916—to his sorrow—she predeceased him, leaving the consolation of their daughter, Tilda, born in 1909.

He would never speak to his daughter about Deadman Creek, not while she was a child. She knew, though, how it ended, from her mother. Em'ly had not been present at the deaths, or at least not quite—she had been down in the ravine with the two remaining horses, her heart trip-hammering against her ribs, convinced that the world was ending just above her. She described to Tilda her sick certainty that all was lost—the terrible heat of the fire; the blood-red flickering of flames against the sky, and the shouts and screams and gunshots from the house. Then suddenly, there he was at the lip of the ravine—Tilda's father. He came tottering out of the smoke and the red-hot cinders, ravaged and soot-streaked and maimed in his right hand, raving and choking that it was over.

Lige Dillashay had been shot dead by the Mormon. Strother Purcell had been thundered to ruin by that godalmighty horse, slung to the ground and stirrup-drug across the field. Em'ly had not seen it, but Three-Fingered Tom had been there. He had gimped after the Clydesdale with such alacrity as he could muster. Finding his friend Strother Purcell still miraculously breathing, Tom had sat with the old man while he passed, afterward wrapping the body and digging a grave — though this did not entirely make sense, as Em'ly herself conceded, not if her own recollection was accurate. Tom would have needed all night to do all that, and surely it had not been dawn when he appeared at the lip of the ravine — though possibly it was. The more Em'ly thought, the more it seemed conceivable that hours *had* passed. How could anyone keep track of time, after all, when the world was ending?

So perhaps it was dawn. Tom appeared out of blood-red daybreak. It was over, one way or the other — and the two of them had to flee, before distant neighbours, drawn by the fire, should arrive with horrified questions. So they fled.

Tilda remained with her father for some years after Em'ly's passing. They owned a small orchard — paid for, local rumour would have it, by a mysterious cache of so-called Mormon Gold — and grew apples and peaches and plums for market. Three-Fingered Tom lived quietly, though certain persistent speculations bat-winged about him, concerning a clandestine past. He never confirmed these, but did not entirely deny them, either.

Late in his life, he sold the orchard and moved with Tilda to Yale, just a few miles west of the roadhouse where so much had begun. Half a century had passed since the events of 1876, and Tom himself was scarcely remembered here. He remembered, though. He remembered everything.

He had long intended to compose a full accounting of the life and times of Strother Purcell, whom he held to be the greatest man he had ever encountered, or heard tell of—and Tom Skiffings had heard tell of them all. He had been jotting notes and sketching out passages, as long as his daughter could remember; Em'ly had done so too, right up until her own premature demise. Now Tom began to confide certain remarkable aspects to his daughter. He intimated, for instance, that Strother Purcell might not have died that night at all—and nor had his half-brother. "They'd both died before, you see—or should've done," he said. "Death can't just haul off men like that, grabbing 'em by the scruff of the neck—not the way he'll do with the likes of me. No, Death needs to *ask* a man like Strother Purcell, and then wait for a reply."

Tom had been talking more and more like this, which concerned his daughter. He had recently turned sixty-two—not truly old, except he'd never enjoyed robust health, or anything resembling it.

It was 1927. They had a small house just above the river, which Tilda was fixing up—a new roof that summer, and plans to build a sun-room in the front. In fair weather, up on the roof, she would see her father hirpling down to the river, across the railroad tracks and past salmonberry bushes. She'd go down herself after an hour or so, to find him sitting, small and withered, on a log. The Fraser churned inexorably past; Hell's Gate to the east, and the mud flats to the west, where in his boyhood the Chinese and Natives had still squatted in mute resolve, sifting for the last specks of gold. Sometimes she wondered if her father could see them still, on mornings when the season turned and the mists hung low and lingered.

"Penny for 'em," she would say, meaning his thoughts.

Most often he'd just chuckle. But sometimes he'd say something outlandish in reply, such as: "Wyatt Earp was shit-scared of him — Weaver told me that. Weaver was a damned fool, but he wasn't a liar." Or: "A whole damned mountainside tried to kill him, in '76. Couldn't do it. You suppose the likes of the Collards had better luck?"

He had heard, from somewhere, the gist of Weaver's Yarn. He scoffed and told his daughter not to believe it — not that business about Bolivia, anyway. But late that summer, he took to hinting that another party had appeared out of the smoke at Deadman Creek: a great ungainly gal with hands like hams and a strawberry birthmark stained across her face, who had followed Lige Dillashay all the way from San Francisco, and was not about to let him die, or his brother either, when she could carry them both so easily to safety. "Shot to ribbons?" Tilda's father said. "Hell, yes, they'd been shot to ribbons. But you want to hear a secret? Here, I'll tell you one." His daughter leaned in close, and he whispered: "They had doctors in the Oregon." He also hinted that others had seen the brothers, long after Deadman Creek — they just never learned the true identities of a maimed evangelist and his towering one-eyed brother, who were ministering to the poor and sick at missions and soup kitchens on the Eastern Seaboard as late as 1912, and thus atoning ten times over for such sins as the two of them had committed.

One afternoon in autumn, Tilda drove him out to the site of the old roadhouse, which Old Tom had conceived an urgency to visit. Tilda had recently come into a possession of an automobile: the half-wrecked relic of one of Mr. Ford's creations, which through the alchemy of mechanical aptitude she coaxed back into operation. She could only imagine what an oncoming motorist might suppose, to see that contraption rattling toward him: Tilda at the wheel, Old Tom blanket-swaddled beside her, neither one of them touching five feet in height — just two pairs of eyes peering over the dash, as if elves had commandeered a

Model T. Tilda took after her father in appearance, though she was stronger than he had ever been, and would be hale and energetic well into her nineties.

The road out toward Hell's Gate was little more than a widening of the old Wagon Road, still narrow and perilous beyond all sense. That afternoon, Old Tom had grown almost young again, pointing out the sites where this event had once taken place, or that one. The ruin of McCutcheon's Roadhouse was still discernible, and the vantage-point where he had first set eyes upon Strother Purcell. But abruptly he'd grown fretful, and told Tilda she must take him back again, to Yale.

"We just got here," Tilda protested. She'd packed a hamper, and planned for the two of them to have a picnic.

"It's late," her father told her, though it wasn't. "She'll be wondering where I am."

"She?"

"Billie."

His sister. She was going to be an actress, Tom said, though at present they helped out their Uncle John. The two of them were all their uncle had, pending the arrival of a French chef from Montreal. Uncle John would be wondering where Tom was, too.

"The chores, you see," Tom said to her. "I got chores."

Tom Skiffings died that winter, leaving his project unfinished. After his death, Tilda discovered whole sheaves of notes in an old steamer trunk, along with draft segments written in her mother's hand. There was a trove of other documents as well: yellowed clippings from newspapers, dating as far back as 1864; personal correspondence between sundry individuals; and long portions of the hand-written journal of Barrington Weaver. Tilda had no clear notion how her father had acquired all of this, but manifestly he had conducted far more research than she had ever imagined.

In 1936, Tilda Skiffings married for the first and only time, to a man named Sturluson. She did not abandon her father's project, however. Over the years, she conducted extensive research of her own, travelling as far afield as North Carolina. Her findings called into question various elements of the account, but turned out—sometimes startlingly—to buttress others. In 1994, long after her husband's death, and at the age of 85, Tilda gathered whole boxes of files about her and sat down at a portable typewriter. Winding the first of many sheets into the roller, she began:

> They were passing into myth before the snow had commenced to fall in earnest on that bleak midwinter afternoon, blurring the hard distinctions of this world. So it is not possible with confidence to say where certainties begin and end.
>
> There were three of them; this much at least is beyond dispute...

–ACKNOWLEDGEMENTS–

This is a work of fiction, and the main characters are entirely fictional, although certain historical figures lounge on the periphery, notably Wyatt Earp and his wife Josephine Sarah "Sadie" Marcus. The two of them were indeed living in the Bay Area in 1892, where Wyatt was managing a racetrack and trying to regroup after a chastening experience in the San Diego real estate market. And the broad strokes of their stories do conform, more or less, to the historical record, although Barry Weaver is far from a reliable narrator and liberties have (to say the least) been taken. Then again, there is lively dispute about the essence of Earp amongst the Earpians themselves, so Weaver has company. Of the various Wyatt Earp biographies, I particularly enjoyed Jeff Guinn's *The Last Gunfight: The Real Story of the Shootout at the O.K. Corral—And How It Changed the American West*; and Allan Barra's *Inventing Wyatt Earp: His Life & Many Legends*. And *Lady at the O.K. Corral: The True Story of Josephine Marcus Earp*, by Ann Kirschner, is a gem. As for nineteenth-century San Francisco itself, I will just say this: no one should, under any circumstances, consider dying before having read Herbert Asbury's classic *The Barbary Coast: An Informal History of the San Francisco Underworld*.

Heartfelt thanks to my agent, Samantha Haywood, and her team at Transatlantic, for much insight, guidance and unflagging support. Special thanks as well to Jude Weir and Susin Nielsen, who read early drafts and suggested vital improvements.

And my gratitude to Susanne Alexander and the splendid Goose Lane gang. My editor, Bethany Gibson, was (as ever) wise and altogether terrific. Peter Norman's copy-edit was (as ever) rigorous and perceptive.

Ian Weir is a playwright, screenwriter, TV showrunner, and the author of two previously published novels. *Daniel O'Thunder* was shortlisted for the Commonwealth Writers' Prize for Best First Book, as well as the Canadian Authors Association Award for fiction, the Ethel Wilson Fiction Prize, and the amazon.ca First Novel Award. *Will Starling* was longlisted for the International DUBLIN Literary Award and shortlisted for the Sunburst Award. Among his extensive television credits are his work as creator and showrunner of *Artic Air* and as writer and executive producer of the acclaimed gangland miniseries, *Dragon Boys*. He has won two Geminis, four Leos, a Jessie, and a Writers Guild of Canada Screenwriting Award.

Born in North Carolina, Ian Weir grew up in Kamloops, British Columbia. He now lives near Vancouver.